The Black Silk Purse

By Margaret Kaine

The Black Silk Purse

The Black Silk Purse

MARGARET KAINE

Allison & Busby Limited
12 Fitzroy Mews
London W1T 6DW
allisonandbusby.com

First published in Great Britain by Allison & Busby in 2018.

A CIP catalogue record for this book is available from
the British Library.

First Edition

ISBN 978-0-7490-2310-2

Typeset in 11/16 pt Adobe Garamond Pro by
Allison & Busby Ltd.

The paper used for this Allison & Busby publication
has been produced from trees that have been legally sourced
from well-managed and credibly certified forests.

Printed and bound by
CPI Group (UK) Ltd, Croydon, CR0 4YY

For all my loyal readers

'And take a bond of fate'

WILLIAM SHAKESPEARE
MACBETH: ACT 4, SCENE 1

Chapter One

Chapter One

1903

Ella withdrew into the shadows, the workhouse uniform thin through years of laundering, offering little protection against the March wind. During the past six years she had become accustomed to cold and even hunger, but no amount of deprivation could take away her dreams. Hazy and only on the fringes of her mind it still lingered, that other world, one of colour and beauty, and these rare visits of Miss Fairchild with her glossy black hair, jewels and furs had become beacons in a life that contained only greyness. Ella glanced over to the waiting carriage with its patient chestnut horses, waiting to step forward to receive the reward of a smile. It might be swift, but with it would come the three words spoken in a refined voice, '*Goodbye, my dear.*' The endearment was like a balm bringing alive the vague remembrance of another voice, loving and gentle. Ella had been six years old when brought to the workhouse, and she had clung to that precious memory at first with despair and later with ferocity. It was her proof, her security. Because of it, she knew the truth: that, despite the taunts and name-calling, she was not a bastard nor was she a foundling.

After catching a glimpse of the well-dressed woman and asking endless questions, Ella had discovered via one of the senior inmates not only the name she sought but also the regular timing of her visits. And since then she had, not without difficulty, contrived to be outside the workhouse in order to wait for her to leave.

Today, she was a bit later than usual, and then the door was opened and with a swish of her skirt she came out, her breath misting the chilly air. Ella moved forward to be seen, rewarded and warmed by the familiar swift smile and the words, 'Goodbye, my dear.'

Ella watched as the footman assisted her into the carriage and looked longingly at her lovely clothes; a dark-green coat trimmed with rich fur, a paler green hat with crimson feathers. Then, all too soon, the coachman was urging the horses and Ella hurried to a door at the side of the tall building and gingerly opened it.

All seemed safe, so she sidled inside. Talon-like fingers dug into her right shoulder. 'And where, girl, have you been sneaking off to? Aren't you supposed to be doing a stint in the laundry?'

Ella twisted round in horror. Miss Grint, one of the officers, had the habit of appearing from nowhere. 'Yes miss, sorry miss!'

'Sorry doesn't answer my question.'

She looked up with defiance into the harsh narrow face. 'I felt sick, needed a breath of fresh air.'

'What, in this freezing cold? Who gave you permission?'

Ella bit her lip.

'I see.' The blow knocked her sideways, the palm hard and stinging across her right ear. 'You idle brat, get back to your work.'

Directed by a violent push, Ella staggered along the corridor in the direction of the steaming noisy laundry. She hated Miss Grint so much it was like a fire in her belly. But she'd show her, just as soon as she was old enough she'd get out of this place, and when she did, she was going to become rich and she'd come back and she'd . . . The stone steps down to the laundry were steep and awkward in her ill-fitting shoes; she picked up her skirt and concentrated.

'Oi! Where do you think you've bin? Get hold of some tongs and lift those sheets out of that boiler.' The woman shouting was in her fifties, her grey hair hanging in wisps around her perspiring forehead.

Ella hurried past her to haul the dripping white linen out of the boiling water and, dodging the splashes, lowered it into one of the long wooden rinsing troughs. All the girls had to learn household tasks to prepare them for work outside, but it was heavy labour for young thin arms. Glancing at the girl whose fainting act had caused the distraction that enabled Ella to slip away, she gave her a grateful grin. It would mean giving away her meagre supper tonight, but it had been worth it.

As the carriage drew away, Letitia Fairchild relaxed into its padded seat, relieved as always that her stultifying visit, decreed in her father's will, was once again over. Despite herself, she still resented how even from beyond the grave he managed to control aspects of her life. Although she had to accept that it wasn't his fault that some ancient relative had once fallen on hard times and spent a few years incarcerated in that gloomy place. He had never forgotten the unfortunates left behind and her father, having benefited by the man's later wealth, had bequeathed to his daughter the duty of visiting the workhouse four times a year. Letitia was generous but also had a keen head for figures and knew that her questions caused not a little consternation, but she was assured from photographs she had seen that this workhouse was little different to any other – after all, the number of poor and homeless in London was vast. And no matter how large the amount of charitable donations to swell the public coffers, more money was always needed to house, clothe and feed the inmates decently.

Enjoying the sound of the horses' hooves on the road, she gazed at the tall houses in the tree-lined roads leading into the city, feeling relieved as they neared her comfortable home in Hampstead. Not the smartest address in London but, as her father had proclaimed, one that spoke of solid respectability and yet might disguise a gentleman's true wealth.

She was entering the hall, her hand already raised to remove her hatpin, when the butler came forward. 'Miss Featherstone is waiting in the drawing room, madam. I told her that I expected you back shortly.'

'Thank you, Forbes. Please serve tea.' She unbuttoned her coat and, passing it over to a waiting maid, swept into the large handsome room. 'Grace, what a welcome surprise.'

The woman seated on the deep-cushioned sofa raised a hand to pat her hair into place. 'I didn't expect to find you out.'

'My duty visit to the workhouse. I've ordered tea but I can't possibly take it until I've washed my hands. You'll have to excuse me a moment.'

'Of course,' Grace frowned. 'You didn't touch any of the inmates, did you?'

Letitia turned at the door. 'No,' she said with an indulgent smile at the woman she regarded as her best friend, 'I didn't touch any of the inmates.'

A few minutes later, as they indulged in tea and scones, Grace was brimming with a snippet of gossip. 'Did you know that Lord and Lady Allaway have gone to Madeira for two months?'

Letitia shook her head.

'I did hear a whisper. Of course, one can never believe all one hears but, apparently, all is not as it should be in that household.'

'In what way exactly?'

'Shall we say that it involves a certain French governess?'

Letitia paused, her cup halfway to her mouth. 'You can't mean it, not Lord Allaway. He must be sixty if he is a day. The old goat!'

'Letitia!'

'Oh, come on Grace. We may be unmarried but we're old enough not to be ignorant of the world.' She glanced at her friend who, at twenty-six, was a year younger than her. She had both a fair prettiness and a good cleavage, and it was widely accepted that most men preferred an 'English rose'. Letitia put a hand up to her black hair, dressed in a chignon. Not only were her own breasts small, but 'handsome' was perhaps the best word that could be ascribed to herself. She had to admit that her assertion had been a trifle exaggerated as their knowledge of men had been confined to one suitor only each. And neither had led to matrimony.

Almost as if Grace had read her mind, she mused, 'Marriage is a subject we never discuss. Don't you think that a little strange among two close women friends?'

'We did discuss Victoria's marriage after she died, agreeing that her excessive mourning for Prince Albert had been the height of self-indulgence.'

'That was over two years ago.' Grace gave a sigh of resignation. 'I wasn't thinking of general conversation, Letitia, but never mind.' She dabbed at her mouth with her napkin. 'I really should get back to Mama. She's not at all well at the moment.'

It was after her friend had left that Letitia went to stand before the glowing coal fire surrounded by the solid-mahogany furniture so familiar to her. A feeling of sadness swept over her as she wondered whether her life would have been different if her own mama had lived. Would she herself have been different? Letitia had always believed that her father had blamed her for the loss of his wife in childbirth. Certainly, he had been a stern parent and there had been little warmth in this mausoleum of a house. There was only one man from whom she had ever received affection and she would always wonder whether his invitation to dine that evening at Eversleigh had been timed to coincide with her expected absence. Certainly, when her social engagement was cancelled and she had joined the two men in the drawing room for cocktails, Cedric Fairchild had been unable to conceal his anger and dismay. She walked slowly across the room feeling a familiar ache in her heart as she thought of Miles Maitland, that idealistic young man with whom she had felt an instant bond. Sensing her father would disapprove, they had felt it advisable to be circumspect about their affection for each other, contriving during those summer months to attend the same social events even, at times, to stroll out into a garden where, in secluded corners, they could find some privacy. Letitia stared blindly ahead, remembering how Miles had hated the secrecy, insisting that he should explain their relationship to her father. But, long ago, she had learnt the futility of dwelling on that fateful night. With an effort she brought her mind back to the present, and as she drew out the chair to sit before her satinwood desk, she reminded herself that unmarried and childless she may be but, unlike countless other women in the same position, her father had at least left her financially secure.

Letitia picked up her silver fountain pen and, unscrewing the top, began to leaf through her diary to enter the date of her next visit to the workhouse. She paused, reflecting that it seemed a little odd that the same girl should be loitering outside again when she left. What was she – about eleven or twelve? All the inmates had their hair cropped to prevent lice but a few brown strands had escaped her cap; her pale face always looked pinched. Could the poor child possibly be half-witted, for why else would she stand out there in the freezing cold?

* * *

Later that evening at the workhouse, Ella trailed upstairs to the long cold dormitory, not only hungry but exhausted. However, she found it impossible to sleep. Not because of the sound of rats and mice rustling and scampering among the eaves – that was a familiar noise, as were the snores and muffled sobs in the room – it was her thoughts that were keeping her awake. Huddled on her straw mattress, she couldn't help thinking about the afternoon's visit. Miss Fairchild had spoken to her again, and Ella had long accepted that never again would she hear the warmth of her own mother's voice, but still her underlying loneliness never seemed to leave her.

And what of that other voice that haunted her, that of a servant woman? Ella couldn't remember her face or her name, but she had never forgotten those terrible words delivered in a hoarse whisper. *'Dearie, promise me you will never forget what you saw. Your ma was killed deliberate, them horses were driven straight at her, and someone oughter pay for it.'*

Chapter Two

It was three months later when, in a Camden tenement with dusty brown linoleum, scratched furniture and cheap fabric curtains, Rory Adare sat by the makeshift bed in the cramped sitting room. His father lay in silence, his once strong and handsome face gaunt and Rory leant over to pull the thin grey blanket higher around his shoulders. But he knew that Seamus, like himself, was waiting for the dreaded thud on the door. When it came, sixteen-year-old Rory went to face the burly man more than twice his age and, grim-faced, held out the coins.

'What do you call this?'

'It's all we've got.'

Grabbing the money, and with a scowl on his pockmarked face, the debt collector pushed past him into the shabby room and strode over to the mantelpiece.

Rory flung himself at him, but even though tall for his age, he was no match for the other man's bulk. Shouldered aside, he watched in horror as their last possession, a French ormolu clock that had belonged to Rory's mother, was tucked inside the thug's muffler and jacket. Seconds later, he was gone, with Rory slamming the door in fury behind him.

He turned to face his father. 'Da, we can't go on like this.'

'I know, son.' But Seamus's voice was weak, and despite his long struggle, it was obvious that he was weakening with every hour that passed.

With desperation Rory knew that there was now no alternative. '*You* could go in Da, you would at least be looked after.'

Seamus shook his head. 'The moneylenders never forget a debt, they'd only hound you, even rough you up. You'd be safer with me in the workhouse. Besides, your mother would have wanted us to stay together.' His voice became a hoarse whisper. 'True to God, I never thought it would come to this.'

Rory could only stare at him in despair. When two years after his wife's death Seamus had been diagnosed with cancer, its swift onset caused his once successful career as a Dublin journalist to falter. As his health continued to fail so did the quality of his writing, and eventually with little income they were forced to sell even their furniture. At first Seamus fought against taking Rory from his studies and their dream of his going to Trinity College, but as their situation became desperate and his mind befuddled by whisky to dull his pain, he disregarded his son's protests and began to insist they should go to London.

'There will be places where I can submit previously published articles. Sure, we'll be grand, you'll see.' But it was his last statement uttered with defiance that revealed the truth. 'Besides, I have no wish to become an object of pity.'

Despite Rory's plea, that same fierce pride had prevented him from accepting any offers of help, and with Rory's misgivings they had come 'over the water' to an unwelcoming London and continued rejections. As the months passed, Seamus's health worsened to such a worrying degree that Rory hardly dared to leave his side.

'Ye'll do no such thing,' he raged when, with their savings gone, a frightened Rory wanted to write to Dublin for help.

'Just for a loan to get you some medical help, Da.'

But even in his weakened state Seamus's temper flared. 'If we had family it'd be different, but no Adare goes begging from friends.' He struggled to raise himself from his pillow. 'I'd never forgive you, lad, never.'

And so there had been no alternative to making the dreaded application, and they were waiting for the visit of the Relieving Officer. There would be no problem with Seamus being admitted to the workhouse, but Rory feared that his own case might be dismissed with contempt. He glanced over at the bed, at his father's grey complexion, at the lines of pain now etched on his face. How could he not accompany him, be on hand to see him, to offer him a son's comfort and love? But would this man they were expecting have the humanity to understand that?

And then the tap came on the door, and on going to open it, Rory saw a small, portly man, red-faced behind his dark moustache and beard.

'Adare?' His voice was sharp.

'Yes, sir.' He stood aside.

The man entered the room with only a cursory glance at Rory. Instead he went over to the bed by the wall. 'Seamus Adare?'

He received a weak nod, and after staring down at him for a few minutes, he wrote in a small black notebook. Then he turned to Rory. 'And you are?'

'Rory Adare.'

'Your age is?'

'Sixteen, sir.'

'Occupation?'

Rory hesitated.

'Speak up boy!'

'He is a scholar.' The strength in Seamus's voice surprised them both.

The statement was written in the notebook.

The man, who hadn't offered his name, began to prowl around the two rooms, looking inside the cupboards and drawers. Apparently satisfied, he said, 'No source of income, then?'

Rory shook his head. 'I was employed as a pot boy, but . . .' His throat dried at the thought of revealing what had happened.

'I suppose it's the usual, sacked without a reference?' His tone was sarcastic.

Rory could only nod, avoiding the man's eyes, but there were no more questions, and later that night, his head on a grubby flock pillow, Rory lay staring into the darkness. To be forced to enter a workhouse was degrading for anyone, but for a man like his father, well-educated and who had mixed with the cream of Dublin literary society to spend the last days of his life in there . . . Rory could hardly bear to think of it. He had little thought for himself, he was young and strong, while nothing on earth would persuade him to remain in such a place, not after . . . he could only close his eyes in misery at the inevitable prospect.

After Ella's stint in the laundry ended, she began to learn needlework, an occupation she found far more to her liking. It was not that she had any special aptitude for the work, but the large room was quieter and the older women talked freely among themselves. Then, on one particular afternoon, knowing that it was time for another visit, she found it hard to concentrate. But she did try to listen to old Agnes, who was helping her with the intricacies of blind hemming. It seemed that her late husband had fought for his queen and country.

'Out in South Africa, he was, fighting them Zulus,' she said, 'and a spear got 'im in the shoulder at Rorke's Drift, so it was a pension after that.' She sucked on a length of cotton before threading a needle. 'But he didn't last long, and the army don't care about widows. Then our Janey went down with consumption and the doctor's bills took what bit we'd got saved.'

Ella dared to ask, 'What happened to her?'

'She couldn't fight it, love. And she wasn't 'aving no pauper's funeral; my Jim wouldn't 'ave wanted that. I got behind with the rent and the blasted landlord sent the bailiffs in. Next thing I know, I was carted off to this place.'

'That's awful.'

'I've 'eard of worse.'

'Agnes, how do some girls manage to get out of here?'

'If they're lucky they get taken on as apprentices, usually to dressmakers or milliners.'

'Not into service, then, you know in one of them posh houses?' The inmate who showed Ella how to sew buttons on, had once worked as a housemaid before falling on hard times.

Agnes shook her head. 'They wouldn't look twice at yer, not coming from this place. Mind you, some go out as servants – or should I say skivvies – in alehouses or to tradesmen's wives or suchlike, but most end up sent back.'

Ella stared at her. 'Why?'

'Thievin', lazy, or up the spout. This place doesn't spawn angels. 'Ow old are yer?'

'I think about twelve or thirteen. I'm not sure when my birthday is. I know I was six when I came in.'

'What, with yer ma?'

Ella shook her head. 'She was killed in an accident.'

'And yer dad?'

'She never told me. I think he must be dead.'

Agnes tightened her lips. 'Then 'ow come you didn't get sent to the orphanage?'

'I was supposed to go but they'd just had a big fire, so I ended up here.'

Agnes thought back. 'Six years ago, you say. Oh yes, I remember, arson was rumoured. Still, this place isn't that bad, it's big enough for the kids to be taught 'ere and not to 'ave to go to school outside. Those who do are looked down on as if they were freaks, poor little blighters.'

'That's not fair.'

'Life ain't fair, you'll learn that. Now, yer seem a decent girl, so work hard and keep yer nose clean. And mind yer don't get on the wrong side of that Miss Grint. If ever a woman was suckled on a sour lemon . . .'

But Ella was glancing up at the clock on the wall, which said ten minutes to four. 'Agnes, if I nip out for a few minutes, will you cover for me? Say I've got a bellyache or something.'

'Why, what you up to?'

'Nothing bad, I promise.' She put aside the skirt she was hemming, and as soon as the officer further along the line bent over another trainee, Ella eased herself out of the room. She met nobody as she hurried along the winding corridors, and on emerging into the blinding sunshine she turned the corner to find Miss Fairchild's carriage close by, drawn into the shade of the building. Feeling daring, Ella walked slowly towards it, drawn in fascination to the chestnut horses. The one nearest to her turned his head and, with a thump of her heart, she gazed into soft brown eyes. This horse would never trample anyone to death, she was sure of it.

'His name's Rusty – go on, stroke him, he won't hurt you.'

She glanced up to see the coachman grinning at her and, with a flutter of fear that was almost enjoyable, moved to place her hand on the horse's long neck. Its coat felt soft, velvety and very warm. She liked it. 'He's hot.'

'He's all right. It's a hot day. What's yer name?'

'Ella.' She glanced over her shoulder, fearful that someone might come out and see her talking.

'What are yer scared of?'

'I shouldn't be out here.'

'Playing truant, eh? I used to do that as a lad.'

'Me too!' The footman came round the carriage and winked at her. He was much younger than the coachman, with curly fair hair. 'Me dad used to take the strap to me, but it didn't make any difference.'

Although the church clock a little distance away struck four, there was still no sign of the visitor and Ella's palms began to grow clammy as she moved back to wait by the wall. She didn't dare to be out here for much longer. What if somebody noticed she was missing and reported it to Miss Grint? Her heart gave a leap of fear at even the prospect.

Chapter Three

Earlier that same morning, Letitia hadn't felt at all inclined to make her duty visit to the workhouse when her maid drew back the blue brocade curtains to let in a stream of sunlight. The Master's office was never a pleasant place to be as the air was always tainted with the staleness of tobacco smoke. She doubted the small window was ever opened. But after a delicious luncheon of salmon, buttered new potatoes, peas, and salad from her kitchen garden, she went upstairs to change. Letitia had for some time been conscious that only once had she obeyed her father's wish that she should, on occasion, inspect some part of the workhouse unannounced. Then, escorted to a cold and cheerless dining hall, she had stood on a platform and looked down on row upon row of women seated on backless wooden forms before long tables. They were of all ages and dressed in the same grey striped uniform and white starched caps, the only sound had been of wooden spoons against bowls, the slurping of watery soup and the heavy footsteps of patrolling officers. Letitia had found the scene one of such abject misery that she hadn't been able to get the image out of her head for days.

Arriving at the workhouse, Letitia descended the steps of her carriage wearing a dark-blue linen skirt and matching coat, with an elaborate cartwheel hat trimmed with crimson silk dog roses. One lace glove carried carelessly, she greeted the female officer waiting at the main entrance to escort her along the winding corridors that led to the Master's office.

William Peaton, a portly man with bushy sideburns and a well-trimmed beard rose from his chair as she swept in. 'May I bid you a good afternoon, Miss Fairchild. I trust I find you well?'

'Perfectly, thank you. And yourself and Mrs Peaton?'

'In good health too, praise the Lord.'

'I trust I shall have the pleasure of seeing her later?'

'But, of course. She will be joining us once our business has been completed. Please.' He came round the desk to fuss over her chair and, once satisfied that she was comfortable, returned to open the large brown ledger before him and, turning it round, passed it over for her inspection.

Letitia removed her other glove and, placing them both on the desk, scrutinised the neat entries. The man opposite remained silent. Eventually, and only when she was satisfied with the figures, Letitia said, 'Again, I must congratulate you, Mr Peaton, on such orderly accounts. Being appointed by the Board of Guardians only after his death, you would not have known my father, but he would have been gratified to see how well the family bequest is being utilised.'

'Thank you, Miss Fairchild.' He held his hand out for the ledger. 'May I relieve you . . . ?'

Letitia smiled and passed it over. Behind her, the door opened to a cloud of eau de cologne and Mrs Peaton, a narrow-shouldered woman with prominent blue eyes and greying hair scraped into an apology of a chignon, came in. 'Miss Fairchild, how delightful.'

Letitia wondered whether in her wardrobe she possessed any other colour but black, although this time she was at least wearing a cameo brooch at her neck. A stony-faced woman of about forty, obviously a superior sort of inmate, followed her in and sullenly placed a tray on the desk. Letitia glanced at the earthenware cups and accepted a cup of tea but declined to take a biscuit. After the usual pleasantries, she made her request.

'I am not certain of your exact meaning, Miss Fairchild?'

She explained about the previous occasion and smiled at them both. 'So, you can see that as a dutiful daughter, I find myself . . .'

William Peaton frowned. 'What exactly did you have in mind?'

'Oh, nothing extensive; perhaps as I have seen where the inmates eat, I might see where they sleep?'

Mrs Peaton answered for him. 'Could I suggest Miss Fairchild, that you inspect our infirmary? You could then also see the care they receive when ill.'

'That would be most satisfactory.'

'Then perhaps if you would like to accompany me?' Mrs Peaton rose and held open the door.

'Certainly, and as I have no doubt that all will be in order, I shall bid you good day, Mr Peaton, until our next meeting.'

Letitia was wary, not at all sure what she was facing. The building was like a warren, the corridors narrow and twisting, but eventually Mrs Peaton opened a door into a cavernous medical ward. The ceiling was high, the windows grimy, but the bedding on the iron beds, if coarse, did at least appear to be clean. Letitia walked at the side of the Master's wife between the rows of beds, conscious of women's weary eyes watching her, filled with pity at the sight of gaunt and wasted faces, by the ugliness of old age. Several patients lay supine, either asleep or exhausted by pain.

'You have doctors in attendance?' she asked.

'We have two medical officers appointed by the Board, who visit on a regular basis. Most of our inmates receive a higher standard of care here than they would where they lived before.'

A couple of nurses gave her curious glances, and Letitia fumbled to find a scented handkerchief to cover her mouth when, to her horror, a crone retched, then leant over the bed to vomit into a pail. A few minutes later, she felt her own bile rise at the stench emanating from a bed further down the room. 'A bad case of diarrhoea, I'm afraid,' Mrs Peaton said.

Letitia swallowed. She had intended to speak to one of the patients in person but horrified at feeling nauseous, was thankful to see another door only a few yards away and began to quicken her pace. 'Thank you, it has been most interesting.'

'Is there anything further I can show you? Our isolation ward, perhaps?'

Still struggling against her nausea Letitia managed to say, 'I don't think I need to take any more of your valuable time, thank you Mrs Peaton.'

When at last the door of the main entrance opened, Ella's feet were feeling hot and heavy in her black boots. She'd been feeling brave after having spoken to the coachman and footman but now . . . Plucking up her courage, she moved out of the shade. Miss Fairchild had paused and seemed to be taking deep breaths.

'Hello, miss.'

The long skirt swished. 'Hello. You always seem to be out here when I come. Tell me, are you waiting for someone?'

'Only you, miss.'

Ella saw her frown. 'Are you saying that when I visit the workhouse you loiter outside in the hope of seeing *me*? Now, why on earth would you do that, child?'

Taken aback by the direct question, hot colour flooded Ella's cheeks. She floundered, 'I don't know, miss.'

'I see. Well, it's very flattering but . . .' Letitia realised that she had left her gloves on the desk in the Master's office. She paused, perhaps the girl would like to earn a penny or two. 'I've left my gloves on Mr Peaton's desk. Would you like to fetch them for me?'

The girl's eyes filled with panic. 'Oh no, I'm sorry, I couldn't, miss. I'll have to go now.'

Letitia watched in bewilderment as she ran towards a side door and disappeared. She hesitated, then decided that she would return herself, and went back through the main entrance.

'You young varmint, I've caught you before, sneaking off!' The voice was a woman's and it came from around a bend in the corridor. 'And what was it this time?'

'I got the stomach cramps.' Letitia recognised the girl's voice.

'And you needed to go outside?'

'I felt sick.'

'You're a lying toad.'

Letitia heard the sound of a hard slap, followed by another, and quickening her pace, saw the girl holding her hand against her ear, one side of her face reddening. She was glaring up at one of the workhouse officers, an angular woman with a narrow, harsh face. 'Now, get back to work, and there'll be a black mark on your record. A troublemaker, that's what you are.'

'That's not true!'

'Don't answer back . . .' Still holding the girl by the shoulder, the woman once more raised her hand, but Letitia's commanding voice stopped her.

'That is enough!'

The officer instead gave the girl a push and she, after a grateful glance at Letitia, ran away.

'Is such treatment necessary?'

'I am afraid so, madam, otherwise we would have mayhem.'

'And your name is?'

'Miss Grint, I am a day officer.'

Letitia inclined her head and gave what she hoped would be interpreted as a smile of acceptance. So deep in thought was she, that when she reached the Master's office it was to give only the lightest tap on the door before entering. Mr Peaton was bending before a safe in the corner of the room, where he was transferring the ledger he had presented earlier to her. He straightened up.

'Miss Fairchild. Is there perhaps something wrong, some query about the infirmary? My wife seemed under the impression . . .'

She smiled. 'Not at all, Mr Peaton, it is just that I think I left my gloves on your desk.'

'Oh, I see.' He leant over and lifted a sheet of paper. 'Ah, there they are.'

'Thank you, and may I bid you good afternoon once again.'

'She caught me,' Ella muttered to Agnes.

'Who did?'

'Miss Grint, she gave me what for as well! *And* she said she'd put a black mark on my record.'

Agnes put down the sock she was darning. 'That's bad, love, really bad. Don't say I didn't warn yer.'

Ella went up to the dormitory that night full of mixed emotions. She had better stop this waiting outside. After all, she wasn't a child any more. Agnes had told her that she was now able to have babies.

'And in a few years, when a man does come near you, keep yer legs crossed until you've got a wedding ring on yer finger. Cos you've got nobody but me ter put yer right, except the parson on Sunday, and he only spouts about sin and hellfire. You take notice of what I say, and you'll save yourself a lot of grief.'

Ella had heard enough 'dirty' talk to know what she was talking about, and the results of it; she wasn't going to be stupid enough to let that happen to *her*.

And then she thought of how wonderful the afternoon had been, what with the coachman and the young footman joking with her, and that lovely horse. And hadn't the visitor stopped Miss Grint from belting her again? But remembering what Agnes had said, Ella began to panic in case the black mark meant that she could never get out of this hateful place.

It was when Letitia was travelling home in the carriage, and the horses turned into the road leading to Eversleigh that she saw the fair-haired man outside its tall iron gates. He was motionless and she leant forward thinking that there was something familiar about the set of his shoulders. Her breath caught in her throat – no it couldn't be . . . She clutched for support at the velvet-clad padding by her side. Her cheeks hot, her pulse racing, Letitia fought the impulse to open the carriage window and peer out. But he must have heard the clop of the horses' hooves as they approached because after a swift glance over his shoulder he was striding away. But she had known him in an instant. Hadn't his image haunted her for the past seven years? And to her consternation her heart had leapt on seeing him. But that, she told herself, was only because it had been a shock. She wouldn't countenance it being for any romantic reason, not after the despicable way he had treated her. But why Miles Maitland would come back to Hampstead, where he had scandalised local society by his hasty departure, she couldn't imagine.

By the time the carriage had drawn to a halt for Jack to open the gates, the distantly retreating figure was no longer visible. But Letitia was sure of one thing, if Miles intended to visit Eversleigh, to call on her, he would find that she was not the naive young woman she'd been when she was twenty. Even to the Featherstones, Letitia had never admitted that in those dark months after his desertion she had formed two base suspicions. Either her father had threatened to disinherit her, or he had offered Miles a bribe to disappear from her life. Why else would the young man who had professed to love her emerge from her father's study ashen-faced and refusing to speak to her. Not only that, but he never contacted her again and, without giving any reason, fled abroad.

Chapter Four

With Seamus taken immediately to the male infirmary, Rory found himself subjected to not only a public bath, but also the humiliation of being deloused and having his head shaved. His scalp felt cold and exposed and he felt sickened at the sight of his reddish-brown hair lying in tufts on the floor, even though he knew it would grow again. What he hated most, though, was the knowledge that he had lost not only his independence, but also his dignity. He was now reduced to only a number.

'Hurry up, lad, I haven't got all day.'

The officer was impatient, and hurriedly Rory put on the drab blue and grey uniform.

'Follow me.'

The sour smell from the dormitory emanated as soon as the door was opened, and Rory gazed in dismay at the grim long room with iron beds crowded together.

'There's one at the far end you can have.' The officer indicated a notice nailed to the back of the door. 'Can you read?'

With compressed lips, Rory nodded.

'Those are the rules – make sure you stick to them.'

But the sight of the dormitory paled into insignificance when

Rory first saw the dining hall. He didn't think he had ever seen a more depressing sight, but taking his place at the end of one of the long tables, found himself grateful for the bowl of greasy stew and a hunk of bread.

Together with the other inmates, he spent that afternoon and every following day, with the exception of the Sabbath, toiling in the oakum room, where he shredded old ropes into fibres, holding them by an iron hook held between his knees. He was told that the fibres, once mixed with tar or grease, became caulking, filling the gaps between wooden planks on ships to keep them watertight. It was this knowledge that Rory clung to as consolation that his labours would, in the future, keep seamen safe. But that didn't disguise the fact that the work was unpleasant nor, as time went on, prevent the calluses on his hands becoming ingrained with grime.

He was allowed to visit Seamus in the infirmary once a week, only to see his father's once tall strong body becoming little more than a skeleton. But he would rouse a little on seeing Rory who, in the short time allotted to him, would murmur of the old days in Dublin. And while he would always miss his beloved mother, he was almost thankful that Mary hadn't lived to see her once proud family brought to such degradation.

When Grace next came for tea at Eversleigh, Letitia was sorely tempted to tell her that she had seen Miles again. But she still rationalised that it would be best to keep her own counsel, at least for now. If he had returned to the area with the intention of staying, the news would soon spread. And if he had merely been passing through, then she had no desire to begin a topic that would inevitably bring back shameful, painful memories.

Grace glanced at her, raising an eyebrow as she looked at the last scone, and Letitia laughed. 'You have it – I'll ring for some more.'

'I shouldn't really, but they are quite small.'

'Heavens, you've a figure to envy.' Coming back from the bell pull Letitia said, 'I think I shall call you Jiminy in future. You remember – Pinocchio's conscience.' She was startled to see distress in her friend's eyes.

'I'd rather you didn't, that's what Peter used to call me.'

'Grace, I had no idea, otherwise . . .'

'How could you possibly have known?'

A silence fell and as she poured herself another cup of tea, Letitia remembered her friend's heartbreak when, several years ago, the man she loved and hoped to marry had instead chosen the Catholic Church. It was Letitia's hope that he would remain there and that Grace would eventually find happiness with a man more deserving of her. 'Well, I have something rather interesting to tell you about my visit to the workhouse last week.'

'I remember you saying that you intended to make a surprise inspection this time.'

Letitia pulled a face. 'And so I did. I visited the infirmary and although all was satisfactory, it was a far from pleasant experience. No, this is something completely different.' She went on to describe how a young girl had come forward to speak to her and then later she had witnessed her being ill-used.

'You must do something!' Grace exclaimed. 'All she did was to go outside without permission.'

'Yes, but why, Grace?' Into Letitia's mind came the memory of a clear young voice, '*To see you, miss*,' and her surprise that the vowels, while not pure, had only had a hint of the Cockney ones that she would have expected. 'I ask you, why would she wait outside especially to see *me*? I have noticed her before.'

Grace was silent for a moment, then said, 'You and I have

talked sometimes of whether we believe that everything in life happens for a reason, that everyone we meet touches our life in some way. What if this is such an instance?'

Letitia stared at her. 'Are you trying to say that she could be meant to be part of my life?'

'Or perhaps you could be meant to be part of hers.'

'Do you know, Grace, there *was* something about her that intrigued me and I've been toying with an idea. What you have just said, fanciful though it may be, persuades me to go ahead. Why don't I . . .' She continued to explain, the tap on the door so slight that she paused only when she noticed Mabel hovering. 'May we have more scones and jam, strawberry if possible?'

It was fortunate that the size of the kitchen at Eversleigh compensated for its lack of light, because the architect who had designed the substantial red-brick house had given scant thought to its servants. The butler, a tall balding man with rimless spectacles, deplored the frequent lighting of the gas burners necessitated by its small windows. 'Of course,' he said, 'the upstairs rooms are blessed with God's light even on a dull day, are they not, Jack?'

The young footman grinned and winked at the plump under-housemaid, who was folding napkins at a dresser. 'They certainly are.'

Henry Forbes frowned at him. 'Have you brushed the jacket I put out? And checked the others in my wardrobe?'

'All is in order, Mr Forbes.' He glanced up at the sound of hurrying steps on the stairs.

'You'll never guess what I just heard the mistress say!'

The butler turned from his task of counting the silver cutlery. 'Mabel, how many times have I told you – what a maid hears in the drawing room, remains there.'

'Yes, but—'

He held up a gloved hand.

Her lips met in a mutinous line. 'More scones and jam please, Cook.'

'Glory, they've got an appetite on them today. A good job I made extra. What about cream?'

'Just jam. Miss Fairchild asked if you have any strawberry.'

'It always was her favourite. Go and fetch some.' She turned to the butler. 'You mustn't be too hard on her, Mr Forbes.'

'A good servant should be like that proverb, Mrs Perkins – "see no evil, hear no evil, speak no evil".'

'You mean like those ivory monkeys I saw in that antique shop? Right ugly things, they gave me the creeps.'

Mabel was already handing her the jam. 'I was never going to speak any evil. You should *know*, Mr Forbes, cos you won't like it.'

He sighed. 'All right, just this once.'

'Miss Fairchild is only going to bring a girl from the workhouse here, to work in the kitchen!'

Cook let out a squawk. 'Over my dead body, she is!'

The butler stiffened. 'You must have misheard her, girl.'

'The very idea,' Cook bristled. 'I'll have no disease-ridden brat handling my victuals.'

'Well, I heard her, clear as a bell.'

'Mabel?'

'Yes, Mr Forbes?' She picked up the tray.

'You have my permission – just this once – to come back and report anything further you hear on the subject.'

Cook was now sitting on a kitchen chair, her legs apart beneath her long white apron. She leant forward. 'I'm perplexed, that's what I am, perplexed. Whatever is the mistress thinking of?'

'I wonder if she means the kid who was hanging about outside,'

Jack said. 'Seemed all right to me, scared stiff of something or someone, though, cos she was playing truant.'

'This gets worse by the minute, I can feel it in me waters.' Cook heaved herself up. 'You put your foot down, Mr Forbes, or we'll all come to regret it.'

'She was a right scrawny little thing, mind, if it *is* the same one I saw. Needs a bit of feeding up, Cook, if you ask me.'

'Well, I didn't.' She turned to glare at the under-housemaid who had started to giggle. 'And you'd better go and begin the linen room, lady.'

Cook watched her go, and said, 'I swear that girl puts a pound on every time she eats a bun.' Her broad face creased in a frown. 'You know, Mr Forbes, we're a happy ship here, I do hope that isn't going to change.'

To Letitia's dismay, her news in the morning room the following day was met with a lukewarm reception. 'I can sense your apprehension, Forbes, but surely it is an act of Christian charity to help an unfortunate child? And it does so happen that the scullery maid has given notice.'

He nodded. 'That is true, there is sickness at home and she is needed there. But forgive me, madam, the highest references have always been required when employing staff at Eversleigh. I take it that you have looked into this girl's character?'

Without the slightest hesitation, Letitia said, 'Naturally.' However, it was with a sense of uneasiness that a few minutes later she watched him leave. Although he would never say so, she knew that he disapproved of her plan and this was not only disconcerting; it confirmed her growing realisation that her decision had been emotive rather than sensible. Letitia thought for some time and eventually decided that she would write a note to Grace, stating her intention to call. It was not her friend's advice she sought but that of her mama. Charlotte Featherstone might have a delicate constitution, but Letitia was not only fond of her, she considered her to be the most intelligent woman she had ever met.

Chapter Five

The Featherstones lived in a handsome stone-built house three miles distant from Eversleigh, in a leafy avenue. Grace's father, who had died from a heart attack at the age of fifty, had been a business colleague of Cedric Fairchild, and their two daughters, introduced to each other at an early age, had remained friends ever since they were young.

Letitia entered the drawing room. Long windows overlooked the garden with its colourful herbaceous borders. Grace and her mother, sitting opposite across a rosewood coffee table, looked up with welcoming smiles. Letitia thought yet again how much they resembled each other. There was the same fairness, the prettiness of complexion; although whereas Charlotte's expression wore a keen intelligence, Grace's blue eyes revealed her more gentle nature.

After being greeted with delight, the first half-hour passed in pleasant conversation and then, once they had enjoyed their cucumber sandwiches and coconut macaroons, Charlotte turned and said with a slight frown, 'Grace has spoken of your interest in a workhouse girl, and I have to confess to feeling both intrigued and a little anxious.'

'It's just that . . .'

Ten minutes later, Charlotte gazed at her. 'My dear headstrong Letitia! Let us, just for a moment, return to the crux of the matter: your decision to become involved with this girl. I detect my daughter's hand in this.' She glanced at Grace. 'Am I correct? Did the initial idea come from you?'

'Not exactly . . .'

'It was my suggestion to bring her to Eversleigh,' Letitia said swiftly.

'I see. Don't mistake me, I can see the appeal of the situation, it intrigues me too, but that doesn't change the fact that Letitia has now placed herself in an invidious position.'

'What do you mean, Mama?'

'I mean, Grace, that she now has no choice but to go ahead with this foolhardy scheme. To do otherwise would convey the impression to her staff that she is indecisive, and that would never do.'

'But what if the duty officer was correct and she is a troublemaker?' Letitia said.

Charlotte considered. 'Tell me, when she approached you, when she spoke to you, was she impertinent?'

Letitia shook her head.

'Was there insolence in her eyes?'

'No, in fact she seemed shy.'

'Then you can only make further enquiries as to her background and hope there are no reports of immorality.'

Grace gave a gasp, and Charlotte looked amused. 'All types of people end up in the workhouse, my dear, although I'm the first to admit that one can never generalise.'

'Don't forget, Mama, that one of Letitia's own relatives, through no fault of his own, spent a period of his life in one of those places. How do we know that this child wasn't a victim of a similar circumstance?'

'You are determined to see life through rose-tinted glasses, Grace. As far as you are concerned, Letitia, I can only advise you that when the girl does arrive in your household, any involvement on your part should be kept to a minimum.'

'But . . .'

'Think about, it my dear. Resentment or jealousy among the rest of the staff will only sit ill on the child.'

Letitia knew that what she said was true, but did that mean that she was going to bring this girl to Eversleigh only for her to remain hidden out of sight in the basement? Because if she and Grace were right in their imaginings, that this girl was meant to be in Letitia's life, or she in hers, then how in the name of heaven was she going to discover why?

Ella was bored. Agnes had told her the law said children had to be educated up 'til the age of ten, and she and a few of the other girls who were good at their lessons were expected to help out with the little ones. On this particular morning, seven-year-old Violet was more interested in picking at the boil on her neck than writing a sum on her slate.

'Press it with your hankie,' Ella hissed as yellow pus spurted out, but Violet had forgotten it.

Ella fished up her sleeve and handed over her own. 'Here, keep it, I don't want the dirty thing back. Give me your clean one later.'

When the doorknob squeaked and Miss Grint marched in, everyone swiftly lowered their heads and Ella felt her stomach lurch when she heard her number called out. She swallowed and slid from the bench while the other children nudged each other, one tweaking the back of her skirt in sympathy as she walked down the narrow aisle between the rows of desks.

'Come with me.' Miss Grint swept out of the open door and, red-faced, Ella hurried behind her.

'Where are we going, miss?'

'You'll soon find out.'

'What have I done?'

'You'll find that out too.'

Ella, whose feet were outgrowing her boots, found it difficult to keep up with the long strides of the figure before her. She felt sick with fear, especially when she saw that they were heading for the Master's office. She wiped her now clammy hands on her apron as Miss Grint knocked on the door. Opening it, she put her hand in the small of Ella's back and pushed her inside. 'Number 85, sir.'

'Ah yes. Thank you, Miss Grint.'

Ella heard her leave and stood before the large desk in the hot stuffy room. Mr Peaton, with his wife seated beside him, was looking down at a brown folder.

'Your full name is . . . ?'

'Ella, sir. Ella Hathaway.'

'And I see you have been with us for several years.'

'Yes, sir.'

'Have you any complaints as to your treatment here?'

She shook her head.

'Speak up, girl.'

'No, sir.'

'Good. Now then, Ella, tell me the truth. Have you been in the habit of waiting outside to see a certain visitor, a Miss Fairchild?'

Ella floundered. What should she do? She could lie, but the Master would believe Miss Grint over her, that was for sure. But if she admitted it, she'd likely get another black mark.

'There's no need to be afraid.' It was Mrs Peaton speaking. Ella didn't trust Mrs Peaton, she'd once seen her pinch a three-year-old girl so sharp that she'd cried. 'Answer the Master. Do you wait outside to see Miss Fairchild?'

Mutely, Ella nodded.

'And why would you do that?'

There was that question again. 'I like to look at her nice clothes.' She saw them exchange glances.

Mr Peaton turned to his wife. 'So, at least we have ascertained that she is indeed the girl in question.'

Mrs Peaton lowered her voice. 'But we have been asked about her background.'

'In her record, there is merely the one transgression, otherwise nothing untoward.'

At the word 'record' Ella became full of panic. This *was* about that black mark! Perhaps if she said she was sorry, that she wouldn't wait outside any more . . .

But Mr Peaton was talking to her. 'Ella, the rules in this workhouse are there to be obeyed, I will not countenance disobedience. Do you understand?'

'I'm sorry, sir, I won't do it again.'

'Yes, well, you are a very lucky girl. I have received a letter from Miss Fairchild, and she is prepared to offer you domestic work in her household.' He glanced sharply at her. 'However, she is relying on my judgement as to whether you can be trusted. What do you have to say for yourself?'

Ella felt rooted to the ground with joy. Then she stared at the impatient bearded face of the man opposite, at the cold face of his wife and panicked. Could they stop her going? She gabbled, 'I've never done anything wrong before, sir. I say my prayers every night and I'm a hard worker, I did well in the classroom, and the laundry, and I'm learning sewing now. I wouldn't let you down, honest.'

Mr Peaton gazed at her for a few moments, then glanced at his wife. When she nodded he said, 'All right, I shall inform Miss Fairchild of my approval and arrange for your release. You will be told when you can leave and then brought to see me again.' He waved a hand to dismiss her.

Ella bobbed a curtsey and, turning, almost stumbled from the room to hurry back along the corridors, the soreness of her feet forgotten. That night when she went up to the long dormitory, too excited to sleep, she watched the tired inmates climbing into their beds. Into her mind came an image of little freckle-faced Teresa, who used to sleep in the one next to her own and when she was frightened in the dark or had bad dreams, Ella would reach out and hold her hand. She had loved Teresa like a sister; a quiet child who had believed that everyone had a guardian angel and never once missed praying every night to her own. When one night, several months ago, she had screamed out in agony and later died of a burst appendix, Ella's grief had stopped her believing in angels, but tonight she began to wonder whether they did exist after all.

Chapter Six

After a whole week had gone by, when the supervisor in the sewing room summoned Ella to be measured, her anxiety changed into increasing dread. Yes, she'd outgrown her uniform, but wasn't she supposed to be leaving? Agnes kept advising her to be patient, but Ella was growing more worried with every day that passed.

Then after another week when the passing days seemed endless, Ella was leaving the dining hall after breakfast when Miss Grint seized her arm and, without any explanation, pulled her along a corridor and down stone steps to an unfamiliar part of the workhouse. Lifting a key from a bunch hanging at her belt, she unlocked the door of a large fusty room with rails of clothes and a brown curtain hanging across one corner.

She began to search along the hangers, taking out first one skirt, then another to hold against Ella. 'This one will do,' she said, putting it over her arm, then lifted down a blouse. 'Go on, put these on, quick as you can.'

Ella scuttled behind the curtain and took off her uniform and apron, then, with excitement, tried on the faded brown blouse and black skirt. Her wrists were longer than the sleeves and the waist of the skirt sagged, but at least it reached to the top of her boots. Before she was able to look in the cloudy mirror, the curtain was yanked open.

'You can leave the uniform there.' She thrust out a hat. 'This should fit.'

Ella put it on, relieved to see that on its brown straw there was a crumpled cream rosebud, at least. The mirror was behind her, but she didn't dare to turn around because Miss Grint was already at the door, key in hand and holding out a grey shawl. 'Hurry up, girl, I've got work to do.'

A few seconds later and back up the stone steps, Ella realised they were heading for the Master's office. 'Am I going out, then?'

'So you do have a brain.'

As she hurried behind her, Ella stuck out her tongue. But even Miss Grint's sarcasm couldn't dampen her spirits.

This time, Mr Peaton sat alone behind his desk, and on seeing her, glanced down at a sheet of paper before him and ticked it. 'Ah yes, number 85. Your release is now in order, all that remains is for me to hand over your personal possessions.'

She stared at him. Did he mean the clothes she was wearing when she came here? Cos if so, they'd be far too small!

Ella watched in bewilderment as he leant down and brought up a shabby hessian bag. That was too small to hold clothes. There was a label tied to it with her name and a date, both written in black ink.

'I shall need you to sign your name at the bottom of this form. You *can* write?'

Tearing her gaze away from the bag, she nodded.

'Good. Here then . . .' He pushed a sheet of paper across the desk and pointed at a line marked each end with a pencilled cross, dipped a pen into an inkwell and handed it to her.

She glanced up at him. 'It is just to confirm that you have received your own property. You may read it if you wish.'

Ella looked at the sentence above the line, pressed her lips

45

together, and managed to sign her name without making a blot.

'Now, off you go and wait at the back entrance for the cart.' He replaced the pen at the side of the inkwell. 'I hope you will show your gratitude to Miss Fairchild by working hard.'

'I will, sir.' Picking up the bag, she almost ran from the room to pause in the corridor, glancing down at it, burning with curiosity. Her fingers began to pull on the drawstring, but . . . she couldn't go without saying goodbye to Agnes.

Ella flushed at the spluttered laughter her hurried entrance brought in the sewing room.

'Take no notice, ducks, yer look fine.' Agnes shook her head at the others.

'I've got to rush, Agnes, but look – my personal possessions.' Ella held out the bag.

Agnes nodded. 'Make sure you put 'em somewhere safe. Now, mind yer manners, keep yourself clean and tidy, and don't pull yer face, even if they give you all the dirty jobs to do.'

'Do you think they will?'

'Bound to, seein' as you're new. Just learn as much as you can and try to stay out of this place.'

'I shall miss you, Agnes.'

The old woman blinked and looked down at the shirt in her hands, at its half-turned collar. 'You're a good kid, Ella. I'll miss you, an' all.'

Rory walked out of the shadow of the workhouse and, raising his face to the warmth of the sun, muttered, 'Thank God!' In the clear daylight he inspected his hands, relieved to see that his harsh painful scrubbing had cleaned their ingrained grime. He could do nothing about the stubble on his head. He may as well have 'workhouse' printed on his forehead – or, heaven forbid, even 'prison'.

Another released inmate was already waiting in the place he'd been told to go to, her florid face breaking into a smile as she saw him approach. 'Flaming 'ell, I'm glad to be out of that place. Mind you, at least they kept me personal stuff safe.' She patted a bulging pocket in her fusty black coat. She winked, 'I'd a bin daft to leave it behind. Didn't you bring anythin' in with yer?'

Rory shook his head.

''Ave they found you a job, then?'

'Yes, I suppose I should be thankful.'

'Me too, cos it means I can cadge a lift.'

At the clip-clop of hooves they swung round to see the cart approaching.

'He's early.' The driver reined in the horse, removed his cap and began to mop his brow with a red spotted kerchief. 'I thought there was three of yer.'

'There's only us 'ere.' She turned to Rory. 'You'll 'ave ter give me a hand up, lad, I'm not as young as I was.'

Not so slim, either, if she ever had been, Rory thought as with no step provided, he struggled to help her into the cart, and was about to go in after her only to hear a high-pitched shout. 'Wait for me!'

Looking over his shoulder, he could see a young girl running towards them, one hand holding on to her hat, the other clutching a small bag against her chest. She gasped. 'I was scared of missing it!'

Looking at the height of the cart and then at her slight figure, Rory said, 'I'll go first, then I can help you up.' From the cart, he turned to see her hesitating. 'Come on!' He held out his hand and she took it and climbed up, stumbling a little before going to sit beside the other female. 'Thank you.'

Rory took a seat facing them both. He never wanted to see this wretched place again. Hadn't his father died there and suffered the final indignity of a pauper's funeral? Rory still felt guilty that he hadn't been able to prevent such shame.

47

But Ella was turning to stare at the forbidding building that had sheltered her for so long, although that lasted only a moment. She was too full of excitement not to want to look ahead, even if her belly was full of butterflies.

The woman next to her said, 'I've only managed to get out cos me debts have bin paid off. Are yer goin' into service, then?'

Ella nodded.

'Well, at least it can't be worse than in there.'

As they turned the corner the horse began to trot faster, and putting a hand on the side to steady herself, Ella held the bag even tighter. She looked up at the blue sky, entranced by the hedges and fields and then astonished by the noise and bustle everywhere when they reached the town. The roads were crowded with people; there were delivery carts and something the woman told her was a horse tram, laughing when Ella held her nose when their own horse lifted its tail. 'Nothin' wrong with a bit of horse muck, it's supposed to be an 'ealthy smell.'

But Ella was now smiling at two barking dogs chasing each other, at a small boy bowling a hoop, and when they passed a man roasting chestnuts, the smell made her mouth water. Once or twice she glanced across at the young man on the cart, thinking that he must be at least sixteen because he was so tall, but he seemed in a world of his own. He hardly looked at the buildings and shops they were passing. When the cart came to a halt at the corner of a side street, the woman began to get up and Rory helped her out of the cart. 'Thanks, lad. Good luck to yer both.'

'Thank you.' Their voices came in unison, and as the horse began to move away, Ella looked across at her remaining companion but he was again lost in his own thoughts. Eventually the roads widened and became quieter, there were now only a few people walking along the pavements, and she contented herself with drinking in the beauty of the trees. She looked down at the bag again, desperate to open it, but resisted the temptation. Whatever was inside, she ought to be by herself, and certainly not on a jolting cart.

Rory, who had managed to close his ears to the chatter of the woman, realised it would be rude to ignore his remaining companion. He looked across at the young girl. Clutching a hessian bag against her as if it contained rubies, she glanced up, revealing wide-set eyes in a thin but intelligent face. As she gave a shy smile, Rory could see short tufts of light-brown hair beneath the straw hat. It was awful that even the female inmates had to submit to having their hair shorn.

He smiled back at her. 'How long have you been in the workhouse?'

'Since I was six.'

The sight of children incarcerated in that place had torn at his heart. 'So all this is new to you,' he waved a hand at the scene they were passing.

'Yes. How long were you in there?'

'Six weeks . . . until my father died.'

'I'm sorry.'

'Missy, this is where you get out.' The driver reined in the horse.

Startled she steadied herself as she got up, while the young man got out of the cart and turned to help her down. She gave him a grateful smile. 'Thanks.'

'Good luck.'

'And you.' Ella watched the horse pull away, and then turned to see tall black gates with a name written in gold saying 'Eversleigh'. She stood for a few moments trying to remain calm, then peered through the glossy iron rails to where she could see a long drive leading to an enormous house. Ella's mouth became dry and, feeling sick with nerves, she put her hand on the shiny knob of the gate and turned it.

Chapter Seven

When, at eighteen, Letitia returned home after her final term at Roedean, Mary Blane had already been appointed as her personal maid. Letitia had been resentful at the time, suspecting that her father had chosen the Scottish spinster, with her Presbyterian values, as another means of control. However, over the years, she had come to not only value Mary's loyalty but to respect her sound common sense. And her calm support, when two years later Letitia had embarked on her ill-fated love affair, had been invaluable. But, and she hardly knew why, Letitia still hadn't mentioned to even Mary that she had seen Miles. He hadn't been in contact, which, to her shame, she had found disappointing. She told herself that was because she had hoped to have her curiosity satisfied about that fateful night, not because of any other foolish notion. And had convinced herself that it had probably been merely a nostalgic whim that had brought him to the gates of Eversleigh.

'It is today that the new girl arrives, madam.'

Letitia was sitting before her dressing table. 'I hadn't forgotten. And she has all that she needs?'

Mary nodded. 'Everything was made according to the measurements sent. And her own clothes will be put in the boiler.'

It was just before luncheon when Letitia wandered over to the large windows in the morning room. And it was then that she saw Ella coming up the drive. Even from a distance, the set of her shoulders revealed a nervous eagerness that made Letitia smile. Then, as she drew nearer, she could only stare at her with a pity that bordered on anger. How could they have sent the girl out dressed in such drab, ugly and ill-fitting clothes? But that anger swiftly turned to dismay when instead of turning left to go round to the tradesmen's entrance, Ella began to walk up to the front door. Letitia made a swift movement at the window, gesticulating, not wanting the girl to be humiliated, but already the sound of the bell was pealing through the house.

Ella's heart was pounding as she waited for the door to be opened, and then she stared in awe at the tall man standing before her. His expression was one of anger.

'Not *here*, girl. Go back down the drive and take the path.'

Her cheeks hot with embarrassment, Ella obeyed and began to hurry away, discovering, just inside the gates, a wide path. She began to walk along it, her breathing now rapid and panicky, although when she turned a corner to see a garden with colourful flowers, she stood and stared at it with amazed admiration. It was the first real garden she had ever seen and, at its scent, her spirits lifted, especially when she saw another door, painted green and not grand like the other one. Ella gave a tug on the bell pull and straightened her straw hat, crossing her fingers that the man in the striped trousers and black jacket wouldn't answer again. To her relief, it was a round-faced young girl, her sandy hair pinned up beneath a starched green cap. Her gaze swept over Ella. 'You've arrived, then. You'd better come in.'

'Thank you, miss.'

'Me name's Rosie. Just wait here for now.'

The floor of the lobby had black and red tiles and there were several doors with voices drifting from the one that Rosie had disappeared through. Ella leant forward to listen.

'And use carbolic soap. I want her washed head to foot, mind, no skimping!'

'Don't worry, Mrs Perkins, I won't.'

'When you others take the water, leave it outside the room. I'll not have it turned into a circus.'

That last voice sounded like the tall man. What did they mean 'washed head to foot'? Did they think she had lice or something?

The maid came back. 'All right, Ella. You're to come with me.'

She clutched her bag in embarrassment. 'I need to . . .'

'What?'

'I need to . . .'

'Oh, all right then, it's out there. Make sure you wash your hands after.'

The lavatory was in a small clean outhouse and, instead of squares of newspaper hanging on a loop of string, there was a roll of thin white paper on the window ledge. Ella went back and, seeing a sink just inside the door, washed her hands with a piece of yellow soap and dried them on a striped towel.

Rosie was waiting and Ella followed her along a corridor, up a flight of steep stairs, on to a landing with several doors. Opening the one at the far end, Rosie said, 'You're to be the scullery maid, as young Betsy left recently. And as I'm the kitchen maid, you'll be sharing in here with me, cos we have to be first up in the mornings, so we can get the kitchen range going.'

Ella stepped inside. The room was small and clean with a sloping ceiling and two narrow beds separated by a chest with three drawers. There was a washstand with a jug and bowl with pink roses on them, with a mirror above, and four pegs on the wall. A small wardrobe stood in one corner and on the brown linoleum was a tin bath with a towel draped over the side.

'That's yours.' Rosie indicated the first bed and, when there came the sound of scuffling outside the door, she waited a few seconds before opening it. 'Give me a hand, then!' Ella hurried over and helped her to carry in three heavy cans of water, which they began to empty into the bath. 'We'll leave some in that one for rinsing. Right, take your clothes off and in you get.'

Ella felt humiliated, realising that she was regarded as too dirty for decent company, but peeled off her clothes and, once naked, climbed into the tin bath. 'I can wash myself,' she said as Rosie began to splash and lather her with green strong-smelling soap. Her protest was ignored.

'Your hair won't take much doing – there's not much of it, is there?'

'We have to wear it short so we don't get nits.' She winced at Rosie's hard and searching fingers.

'Clean as a whistle,' she pronounced. 'Stand up.' She filled a jug from the saved water in a can and poured it over Ella's head. 'You can get out now and dry yourself.' Handing over the rough towel, Rosie stood back and her voice was sharp when Ella went to pick up her clothes. 'No, leave them there! You'll find some fresh ones in the bottom drawer.'

There were three pairs of knickers, two vests and a couple of pairs of stockings and garters, laying folded and new. As she hurriedly put on some knickers, she turned to discover that Rosie had taken out of the wardrobe a green dress and apron exactly like her own, and a pair of black boots that looked brand new. Ella caught her breath. 'Are they for me?'

'Well, they're hardly my size.'

Ella dressed herself, fumbling with the buttons, and stood still while Rosie pinned on the cap. 'Boots fit all right?'

'Yes, thank you, miss.'

'You don't have to call me miss.'

Ella darted an apprehensive look at her hessian bag lying on her bed, and Rosie tapped the front of the open drawer. 'You can keep your stuff in there and, as long as you respect my things, I shall respect yours. Understood?'

With a flood of relief, Ella said, 'Yes, miss—I mean, Rosie.'

'Right, we'll get the bath emptied later, come on.'

Feeling self-conscious in her new outfit, Ella began to follow her back along the corridor only to be mortified when her belly gave a loud rumble. For the first time, Rosie softened and she laughed. 'It's roast mutton today, followed by apple pie and custard. I bet you never got that in the workhouse!'

'This is the kitchen,' Rosie said, as she led the way into a large room. But Ella was too conscious of the sea of faces staring at her to look around. She followed the other girl along the long table where every chair was occupied except for two opposite ones at the end. 'You're to sit there.'

Ella began to pull out the heavy chair only to make a scraping sound on the floor. 'Lift it!' Rosie hissed. That worked, and Ella thankfully slid into her place.

The man sitting at the head of the table was the stern one who had opened the front door. As he rapped on the table with a spoon, all murmuring ceased.

'This is our new scullery maid, Ella Hathaway, everyone. Ella, I am the butler and you will address me as Mr Forbes. On my right is Mrs Perkins, who is the cook. Rosie will introduce you to the remainder of the staff later.'

There was a murmur of greeting and she felt her colour rise, not knowing whether she was expected to say anything. But conversation began again and Ella bent her head to gaze down at the green shiny tablecloth. But curiosity won and within seconds she was glancing up and around, only for her eyes to widen at the size of the meat being carved by the butler, and then at the serving dishes filled with vegetables, which Rosie was placing at intervals down the table. When Ella's own plate was passed along to her it had not one, but two slices of mutton. The young man next to her held out a dish of golden roast potatoes and, feeling unsure of her behaviour, Ella took just one. 'Go on,' he whispered, 'have some more.'

She helped herself to another three and a spoonful of every vegetable. When the gravy wasn't watery, but a lovely brown colour, she could wait no longer and picked up her knife and fork, only to hear a loud rap on the table.

Ashamed she'd forgotten about Grace, Ella bowed her head as the butler spoke the few words of prayer but, as soon as she saw someone else begin to eat, she hungrily plunged her fork into a small roast potato. It was hot and fluffy in the middle, and the meat wasn't chewy at all – it tasted lovely. Next, she tried the carrots, and was forking up some peas when—

'We don't do that here!' Ella looked up to see that the butler had put his own cutlery down and was glaring at her. 'Our newest member of staff, everyone, needs to learn that in this house, certain standards are expected. One does not bend down to food and shovel it into the mouth. Please sit up straight, Ella, eat your food slowly and mend your table manners.'

She was mortified, her face crimsoning so much it hurt. To take your time at the workhouse meant that another inmate would pinch what was on your plate, at least when the supervisor wasn't watching. Taking a deep breath, she straightened her shoulders and watched Rosie put only a small portion on to her fork before lifting it to her mouth. She also ate with her mouth closed. Ella began to copy her.

A few minutes later, she began to take notice of the others around the table. She and Rosie were the only ones wearing a green uniform. The plump woman who was the cook wore a large white apron and on the other side of the butler was a severe-looking woman in a grey dress with a white collar. There were two maids in black and white uniforms and, besides the young man next to her, she could see another footman – who turned his head and winked. Ella gave a shy smile back, remembering him from when she'd stroked the horse outside the workhouse.

Several minutes later, the used plates were passed along to the end of the table and Rosie leant across to say to Ella, 'Come and help me, then.'

She remembered to lift her chair back and began to stack the plates, putting the cutlery on top. The pile felt awkward and heavy and, feeling as if all eyes were watching her, with great care Ella carried them behind Rosie into a small room to leave them at the side of a sink. Once back in her place, she found herself gazing down at a dish of golden brown pastry, oozing with apples. She also knew that she couldn't manage a single mouthful.

'Something wrong with it, girl?' The cook's voice rose above the conversation.

Startled, Ella said, 'It looks wonderful, miss, only I'm full up.'

'I expect,' the butler said, 'that Ella isn't used to such rich food, Mrs Perkins. The pie is excellent.'

'Yes, well I was taught that it was a sin to waste good food, but then I was brought up proper.'

A few laughed but Ella just stared ahead. She'd been the butt of many a taunt and had learnt to ignore them. Even if she was sarcastic, Mrs Perkins could never be as bad as Miss Grint and, if she cooked meals every day like this one, Ella was prepared to forgive her anything.

Chapter Eight

Rory turned to watch the girl go in then, as the driver pulled away, found himself thinking that, despite her poor start, there had been nothing coarse about her. Rory remembered how he had soon discovered that a woman could be crude when he went to work at the inn. As a pot boy he had been the butt of many a lewd joke from gin-sodden women and forced to accept it as a hazard of his job.

The landlord's blowsy wife was another matter. Her fondness for not only revealing her ample cleavage, but brushing against him in the corridors with a whispered invitation, he had coped with, but it was when she made a grab at his groin that he reacted. Staggering back from his violent push, she had spat at him and he discovered the truth of the saying 'hell hath no fury like a woman scorned'. Her revenge had been to have him dismissed without a reference and to spread a rumour that he was not to be trusted.

But that, Rory told himself, was in the past. It was the future he must think of now and he found himself thinking of the young girl from the workhouse. Despite her gentle manner, she must have a core of steel to have survived for so long in there. Strange that she didn't have a Cockney accent, just a slight one, and as for the way she had lifted her chin and straightened her shoulders in those ridiculous clothes . . .

Deep in thought, Rory was late in realising how far they had come and, seeing a street sign, put on his cap and pulled the peak down over his eyes. The inn where he was to work – the request for a pot boy had arrived coinciding with his release – would be only a few streets away from his previous home. He pushed aside the memory of that with its inevitable reminder of his father. There would be time for reflection, for grieving in the dark hours of the night. Shoulders hunched, he leant forward on the hard seat, dreading the coming job. And then wondered whether he really did have to take it. His father had done his best to provide him with a fine education, surely he should try to put it to use? Anyway, what had he got to lose? With adrenalin beginning to rush through his veins he called, 'Could you stop here, please?'

The driver flung over his shoulder, 'I was told to take yer—'

'It's all right. I can make my own way now.'

He steadied himself as the horse drew to a halt and within seconds he was standing on the pavement. Another young inmate due to be released could have the job, one who would be grateful for it.

When the cart pulled away, Rory gazed after it for a moment, then felt the euphoria of being free, of being able to choose his own way and, with vigour, he began to head in the direction of Hampstead and away from the area of Camden where he and his father had struggled to survive. For some reason, he had a good feeling about the day and was even hoping that he could find a clerical position; after all, he did have a good hand, excellent grammar and an aptitude for mathematics.

His long stride soon covered the distance and when he reached the high street and saw a bank, with confidence in his ability, he turned into the double doors and entered a wood-panelled interior similar to that of the Dublin bank his father had used. The atmosphere was one of quiet industry, with several clerks sitting behind a long mahogany counter, in front of which was a gentleman in a wing collar and top hat attending to his business. The first position had, in gilt letters, the word 'Enquiries', so Rory headed towards it.

'No, you don't, sonny!' The hand that grasped his shoulder was firm and belonged to a heavily built man in a gold-braided uniform. 'What possible business can you have in an establishment like this?'

'I'm looking for work.'

'And you think we employ riff-raff do you? Out you go!'

'But . . .' Frogmarched to the door, Rory was given a rough push that caused him to stumble down the three steps, to the sniggers of a couple of urchins. Furious and humiliated, he walked on until he reached a shop's large plate window and stared at the reflection of an unkempt youth; his hair shorn close to his head, wearing a shabby brown jacket, sleeves short at the wrist, ankles showing beneath his trousers and a dingy grey shirt. The window fronted a Gentlemen's Tailors and, as he stared at the long jackets and pinstriped trousers, fine shirts and stiff collars, Rory realised the hopelessness of his situation. Disconsolate, he turned away, deep in thought, only to be tantalised by the heavenly aroma of warm bread. Going forward, he peered through the door of a grocer's shop to see freshly baked rolls in a white cloth-lined basket. He did have a few coins; had he enough for just one roll, as well as to pay for a bed for the night? But looking up at the cloudless sky, he decided that he could sleep on the Heath. He looked with hunger at the rolls again, then the prospect of the following day and perhaps even the day after that came into his mind. This morning he had at least been given breakfast, even if the porridge was lumpy and cold. With gritted teeth he walked on, thirsty and hoping to come across a public water tap. His only option would seem to be manual work and, deciding that he would have a better chance by exploring the side roads, he turned down the first one.

But by late afternoon, the optimism he had felt earlier was dwindling. No matter where he'd applied, he'd been humiliated and often sworn at. One rough and burly builder had shoved him out of the way with contempt and it was obvious that, unless and until he could smarten himself up, he was wasting his time. Fear of vagrancy and the workhouse again began to rise, and Rory shuddered. To go back to that place and submit himself to delousing and the loss of liberty? Never!

Hands dejectedly in his pockets, he came to a more residential area and saw that, amongst the large Victorian villas, there was one proclaiming 'Private Hotel'. He stood for a moment and stared at the whiteness of the net curtains and the gleaming brass nameplate. Rory wiped the back of his hand across his perspiring forehead and, lifting first one foot and then the other, rubbed his scuffed shoes on the back of his trousers. Squaring his shoulders, he went beyond the railings and down the stone steps to knock on the brown-painted door.

It was opened by a young girl in a mob cap and green apron who muttered, 'What?'

Someone took her arm and pulled her aside. 'Haven't you learnt any manners yet?' An apple-cheeked woman in a long white apron, her greying hair in a bun, appeared. 'Can I help you . . .' her voice trailed away. 'You get on with yer work, May, I'll see to this.'

Rory began, 'I'm sorry to bother you, but I wondered if there was any work available? I'm willing to try anything.'

'Oh, you are, are yer? And what makes you think we'd take on someone straight out of prison?'

Rory shook his head. 'Not that, the workhouse, and I can only apologise for my appearance.'

Her expression softened. 'Well, we can all fall on 'ard times, and I must say you speak nice.' She began to close the door. 'But the truth is we've got all the staff we need.'

'Even a couple of days would help. Please.'

'I'm sorry, we'd never take in someone off the street.'

With the closing of the door, Rory went back up the steps and stood for a moment looking along at the other tall and substantial houses. But what was the point in trying? With fury, he kicked a stone into the gutter and then, in desperation, began to make his way back to the high street, where at least he could have another drink of water. Then, within seconds, walking towards him came a finely dressed man using a silver-topped cane and, as Rory watched, he suddenly paused, patted his jacket and then with a frown began to search the inside pocket with a growing look of alarm.

Rory guessed that he'd lost his wallet. As the man stood uncertainly, Rory made his way past him, seemingly unnoticed. Then, as soon as he turned the corner and into a treelined deserted road, he could see it. Only a few yards away, with the sun glinting on its gold initials, a black leather wallet lay before him in the centre of the pavement. Rory quickened his step, darted a glance over his shoulder and, on blind impulse, swooped to secrete the wallet inside his jacket. Immediately, he heard distant footsteps and, his heart beating furiously, gave a furtive glance over his shoulder. The man was retracing his steps. Rory hurried away, walking swiftly down one road, then crossing over to another and, to his relief, in the next one he came across a small side alley. The only sign of life was a black cat perched on a high wall, its green eyes watching him warily. Rory slipped inside and, standing by the wall, turned to half-shield his body. His heart racing, hardly able to believe what he had just done, he took out the wallet, hesitated and then slowly opened it. Inside were compartments for visiting and business cards and then, using his thumb, he pulled aside the leather edges of a pocket to see, neatly inserted, several five-pound notes. With shaking fingers, Rory counted their thin white edges and stared down in disbelief: his hand, that only yesterday had been black from shredding oakum, was now holding a wallet containing the vast sum of fifty pounds!

Chapter Nine

At Eversleigh, Ella was feeling exhausted by the preparations for a dinner party being held upstairs. The word 'party' to Ella had conjured up pictures she'd seen of children with balloons and pretty dresses, but Rosie had explained that it meant that Miss Fairchild had invited several guests to dine with her. 'It's what the rich do so they can socialise and indulge in intelligent and cultured conversation. At least, that's what Mr Forbes told me.'

'What does "cultured" mean?'

'I dunno. I suppose educated and one of the gentry.' She looked at the potatoes Ella had just peeled. 'You'd better get all them eyes out or Mrs Perkins will 'ave yer guts for garters!'

Ella looked down at her reddened hands and taking an offending potato plunged it back into the cold water, working her way through the remaining pile. Once this task was finished, there was a basket of carrots, freshly brought in from the garden, to scrape. She glanced down at them, relieved to see there wasn't much soil clinging. Luckily, everyone had been too busy to pay Ella much attention and she'd managed to keep out of Cook's way, whose face had become more flushed and perspiring with every hour. So far, she thought, as she rubbed an ache in her back before bending to lift the basket of carrots, she didn't mind working hard. It was wonderful being here. Ella just needed two things to happen: to see Miss Fairchild so that she could thank her, was one; but the other was more desperate – she was itching to open the hessian bag. But even though it lay only feet away in her private drawer in the bedroom, she wasn't going to open it in the dark. And definitely not when there were prying eyes around. So far, there had been no chance at all.

'Rosie?' She turned as the kitchen maid came in to fetch the prepared potatoes. 'When will I see Miss Fairchild?'

'I've only seen her once meself – close to, like. When you've bin 'ere a month she'll summon you to the morning room to ask how you've settled in. Cor, it's lovely up there. You should see the furniture and the mirrors . . .'

'Rosie?' Cook's voice was a screech.

'I'm on me way, Cook.'

'I should think so too,' Ella heard Mrs Perkins say. 'There's no time for gossiping with that workhouse girl! 'Ere, let me see those spuds.'

Ella held her breath but, to her relief, there came no complaint.

Letitia was seated before her triple mirrors, admiring her maid's expertise as she dressed her hair. 'You are sure that the girl is settling in?'

'Yes, madam.' A hint of a smile was in Mary's voice. 'Spunky young thing, she is.'

'Spunky?' Letitia raised her eyes to meet those of her maid. 'That's a strange word.'

Mary laughed. 'It's one we use in Scotland, from the old Gaelic for spark. I mean that she's spirited, that she'll stand up for herself.'

'Has she needed to?'

'Not exactly, I can just tell.' She finished arranging Letitia's hair into coils at the side of her head. 'I thought perhaps the long garnet earrings and choker, madam – they would look well with the rose shot silk.'

'I think you are right, Mary.'

Several minutes later, after the stiff-backed older woman had left the room, Letitia gazed in the mirror reflectively. At least this evening's dinner party, one of the regular ones she hosted in return for received hospitality, would prevent her from constantly wondering about Miles and his motives. She was certainly hoping that the evening would be a stimulating one as she always chose her guests with care, believing there should be fresh faces as well as familiar ones. Grace and her mother, of course; James Manners, her accountant – her father's view had been that it paid to treat one's man of business as a social equal – was bringing his new fiancée; the local Member of Parliament would be accompanied not only by his wife but also a visiting nephew; and the vicar would be introducing the new curate. Letitia was hoping that Grace would find – always supposing that at least one of the unfamiliar male guests proved to be single – a new suitor. She, herself, despaired of meeting another man to whom she was willing to give her heart. Her only consolation was that, although Miles may have shattered it into fragments, at least she knew what it was like to be in love. And, despite herself, an image came to her yet again of the man she'd adored, standing and staring through the gates and up the drive to the house. Yet she had received no letter, no request to see her. Nor had there been any rumour of his return. If she hadn't been confident of her own sanity, she might have believed the man she had seen to be a figment of her imagination.

At last, feeling satisfied with her appearance, she rose from the velvet stool and went over to the bed to collect her evening bag before making her way down the wide staircase to the drawing room. Forbes had everything in readiness: on the sideboard were two large silver trays, one with decanters and bottles and the other with glassware. The two footmen were waiting to serve.

Her first guests were punctual, Forbes announcing the vicar and his new curate, whose prominent teeth weren't helped by him suffering from a stammer. Letitia tried to put him at ease, relieved when Grace and her mother arrived. Then, hearing a booming voice in the hall, she resigned herself: Charles Bentley, their local MP and invited purely to return hospitality. With a satisfied paunch, not only did he eat like a pig, but, with every glass of wine, he became more voluble, while his wife Jane, her fair prettiness now fading, lived in his shadow. However, when the group came into the room, Letitia was encouraged to see that the visiting nephew, Mr Edward Melrose, looked to be rather interesting.

After the introductions, Letitia smiled at him. 'I'm so pleased you were able to join us. Do you plan to stay long in London?'

His own smile lightened his serious countenance.

'I hope for at least a month, Miss Fairchild.'

'And I believe that you live in Oxford, somewhere I've yet to visit.'

'You would admire the "dreaming spires". I'm most fortunate – my parents have a house there.' Her mind registered that he made no mention of a wife.

With Charles then monopolising the conversation, Letitia moved away to greet her accountant James Manners and his new fiancée Miss Sarah Walters, a slim dark-haired girl in cream satin. On enquiring whether they had set a date for the wedding, James, who always wore an owlish expression, smiled down at his chosen bride. 'We thought the end of September.' Letitia found herself envying the obvious affection between the young couple, although not even to Grace would she admit such a weakness. Nor that lately, the shutter in her mind was, after all these years, refusing to remain closed. She glanced down at the cluster of diamonds on Sarah's third finger, smiled at them both and offered her congratulations.

Careful to circulate among her guests, it was a welcome

sound when the grandfather clock struck the hour and Forbes announced dinner. Accepting the proffered arm of Charles as the highest-ranking guest, Letitia led the way into the dining room. Furnished in mahogany with burgundy flocked wallpaper, it could feel oppressive, but not this evening. The table was elegantly set with its centrepiece of white and pink roses and the crystal glasses and silver cutlery sparkling beneath two large candelabra. Letitia waited until everyone had found their place card before sitting at the head with Charles on her right. He droned on through the first course of watercress soup, only giving her respite when he concentrated on the entrée of chicken vol-au-vents. Letitia turned to the nephew and found that his dry wit and sharp observations of public figures delighted her.

'I take it that you have no leanings towards a political career?'

He laughed. 'Ah, but there you are mistaken, Miss Fairchild. The secret is not to take oneself or others too seriously. I am in fact intending to stand at the next election.' He lowered his voice and leant towards her. 'Don't tell my uncle, but I'm intending to stand as a Whig.'

'A Whig?' Surprise had caused her voice to be louder than she intended and, to her consternation, Charles swung round.

'Miss Fairchild, I never thought to hear such a word at Eversleigh.'

'It is only a name and surely in any discussion of the government, one must include all political parties?'

He took a slurp of his wine. 'Damned strange ideas some of you young people have.'

Letitia couldn't resist it. 'You mean, for instance, that some of us believe that women should have the right to vote?'

There was a choking sound from her left, but she wasn't going to let him off that easily. 'I do hope, Mr Melrose, that you support women's suffrage?'

His gaze met hers. 'I haven't given it much thought, Miss Fairchild.'

'But you must, both of you. It *will* come, you know.'

'Absolutely.' Charlotte Featherstone, sitting near enough to overhear the conversation, smiled sweetly.

Charles turned to her. 'My dear lady,' he began, but his next course – fish in white wine with asparagus – began to be served and Letitia repented and introduced a new subject by asking Charlotte if she had seen the new play at the Adelphi. She shook her head. Turning to ask Edward whether he had seen it, Letitia saw that his gaze was not only straying across to Grace, who was wearing a lovely gown of delphinium blue, but lingering on her fair curls and promising décolletage. In fact, as the evening progressed through another four courses, she noticed him cast several surreptitious glances. Then, the whole table was forced to wait, as after his cherry tart, Charles took an alarming amount of cheese.

At last Letitia felt able to rise. 'Ladies, shall we retire to the drawing room?' Leading the way, with a rustle of skirts behind her, she stood aside at the door and drew Grace back. 'Tell me, what do you think of Edward Melrose? I saw him glance at you often during dinner.'

'I have hardly had the opportunity to speak to him.' A flush rose to her face.

As Grace went to join her mother on a velvet sofa, Letitia followed her with lowered spirits. She knew her friend so well and would of course be delighted if she were to find happiness with Edward Melrose. But yet again, Letitia couldn't help wondering if she was destined to spend her life without love, or ever discovering the joys – or otherwise – of the marriage bed.

Chapter Ten

Rory was exploring Hampstead Heath, having soon realised that, despite possessing the wallet, he would still have to sleep in the open. It would have been the height of stupidity not to, as registering at a common lodging house, which was all his appearance fitted him for, would have aroused suspicion as soon as he tried to pay the bill. The sight of a five-pound note in the hand of someone who looked like a vagrant would be enough either for a law-abiding citizen to call a constable, or a rogue to rob him. Out here, there might be a few people walking their dogs, but at least he was away from prying eyes. Eventually, smiling at the high spirits of a collie who was prancing around its owner, he began to search for a good place to sleep. Fearing that some ruffian might rob him or worse, he finally chose a spot that was not only secluded but provided dense foliage on three sides. Then, after searching for a few broken branches, Rory put them in front as extra security.

It was too light at first but, even when darkness fell, sleep proved elusive with the discomfort of the uneven ground and growling hunger pains. And he found it impossible to stop his mind racing, planning first one course of action and then another, wondering whether to return to Dublin or perhaps to sail to America. Dublin tempted him; he had friends there. But people would ask what had happened to his father and why there had been no notice of his death. Rory could never let it be known that Seamus had died in a workhouse. As for America, wasn't it the first choice of many an Irishman wanting to emigrate? Or, with the advantage of the fifty pounds, should he try to make his fortune here in England? It was almost dawn before he drifted into an uneasy sleep, only soon to be disturbed when first one bird greeted the day, then several more and soon their chorus rose to its full glory. The sound was so pure, so beautiful, that Rory sat up to lean back against the gnarled trunk of the oak tree and, as he listened, there came into his mind the image of his mother who had loved to feed the birds in their garden. Rory, who had inherited her dark, slightly reddish hair and grey eyes, remembered how, when he was small, she would open wide her arms for him to run into and, as he grew older, she would encourage him in his studies. A boy of only twelve when she died, Rory had stood in tears at one side of her bed with his father at the other, as they watched the gentle Mary draw her last strangled breath. And with that memory there came another – of how she would often sit in an armchair by the window, her lips murmuring as her fingers counted her black rosary beads. And he knew that if she had lived to see her only son a thief, the shame would have destroyed her.

Rory swallowed, his throat dry, and, in the deserted woodland, took out the wallet and gazed down at the white banknotes. His mother had of course known only the good times, the days when Seamus had been a regular columnist. And he tried to convince himself that it was easy to judge others if you had never been hungry or homeless, facing a bleak future. But his guilt still lay heavy upon him and, replacing the wallet inside his jacket, he rose to his feet intending to explore the rest of the Heath, only to hesitate. The birdsong had ceased and the sky, earlier promising good weather, was beginning to darken with heavy grey clouds. Rain began, then the drops became faster until it developed into a downpour and, pulling on his cap, he drew further back into the shelter beneath the thick branches of the tree.

Sunday mornings at Eversleigh brought a change of routine. Expected to attend a church service, the servants had to provide only a simple luncheon for their mistress. However, other duties in the household were as normal and Rosie shook Ella awake at five-thirty. After both girls had rinsed their faces with cold water, they made their way down the backstairs to the empty kitchen. Ella's first duty was to stoke the kitchen range to give a good heat, but Rosie soon lost patience with her efforts. Pushing her aside, she took over the task herself. 'You need to do it like this, give it more strength.'

'Sorry, I'll try and get it right next time.'

'You do know how to scrub a floor?'

Ella remembered seeing a yellow block of soap. 'Soap and water?'

'Yes, and rinse it well, we don't want folk slipping. That water on the range should be hot enough. You can make a start in the scullery.'

Several minutes later as Ella scrubbed hard, Rosie called, 'What religion are you?'

'Christian, I suppose.'

'I know that, silly, what church do you want to go to?'

Ella hesitated.

Rosie came to the scullery door. 'Never mind, you can come with me, I'm C of E. Only we'll 'ave to sit at the back, cos it's only the nobs who can sit in the front pews.' Rosie frowned and peered up at the sky from the window. 'It was that hot in the night, and now it's raining. And you haven't got a brolly, 'ave yer?'

Ella shook her head.

'You'll 'ave to share mine, I just hope me Sunday best don't get wet! But you'll be expected to go, like the rest of us.'

Ella was wondering if Miss Fairchild would be there, when Rosie said, 'Although between you and me, Jack isn't a believer. He hasn't 'alf got some funny ideas.' She lowered her voice. 'He says – though not in front of Mr Forbes – that we're all descended from monkeys!'

Ella gasped and leant back on her heels. She liked Jack, with his cheeky grin, but she hadn't thought him soft in the head. 'Does the service take long?'

'Depends on how much of a windbag the parson is. Usually about an hour and a half.'

Ella drew a breath as a sudden thought struck her. She paused, then raising her voice said, 'Is the house left empty?'

Rosie, who had gone to fill kettles ready for morning tea, called, 'No, the footmen take turns to stay behind.'

Head down, Ella scrubbed even more furiously. All she needed to do was to pretend to be ill and then they'd have to go without her, wouldn't they? She knew how to because she'd been told that as soon the other servants came down, as scullery maid, she would have to empty their chamber pots and then wipe them out with a cloth soaked in vinegar. Ella had been dreading it, but now she was hoping that the contents of one would be stinky because that would make her retch and, if she stuck two fingers down her throat, it would be easy to make herself sick. But, to her dismay, when the time came, there were just three chamber pots to empty, all containing only urine. She still hated the job, though.

With reluctance, Ella made herself forego breakfast. She shook her head as porridge was passed along the table and, after looking longingly at the Sunday treat of crisply fried bacon with a sausage and tomatoes, she pushed her plate aside and clasped a hand to her mouth. Not waiting to lift the chair, which then squeaked as she pushed it back, she rushed out of the room, after which she went to the lavatory, put the lid on the pan down, sat there for a few minutes and then pulled the chain.

She returned to a few glances of concern, although not from Mrs Perkins, who glared at her. 'I hope you 'aven't brought something nasty from that workhouse.'

Ella shook her head. 'I think it must have been something I ate.'

'Not in this house, young lady!'

Realising her mistake, Ella said swiftly, 'I mean, I'm not used to eating so much.'

'That makes sense, Cook,' the butler said. 'It will take time for her system to adjust.'

Once back in her place, Ella nibbled at a piece of toast and sipped at a cup of tea. Then as the others chatted, she rushed out again.

As soon as she returned, Mr Forbes said, 'No church for you, my girl, we don't want you showing us up. You'd better go back to your room and lie down.'

'What about the dishes?' Ella knew that washing the used crockery was her next task.

'Rosie's done them before, she can do them again. One of the maids will help her.'

'Yes,' Mrs Perkins said, ignoring a look of outrage from the one nearby. 'But, Ella, don't you forget that you'll owe them both a favour. And take a basin with you!'

Ella obeyed, not without feeling some guilt, but that vanished as soon as she reached her bedroom and saw the chest of drawers. The hessian bag was in the bottom one, lying beneath her underwear. Perhaps she should have waited until Rosie had her half-day instead of telling lies, but then she shook her head, knowing that she would never be able to sneak up to her bedroom, not in the daytime. Mrs Perkins would keep her too busy. But now, once Rosie had been able to change her clothes, at long last Ella would be able to see what was inside the bag.

The waiting time seemed endless to Ella as, with the basin on the floor beside her, she lay on her narrow bed, ready to feign sleep as soon as she heard Rosie's footsteps. Gradually, her thoughts began to drift back to the workhouse and all that had happened the day before. Mr Peaton handing over her personal possessions, Miss Grint being spiteful by choosing such ugly clothes and how, even though Agnes had bent her head to her sewing, Ella had seen tears in her eyes when saying goodbye. There had also been the young man who had talked to her and helped her on and off the cart. He had seemed so sad. His voice had lingered in her mind. There had been an Irish woman in the sewing room who spoke like that . . . and eventually Ella's eyelids began to grow heavy.

Chapter Eleven

In the Anglican church of St John-at-Hampstead, the vicar, having succumbed to a migraine, had delegated the service to his stammering curate. What the young man had been trying to convey in his sermon, Letitia had no idea and, losing patience, became immersed in her own thoughts. And they were not pleasant ones because the door in her mind she had kept locked for so many years had been opened because of Miles's sudden unexpected appearance. The painful memories came flooding back, especially the one sentence that she wished he had never uttered. *'We have reached the stage, my darling, when it would be dishonourable not to speak to your father.'*

As they had planned, Miles arrived at Eversleigh at a time when Letitia knew her father would be in his study and she had positioned herself on the broad landing where, unseen, she would have a clear view. She watched as he handed his hat to the butler and heard his clear voice. 'Mr Miles Maitland to see Mr Fairchild, if that is convenient.'

Letitia was certain that her father would agree to see him, as Miles was the architect engaged on one of his business projects. Forbes returned to escort her suitor to the study and Letitia waited with both impatience and trepidation; she was well aware of how strong-minded her father was. But while Miles may not be wealthy, he was both well educated and had a profession and surely, she'd thought, if he told her father that they loved each other . . .

The minutes ticked by and it seemed an eternity until, just as the grandfather clock in the hall began to chime the half-hour, Forbes made his way across the hall and went into the study. Letitia poised, ready to run down the stairs and join Miles, but he was already striding out, his face so ashen that she felt a painful leap of fear. She leant over the balustrade. 'Miles?'

He halted, became still for a moment, his head bent. He didn't even look up, and Letitia, seeing the butler stand aside after opening the front door for Miles to leave, flew to her bedroom and to the window. With a hand lifted to wave, she remained at the window, watching with bewilderment and despair as he walked down the long drive, opened the tall gates and, to her horror, left without a backward glance.

Utterly confused, Letitia turned and rushed down to the study where Cedric Fairchild stood before the mahogany fireplace. His stance was rigid but she refused to quail before the beetle-browed look she knew so well.

'Papa . . .'

'Never, do you hear me, Letitia? Never!'

'But we love each other.'

His voice was icy. 'Don't question my judgement. You are forbidden to see him again, or ever to mention his name in this house.' He stalked past her, leaving Letitia feeling stunned and almost in tears. She fled back to the refuge of her room, shaking with resentment. How dare he dominate her life in this way. She was no longer a child – did her wishes, her hopes, count for nothing?

When the days went by with no word from Miles, Letitia wrote to him in eagerness, explaining that in another year she would be of age and no longer need her father's permission to marry. She received no reply to that or to three others. With determination, and with Mary accompanying her, Letitia went to the tall house in which Miles had taken rooms, only for a disdainful woman to inform her that Mr Maitland had departed without leaving a forwarding address. And when rumour filtered through that he had gone abroad, Letitia was at last forced to accept that her romantic attachment was over.

Angry and bewildered, she again confronted her father. 'Please, Papa, you must tell me what happened when Miles came to see you.'

His answer was curt. 'Do not make demands of me, Letitia.'

'But I have a right to know.'

He remained silent, continuing to sign documents on his desk. She had hovered a few seconds, then, when he didn't meet her gaze, she had known better than to pursue the matter. All that remained was her bitterness, and that was when the distance between them, always wide, became a permanent chasm and it remained so until his death.

As the curate's voice wavered, and at last he came to the end of a sermon that must have been an equal ordeal for himself and his congregation, Letitia tried to bring herself back to the present, but her recent sighting of Miles outside the gates of Eversleigh made it almost impossible to concentrate on the prayers and hymns. Why would he come back and risk being seen? And again the old doubts and suspicions were returning, unworthy but persistent. Had her judgement of his character been so mistaken? Had his ashen face as he emerged from the study been through guilt? Could it really be that Miles had accepted a bribe to disappear from her life, his only interest in her having been her future inheritance?

When the service ended, and with the reflected light of the stained-glass windows promising sunshine outside, she began to make her way back down the aisle inclining her head to acknowledge acquaintances and then her gaze roamed over the back pews. But the one face she had hoped to see wasn't there. Puzzled, Letitia frowned. Surely Ella should have attended the service together with the rest of the staff?

Chapter Twelve

When Ella, on opening her eyes to see Rosie's uniform lying on the other bed, realised that instead of having to pretend, she really had fallen asleep, she was furious at having wasted some of her precious time. Hurriedly, she sat up and went over to the chest of drawers, bending with eagerness to open the bottom one, and, in disbelief, found that it was jammed. She pulled harder without success, then, kneeling down and gripping the handles tight, she tried again. It was no use, the drawer still refused to budge. Angry and disappointed, Ella couldn't think what else she could do until she remembered that she wasn't alone in the house. Hadn't Rosie told her that one of the footmen would be staying behind?

Dusting the front of her skirt, Ella raced down the backstairs to the kitchen, where she found Jack, his shirt unbuttoned, sitting in Mrs Perkins' comfy chair and reading a newspaper. 'I thought it was a herd of elephants coming, you must be feeling better.'

'I am.' Her voice was breathless, 'Jack, do you know anything about drawers?'

He exploded into laughter. 'Now that's a question to ask a man.'

Ella felt her face go red. 'I mean drawers in a chest.'

'Why?'

'I need to get something out and the drawer's stuck.'

He sighed. 'OK, I'll come and have a look.'

Ella led the way up to the female servants' landing and to the room she shared with Rosie. 'It's a good job there's nobody else in,' Jack said. 'I'm not supposed to come along 'ere, you know.'

'I won't tell, honest. It's this one.' She pointed to the drawer.

'You hold the chest steady.'

She did, pressing down with all of her strength and, after two massive tugs by Jack, the whole drawer fell out, spilling some of its contents. Ella grabbed her undergarments and he grinned. 'Don't worry, I've got two sisters at home.' He put the hessian bag back in the drawer. 'Can you pass me some soap?'

She fetched the green block from the washstand and watched as he rubbed it along the rims of the drawers. 'There, that should do it.'

'Oh Jack, thanks.'

He tested the drawer and said, 'It should be fine now, and one good turn deserves another. Yer never saw me reading the paper down there, did you?'

She shook her head.

'Good kid.' He went out, closing the door behind him, and within seconds Ella was sitting on her bed with the hessian bag on her lap. The knot on the cord was so stiff that it took her ages to ease it, but at last, her now sore fingers managed to loosen the drawstring. The first thing she saw squashed inside was a small rag doll. As Ella took it out to gaze at its red plaits and crumpled red and white spotted dress, she wondered whether it had been her favourite toy – certainly, already within her was a flicker of familiarity. After holding it for a few seconds, she put it aside to see that beneath it lay a child's reading book and under that cleaning cloths and an old duster. Disappointment washed over her and then, as her fingers delved further, she felt something smooth and silky and discovered that the hessian bag had covered a black silk purse. With growing eagerness, she pulled it out and, with relief, found the smooth knot of its drawstring easier to undo.

Ella hesitated a moment, then, opening it, she looked inside. A small blue velvet box had tucked beside it a leather-covered book with a silver clasp and a cream envelope. With great care, she took them out and put them on the brown candlewick bedspread. There was also a tiny blue velvet pouch and a folded sheet of paper. Making sure the purse was now empty, she put it aside and, her face burning with excitement, she unfolded the sheet of paper.

The lined paper was thin, the words written in pencil.

This bag was in a drawer in Mrs Hathaway's room. I put it in another to keep it safe. The rags and duster should keep it from nosy parkers. I sent it with the child. Violet Rutter.

Ella read the lines again and when she picked up the leather-covered book, she had a vague sense that she had seen it before. Gazing down at the shiny clasp, and with a tight feeling in her chest, she opened it. Inside in black ink was the name, *Selina Maria Hathaway, 1889.* Ella stared at it, wondering if it could be her mother's name. She turned the page. There were lines and lines of words written in the same slanting handwriting but, with bewilderment, Ella found that they didn't make any sense. The letters were the same as the ones she knew, but the words were different from any she had seen. Leafing through the book, she discovered that except for some blank ones at the end, all of the pages were the same.

Puzzled, she put it aside, and gazed with uncertainty at the long envelope. It looked so important that she felt scared about breaking the seal so, instead, she picked up the velvet pouch and, finding inside a tiny gold coloured key, inserted it into the lock on the box. It turned with ease and a faint click. She paused, then put the blue velvet box on her knees and lifted the lid.

Minutes ticked by as a shocked Ella stared down at its contents. The box was divided into two sections; in one rested a pearl necklace and a gold locket on a chain and, in the other, two sparkling rings, a brooch and a pair of pearl earrings. She felt bewildered; how could these beautiful things belong to her? Her first thought was that Mr Peaton must have made a mistake. Then Ella shook her head because hadn't the note said that the purse was found in Mrs Hathaway's room, and wasn't Ella's own surname Hathaway?

Struggling to make sense of it, Ella could only think that if, as she'd been told, she had been sent to the workhouse after her mother's death, then Selina Maria Hathaway must be her mother's name. And as these were her personal possessions, then there had been no mistake. She had always had a hazy memory of a loving, gentle voice and, taking out the delicate chain and placing the locket on her palm, she thought how pretty it was with a tracing of rosebuds around the edge. There was also a little catch at the side that moved when she pressed it, and the locket sprang open to reveal inside a tiny curl of baby hair. Ella touched its softness, and it was then that the tears came. Here, in this small room where there were no prying eyes or listening ears, she was at last able to cry out the long years of unhappiness. She wept for her missed childhood and the love she would never know, and it was some time before she could dry her eyes to gaze down at the locket still clutched in her hand. She so longed to wear it, to have it close with her, and surely if she wore it safe beneath her uniform . . . She put the locket down, unbuttoned the top of her dress and, after fiddling with the tiny clasp on the chain, managed to fasten it around her neck. Going over to the small mirror above the washstand, Ella held up the chain so that the locket could nestle below her throat and stood admiring its reflection. Her own, she hated, considering herself plain, although Agnes had told her that when her hair grew it would make all the difference. 'Stands to reason,' she said. 'It's a woman's crowning glory, her hair.'

Ella could only hope that she was right. Now, she only had ugly brownish tufts, but at least her cap hid them from sight. She fastened her dress and looked down to make sure that the shape of the locket didn't show through it. She couldn't have borne people asking nosy questions.

It was as she went back to the bed, intending to try on the ring, that the grandfather clock in the hall struck the half-hour and, with a pang, Ella realised that her precious time was now almost over. Suppose Rosie came back early and hurried upstairs to change? Swiftly Ella locked the box, replaced the key in the pouch and put everything in the same order back inside the black silk purse. Wrapping it in a petticoat, she pushed it to the back of the drawer and put her spare nightgown on top. As Rosie and Jack had already seen the hessian bag, so that it didn't look empty, Ella put a liberty bodice and some stockings inside and placed the bag at the front.

Then, deciding to go downstairs and to heat some water for the churchgoers' tea, she went to the mirror to put her cap on. She wasn't daft, she knew the jewellery was probably imitation – or paste, as Agnes had called it. But Ella, with the locket feeling warm against her skin, at that moment didn't care whether her jewellery was real or not, she'd have to be starving to death before she would part with any of it.

Chapter Thirteen

Rory, his jacket collar up, had been huddled beneath the dripping oak tree on Hampstead Heath for ages, thankful for the small area of dry ground around its broad trunk. Even though the downpour had long reduced to a drizzle, it would still soak into his clothes and it had been a long disconsolate wait with little to distract him. His thoughts had not been happy ones.

It had been ten days ago when, on his way to the oakum room, Rory had felt the heavy hand on his shoulder. And he had known without being told. His voice quiet he said, 'When?'

'About two o'clock this morning, sudden like.'

'Can I see him?'

There was a nod and, on legs that felt weak yet heavy, Rory followed the burly officer along several corridors and up a flight of stairs to a black-painted door. 'In there, lad, I can't give you long, they'll be coming to remove him.'

Rory opened the door and stepped into a small white distempered room with little sun entering its tiny window. The room was square and bare except for two trolleys; one was empty and laid out on the other was a long shrouded outline. Taking a deep breath, he crossed the small space and, lifting the top of the threadbare sheet, pulled it back to gaze down at the gaunt face of the man who had been his father and his best friend. Rory felt love and grief sweep over him, wishing in one way that they had never left Ireland. They had no living relatives, but at least in Dublin they'd had friends, and then perhaps his father's final weeks wouldn't have been spent in this godforsaken place. Rory struggled against tears as he placed his hand over his father's lifeless one. 'Goodbye and God bless you, Da, thank you for everything.' It was as he bent to kiss the cold forehead, and before he could say a prayer, that he heard the sound of footsteps and the door was flung open.

'Off you go, lad!' One man jerked his head, while another pushed past him carrying a large hessian sack. Rory turned away from their grisly task, shame flooding through him that he was unable to prevent this last indignity. With hunched shoulders, he fought tears as he made his way back down the stone stairs and, unable to face the oakum room, he found privacy in a cubicle in the empty latrines. There, he began to weep as if his heart would break, his only consolation knowing that Seamus had received the Last Sacraments only a few days before.

Now, with tears rising again, Rory brushed them away, dodged a dripping branch of the tree and thought that, despite all his despair, at least his father had never lost his faith. Whereas I, Rory thought, don't seem to be certain of anything any more. And with hunger gnawing at his stomach, his relief was profound when at last the drizzle slowed. He set out across the deserted heath towards civilisation, where the high street was deserted: the shop windows were blank with either their blinds drawn or windows shuttered and, as it was Sunday, there was no hope of anything changing. The only sign of movement came from a mongrel relieving itself against a drainpipe and it looked curiously up at Rory as he went to find the small baker's he had previously been tempted to enter.

A canny baker would find many uses for stale bread, but that didn't mean there might not be something, however small, that Rory could salvage. He continued along the pavement counting the shop doors until he turned into a side street. After several yards, he found the back alley he had hoped for and, recounting the gates until he came to the one he sought, he hoisted himself up to the top of it and dropped down the other side. In the yard inside a small recess was a large dustbin and Rory eased off the lid and looked inside. There were no loaves of bread, but he could see a cluster of fancy cakes covered in green spots of mould, and beside them a small, partly eaten fruit cake. Closing his mind as to whether human or animal teeth had bitten into it, he wiped his hands on the seat of his trousers, and seconds later the fruit cake was inside his jacket. Rory managed to replace the bin lid without causing it to clang, climbed back over the gate and, thinking it unlikely that anyone would deliver on the Sabbath, remained in the empty alley. He took out the cake, turned it to its 'good' side, and, tasting it to find it chewy but full of currants and sultanas, he soon devoured it. Then he went to find the public tap he'd used the day before so that he could wash his now sticky hands, after which he cupped them to drink the cool water before splashing more over his face and drying it with his handkerchief.

It was as he straightened up that he became aware of movement on the opposite side of the road. A group of people was about to turn a corner, among them two young girls wearing black lace mantillas. Realising that they must be going to Mass, his first instinct was to follow them, and then he paused on the kerb. Hadn't he, during the long wait on the Heath, come to the conclusion that he would be a hypocrite to attend? He dug his hands into his pocket and, at the prospect of a long and lonely day ahead, began to kick loose stones into the gutter.

It was then that he heard a commotion. On turning, Rory saw an elderly man collapse to the pavement, while a burly youth fled with a cap in one hand and a walking stick in the other. Furious, Rory moved to chase after him, but the ruffian, fleet of foot, had already disappeared and instead Rory hurried to help the victim to his feet.

'Thank you.' Rheumy blue eyes beneath a shock of white hair looked at him with some suspicion and Rory could see what he was thinking.

He shook his head. 'I'm a passer-by, not an accomplice, sir. That was a terrible thing to happen, you must be shaken.'

'I confess I am, somewhat.'

He winced, and Rory said, 'Are you hurt?'

'It is just my arm but if you would kindly help me across the road?'

'But of course.'

Even with Rory's support, the victim's gait was unsteady. 'You relied on your stick, sir.'

'I did indeed, young man. He's not gained much, just a decent cap, but the stick if not of monetary value was an old friend.'

On learning that his companion was going to Mass, Rory insisted that he continued to lean on his arm.

'I am indebted to you.'

They walked slowly up the hill to their destination and, just as they reached it, a brougham pulled by a chestnut bay drew up. A middle-aged man, his face florid beneath bushy eyebrows called, 'Good morning to you, Mr Braithwaite. And what is all this?'

'The gentleman has been robbed, sir.'

Descending from the brougham, he said, 'What? Mr Braithwaite is this true?'

'I'm afraid so.'

'Then that's an end to it. I've offered to bring you several times, and now I'll brook no argument.'

Mr Braithwaite, taking his hand from Rory's arm began to search inside his pockets.

'Did he get your wallet, man?'

'I didn't have it with me, just change for the collection.' He turned to look at Rory. 'Son, you have been a Good Samaritan, and I'm grateful to you. Unless I am mistaken, you could make use of this.' He held out a shilling.

The florid-faced man blustered, 'Now, Mr Braithwaite, I must protest.'

'It's not necessary, sir. I was glad to help.'

'Please, let me have the pleasure of helping you.'

Rory, although conscious of the wallet inside his jacket, knew that it would be churlish to refuse. 'Thank you, sir, I appreciate your kindness.'

As the two men went into the church, Rory saw, with some unease, that his benefactor's coat bore patches on the elbows. Putting the money in his pocket he began to walk back along the road before slowly coming to a halt. Wasn't it his duty? He swung round and seconds later was opening the door into the church and crossing himself with holy water from the wall-mounted font. Rory entered into the familiar atmosphere of incense and candle wax where, on the main altar, a fair-haired boy in a white cassock was lighting tall candles. A task Rory had performed so many times. The interior of the church was a fine one with tile mosaics, historical paintings and sculpture, and, it being early for the service, there were only a small number of worshippers in the pews as he made his way towards a side altar. There, standing before a stand of votive candles, he put one of his few coins into its box and chose a thin white one. Holding it to the flickering flame of another, he inserted it into a vacant holder and then knelt to pray for the souls of his parents. In the silent and reverent atmosphere, his chaotic thoughts began to calm and, after rising, he changed his mind and, deciding to stay, made his way to a back pew. The congregation was now beginning to file in and he watched the two young girls in mantillas move along their front pew to make room for an elderly woman. In the opposite seat sat Mr Braithwaite and his friend, and then soon the church was full as everyone waited for the organist to herald the arrival of the priest and his procession of servers.

Within minutes, Rory was listening to the Latin liturgy that had been so much a part of his childhood. He had always loved the beauty of the Mass, but it was when the priest stood in the pulpit and began with the words, 'Today's Gospel is taken from the teachings of St Mark, 8:36. *"For what shall it profit a man, if he shall gain the whole world, and suffers the loss of his own soul?"* that Rory felt his throat tighten with shame. When, afterwards, his guilt forced him to remain in his seat as others went forward to receive Holy Communion, his thoughts were dark. This old church, its walls silent with the prayers of past generations, was compelling him to face up to the bleak truth about what he had done. The wallet with its fifty pounds was his personal thirty pieces of silver for, by keeping it, hadn't he betrayed his parents and all they had taught him? Did he want to carry the burden of that knowledge for the rest of his life? What did it matter that lately he had begun to question the Catholic doctrines – nothing could change the distinction between right and wrong. I must have been deranged, Rory muttered to himself, and ten minutes later, the service over, he was moving along his pew to genuflect and walk out of the church and into sunshine. Only now, he had purpose in his stride.

Chapter Fourteen

At Eversleigh, Ella had been waiting for everyone to return and, as soon as she heard signs of their arrival, she began to make the tea, proud of her neat layout of cups and saucers on the table and hoping everyone would be pleased. A tray had already been prepared with a pretty china cup and saucer, and she guessed that this was intended for Miss Fairchild. Ella hadn't seen Jack since he had helped with the drawer, but she could see that he'd shaken up the cushions on Cook's chair, giving no indication that anyone had sat there.

Mrs Perkins was the first to enter the back door. 'Glory be, I'll say it agen, why ever did that poor young man join the clergy? It must be hell on earth for 'im, trying to give a sermon.'

Gloria followed her in. 'It was hell on earth for us, you mean. Hey, well done, Ella, a cuppa all ready and waiting. Don't worry, you didn't miss much.'

Only the chance to see Miss Fairchild, Ella thought, but touching the outline of the gold locket nestling beneath her dress, she had no regrets. As the others began to file in, she bent to lift the huge brown teapot, struggling a little with its weight.

'You're feeling all right now, I suppose?' Cook's glance was shrewd and suspicious.

"Ere, let me take it,' Jack said.

'Leave her alone, she's got to learn,' Cook snapped, and, biting her lip, Ella managed to transfer the pot to the table, relieved when Rosie came in and, removing her hat, offered to pour. Ella stood back as the rest of the staff followed, intrigued by the way that everyone looked different in their Sunday best. Even Mrs Perkins, in a hat with a frothy feather, didn't look so severe, while the parlourmaids, one dark and pretty, the other fair and round, although dressed soberly, revealed a taste for pretty straw hats, each with a different coloured ribbon.

'I thought Miss Fairchild looked very well in that cream muslin,' Cook said.

Miss Blane, whose Sunday best differed little from her usual black except for a cameo at the neck, nodded in agreement. 'It is a colour that suits her.' She swiftly drank her tea and then attended to her mistress's tray. 'Jack, the carriage will be needed at three o'clock, as she intends to take tea with Mrs Featherstone.'

'Just look how the sun's coming out, I wish I'd got *my* half-day,' Mabel, the fair-haired parlourmaid said with a sulky look.

'Aren't I the lucky one!' The other parlourmaid, the one who Ella considered prettier, glanced at the butler. 'I might be late back, Mr Forbes, you won't lock me out, will you?'

'The door will be secured at ten o'clock, the same as always, Gloria.'

She turned away from him and pulled a face. Ella saw Mabel give her a nudge and wondered whether Gloria had a follower. Agnes had told her that was what young men who wished to court a servant were called. And that such 'goings-on' were disapproved of by the mistress of a household.

'Makes yer wonder, don't it,' she'd said. 'If it was left to the nobs, we working classes would never 'ave any bleedin' fun.'

Ella wasn't surprised that Gloria was being courted and looked with envy at her dark curly hair. She hated her own, which was boring and mousy, her only consolation being that Agnes had told her that there was a good chance the colour might change or deepen. She'd said, 'Just give it time, love, you might be both lucky and surprised.'

Delighted to see that Cook had put some biscuits on the table, Ella rather self-consciously took one. She began to count the members of staff including herself; there were nine indoor ones – no ten – she'd forgotten about the under-housemaid, who hadn't wanted tea and had gone straight upstairs. And Ella had seen two men working in the garden. Then there was the coachman, who had a wife and lived in rooms over the stables. Just fancy all those people to look after one person. But then she supposed that if you were born a lady, like Miss Fairchild, your whole life would be different from ordinary people.

Jack came into the kitchen and with a swift wink at Ella said, 'Good sermon, was it?'

'Don't ask,' Mabel said. 'Flamin' waste of time.'

'Maybe,' said the butler. 'But I would like respect in this house towards the clergy; I don't suppose the unfortunate young man is any happier about it than we are.'

'Quite right, Mr Forbes,' said Cook, replacing her cup and saucer. 'And it's time to get changed, everyone. Ella, leave this crockery, you can see to them later. I want you to set to and wash those lettuces Bert's left in a trug outside. There's cucumbers too, so slice those – and thin, mind. Rosie can do the tomatoes when she comes down – I'm a bit particular about them.'

Ella did indeed 'set to' and, having discarded three caterpillars before feeling satisfied with the lettuces, she started on the cucumbers. But it wasn't as easy as it looked; somehow the knife seemed to slide and cut crooked so that it was a struggle to achieve thin slices. She stuck her tongue between her lips to concentrate and began again. By the time Rosie came to check on her, the pile of acceptable slices was dominated by the pile of rejects. 'Flippin 'eck, what on earth have you done?'

Ella felt a leap of fear. 'I've tried ever so hard.'

'You're supposed to peel the bloomin' things. 'Ere, give 'em to me.' Rosie scooped up Ella's efforts, went out and seconds later returned. 'I've put 'em beneath the hedge, away from where Bert's working. They can go on the compost heap later. Besides, that knife you're using's no good, you need this one.' She went to a drawer to select another. 'And get on with it, cos Cook will expect 'em finished by the time she comes back.'

Letitia was sitting before her dressing table, attempting to tidy her hair after removing her hat when, after a tap at the door, Mary brought in tea. 'Thank you, I can't deny that I'm ready for it.' She turned. 'Have you any idea why Ella wasn't in church?'

'The girl wasn't well, vomiting, I believe, madam.'

Letitia stared at her in alarm, worried that her philanthropic gesture may have brought infection into the house. 'It's nothing contagious?'

Mary shook her head. 'I believe the cause to be a change in her diet. She was fine when we returned.' She picked up a tortoiseshell comb and completed Letitia's task. 'Now, unless you need me for anything else, madam, I'll away to my mending.'

Letitia smiled and shook her head, still unsure whether to confide in Mary that she'd seen Miles outside Eversleigh. And then she became thoughtful. It may be fanciful, but she still had this strange sense that Ella had come into her life for a reason. And she didn't want to wait too long before having an opportunity to see and talk to her again. Honestly, these unwritten rules of society were so frustrating. Would the rest of the staff really think it was showing favour for her to send for Ella before the usual month?

Chapter Fifteen

In Hampstead High Street, Rory found it a strange sensation to be retracing his steps of the day before. Turning the corner and walking along the street where he had found the wallet, he remembered how he had bent to scoop it up and secrete it in his jacket, his hurried walk away from the scene, the way his heart had beaten so fast that he could hardly breathe. And then the furtive hiding in the alleyway, his euphoria on discovering the ten five-pound notes – he had felt no shame, had thought only of himself. Hot with guilt and taking out the wallet once again, Rory checked the address on one of the business cards. The gentleman who had been approaching him, the one he had swiftly passed, must be this Professor C. R. Dalton, which must mean that he was an academic.

Rory had waited for what he judged to be an appropriate time, one when church services would be over, but he still hadn't thought of a believable story. He could say that he had only just found the wallet. But no one would believe that because a search of the adjoining streets would have been undertaken by the servants. Would it be safer just to hand the wallet to whoever opened the door? But he could be detained, as its loss would have been reported to the police, and Rory had no desire to fabricate a statement because he wasn't sure of his ability to lie before authority. If he obeyed his conscience, he would tell the truth but the possible consequences of that made him shudder. And if he did manage to hand over the wallet, and leave with his freedom, he would merely be left in his original predicament, penniless. And a venal part of him, even if it was due to need, was hoping that the professor would be so grateful that he might offer a small token of appreciation. The thoughts whirled in his mind, and he still hadn't come to a decision, when he reached his destination and stood at the foot of the steps of number 35. Rory paused and looked up at the two white pillars framing a polished mahogany door with a fine stained-glass skylight and a gleaming brass doorbell. He removed his cap and, after wiping the dust off his shoes on the backs of his trousers, went up the steps, his palms clammy with nerves. On reaching the top, and before he could change his mind, he reached out to the bell, only for his hand to fall to his side. Stepping back from the now open door, Rory stared into the glare of a butler.

'What on earth? Be off with you!'

'I, er . . .'

'What is it, Craven?' Rory recognised the gentleman behind the butler from his silvering hair and neat goatee beard. He seemed about to leave.

'Excuse me, sir, but would I be addressing Professor Dalton?'

'Yes, I am Professor Dalton.'

He frowned, and the butler moved forward. 'I'll deal with this, sir.'

Rory ignored him, his gaze holding that of the professor. 'Could I ask you to give me a few moments of your time, Professor?'

'Can you give me any reason why I should do so?'

Rory forced out the words, 'It concerns your wallet, sir.'

Again a frown, but his expression changed. He removed his grey kid gloves and, putting them into his top hat, handed them back to the butler. 'Craven, please show this, er . . . this young man into my study.'

The butler looked at him, aghast. 'Are you sure, sir?'

'Do as I say, Craven.' The professor's tone was quiet but carried with it the authority of a man used to being obeyed. He turned and began to walk back along the maroon and black tiled hall.

Rory found his arm seized in a surprisingly strong grip by the butler, who hissed, 'One false move, sonny, and I'll fetch the constabulary.'

If he'd felt nauseous before it was nothing to how Rory felt now, because he had abandoned any intention of lying, of trying to wriggle out of his crime. He was going to tell the truth because only then would he be able to live with his conscience. Otherwise he knew his guilt would be a shadow on the rest of his life. And when, after a nod of dismissal, the butler had left – Rory was convinced he would be outside with his ear to the door – the professor settled himself in a green leather armchair behind a large rosewood desk. 'Your name is?'

'Rory Adare, sir.'

'Hmm. Irish, I take it?'

'From Dublin, sir.'

'So,' his voice was quiet. 'Tell me about my wallet.'

Rory swallowed, then, taking the wallet from inside his jacket, in silence he held it out. The professor gave a swift glance at Rory and then, taking it, he riffled through its contents with a growing look of disbelief. 'There is nothing missing. How did it come into your possession?'

'I found it, sir. It was lying on the pavement in the next street. It was just after I had walked past you yesterday and, seeing you searching in your pockets, I guessed then you had either lost your wallet or had it stolen.'

Now the professor's gaze was piercing. 'So you have had this in your possession all that time?'

Rory nodded. 'I had intended to keep it but . . .' As he gazed at the man before him, immaculate in a grey coat, his shirt pristine, his necktie displaying a gold pin, he felt even more ashamed of his own shabbiness. A night in the open must have made it even worse.

The professor spoke slowly. 'Are you telling me that you intended to steal it, only to change your mind?'

Again Rory nodded. 'I'm ashamed to say that I gave in to temptation, convincing myself that as I had found the wallet rather than stealing it from you, I wasn't a thief.'

'I believe that there is such a crime as unlawful possession.' Again, the professor's gaze seemed to Rory to be an evaluating one, and his stomach gave a painful leap of fear.

'I can only apologise, sir. I've never done such a thing before.' He hesitated. 'I hope you won't inform the police. As you said yourself, everything is intact.'

'I can't deny that I am relieved to have it returned.' His gaze swept over Rory. 'Workhouse clothes?'

'Yes.'

'How long were you an inmate?'

'Only a month, sir, until my father died.'

The grandfather clock in the hall chimed the hour and the professor leant forward. 'I am afraid I am expected elsewhere. Would you say nay to some food and perhaps some fresh clothes? I am sure my housekeeper could find something suitable.'

Astonished, Rory said, 'I would be most grateful, sir.' Not only was this a gesture he had never expected, but it seemed to mean that the professor wasn't going to involve the police. Then, his gratitude was tempered by a sudden panic. This could be a ploy to keep him here until a constable arrived.

The professor gave a slight smile. 'It is a sincere offer, you have nothing to fear. You interest me, young man.' He rose and went to the embroidered bell pull at the side of the mahogany fireplace, whereupon the butler entered so swiftly that Rory knew his suspicion had been correct. 'Craven, I plan to return by late afternoon and will then see this young man again. Meanwhile, I would be obliged if you would take him down to the kitchen to be fed. Also, ask Mrs Walters if she can find him some other clothes.'

'Of course, sir.' His face was impassive, but once Rory was in the hall, the butler gave him a push in the back and, taking his arm, marched him to the rear of the hall. 'Down there,' he hissed, indicating a flight of stairs, 'and I'll be right behind you, so watch yourself, laddie, that's all.'

Rory, after another shove when they reached the bottom, entered a large whitewashed kitchen with gleaming copper-bottomed saucepans on a high shelf around its walls. Sitting at a large oblong table were several servants finishing a meal. Heads turned, and on seeing Rory with the butler behind him, there came sniggers. One young footman held his nose. 'Cor blimey, look what the cat's dragged in.'

'That's enough of that, Charlie,' the butler snapped. 'Mrs Walters, the professor wishes this lad to be fed and given a clean set of clothes.'

The woman he spoke to, round-shouldered with greying hair in a bun and a bunch of keys at the waist of her black dress said, 'Well, I'm sure Cook can find him some leftovers. But as for clothes, he's a bit skinny for any I can think of.'

'That won't matter, better a bit big than too small like those he's got on,' the Cook said, her gaze appraising Rory's thin wrists and ankles. 'You look as if you need feeding up, me lad.'

Charlie said, 'Where did the professor find *him*?'

'Rather the reverse,' the butler told him, 'and I'd thank you not to pry into the master's business.' He settled himself into a chair at the head of the table, ostensibly reading a newspaper, but there was tension in him. Rory knew that a vagrant such as himself being brought into the house – and by the front door – was an action that any respectable butler would abhor. And it was understandable, because on his shoulders rested the safety not only of his master, but of the household too. As for the shoves, Rory had received far worse in the workhouse.

In an effort to reverse the butler's first impression of him, Rory said in a respectful tone. 'Mr Craven, my name is Rory Adare.'

The butler looked at him over the newspaper but didn't answer.

The housekeeper sniffed. 'Irish,' she said.

Rory managed not to retort. Since he and his father had come 'over the water', he'd discovered that many people viewed his countrymen as both inferior and feckless. Yet even though The Great Famine in Ireland was only five decades before, there seemed little shame or guilt felt by the English about the appalling disregard – even callousness – shown by their government.

'I'll be glad to feed him, but not in that state.' Cook gave Rory an encouraging smile.

'So it's a bath first.' The housekeeper gave a heavy sigh. 'You two girls jump to and fetch the hot water, and don't look like that! If it's the master's wish, it's not our place to complain.' She studied Rory's build. 'Hmm. I'll pick something out and bring it down. You'll need a towel as well.' She walked away muttering, 'As if I hadn't enough to do.'

Rory remained with uncertainty at the bottom of the stairs as, with a few curious glances, the other servants began to leave the kitchen. The only ones remaining were the Cook, who was busy inside a large cupboard, and a young scullery maid who was trotting in and out removing the dirty crockery. Rory, reminded of the young girl on the cart, hoped once again that she was being well-treated. But, uppermost in his mind was the puzzle of what exactly lay behind Professor Dalton's statement, 'You interest me, young man.'

Chapter Sixteen

With his ablutions finished in the servants' downstairs bathroom, Rory felt far more comfortable. The workhouse cast-offs had been taken away with a replacement pile left outside the door and, his short hair still wet, he drew on a pair of well-worn black trousers, relieved to see that they didn't dangle above his ankles. The shirt was so soft against his skin that he cared not a jot that it was darned in places and, while the grey jacket felt wide on the shoulders, at least it was long enough in the sleeves.

He went back into the kitchen to find it empty apart from the Cook, who beamed at him and indicated a place set at the table before a plate containing two slices of thick ham and a small slab of cheese. A bowl of garden salad was beside it accompanied by two buttered hunks of bread. Beyond it was a small plate with a slice of fruit cake. 'Sit you down,' she said.

Rory was so hungry that he felt almost emotional at the sight. 'I can't thank you enough.'

'Aye, well a growing lad needs nourishment and you look as if you've not had much for a while.'

Rory began to eat, trying not to bolt down the food. The moist ham was full of flavour, the cheese had a sharp tang and the bread was fresh. The salad was refreshing and, as he reached for the fruit cake, Cook placed at his side a mug of strong tea. He looked up at the buxom grey-haired woman, realising that she had deliberately remained silent throughout his meal. 'That was wonderful, thank you. You've been very kind to me.'

'And why shouldn't I be? Twenty years I was married, until Mr Marriott passed away. I had a boy of my own once, he'd have been just about your age, if he'd lived.'

'I'm sorry about that. I'm sixteen.'

'Aye, I thought as much.'

He glanced around. 'Is there anything I can do to help? Maybe polish shoes or something?'

She looked at him. 'Some mother's brought you up proper, if I'm not mistaken.'

He smiled at her. 'Yes.'

'No longer here?'

He shook his head. 'Nor my father.'

'It's tough when you lose them young.'

Rory was about to rise from the table when the butler returned. He gave Rory a sharp glance. 'Professor Dalton wished to see you again when he returns, so I hope you're not about to scarper.'

'Of course not. As I've just said to Cook, I'm quite willing to offer my labour in return for her kindness.'

'I was the one who sorted out your clothes,' snapped the housekeeper bustling in.

'Of course, I'd like to thank you too.' Rory looked down at his scuffed boots. Maybe if he offered again? 'I could polish the shoes?'

'All right, but it looks to me as if you need another pair yourself.' Cook gave a meaningful glance at Mrs Walters, who sighed.

'All right, me head will never save me feet. I'll 'ave a look in the bag I've put by for the poor. What size?'

'I was size eight, but I'm probably size nine now. Mrs Walters?'

'Yes?' She was already moving towards the door.

'If there was a pair of socks without holes?'

'It'll be a top hat next!'

Shown to where the boots and shoes were kept, Rory heard one of the maids whisper, 'You don't suppose he's a by-blow do you, of the professor I mean?'

'That's a dreadful thing to say.'

'He's a man, ain't he? It wouldn't be the first time a toff has . . .'

The murmuring faded into the distance and Rory grinned. By-blow, indeed!

He could just imagine what his mother would have said about that suggestion!

Displayed on the back wall of the kitchen were rows of bells and, later that afternoon, the tinkle of one below a sign proclaiming 'Study' signalled Professor Dalton's return. Rory had just come to the end of the row of boots and shoes. It hadn't been too onerous a chore as he'd often applied blacking to both his own and his father's shoes, dubbin too, at times, in order to keep them waterproof.

'Get those hands washed!' The butler, now wearing his black jacket over his waistcoat, came into the passage where Rory was sitting on a small bench. 'In case the master wants to see you straightaway.'

With some trepidation, Rory got up and went into the scullery, where the young maid handed him a nail brush.

'Thanks.'

'What do yer think he wants yer for?'

'I have no idea.' He managed to keep his voice calm and had only just dried his hands on a rough striped towel, when the butler returned.

He jerked his head. 'Upstairs!' Rory followed his stiff-backed figure up the backstairs and along the hall to the study where the butler opened the mahogany panelled door and, standing aside, gestured to Rory to enter.

'Thank you, Craven.' Professor Dalton, again seated in the green leather chair behind his desk glanced at Rory's appearance. 'An improvement, I think. You are no longer hungry I take it?'

'No, sir. And I've given my labour to repay your kindness.'

His mouth twitched. 'I see. In what capacity, may I ask?'

'Acting as bootboy. There was a backlog due to your previous one having left to join the army.'

'Yes, it will be the making of the boy. That isn't an avenue you have explored for yourself?'

'No, sir.'

The professor reached forward and, taking a pipe from its rack, he opened a leather pouch and began to take out tobacco. As he pressed it into the bowl he said, 'As I said before, you interest me. I'd like to know of your family, your background.'

Rory gazed at him, searching his eyes. Was this just idle curiosity, was this man merely seeking diversion on a Sunday afternoon? Or, and the possibility struck a chill in his bones, was he still undecided whether to have Rory arrested as a thief? With some apprehension, he began to talk, hesitantly at first, relating how in Dublin after his father became ill his political articles had gradually been rejected and his regular newspaper column axed. But soon the words came flooding out.

The professor with his pipe now lit, leant back in his chair and remained silent and attentive. Then at the mention of Mary's death, he raised a hand. 'It was pneumonia, you say, not tuberculosis?'

'Yes, sir. My father and I were both with her at the end.' Rory felt his throat thicken and swallowed.

'And later on you decided to come to England. Why was that?'

'He became so ill that it affected his work and, mistakenly as it happened, he thought he would have more chance of success here in London.' Rory gazed at the professor. 'How could I have told him that because of his illness his judgement was no longer sound? At his insistence, I continued my studies at the public libraries, but when his health became worse and we finally ran out of money, in desperation I took a job as a pot boy at a nearby inn.' He saw the professor raise his eyebrows when Rory explained how and why he was dismissed without a reference. 'And then my father's condition became such that our only solution was the workhouse, and he refused to enter without me.'

'Do you think that the hardship you found there changed your character?'

Rory remained silent as he sought an honest answer, then said, 'I think in some ways it will have strengthened it.'

'You don't consider keeping my wallet to be an act of weakness?'

Feeling the heat rise in his face, Rory said, 'Yes I do, but I attribute it to the shock of bereavement and living as a vagrant.'

For one long moment, the professor drummed his fingers on his desk, while he held Rory's gaze. Then he gave a nod.

Rory felt a leap of fear, only too aware that a constable could still be called.

'I am in need of help with a book I am writing.' Professor Dalton's tone was brisk. 'Someone to carry out general research and to keep my papers in order, that sort of thing. I take it you would be capable of that?'

Rory stared at him in shock, so dumbfounded that at first he didn't answer. Then, 'You mean you are prepared to . . . ?'

'Trust you? Yes, I am. Again, would you be capable of that?'

Rory pulled himself together. 'Perfectly, sir.'

'Good. You have demonstrated that you are articulate and you claim to have knowledge of Latin. I assume that you have copperplate handwriting?'

Rory could only nod, his mind still reeling. Not only to be offered a position when he was unable to supply a reference, but to be able to spend his days in the world of books and academia. He couldn't believe his good fortune.

The professor looked at him thoughtfully. 'Rory, one lapse can be forgiven, I think.' He rose. 'We'll go into further details tomorrow morning and, in the meantime, I am sure my housekeeper will be able to find you a bed.'

'I can't thank you enough, sir.'

'Then I trust I won't have cause for regret.'

Straightening his shoulders, Rory met his keen gaze and held it. 'Professor Dalton, I give you my word.'

Chapter Seventeen

On a glorious day during the following week, Letitia decided to send for Ella. With sun streaming through the tall windows into the morning room to burnish the walnut side tables and with a display of crimson roses before the Adam fireplace, she thought it would be an altruistic gesture to share the scene with the young girl. After all, there would have been little colour or beauty in her life, which was probably why she had waited outside the workhouse with such persistence. Someone dressed in colourful rich silk and a hat embellished with feathers must have seemed like a visitor from another world.

She wondered whether Ella would react in the same way as previous scullery maids dutifully summoned to Letitia's presence? Overawed and tongue-tied, looking down at their feet and fidgeting, patently relieved when the butler came to escort them back to the servants' hall? She rose from her chair and, going over to the bell pull at the side of the fireplace, waited for the butler to come in. 'Forbes, please would you bring the new scullery maid to me.'

Letitia saw his surprise but ignored it. 'I take it there have been no problems as yet?'

'Not so far, madam.'

She inclined her head and, as he left with a carefully controlled expression, she went to sit before her escritoire where, drawing towards her a sheet of cream vellum, she unscrewed her fountain pen and with its gold nib wrote, at the top of the page, Ella's name together with the date. At least this would be a distraction from her chaotic thoughts because she'd had not a moment's peace of mind since seeing Miles. Every time the post was brought into the drawing room, her heart would leap in case there was a letter from him. It wasn't that she had any silly romantic notion of a reconciliation, because Letitia considered his treatment of her too base for that to ever happen. But she did have an increasingly burning desire to know the truth, however hurtful it may be.

Ella, scrubbing at a pile of carrots, didn't hear Cook come to the door of the scullery until she snapped, 'Tidy yourself, girl. Miss Fairchild wants to see you.'

Twisting round, Ella stared at her. 'But Rosie said it would be a month.'

'Well she was wrong. Hurry up – you don't want to keep the mistress waiting. And take that sacking apron off.'

Ella obeyed, and then, her stomach churning with nerves, she washed and dried her hands before hurrying into the passage. Mr Forbes, waiting with ill-concealed impatience, told her to straighten her cap and, standing on tiptoe before the mirror, Ella also tucked in stray wisps of hair. She could only think that Miss Fairchild had found out that she'd lied to avoid going to church and her face was burning as she followed him up the backstairs, and, for the first time, into 'upstairs'. Soon they were crossing a hall where her heavy boots made a noise on the black and white tiles, while a grandfather clock began to strike the hour. The butler opened a wide cream panelled door and, standing in the entrance, said, 'The scullery maid Ella, madam.'

There came the voice she remembered so well. 'Thank you, Forbes.'

He moved aside, gestured to Ella to go forward and, as she tentatively stepped inside, he left, closing the door behind him. Miss Fairchild, wearing a blue dress with white lace at the high neckline and at the cuffs, was sitting before a writing desk. She turned and smiled. 'Good morning, Ella.'

'Good morning, miss.' Her voice came out as little more than a whisper.

'I won't keep you a moment, my dear.' She bent her head and continued writing.

Ella dared to look around the large room, staring in admiration at the white fireplace and pale walls in the prettiest shade of green she had ever seen. She glanced back at Miss Fairchild but she was still busy, so Ella gazed around once more. There were small tables in a lovely golden wood, on some were china ornaments, and on others fringed lamps. Rosie had told her about the mirrors; Ella especially liked the huge gold-framed one hanging over the mantelpiece. With the air full of the delicate scent of roses and the carpet so soft beneath her black boots, Ella felt awkward, especially as there was a stain on her skirt.

'Do you like the room?'

Startled, Ella saw that Miss Fairchild had turned and was watching her. 'Oh yes, miss, it's beautiful.'

'Miss Fairchild, Ella. Try to remember always to use the person's full name.'

She swallowed. 'Yes, Miss Fairchild.' Ella looked at her, trying to guess if she was cross, but no, she was smiling.

'So, how are you settling in at Eversleigh?'

'Very well, thank you, miss . . . Miss Fairchild.'

'Good. I was sorry to hear that you were unwell last Sunday. But you are fully recovered now?'

Ella nodded. She wasn't going to admit anything until she had to.

'That's good.' Her voice was gentle. 'I asked to see you, Ella, because I realise how very different all this must be from what you are used to. And also because I want you to try to listen and learn – in that way you will gain experience.'

Ella felt a flood of relief. It wasn't about the lying, then. She'd decided never to do that again, it wasn't worth the worry!

'Perhaps you could tell me what you have learnt so far.'

She floundered. What could she say? That Rosie had shown her the best way to stoke the range, and that she was getting better at washing the dishes? She hesitated – better not to mention the chamber pots. 'I've found out that cucumbers need to be peeled, and how to slice them thin, how to make a proper cup of tea . . .' Her voice trailed off.

'I think that is an excellent beginning. And you are happy?'

'Oh, yes, thank you, Miss Fairchild.'

There was a short silence, then, 'I would be interested to know more about you, Ella. I understand that you were only six years old when you entered the workhouse.'

She nodded. 'I think so. I was taken there after my mother was killed.'

'I'm so very sorry. Was it in an accident?'

Ella shook her head. 'No, she was killed deliberate, I saw it happen.'

'But you were only a child, are you sure you weren't mistaken?'

Ella shook her head again. 'Someone else saw it, a grown-up. All I remember is promising never to forget what I'd seen.' There had been little likelihood of that, especially in those first few weeks in the workhouse. The nightmares had caused her to wake up in terror at the images, her mother's muslin skirts dirtied and stained with blood, her body in a heap beneath the hooves of the black horses.

'And to whom did you give that promise?'

Ella felt foolish. 'I can't remember her name, only her voice.'

Her gaze met the concerned one of Miss Fairchild. 'My dear, you are very young to dwell on such a tragedy and I have heard that sometimes memories cannot always be relied upon. My advice is to try to put it out of your mind until you are older.' She paused and her smile was warm. 'But I am very pleased to see you making such good progress. You may return to your duties now, Ella.'

'Thank you, Miss Fairchild.' Ella, wondering whether she was supposed to curtsey or something, managed a clumsy bob. Then she turned to grasp the gleaming doorknob and opened the door. Mr Forbes, who had been waiting in the hall, came forward to close it. 'Off you go then, and don't clatter down the stairs.'

In the morning room, Letitia, who had hidden a smile at Ella's uncertain attempt at bending her knee, mused that her impression had been a favourable one. The girl not only seemed quick to learn, but her glance around the room when she'd thought herself unobserved had been an appreciative one. However, Letitia thought that the story about her mother's death seemed implausible. It was more likely that the only way the girl had withstood the deprivation of the workhouse was to weave stories in her imagination, to dramatise her early life. And at such a young age, it could easily happen that, as time passed, the line between fact and fiction became blurred.

She became thoughtful. There had been sincerity blazing from the girl's eyes, distress too, when she'd talked of her mother. Letitia recalled a recent interesting conversation concerning Dr Sigmund Freud, whose theories she found fascinating. Would he not consider that carrying a tragic conviction such as this might well cause long-term psychological harm?

Chapter Eighteen

During the following weeks, Ella, heeding the advice of both Agnes and Miss Fairchild, concentrated on learning as much as she could. She scrubbed floors and prepared vegetables, watching others and asking questions that might prevent Cook from finding fault with her. Ella was constantly wary of her moods and sharp tongue, but nothing could spoil her appreciation of the food she provided. She would pour Cook's sweet custard over jam and suet roly-polys, treacle sponge puddings, fruit crumbles and pies, with as generous a hand as she dared.

Rosie told her that they were lucky to have such good food. 'You should 'ear the tales me sister tells. She's in service in Bayswater. Nothing but lumpy porridge every morning and, as for the dinners, she says the portions wouldn't feed a seven-year-old. The skinflints even ration the tea.'

'Miss Fairchild is an angel,' Ella said.

'Yes, well you're biased, seein' as she saved you from the workhouse.'

But Ella's mind was full of anticipation of her first Sunday half-day. Looking forward to it with increasing impatience, she was thrilled that she would be able to sally forth in her 'Sunday best'. Her dress might be a dull grey, but it did have a white collar and each time she wore it to church services, Ella felt almost grown-up. She found the rest of the congregation fascinating; the bewhiskered gentlemen, the fine clothes worn by their wives, and would gaze with wistfulness at their cherished and well-dressed children.

To her delight, on Sunday she didn't have to wash the dishes after the luncheon of cold collation of ham and salad, enabling her to set off early down the drive. Most of the other servants went to visit their families on their half-day, often begging from Cook some leftovers from the pantry, but for Ella it was the world outside the tall iron gates that beckoned. Wearing her straw hat, she stood outside and lifted a finger to pull forward a strand of her hair, anxious for it to grow, hoping that it would curl or wave. She couldn't wait to have long hair – Rosie and the parlourmaids all had long pretty hair, even if most of the time it was hidden beneath their caps.

She walked briskly, her black boots clipping the pavement, loving the feel of the sun on her face, the sound of the soft rustling of a breeze amongst the trees as she passed. A bird sang, its trilling notes soaring and, as behind their tall hedges were other large houses, she would pause to peer through the gates but, in her opinion, none was so fine as her own. She giggled to herself at thinking of Eversleigh in such a way, but then it *was* where she lived, wasn't it? And so, with the eagerness of youth, Ella, remembering Jack's directions, eventually found herself in Hampstead High Street. She'd been warned that all the shops would be closed, but she was still able to see glimpses of their merchandise by bending to look beneath the blinds, or sometimes through the narrow windows of their doors. She hadn't any money to buy anything, at least not yet, not until she received the first instalment of her wages. At the heady prospect, her face broke into such a beaming smile that an old man shuffling past gave a toothless grin in reply. 'Afternoon, missy.'

'Good afternoon. I want to get to the Heath. It is this way?'

He nodded. 'It's a fair step, mind, and not a place to go on your own.'

But Ella, after thanking him, was already moving away. His warning didn't worry her because she was no shrinking violet. Hadn't she survived six years in the workhouse? She was further reassured by seeing several other people ahead, and they all looked perfectly respectable. And then, at last, she found herself facing a vast expanse of open space and she could only stand and gaze in wonder. It was not only that she had never seen so much grass, there were also so many trees, and all in differing shades of green. 'It's beautiful,' she breathed, hardly able to believe that, while she'd been shut away behind high walls, there had been this glorious world outside. She could feel the springiness of the turf beneath her feet and breathe in the smell of earth, foliage and fresh air. At first, she felt a little nervous and stood there for several minutes just looking around and then began to walk on, wanting to explore further, her body feeling light until, with joy bubbling inside her, she could contain it no longer. With a swift glance over her shoulder, and seeing the nearest people were some distance away, she began to run, really run for the first time in her life. Removing her hat, she held it out behind her, loving the feel of the breeze on her hair, beginning to laugh aloud, raising her face to the sun, exulting in her new-found freedom. When she eventually slowed down, her breathing rapid, her lips were still smiling and it was with reluctance that she replaced her hat and began again to walk in a sedate manner.

She heard movement on the turf behind her, and turning to see a young man approaching, flushed scarlet to realise that he must have seen her running like a wild thing.

'Don't you remember me?' His voice was cheerful, even teasing.

Ella stared at his reddish-brown hair and stiff white collar, then, on the fringes of her mind, came an image of the sad young man she had talked to on the day she left the workhouse. 'You were on the cart.'

'Yes. I recognised you straightaway.'

She gave a shy smile. 'You look different.'

He nodded. 'I've been fortunate.' He gestured at his jacket and grey trousers. 'I'm a bit better dressed than I was last time. You look nice too. Whoever it was who gave you those clothes in the workhouse . . .'

'That was Miss Grint. She was always hateful to me, and I'll get my own back one day.'

He smiled.

'No, I mean it,' Ella told him.

'I was only in there for a month and that was too long,' he said. 'I intend to come up here, whenever I can, to get some fresh air, weather permitting. Are they treating you well where you are?'

'Yes, I've never been so happy.'

'I'm glad to hear it. My name is Rory Adare, by the way.'

'I'm Ella, Ella Hathaway.'

'Look, shall we walk together? It's not really safe, you know, to come up here by yourself. I tell you what, let me show you where I spent that first night.' As he fell into step beside her, he explained how he'd decided not to take the position of pot boy that the workhouse had arranged. 'It was a risk, indeed most would say a foolish one. And it wasn't easy . . .' He looked troubled for a second, then smiled at her. 'But it all worked out in the end.'

Minutes later, Ella was staring first at the wide branches of the oak tree and then at the uneven ground beneath it. 'Weren't you scared, out in the open like this?'

'I'm able to look after myself, I'm young and strong. It did pour with rain, though, first thing, and I was trapped here for ages.'

Ella remembered that wet morning. It was when she had struggled to open the drawer in her room, and her hand instinctively went to feel the shape of her locket beneath her dress.

Rory was thinking that the girl didn't look quite such an oddity now that she was wearing half-decent clothes. Although she still had that awful cropped hair, which was why even at a distance he'd guessed who it was. Fleetingly, he wondered what she would look like when it had grown. The scene where she had been running with such abandon had seemed to capture the very essence of freedom. So much so that he'd felt his own spirits rise. Not that he would dream of referring to it because she must have thought herself unobserved. What a coincidence that they should meet again, although perhaps not so surprising as they both lived fairly near to the Heath. He was glad that he'd seen her, although he must warn her again about wandering around on her own. Rory knew so few people that he didn't mind that she was that much younger, it was just good to have company.

Chapter Nineteen

Just over a week later, Letitia, seated on the chintz sofa in the morning room, was immersed in *The Times* when Forbes brought in the morning post. She glanced up, saw the cream envelope on the salver, and knew immediately that it was from Miles. How could she forget those strong curved strokes of black ink? Not that he had risked writing to her here, but notes had often been passed between them.

She kept her voice calm. 'Thank you, Forbes.'

Letitia's hand trembled as she gazed down at her name written in that familiar flowing script, and then, taking her ivory paperknife, she slit open the vellum to extract a single sheet of paper.

My dear Letitia,

I have thought of you so many times during the past seven years, and I hope with the utmost sincerity that you are both well and happy. I am, at the moment, in London, it may even be possible that you caught sight of me when I walked to the gates of Eversleigh. However, it has taken some time to gather the courage to ask whether you will agree to see me.

I am hoping that you will find it in your heart to do so as

I have a desperate wish that there should be truth between us.
And so, unless I hear from you to the contrary, it is my intention
to call on you at four o'clock on this coming Friday.
    Be kind to me, Letitia, this has been a decision made after
much heartache – I really do need to see and talk to you.
    With deep affection,
    Miles

She read the letter again, trying to read between the lines, to interpret each word's meaning and nuance, then the letter fluttered from her hands and into her lap. Did she even need to consider? She would be a fool to turn down his request. Hadn't she longed, herself, with desperation, to know exactly what had happened in her father's study that fateful night? But if Miles was at last going to confess to it, what had changed, why had he waited until now?

Letitia glanced down at the embossed name of a prominent hotel in the centre of London. And again, the suspicion insinuated itself. Had her father financed Miles, offered him a lucrative contract, letters of reference, the chance to make his fortune abroad? Temptations any young architect would find attractive. And if Miles had been told that Letitia would be disinherited if she married without her father's permission . . . What was the old saying, 'love flies out of the window, when poverty enters the door'?

And yet, though her logic could believe that scenario, in her heart she found it difficult. She had so believed Miles to be a man of integrity.

It was later that day when she at last confided in her maid that she had seen Miles outside the gates of Eversleigh, and after telling her about his letter, Mary was not slow to express her indignation. 'If you don't mind my saying so, madam, he's got a barefaced cheek to show his face again in this house.'

'And I am sure many would agree with you. But, Mary, please keep your own counsel about this.'

'Of course, but, apart from Mr Forbes, I doubt if anyone else would recognise him. We have had several changes of staff since then. Madam, I may be speaking out of turn,' Mary's forehead was creasing in a heavy frown, 'but please take care. Last time,' she bit her lip, 'well, I wouldn't like to see you hurt like that again. And charming men can be like snakes – or so I'm told.'

Letitia gave her a smile that portrayed more confidence than she felt. 'Don't worry, Mary. I intend to remain on my guard.'

The few days before the expected arrival of Miles seemed an eternity until Friday dawned. The weather was warm, with sunlight streaming through the windows when Letitia awoke, and, after her hot chocolate, she lay back against her pillows, her stomach twisting in knots as she tried to imagine the forthcoming scene. Would she be able to remain, as she hoped, calm, confident and in charge of the situation? At the moment, she found it even difficult to decide what to wear, later choosing an elegant long skirt in emerald green and a favourite high-necked ivory blouse that gave warmth to her complexion.

Letitia could only pick at her breakfast and, not until the mantel clock in the morning room displayed ten, did she rise from the sofa and go over to the silken bell pull at the side of the fireplace.

Within minutes, the butler entered. 'Please close the door, Forbes.' Then Letitia said, 'I wish to speak of a confidential matter. I am expecting a visitor this afternoon at four o'clock and I would request that his identity remain between ourselves.'

'You can be assured of my discretion, madam.'

She hesitated, then said quietly, 'The gentleman's name is Mr Miles Maitland.' She saw his eyes narrow before his normal impassive expression returned. 'I wish you to greet him yourself and for refreshment to be served on his arrival.'

'I understand, madam.' His tone was one of stiff restraint.

Knowing that he would have some remembrance of the way Miles had fled her father's study that night, of her own distress in the weeks that followed, Letitia said, 'Thank you, Forbes, that will be all.'

The following hours were the slowest to pass that Letitia could remember. Embroidery was inconceivable and her hands were too unsteady even to write letters. She managed to be distracted, a little, by the current issue of *Vogue*, but scarcely ate any luncheon. And then, at last, came the peal of the doorbell and, her ears straining for every sound, she heard Forbes's swift footsteps cross the hall.

'Good afternoon. I think Miss Fairchild is expecting me.'

Oh, that remembered voice, that slightly husky tone. Letitia resisted the impulse to rise, to stand in the middle of the room, and instead smoothed her skirt, touched her hair and remained seated in what she hoped was a confident manner on the sofa.

The door opened. 'Mr Maitland, madam.' As the tall man came into the room, the butler retreated, closing the door behind him.

Letitia rose and, summoning her composure, she held out her hand. 'Good afternoon, Miles.' He was still as handsome, still with that characteristic intensity.

He gazed steadily at her for a moment, his handshake warm. 'It is good to see you, Letitia.'

She forced a smile. 'Please,' she gestured towards an opposite armchair and, as they were seated, the grandfather clock in the hall chimed the hour. 'You are very punctual. And you are well?'

'Thank you, I am. I trust that you too are in good health?'

She merely inclined her head. He seemed ill at ease, convincing her that, as she had hoped, he had come to Eversleigh to offer a belated explanation. A guilt-ridden one, she imagined, her attitude hardening as she saw how prosperous he looked.

'Letitia, I do appreciate your generosity in agreeing to see me.'

'I was curious, Miles.' There came a tap at the door and a parlourmaid entered carrying a tray and placed it on a low table. 'Thank you, Gloria, I will pour.'

With a sly look at Miles, the girl went out, closing the door behind her with exaggerated care.

There followed the coffee ritual of whether black or white, the pouring, and the passing of cups, with Letitia's comments polite and formal. There was little spontaneity from either of them, merely awkwardness, while the tension in the room mounted. The plate of biscuits remained untouched.

Then Miles slowly replaced his cup and leant forward. 'This is not merely a social call, Letitia, I would not have been so crass as to request that. Nor is it an idle curiosity to see you again.'

'I hope not, Miles.'

He shook his head. 'I have something to tell you that has weighed so heavily on my conscience that I scarce know how to begin.'

She looked at him and her voice trembled. 'Do you know, Miles, the worst aspect of it all was the bewilderment, no word, not even a letter.'

His gaze searched hers, his own troubled. 'I am sorrier than I can express. I have to admit that I was surprised to learn that you have never married.'

'When one suspects that proposals are out of interest in my inheritance, rather than myself . . .'

'I don't remember you as a cynic.'

'Life changes one.'

He ran his fingers through his dark hair, a gesture she had known well. 'I can't blame you for being bitter, but I am hoping that you will find it in your heart to understand why I acted as I did. We were so close, Letitia. Do you remember how we would often finish each other's sentences?'

'I remember many things, Miles.'

For one long moment he didn't speak, then he said, 'That last evening, when I came to Eversleigh, is one that will be with me until the day I die. I have been torn apart ever since, consumed with not only guilt because of the way I fled, but, even now, by uncertainty as to whether I should tell you the truth.'

'I am no longer a naive young girl, Miles.'

He looked at her, his expression now drawn. 'I can see that, Letitia.' He drew a deep ragged breath. 'I discovered something about myself that night, which came as not only a profound shock, but one that shook the foundations of my life. At first, when my admission of our affection for each other was met with such revulsion and horror – even now I can remember my humiliation, my anger. But what followed . . .'

'How much?' Letitia's voice was as sharp as a splinter. 'How much did he pay you?'

Miles made an involuntary movement towards her. 'No!'

'What else do you think I have wondered all these years? Had my father threatened to disinherit me? Had he offered you money to leave the country? You forget, Miles, I knew what he was capable of.'

His expression was one of sadness. 'You found it in yourself to believe that?'

She looked at him, seeing what she thought was sincerity in his eyes and remembered how, before that night, she would never have doubted him. 'I fought against it for a long time.'

He got up and began to pace the room, then slowly returned to sit beside her. She could see anguish in his eyes as he said, 'I know of no way of softening this.'

It was several minutes later when, leaving her sitting motionless on the sofa, Miles rose to stand and gaze out of the tall windows. Letitia's mind and heart were reeling with horror, every instinct rebelling against what he had just revealed. That when he came to see Cedric Fairchild in his book-lined study, the words her father flung at him had rocked not only his world but now her own.

'Not a court in the land would allow you and my daughter ever to marry. Not when you are my natural son.'

Letitia felt bile rise in her throat at the remembered image of an ashen-faced Miles emerging to cross the hall and leave. And then she felt the full impact of what this news meant and turned to Miles with bewilderment and anger. 'But why on earth didn't you tell me? Have you any idea of how hurt I was, how heartbroken? To just leave like that, without even a word?'

He turned, and his gaze was anguished. 'I was in a state of shock. Afterwards, I could hardly sleep for days wondering whether or not to write and tell you what had happened. I still think I was right in keeping it from you. Letitia, try to put yourself in my place. What would I have achieved by destroying your world, ruining your relationship with your father? He was the only family you had. And believe me, the secret would somehow have leaked, it would only have taken raised voices for the servants to get wind of it and for the scandal to spread, and then you would have been subjected to the unthinkable. Pitying and shocked glances, speculation about what had taken place between us. I was never going to subject you to that.'

Her eyes filled with tears and she shook her head. 'You were wrong, I would rather have known. I was so unhappy, Miles, and for such a long time.'

He looked down at his hands and his lips twisted. 'I'm so very sorry.'

'How do you know Father was speaking the truth?'

'My mother confirmed everything.' He came to again sit beside her. 'Letitia, listen to me! We did nothing for which you should reproach yourself. Yes, I held you in my arms and kissed you, and we wanted to marry, but we did nothing wrong, there was no intimacy between us.' But in despair she could only stare at him. No matter what he said, she knew that she had been in love with him and it appalled her. Even if at the time she hadn't known that Miles was her half-brother – surely some instinct should have protected her?

Chapter Twenty

'He was ever so good-looking,' Gloria told the others in the kitchen. 'You don't think Miss Fairchild has a beau? Now wouldn't that be something to celebrate, Mr Forbes? I love a nice wedding.'

'Don't talk nonsense, girl.'

Ella who could hear their conversation from the scullery wondered why the butler sounded so angry. She'd never seen a wedding, and tried to imagine Miss Fairchild with a veil over her face – she had seen a picture of a bride once, but even then couldn't understand why her face was hidden. Suppose it was someone else pretending to be her and the bridegroom married the wrong person?

Later, Ella's mind was full of thoughts about her approaching Sunday afternoon off. She was hoping that the weather would be fine because she and Rory had arranged to meet on the Heath. She liked him a lot, she really did. Although he hadn't been the only one to warn her about going up to the Heath on her own. When she'd returned to Eversleigh, Jack had been furious. 'Ain't yer got *any* sense in that 'ead of yours?'

'Nobody said anything.'

'I suppose you're blaming me, seein' as I told you about the Heath in the first place. But I did say it was best to go with somebody.'

'I thought you meant cos of finding the way.'

Ella hadn't mentioned Rory, not wanting to answer curious questions, and then her musings were disturbed by a screech.

'Rosie! What's the matter with you lately? You're as much use as a wet lettuce.'

Ella looked round the scullery door to see Rosie bend to pick up a bag of sugar that she must have dropped.

'Be careful! Look, it's split on one side.' Tutting, Cook pushed her out of the way. 'Here, give it to me and go and fetch a brush.'

Rosie, her lips pressed together, went out into the corridor, and Ella returned to scrubbing at a burnt pan with sandstone. Poor Rosie, something did seem to be wrong with her; lately, she hadn't wanted to chat at all when they went to bed. Once Ella had heard what she thought were sobs from the other girl, but hadn't dared to ask in case she was thought nosy.

But that same night, once they had undressed and put on their nightgowns, Ella was so shocked by the wretchedness in the other girl's eyes that she blurted, 'Rosie, what's wrong? You can tell me, I won't tell anyone else, honest.'

Rosie's eyes were brimming with tears. 'I can't . . . I don't know what to do. If only I could go home.'

'Is it your mother again? Is she worse?'

She shook her head, dabbing at her eyes with her hanky. 'There's someone I need to see, and I haven't got a half-day for ages cos I was given a whole one last time, what with my mum being ill.'

'Can't you explain it to Mr Forbes?'

Her expression was one of horror. 'No, he'd want to know why.'

'It's really important, seeing this person?'

'More than you can imagine.' Her eyes filled with tears again.

Ella stared at her, distressed to see dark circles beneath her eyes, her lips twisting in despair. Rosie had been so good to her, showing her how to do things, never prying into Ella's belongings.

The words came out in a rush. 'You can take my half-day on Sunday, if you like.'

Rosie stopped dabbing at her eyes and stared at her. 'What? Do you mean it?'

Ella nodded, hardly able to believe that she'd thrown away her chance to see Rory.

'I don't know if Mr Forbes would let us.' Rosie's expression was one of doubt. 'And he'd want to know the reason.'

'Not if I said it was my idea.'

'But what could you say?'

'I'll think of something, you'll see.'

Stunned, Ella found herself clutched in Rosie's swift and tight embrace. She could remember only little Teresa ever hugging her, and that was only before she was taken away to the hospital to die.

Later, she lay awake staring into the darkness, worrying both about Rosie and the excuse she could make to the butler, but her fear most of all was that Rory would think she had let him down. It would be awful if he waited a long time for her. And yet she had no way of getting in touch with him. Even if she knew where this Professor Dalton lived, how could she write a letter without paper and an envelope?

In an effort to distract herself, Ella thought of her secret in the bottom drawer of the chest. She was longing to open the black silk purse again, but she had never once been alone long enough. Cook was always at her heels, filling any idle moment with another task, and besides there was always the risk of Rosie coming in.

The idea came slowly. If things went as planned on Sunday, once Rosie had left, why shouldn't Ella plead a headache and come upstairs to lie down, safe in the knowledge that she wouldn't be disturbed. Ella stifled a yawn, beginning to feel more content. She was disappointed at not being able to see Rory, she really was, but at least she had something else to look forward to.

'Just to say thank you?' The butler's voice was incredulous and Ella felt the guilty flush in her face increase.

'Rosie's been that good to me, Mr Forbes, being patient when I made mistakes, and I can't buy her a present or anything.'

He gazed down at her, his forehead creasing in a frown. 'All right, but only this once, mind. I can't have swapping and changing with the staff roster, it would cause chaos.'

'I promise.'

'All right, off you go.'

Ella went back to the scullery and a few minutes later Rosie came in and hissed, 'I saw you follow him into the corridor.'

Ella whispered, 'I told him it was my way of thanking you for showing me how to do things. Anyway, he's agreed.'

Rosie's eyes lit up, then she scurried away as there came a screech from Cook. 'Rosie, what are you doing in there? I need these eggs separating.'

Ella stared down at the muddy water she was using to wash soil off potatoes, certain now that she wouldn't be able to see Rory on Sunday. It was stupid to mind, especially when she had her other plan, but the truth was that she minded very much. And what she later overheard didn't help to raise her spirits.

'I thought it a very generous gesture.' Ella could hear the butler's deep voice as she returned from the lavatory. She paused outside the kitchen.

'I wouldn't 'ave thought a girl from the gutter would have any finer feelings.' It was Cook's voice, dispelling Ella's hopes that she had softened towards her.

'Now then, Mrs Perkins, we neither of us must allow our

128

prejudices to get in the way of fairness. You can't deny that she performs her duties well. And she has gone up in my estimation. Unselfishness is a rare attribute in the young.'

Ella felt even worse about planning to lie to Cook on Sunday. As for letting Rory down, after asking herself what he would have done in her place, faced with a weeping Rosie, it was a small comfort to feel convinced that he would have done exactly the same.

Chapter Twenty-One

On the other side of Hampstead, Rory was struggling to contain his anger in the servants' hall at number 35, where, downstairs, he felt that he was still regarded by some with reservation, even, at times, with suspicion. Certainly, Charlie never lost an opportunity to pass a snide remark, although he took care only to do so when they were alone.

But, on leaving the house ten minutes later, his spirits rose at the prospect of spending the morning at the British Museum. In the library there, he would be able to lose himself in his work, searching for and perusing facts needed by Professor Dalton for his manuscript. Rory had discovered that philanthropic gestures were no strangers to the professor, and his admiration for his learned benefactor grew daily. The fact that his chosen area of expertise was history rather than science was an added bonus, Rory's own inclination leaning in the same direction.

After boarding a tram that wound its way to his destination, he thought ahead to the coming weekend, finding himself looking forward to seeing young Ella again. She was so full of courage and eagerness. What the future held for her, he had no idea, but he did hope it would include a better life than working as a servant. Her education, though, would only have been basic, but she seemed an intelligent girl and maybe he could be of some help to her. He must ask her exact age, whether she liked to read, even whether she had ever read an actual book all the way through. Probably, he thought, she would only have had access to tracts from the Bible or, and here his lips twisted with cynicism, tracts on the glory of the British Empire.

It was as he alighted that he saw the young boy, aged around ten, his pale face pinched with hunger. Not an uncommon sight in London, but it dampened his mood. Then, as Rory drew nearer, the boy went to approach a well-dressed gentleman walking towards him and held out the palm of his hand. Appalled to see the man raise his silver-topped cane and bring it down so brutally that the child cried out with pain, Rory increased his stride and called, 'Was that necessary, sir?'

The florid-faced man looked at Rory's cheap clothes and his dark moustache quivered with fury. 'You don't fool me. You're in it together, thieving ruffians out to snatch my wallet. I've a good mind to call a constable.'

The boy said, 'Quick, scarper.'

Judging it advisable, Rory's long and hurried stride kept up with him as they weaved along a couple of side streets before drawing to a halt. He looked down at the grubby small head. 'Haven't you got a home to go to?'

'No, mister.'

'But where do you sleep?'

'Under the arches.'

Rory guessed that he meant the railway arches. 'Your parents?'

'Dead, mister. And I ain't goin' in no workhouse, neither.' He began to edge away, his expression wary.

'What about food?'

Again, he shrugged. 'There's always sumthin' in the bins.'

Rory winced, remembering his own foraging that time, looked at the thin face before him, seeing the defiance in his pale-blue eyes. 'But what about when winter comes? You're very young to be on your own.'

The boy's lips met in a mutinous line. 'I know kids who've died in the workhouse and bin beaten in them orphanages. I can look after meself.'

Looking at the determination in his eyes, Rory was tempted to believe him. 'What's your name?'

'Albert.' He drew himself up. 'I'm named after the prince, just like the Albert 'All.'

Rory grinned. 'And a fine name it is too.' He handed him a couple of pennies, wishing he could have given him more. 'Spend them on food now, nothing else.'

'Ooh, thanks, mister. I will, I promise.' He ran off, the coins clutched in his hand.

Rory watched him until he was out of sight. London, despite being one of the richest cities in the world, had a vast underbelly of poverty. He'd seen beggars starving to death in alleyways, despair and poverty causing men to turn to the 'demon drink', as the Temperance Movement called it. His father would have smiled at the term and quoted George Bernard Shaw, who had once described whisky as 'liquid sunshine'. But then Seamus Adare had, until his last few years, lived a civilised life.

Rory made his way to the British Museum where, as he was in possession of a reader's ticket, he was able to enter the vast circular reading room. He also had access, at number 35, to Professor Dalton's personal library and, as humanity and its deprivation was a subject that interested him, he was determined to take advantage of its books on theology and philosophy. After all, such a facility wouldn't always be at his disposal, as the professor only required his assistance in the compilation of the new book. He pushed aside the question of what his future would hold once the book was finished.

The following day at Eversleigh, Rosie was showing Ella how to slice runner beans. 'My ma used to call 'em "little boats" to make us kids eat 'em. Straight from the garden, they were. Me dad wouldn't allow any flowers to be grown, not with six kids to feed.'

Ella, who loved hearing about Rosie's chaotic home and childhood, copied her instructions – using the correct paring knife helped – and, after some misshapen pods, mastered the skill. 'Does this person you want to see today know you're coming?'

She shook her head, and glancing at her, Ella could see determination in her eyes instead of despair. It made her feel good inside, knowing it was due to her impulsive offer. She turned to see Rosie gazing at her. 'You know, yer hair is beginning to grow a bit.'

'I wish it wasn't such a dull colour.'

'There's time yet for it to deepen. Some browns can look lovely.'

'You're a kind person, Rosie. I hope you come back on Sunday feeling better.'

'You're not the only one!'

Ella took the prepared runner beans into the kitchen where Cook, having put three apple pies to bake in the oven, was sitting at the table talking to Gloria. 'What do you think's wrong with Miss Fairchild?'

Ella hovered to hear the parlourmaid's reply.

Gloria shrugged. 'I dunno. But when I took her morning elevenses in, she was still very quiet, pretended to be reading.'

No matter how Letitia tried to blank images of that romantic summer from her mind, nor to remind herself that the number of times Miles had held her in his arms and kissed her had been few, deep within her lay a kernel of shame. And, to her dismay, this tended to overshadow the joy she should feel that, rather than being alone in the world, she had a half-brother. Within time, she knew, the discovery would bring her warmth, a sense of belonging, but as yet she felt too distraught, too full of guilt. Incest. The terrible word kept emerging to lie on her conscience, even though she knew Miles was right; they had not, thank God, shared such intimacy. But her thoughts were not only of herself, but of the betrayal of her mother. Had she been aware that she had been betrayed? That during their marriage her husband had fathered another child?

So far, she had managed not to respond to the concern she could see in Mary's eyes, to resist the temptation to confide the shocking truth to her, even though she could see curiosity in her eyes and the question trembling on her maid's lips. For Letitia, it was all too raw to put into words.

Miles had suggested that they meet again at his London hotel, where there would be no risk of servants overhearing their conversation. 'But not immediately, you will need some time to yourself.'

At the time, her mind had been numb, but now she could see the sense in waiting a short while. There would be so much to discuss between them and her mind needed to be clear. She didn't even know whether Miles intended to take up residence again in England, although she doubted that it would be in Hampstead.

Chapter Twenty-Two

Early on Sunday afternoon, Ella went to and fro from the scullery, clearing the table and washing the crockery from their cold luncheon. She loved this meal of the week, never before having tasted home-cooked ham, raised pork pies, pickles and chutney, with crisp salad leaves and greenhouse tomatoes. She was feeling virtuous, too, despite a twinge of guilt for the fact that she was going to tell a lie, because she attended morning service at St John's Church with the rest of the staff.

And, as she wiped the dishes dry, she was conscious that her body was at last beginning to fill out. Her legs were no longer like matchsticks, and, to her secret pride, there was even a hint of a growing bust. Every night, she brushed her hair a hundred times, impatient for it to grow, but nature wouldn't be hurried.

Ella's only problem was that she felt apprehensive in case, that afternoon, Rory took offence because she had let him down. What if he waited and waited and she'd made him feel stupid? He might not even bother to come to the Heath the next time she had a half-day. And then she fretted whether he would remember that was only once a month, because only then would he be able to work out the date. But she tried to push that worry from her mind, and once she had completed her tasks, Ella wiped her hands on the roller towel, took a deep breath and, on going back into the kitchen, composed her expression into a woebegone one.

The butler was nowhere to be seen, Cook was sitting with her feet propped on a footstool, while Gloria was darning one of her black stockings. She sucked her finger after pricking it with her needle, 'Blasted thing!'

'Don't let Mr Forbes hear you using such language.' But Cook's eyelids were already heavy and, following the pattern of the past few weeks, Ella knew that she would soon fall into a deep doze.

'I've got a bad headache,' she said in a plaintive voice. 'I've done all the pots, though.'

'Better go and have a lie down then.' Cook yawned. 'I'll have forty winks I think.'

Ella made her way up the backstairs, feeling ashamed that she could lie so easily. But then she'd had a lot of practice, because telling the truth to Miss Grint had usually resulted in a clout.

Once inside her bedroom, however, Ella had no other thought than to look again at her personal possessions. Retrieving the nightgown from the back of the bottom drawer she unwrapped it, opened the black silk purse, and laid out its contents on the brown candlewick bedspread. She held the rag doll against her cheek for a moment before gazing down at her treasures, moving them into a neat line, wondering which to look at first. The blue velvet box drew her like a magnet. After unlocking it with the tiny key, as the lid opened, sunlight from the window caused the jewellery to glitter so much that she caught her breath. It was all even more beautiful than she remembered.

She decided to try on the pearls. She had seen Miss Fairchild wearing pearls. Ella undid the top buttons of her dress, took out the pearl necklace, and went to stand before the small mirror on the wall. The clasp was fiddly but, once it parted, she lifted her arms to fasten it behind her neck and let the pearls fall in a creamy string around her throat. She touched their cool silkiness and went to fetch the matching earrings. Removing her cap, Ella clipped them on and then stared in wonder, turning her head so that the small droplets swung. Somehow, her face didn't look so plain, especially as her cap was covering her stubby hair. As she stood there, Ella held her gold locket for a moment, thinking of her mother as she always did when she touched it. A wave of sadness swept over her; it seemed so unfair, to have these lovely things and then to die so young.

She kept the pearl jewellery on and, going back to the bed, tried on one of the rings. Its blue stone was lovely and sparkly but slid off her finger, as did the other ring with several smaller stones. Ella wondered whether they had been presents bought by her father. How she wished she knew something, anything about who he was. And then her glance fell on the leather-covered book. It might be in a foreign language but hadn't her mother's name been in it? What if her father's name was mentioned too? With eagerness she opened the silver clasp and, after reading the inscription again, she began to pore over the pages. Frustrated and impatient, Ella wished her mother had written in English. Of course, she could have been a foreigner, although that seemed doubtful as surely Ella would have somehow known that. Page after page, she scanned, unable to make sense of a single word, and couldn't see any sign of a man's name. But she slowly realised that one initial began appearing, first, now and again, and then frequently. Ella frowned, thinking hard. What could the initial J stand for? James maybe? But it could be anything, perhaps not even a person. It could be a place. But why not put the full name? Had it been a secret? Had her mother written in a foreign language because she had something to hide?

'It's a mystery,' Ella muttered and, closing the book, instead picked up the envelope. Should she open it while she was safe from anyone coming in? She looked at the slightly rough and thick paper, and at the intact red sealing wax. She still felt too nervous. It wasn't even addressed to anyone.

The thin folded piece of paper was next, and she read again the pencilled lines. *This bag was in a drawer in Mrs Hathaway's room. I put it in another to keep it safe. The rags and duster should keep it from nosy parkers. I sent it with the child. Violet Rutter.* Ella concentrated, trying to remember whether the name meant anything to her, but without success. She knew a woman had been holding her hand when she had seen her mother knocked down by the horses, but Ella couldn't remember her face, only a vague recollection of her voice. There was so much she longed to know, to discover. But since coming to Eversleigh, Ella had come to realise how ignorant she was. And she'd been thinking, lately, that it might be better to put her personal possessions away, to wait until she was grown-up. She could then ask for help from Miss Fairchild about the book; even if she didn't know this language, she might know someone who did.

'I'll be older then,' Ella said aloud. 'I'll be able to understand more. And as for you,' she said looking down at the envelope. 'Suppose I do open you, it would only make it easier for someone to read what's inside.' After all, she thought, they've all been hidden away for the past six years, so why not for longer.

She remained deep in thought for quite a long time and then, with determination, replaced everything in the black purse and disguised it inside the nightgown. She'd managed, so far, to keep her secret, and, straightening up from the chest of drawers, she intended to continue to do so.

* * *

Rory, waiting for Ella beneath the same oak tree where he had slept that first night, was not at first unduly concerned that she was late. Then, as time passed, he realised that she wasn't coming, which could be either because she was unwell, or simply unable to take the time off. He wasn't going to wait any longer – not only was he beginning to feel conspicuous, he was missing the chance of healthy exercise. With a last look in the direction he expected Ella to come, he began to stride out, somewhat surprised that he felt so disappointed. They had been good companions that last time as they strolled in the sunshine. He liked talking to her, seeing her eyes light with merriment if he said something funny. He also enjoyed her admiring expression when she looked up at him. I feel taller when I'm with her, he thought – it was so rare nowadays that anyone treated him with respect. He knew that it was mainly because of his hair, which screamed that he was an ex-inmate of the workhouse or gaol. He dreaded to think how Ella felt about her own appearance, but then she was still very young to worry too much about such things.

He walked on, facing a light breeze, feeling his spirits lift and deciding that, while cities had their advantages, nothing could compare with this feeling of freedom that wide open spaces brought. I'll never forget how lucky I am, he thought. At least that is one thing that being an inmate in a workhouse has taught me.

Chapter Twenty-Three

It was late that Sunday evening when Rosie eventually returned, and Ella, who was making cocoa for any servants who wanted it, turned with eagerness, hoping to see her friend smiling.

But Rosie's face was crimson, her head held high in defiance. She put down her basket, now empty of the leftovers that Cook had sent for her family, and faced them all.

'I want ter give in me notice, Mr Forbes.'

All heads swivelled towards her.

'I beg your pardon?'

'I'm leaving to get married.'

Ella felt dumbfounded. Married? But that was wonderful, and then her spirits crashed at the thought of how much she would miss her.

Cook was the next to speak and her voice was harsh. 'Rush job, is it?'

Rosie nodded while Ella caught her breath.

'Well, at least the scoundrel is marrying you. But I'm disappointed in you, Rosie, I really am. I thought you'd got more sense.'

Ella cast a scared glance at the butler only to see his

expression hard and his eyes – she had never seen them so cold.

'I am appalled, Rosie, that you have brought such shame into this house. The mistress will have to be told, you know that.'

'Yes, Mr Forbes.' But Ella noticed that although her voice was steady, her eyes were bright with tears.

'You can stay this one night and that is all. Pack your bags and I shall see you first thing in the morning.' He jerked his head, and Rosie – after a swift glance around the room at the others – hurried out of the kitchen. Ella could hear her tread on the servants' stairs and, in the midst of shocked murmurs, she began to make haste with the cocoa so that she could join her.

When she burst into their bedroom, Rosie was already packing her belongings. 'Jim works on his dad's farm,' she told Ella. 'And he never hesitated, not once, when I told him I was in the family way. The banns will be read out next Sunday, and three weeks after that I'll be Mrs Fowler.'

Ella sat on her bed. 'Don't you feel even a little bit . . . ?'

'Ashamed?' Rosie turned to her. 'I was at first, but let me tell you something, Ella, yer body doesn't always do what yer head says. It was only the once, anyway. I'm not a bad girl, whoever says so. Me pa was a bit fierce at first, and Mum had a few tears, but they like Jim and, as his father's on his own now, my help in the house won't go amiss.' Rosie finished her folding. 'Look, young Ella, don't you go copying me. I've been lucky. But you – you've got no family and if the bloke did a runner you'd probably end up with someone cutting you with a rusty knife. Yer know – a backstreet job. You do know what I mean?'

The sewing room had taught Ella much more than how to sew a seam and darn; she had heard enough horror stories of young women bleeding to death to know what Rosie was talking about.

As for Ella getting herself into such trouble, hadn't Agnes told

141

her to wait until she had a ring on her finger? Not that Ella could imagine herself ever wanting to lie down with a man. And Rosie was right, she had been lucky. If the father hadn't offered to marry her, the poor little baby would have been a bastard. And Ella hadn't heard that ugly name used without knowing the cruelty of it.

It was a few days later, when enjoying scones and strawberry jam in the Featherstones' drawing room, that Letitia mentioned her regret at having to dismiss her kitchen maid without a reference.

'It does seem harsh, but what choice did I have?' She replaced her cup onto its fluted saucer.

'You did say that Rosie is to be married,' Grace said, 'so hopefully she won't need to seek another position.'

'That's true.' Letitia felt somewhat reassured. 'But further on the topic of servants . . .' Letitia told them about the morning she had sent for Ella, and of the girl's suspicions regarding her mother's death.

Grace asked, 'I don't suppose she mentioned anything about a father?'

Letitia shook her head. 'No, but we can probably assume the worst.'

Charlotte spoke slowly. 'You mustn't encourage her, Letitia. What if there should be a grain of truth in her accusation? Can you imagine what a can of worms you would open for this young girl? Having settled in at Eversleigh, her life would be turned upside down, especially if the law became involved.'

'I hadn't considered that.'

'My advice is to leave well alone, at least until the girl is much older.'

'As always, you are right.' She smiled at Charlotte, remembering how, as a small girl, she had envied Grace for being her daughter.

Charlotte rose to ring for more tea and Letitia noticed Grace's gaze stray to a vase of crimson roses, their velvety petals reflected in the mirror behind. 'They wouldn't be from a certain prospective Member of Parliament, would they?' she teased.

Grace's voice was quiet. 'They arrived this morning.'

'Do you like Edward, Grace? Really like him – you know what I mean.'

'Yes, I do.'

Letitia turned to her on the sofa and touched her hand. 'I'm so pleased, you deserve to be happy.' She saw pink shade her friend's cheeks.

'A sentiment with which I entirely agree,' Charlotte said as she returned to her chair. Letitia tried to suppress a feeling of jealousy, knowing that she, herself, would have welcomed an approach from Edward. But at least Grace would be marrying a man of intelligence, someone who had a sense of humour. Her previous suitor had been far too bookish and pious.

'I must tell you, Letitia, about Lady Langley's parrot,' Grace said, beginning to laugh.

'Parrot?'

Grace nodded. 'It's called Alfie and when I was taking tea with her the other day, it squawked across the room, "Choccy biscuit, let's have a choccy biscuit". It was hilarious!'

Letitia also began to laugh. 'Don't tell me that there were chocolate biscuits on the plate.'

'Absolutely, that's what was so amazing. Apparently, he can say dozens of words.'

'Perhaps I should consider a parrot to keep me company.' Letitia looked at these two dear people, longing to confide in them, to reveal what was foremost in her mind. They had both been fond of Miles. But, with difficulty, she managed to resist the temptation, as she had decided that her best course of action would be to say nothing to anyone until she had seen and talked with Miles again. And she felt too bruised, yet, to talk in a rational manner. Grace had already expressed concern that Letitia looked pale and a little tired, which was, of course, due to her nights of disturbed sleep. She had discovered that just before dawn was the worst time and she still worried that her mother may have discovered her husband's infidelity. Letitia hated to think of her being hurt and bewildered, perhaps so unhappy that it affected her health, even contributing to her dying in childbirth. And then her own long ago feelings of loneliness would surface, and Letitia would find herself reliving her motherless and cold childhood.

When, after leaving the Featherstones', she sat in the coach as it took her home, she thought again of the advice Miles had given her before he left Eversleigh. 'You will need to give yourself time. But I promise that you will come to accept the situation, just as I did. After all, we have no alternative because there is nothing in the world that either of us can do to change it.'

Chapter Twenty-Four

It was the following week when Professor Dalton sent for Rory. Anticipating a request for some aspect of research, he left the small downstairs room, which was previously used for storage and now allocated to him for his clerical labours, and his mood was calm as he swiftly went up the backstairs. He was beginning to feel at home in this tall and comfortable house, his relationship with the other staff now becoming more friendly. The only exceptions were the professor's sombre valet, although he kept himself apart from everyone, and, of course, Charlie. The young footman's animosity still hadn't lessened, and Rory would often have to bite his tongue on an angry retort and, on occasions, even to unclench his fists. But his position in the household was too valuable to risk losing for the sake of a moment's satisfaction. He had come to the conclusion that Charlie's resentment stemmed from the fact that Rory was both Irish and a Roman Catholic. He sometimes wondered whether bigotry would ever be eradicated, with his own country being one of the worst offenders.

After a light tap on the door, he went in to stand before the large mahogany desk.

'Good morning, Rory.'

'Good morning, sir.'

Professor Dalton put down his pen and, leaning back into his chair, made a steeple of his fingers. 'There is something I need to discuss with you.' His expression was serious and Rory felt a stab of alarm.

'Is there some problem with my work, sir?'

He shook his head. 'No, you can rest assured on that point; in fact, your help during the weeks you have been with me has been invaluable.'

Been? Rory tensed. He had thought that, as the book needed several more chapters, his position would be secure for months yet.

Professor Dalton opened the small right-hand drawer of his desk to retrieve a letter. 'Several weeks ago I received an offer of a visiting professorship. And, as the opportunity to study and live in a different culture appealed to me, I have been involved in correspondence on several occasions. Yesterday, I received a letter of confirmation. It will mean my leaving England, and very soon. I shall be away for one year.' He laid the paper before him on his leather-bound blotter and began to unscrew his fountain pen.

Rory felt almost sick with disappointment. He had so enjoyed the work, had felt secure here. He dreaded the thought of being homeless again.

'I sent for you, Rory, to ask whether you would be prepared to accompany me to New York.'

Rory's throat closed with shock.

'I shall hope to complete the book during that time. But you have no need to make an instant decision. If you could let me know by the end of the week.'

'I have no need to consider your offer, sir.' The surge of relief Rory felt was so profound that he almost stammered. 'I'd be happy and honoured to accompany you.' He couldn't believe his good fortune. When he was stranded on the Heath, hadn't he fantasised about going to America, the place which had welcomed so many of his countrymen?

The professor smiled. 'I am pleased to hear that, Rory. It's a challenging prospect for both of us. I have never visited our colonial friends, but I'm sure we will both get on famously. I intend to leave in a month's time, but as I haven't yet informed anyone else, I would be obliged if you would respect that.'

'You have my word, sir.'

When Rory left, closing the door quietly behind him, his step was full of excitement and once back in his small room he paced it, too restless to concentrate, his mind whirling with thoughts of what lay ahead. He knew that he would never be able to repay the kindness he had received at the professor's hands. Hadn't he arrived on his doorstep a common thief, even if he had repented and brought back the wallet? When Rory thought of the picture he must have presented, unkempt and shabby, and now for the professor to include Rory in his plans, enabling him to cross the Atlantic, to see America and the famous Statue of Liberty. This was an opportunity beyond Rory's wildest dreams. Especially as he would be going to New York as the professor's research assistant, which meant that he would have security. And who knew whether, at the end of twelve months, he would come back to England? After all, it hadn't been exactly kind to either himself or his father. He couldn't wait now to be able to study a map of New York, and to learn more of its history.

It wasn't until late that evening that he thought of Ella, wondering whether he would have a chance to see her before he left. He had hoped so much to be able to help the girl, to encourage her to widen her horizons and improve herself. Mentally, he calculated when she was likely again to have her next Sunday half-day, discovering that it was less than three weeks away. But he wouldn't rely on that; instead, disregarding the weather, he would go to the Heath each following weekend. She was unlike anyone he had ever met, and he didn't think he'd ever forget her determined young face as she had climbed down from the cart to face an unknown employer and an uncertain future. Now that was what he called courage. Rory paused, feeling a smile come to his lips as he remembered how Ella had run with the wind, her arms outstretched, exulting in her freedom. It was a pity that he had no artistic ability to capture the image, because it would have made a most visual and uplifting painting. With her hat removed and her ugly shorn hair, it would have served to be a poignant reminder of the hardship of life in the workhouse.

But Rory's thoughts now were full of the adventure that lay before him. Who knew what would happen in America, something might even change his life for ever.

Chapter Twenty-Five

'The mistress will not be requiring luncheon tomorrow, Mrs Perkins.'

The butler, returning from the drawing room, removed his jacket and sat at the table to read the morning paper.

'Why's that then, Mr Forbes?'

Ella, a silent spectator, saw the butler's expression harden. 'As I was not made aware of that information, I cannot tell you.'

Cook's eyebrows nearly hit her hairline at his brusque tone. 'Well, it will be something simple for all of us, then. I could do with a breather, and I don't care who hears it.'

'My gran had varicose veins, Mrs Perkins, they used to plague her something terrible,' Mabel said, and then nudged Gloria who began to giggle.

'It's no laughing matter,' Cook snapped, 'as you'll no doubt learn when you begin to get a bit of sense.'

'And I,' the butler said, with a rustle of his newspaper, 'would like a bit of peace to read about what's happening in the country, if you don't mind.'

'Yes, Mr Forbes.' Mabel pulled a face. 'We're just on our way to see to the bedrooms on the top floor.' But, even as the two parlourmaids hurried up the backstairs, the butler was moving away to his own pantry.

Cook saw Ella hovering by the scullery door. 'What you can do, my girl, is to sandstone that sink. There's no excuse for brown stains.'

Ella turned and, seconds later, was scrubbing until her hands and knuckles were red and sore, before standing back to survey the result of her labour. It was a good feeling to make things look nice, but she was already finding that Rosie's absence was making her own work harder. And she did miss her. After all, the only friends she had were Rosie and Rory. Her mouth broke into a smile thinking what good names they would be for twins, a girl and a boy. The only twins she'd met were two shrunken old women who she used to see sitting together in the workhouse dining hall. As alike as two pins they were, even to the whiskers on their chins. Ella intended never to have a hairy face, no matter how old she was. She'd pull them out or cut them off with some small scissors. Now that Rosie wasn't there to tease her about vanity, Ella was staring at herself ever more often in the small mirror in her bedroom. Her face did seem different, fuller somehow, but what she was most impatient about was for her hair to grow. And her desperate hope was that it wouldn't be completely straight.

Cook's voice in the doorway made Ella jump. 'The new kitchen maid is starting this week. So mind yer manners, and try to help her as much as you can.'

'Of course, Cook.' Ella's spirits lifted. 'What's her name?'

'Pansy.' Cook swung round to Jack who had let out a guffaw. 'And I'll have none of that, either. Nobody can help the name they're christened with.'

Ella dried her hands and went into the kitchen. 'What's wrong with the name Pansy?'

'Gawd, you're as green as grass,' Jack said. 'I don't know how you managed it – weren't there any—'

'That's enough!' Ella swung round to see the butler approaching.

'I leave for a few minutes and what do I find? Ella, I think one of the parlourmaids had better enlighten you in private, and after that the subject is closed.'

It was Gloria who later followed Ella into the corridor and whispered in her ear. Ella felt the heat rise in her face so much that it almost burnt. 'I never—'

'No, well I don't suppose you'd come across them in the workhouse. But mark my words, Ella, it's no advantage to be ignorant of the ways of the world.'

'Thank you, Gloria.'

'Anything else you need to know, just ask me.' Gloria hesitated. 'I wasn't keen on your coming 'ere at first, but I was wrong. You're all right, Ella, a good little worker.'

Ella felt a flush of gratitude. She'd been a little in awe of Gloria, who she admired not only because she was pretty, but also because she had that most romantic of things: a young man.

Letitia had deliberately refrained from requesting her coach until the day before she was due to meet Miles, although she was long resigned to the fact that in any household with servants it was almost impossible to guard one's privacy.

The previous week, on the pretext of wishing to enjoy some fresh air, she had herself walked down the long drive and made her way to the post box. A letter addressed to Mr Miles Maitland, if left on the salver on the hall table, would most surely have caused speculation.

'I shall be lunching in the City tomorrow,' she said that evening, turning to watch as Mary lifted out of the wardrobe an ivory crêpe de Chine blouse. Letitia considered it a trivial bore to have to change for dinner when she was dining alone, but knew that any departure from the custom would lose respect from her staff.

'So I heard, madam.'

'Nothing escapes you, does it?' But Letitia was smiling and her eyes met the curious ones of her maid. Then, knowing that she could trust her, she continued, 'I shall tell you who I am meeting and where, but it is in the strictest confidence, even from Forbes.'

Her eyes wary, Mary nodded.

'I would imagine that this may not come as a surprise to you. I shall be lunching with Mr Miles Maitland at his hotel.'

'Forgive me, but is that wise?'

Letitia could see both fear and consternation in the other woman's eyes. She could, of course, reassure Mary by telling her the truth about Miles but not yet, in fact it may even be never. She had no desire to tarnish her father's reputation in his own household unless there was no alternative.

'I appreciate your concern, Mary, but in this instance you will just have to trust my judgement.' She smiled. 'So, shall we decide on which outfit I should wear?'

Chapter Twenty-Six

Only when Letitia was travelling into the City did she realise how much popularity the newfangled motor vehicles were beginning to gain. Was this a portent of the future? Although, surely, horses would never completely be replaced, especially in the case of hansom cabs? But her thoughts soon became personal ones, her anticipation of seeing Miles, tinged with apprehension. The hotel was not one she was familiar with, apart from its famous name, and, when the carriage drew to a halt and the footman came round to assist her out, Letitia mentally registered its air of discreet opulence. The young man she had known would never have been able to afford such accommodation and her curiosity became more intense. She was hoping that in the next few hours she would learn more about his life during the past seven years.

'Thank you, Jack.' She went forward to speak to Tom. 'I shall arrange for a telephone message to let Forbes know when I wish to return home.' For the first time, Letitia fully appreciated the convenience of that other newfangled invention which, since its installation twelve months ago, was still regarded with suspicion by most of her staff.

Lifting her skirt with one gloved hand, Letitia ascended the short flight of steps to the entrance where a commissionaire resplendent in burgundy and gold braid doffed his top hat and, opening one of the gleaming glass doors, ushered her into the interior. She saw Miles at once. He was sitting in a relaxed position in the foyer reading the *Financial Times*, and she paused for a moment by a marble pillar, feeling, to her faint surprise, a sense of pride. He looked so assured and so confident, every inch a brother to be proud of. She had decided to ignore the prefix of 'half', even if it was more accurate. At that moment Miles glanced up and, on seeing her, rose and came forward. They both hovered uncertainly, and she moved forward to kiss his cheek.

With a grateful smile, he said, 'Letitia. How are you?'

'I am quite well, thank you.'

'I have arranged for a quiet table in the restaurant, I thought it would be more private to talk there.' He led the way and she noticed so many things; the assured way that he summoned a waiter and, once again, the expensive cut of his clothes. Whatever he had done in America, her brother had obviously prospered.

Once their drinks order had been taken, he said, 'How have you been? I have thought of you often.' His eyes were anxious.

'I can't deny that life has been difficult – I'm afraid that our previous relationship still rests uneasily on my conscience.' And it did. Just as she, even now, was finding it difficult to sit opposite him without remembering all they had been to each other. She hesitated, feeling unsure. 'There is one thing that still puzzles me. Miles, I can understand why you didn't tell me the truth about our relationship while father was alive, although I still think you were wrong not to do so, but it is two years now since he died. Why not then?'

He was quiet for a moment. 'I didn't know immediately, as we take a London paper only occasionally. Not that I would have been crass enough to have attended his funeral.' He looked across at her. 'I don't know what to say, Letitia, other than I procrastinated. When my mother died six months ago, I came over to England to attend to her affairs and almost wrote to you then, but somehow the moment passed.'

'Was I so difficult to face?'

'I wasn't sure that you would even agree to see me. And it wasn't something I wanted to put in a letter – that would have been the coward's way.' He paused. 'I'm sorry, Letitia, maybe I could have handled things better. But I am glad that I did meet my father, even if it was only twice. You remember how appalled he was when you unexpectedly joined us for dinner that time?'

'I never did understand why, what reason there could be to generate such an aura of tension, even hostility. It was a most uncomfortable meal, although each time our gaze met we felt . . .'

'Drawn to each other?'

Letitia nodded. 'Now that I know the truth, it explains much. You harbour no resentment? That you grew up without a father's guidance?'

'I wouldn't be human if I didn't. Not at the time, of course, because I thought my mother a widow. What I find difficult to understand is that he had no curiosity about me. I was under the impression that my invitation to dine that night was to discuss some alterations to Eversleigh.' He shook his head. 'Now I realise he just wanted to see how I'd turned out. I still wonder whether he would have ever told me the truth if it hadn't been for our affection for each other.'

'You said that you confronted your mother about the affair.' She looked at him with sympathy. 'That must have been so difficult.'

'She said, and I believed her, that she didn't discover he was married until she had to tell him that she was pregnant in the hope that he would marry her. Perhaps I'm being cynical, but I doubt he would have done so even if he'd been free. Not someone who used to be a shop girl, even if it was at Liberty's.'

'But Liberty's have a very high standard.' She was thoughtful. 'It is true that he could be the most dreadful snob. Is that how they met?'

'Over the glove counter, I believe. Like a penny dreadful, isn't it? I think she genuinely loved him, although she never saw him again after my birth. At least he settled a financial trust on me, which continued after his death. Much of what I have achieved, Letitia, would have been otherwise impossible. I am grateful to him for that.'

She gazed at him, remembering how Cedric Fairchild had always been just in his dealings with their servants, and indeed had never treated her unfairly. Although, she thought with sadness, he had always kept her at a distance and, even when she had dutifully pecked him on the cheek, he had never shown her the slightest warmth. She took another sip of her sherry and, as they discussed the menu, she began to relax more. Letitia chose a light consommé, crab mousse, and Dover sole, while Miles ordered more hearty fare – vegetable soup, whitebait and rib of beef.

During lunch, she brought him up to date with news of mutual acquaintances and it was not until they were waiting for their desserts that she broached what she saw as their 'problem'.

'What is going to happen now, Miles? Do you intend to stay in England?'

He shook his head, inserted his hand into the inside pocket of his jacket and, taking out a wallet, said. 'I would like to show you something.'

He held out a photograph and, after a slight hesitation, she took it and gazed down at a sweet-faced young woman with a little fair-haired child by her side.

'Katharine and I were married four years ago,' he said quietly. 'And we have been blessed with little Letty.' He smiled into her astonished eyes. 'She is three years old and named after you – an absent aunt, but one that I hope will become much-loved.'

Letitia caught her breath. 'But that means that . . .'

'I have no secrets from Katharine.' He leant forward, his voice intense. 'That is how I know that what we had bore no resemblance to the love a man and a woman can feel for each other.' His voice softened. 'Letitia, no fault can be attached to either of us. I think you were lonely in that mausoleum of a house and in love with the idea of love, rather than the reality. And I was a foolish but flattered young man. If we felt drawn to each other in an affectionate way, then at least we know why.'

She turned her head away, relieved when a waiter stopped at their table with the distraction of flaming their crêpes Suzette. Ashamed of the sharp jealousy that pierced her, because she was only too aware that if things had been different between them, then that happy life could have been hers. And to think that during all those years, while she had been living with hurt and bewilderment, Miles had been able to find not only true love but fatherhood. She tried not to feel bitter and, knowing that she must say something, as soon as the waiter moved away she said, 'You are a very lucky man.'

Little more was said until they had both finished eating when they took their coffee in a room overlooking a garden, sitting side by side before the window.

Letitia was the first to speak. 'I am moved, Miles, that you have named your daughter after me, and thrilled to find that I have a niece. Please thank your wife on my behalf, it was a very kind gesture.' Even to herself her words sounded stilted.

'I am hoping that one day you will be able to thank her in person.'

Letitia thought again of the images of his wife and child. She was being both self-pitying and selfish to resent his happiness. And little Letty had looked delightful; it was an appealing thought that she might be able to hold a small child in her arms.

She looked up to see Miles watching her, a gentle expression on his face, and said, 'I'm so glad you came back, that you told me the truth. And I would very much like to visit your home. But if you aren't staying in England . . .'

He smiled. 'What were you told all those years ago, about my sudden departure?'

'The rumour was that you had probably gone to America.'

He gave a quiet laugh. 'It's amazing how an odd word here and there can be transmitted into fact.'

'Are you telling me that you didn't go to America?'

He shook his head. 'I had previously mentioned in conversation that I thought it was a country of opportunity, but nothing more.'

'So,' she said feeling intrigued. 'Where did you go?'

'Ireland. Originally, I went to Cork but, when I married Katharine, we settled just outside Dublin. So you see, Letitia, a visit from you is not beyond the bounds of possibility.'

Startled, she gazed at him and said, 'I'll give it some thought.' Then she added, 'I would have to confide in my maid, otherwise the staff would think it odd for me to travel without her. But I trust her absolutely.'

His face lit up. Miles took out a small pocketbook and began to write in it. 'This is the address. If you write to Katharine using her maiden name, then she can address my reply. A feminine handwriting would be advisable, don't you think?'

Watching him tear out the sheet of paper and pass it over to her she laughed. 'It all feels very cloak-and-dagger.' Letitia looked at him with sympathy. 'You must have missed them, these past few weeks, your family I mean.'

'Letitia, you can have no idea.' He shrugged. 'I did have business matters to attend to, but I regret now that I procrastinated so much before coming to see you. Fortunately, Katharine is very understanding.'

Letitia gazed at him, wondering if he realised how poignant was his first sentence.

Chapter Twenty-Seven

It was Sunday afternoon, and Ella looked up at the blue sky thinking how lucky she was that the weather had changed. Even though it was only September, yesterday had been as cold as winter. She was enjoying being able to experience the seasons, even if her time outdoors was necessarily limited to the odd message to a gardener, carrying in a basket of vegetables or, on a rare occasion, helping the thrice-weekly laundress to hang out the washing.

But that afternoon, as she walked with eagerness down the long drive and out of Eversleigh's gates, she was going to spend among the trees and open spaces of the Heath, and not only that but she was hoping to see Rory again! Her anticipation was keen, her hopes high, as she made her way to the spot where last time they had arranged to meet. She didn't want to think about the possibility that he might not be there because, despite the warnings not to go onto the Heath alone, Ella wasn't sure that she'd be able to stop herself, because the wide, open space drew her like a magnet. She'd felt so free; walking on the spongy grass, seeing people with their dogs, and families with their children. And she could always be sensible, not go wandering off into secluded places.

But then her heart skipped a beat because she could now see

Rory, standing tall, his hand lifting in a wave when he saw her approaching. 'Well, young Ella. And where were you last time?'

'I've got a good excuse, honest.' As they turned and walked further on the Heath, she told him about Rosie, her face colouring when it came to the part about her being pregnant. 'She was so worried and upset, Rory, I had to offer her my half-day. You do understand?'

He smiled as he looked down at her. 'Of course I do.' He frowned. 'But surely you didn't miss having a half-day altogether?'

'I don't know, nobody said anything about that. I suppose I must have, seeing it was my idea.'

'And is there a new girl, to replace Rosie?'

Ella nodded. 'Someone's starting this week.' She had mixed feelings about it. While she would be glad not to have to shoulder her share of a kitchen maid's duties, it had been wonderful to have a bedroom to herself.

'Listen!' Rory caught her arm and pointed to the sky. 'See that skylark hovering in the air? Can you hear it?'

Ella shielded her eyes against the sun and saw a small graceful bird.

'Oh yes.' Entranced, she stood by Rory's side as they watched and listened to it for a few minutes before walking on. 'I wouldn't have known the name of it, though. I don't know much about birds, except for robins.'

She glanced down at the square brown paper parcel he was carrying, wondering if it held sandwiches. 'What's in the parcel, is it a picnic?'

He laughed. 'No, it isn't. Haven't they fed you at Eversleigh?'

She felt embarrassed. 'Yes, of course!'

'Haven't you ever eaten outdoors?'

She shook her head.

'I'm sorry, Ella,' his voice was soft. 'Maybe one day we will picnic together, but not today, I'm afraid.'

They continued strolling along, with Ella interested in everyone they passed. She turned to see Rory watching her, his forehead creased in a frown. 'Will you promise me something, Ella? Don't come up on the Heath alone, ever. It's too risky for a young girl, as I told you last time. And once you're a young lady, it wouldn't be seemly.'

'I'll only come when I'm meeting you, then.'

He hesitated. 'That's something I want to talk to you about. Let's take a breather, look there's a good spot over there.' He led the way to a large oak tree. Once they were settled on the grassy ground beneath it, their legs stretched out before them, he noticed how much smaller Ella's black boots were than his own, and smiled to himself. He glanced at her young eager face, which she constantly lifted to enjoy the sun and fresh air, at the tufts of brown hair escaping her ugly straw hat, and then into the expressive eyes facing him as she turned. 'It's lovely here, isn't it?'

He nodded. 'I have some news, Ella.' He told her of Professor Dalton's offer and that he'd decided to take it. 'I'd be mad not to go to New York. I can't believe how lucky I've been since I left the workhouse. A job I enjoy, a roof over my head, and then a chance like this.' He smiled down at her stricken face. 'And I met you, of course.'

'So you won't be here next time? If I come to the Heath, I mean.' Ella was horrified. She'd only just lost Rosie, she wasn't going to lose Rory as well?

'I'm afraid not, and for a long time after that, at least a year.'

Stunned, she said, 'A whole year, but that's ages.'

'I could write to you, if you like.'

But a dejected Ella was struggling to cope with his news. Without

Rory there would be no one to understand what her previous life had been like. The workhouse had been a special bond between them.

'Ella, *would* you like me to write to you?'

'You mean a letter all the way from America?'

'That's right. It might take a little time to arrive, though. I know your surname, it's Hathaway – see what a good memory I have? – and the name of the house is Eversleigh, isn't it?'

She nodded.

'And remind me of the name of the road.' He scribbled it on a scrap of paper. Then seeing her downcast expression, Rory began to undo the string on the parcel. 'I've brought you a present.'

In astonishment she watched him begin to remove the string. 'For me?'

'Especially for you.'

As he straightened out the brown paper, Ella saw a dark-red book. 'Is it for me to keep?'

He laughed. 'Yes, yours to keep.' He took one of her rough and reddened hands in his own. 'Life hasn't treated you well, Ella, but you're an intelligent girl. Would you do something for me?'

She looked down at his hand holding hers, and felt warm inside. 'Of course I will, I promise.'

Gently removing his hand, Rory picked up the book. 'Whenever you hear a word spoken and you don't know what it means, I want you to find it in here. See what it's called? *Chambers Twentieth-Century Dictionary*, and it's the latest edition. Have you used a dictionary before?' When Ella shook her head, Rory said, 'Look, let me show you how it works. Give me a word to look up, one that puzzled you.'

She pressed her lips together as she concentrated, then said, 'Mr Forbes uses long words. What does "alacrity" mean? That's what he says to Jack, "a bit of alacrity, if you don't mind".'

'Perfect.' Ella took the book from his outstretched hand. 'Go on, open it.'

Ella opened the stiff cover and on the first page saw written: *To Ella, with my affection and best wishes, Rory Adare. 1903.* She wanted to read it again, but Rory was urging her on.

'Can you see how each page is alphabetical? Your word will be at the beginning as it begins with "a". What you do next is to find the following letter which is "l".'

Ella soon found the first page with 'al' on and then her gaze ran down the column. 'It's there,' she exclaimed.

'I knew you'd be a quick learner.'

Triumphant, she read out the meaning, then lifting her head gazed at him. 'So all Mr Forbes means is for Jack to get a move on.'

Rory laughed. 'Exactly! But knowing the correct word for something is essential, Ella. You'd like to feel and sound more educated, wouldn't you?'

'Improve myself, you mean?' She gave a vigorous nod.

'Good. I hardly think you want to remain a scullery or kitchen maid for the rest of your life.'

'I could be promoted one day to a parlourmaid.'

He smiled. 'Indeed you could. And that would be fine. But I have a feeling that one day you might want more, and it will do no harm to exercise your brain.'

She turned to him. 'Why are you being so kind to me? This must have cost a lot of money.'

'Maybe it's because I think you're a bit special,' he said, and then rose to his feet. 'Will you do me a favour – run on ahead just as I saw you do last time? You were the epitome of freedom.' He grinned. 'And you can look that one up later.'

She gave him the book to hold, her spirits now rising. Rory might be going away but she was thrilled that he'd brought her a goodbye present. Ella took off her hat, glanced at him with a wide smile and began to run, lifting her face to the sky, her arms outstretched as if she was flying, and then, for sheer fun, she began to twirl round, just a couple of times, before she turned to face the approaching and smiling Rory. She intended to surprise him when he came back and saw how much more educated she was, and then he'd think she was even more special.

Chapter Twenty-Eight

1909 – Six years later

Ella replaced the figurine on the walnut side table in Eversleigh's drawing room before going into the library, a room she refused to delegate even though she was head parlourmaid. She just wished she could curl up in one of the armchairs and spend hours reading. At least Miss Fairchild allowed her to borrow books, with the butler, having appointed himself as Ella's mentor, recommending authors and titles.

It was later, when she was in the linen room and neatening piles of sheets and pillow-cases, that she heard the sound of the door closing behind her and, swinging round, faced the new and already predatory footman. 'The rule is that *that* door remains open!' Her voice was sharp.

He moved forward, smiling with confidence and she backed away against the shelves, but in the confined space it was easy for him to grasp her shoulders. 'Come on, 'ow about a kiss and cuddle?'

'Get off!' Ella struggled against his strength, twisting her head from side to side, horrified when one of his hands grasped the back of her head, making her helpless to avoid his mouth from covering her own. As his lips hardened, Ella writhed in his grasp, feeling him pull at her bodice, his fingers on her bare skin roughly probing, pushing her locket aside. Livid, she managed to bring her knee up hard, triumphant as she felt it smash into its target.

'You bitch!' With a howl of pain he doubled up and she dodged past him, pulling open the door, fleeing down the backstairs, her breath coming in gasps as she hurriedly fastened her bodice and straightened her cap. Safety lay in the kitchen, where the staff were seated around the table for elevenses. The subject under discussion was Miss Fairchild's purchase of a motor car.

'Scared stiff, I'd be, to get into one of those things,' one of the maids said. Harriet and her twin sister Lizzie had only recently joined the staff.

Ella wasn't listening, in a quandary and unsure what to do. Already, because of her, one footman had been dismissed without a reference and this would mean another on her conscience.

The butler's deep voice broke into her thoughts. 'Ella!' She turned to see him gazing at her, his eyebrows raised. 'It's not like you to appear in disarray.'

Conscious of everyone turning to look, Ella felt heat rise in her cheeks as on hurriedly checking the buttons on her bodice she realised that one was gaping open. Embarrassed she amended things. 'I'm sorry, Mr Forbes.'

'Where's that young jackanapes?' Cook made no secret of her dislike of the new footman. Then she drew her eyebrows together. 'Come on, Ella, out with it!'

She muttered, 'Honestly, I did nothing to encourage him.'

'Looking the way you do, you don't need to,' Cook snapped.

Ella saw the butler's lips tighten. 'The truth, please.'

She knew she had little choice but to tell him because Myrtle, the new scullery maid was both pretty and a bit dim – a vulnerable combination. 'He cornered me in the linen room, and well . . . I managed to get away.' She bit her lip. 'I can't believe it's happened again, I wish Jack had never left.' The previous year he had achieved his life's dream by marrying the daughter of a publican.

Cook sniffed. 'It's not right that a girl can't feel safe in her own home.'

'And I don't need to be reminded of it. You may leave the matter with me, Ella.' Stony-faced, Mr Forbes rose and, after he'd left the kitchen, they heard his determined tread on the stairs.

'It'll be curtains for that young man,' Cook said, satisfaction in her tone.

'And so it should be. A pity he doesn't think with his brain instead of what's in his trousers.'

'I just hope Mr Forbes won't blame me.'

'Of course he won't, but you'd better put yourself straight.'

Going out to the corridor to look in the mirror, Ella was horrified to see how unkempt she looked. In her struggle she'd lost hairpins and, as a temporary measure, she managed to tuck up the loose strands of hair and secure them beneath her cap. Although her dress was now fastened up, a couple of buttons were hanging by a thread. Still shaken, and in need of fresh air, she went outside to the stable. 'How are you, Rusty?' She ran her hand down his long neck and the horse turned his head and nuzzled to her pocket. 'Sorry, I haven't got a carrot this time.' She leant into him and rested her head on his mane, loving the smell not only of him but the warm hay in his stable.

'Is that you again, Ella?' The coachman stood at the entrance.

'What will happen to him, Tom? When Miss Fairchild stops using the carriage?'

'Don't worry, she's already got a good home lined up for these two, over with those friends of hers in Ireland. The Irish are great horse lovers. And you needn't worry about me, neither

– I'm to learn how to drive the new motor and be a chauffeur.'

'Good.' She smiled at him. 'I'd better get back; Miss Fairchild's got company.'

The drawing room was filled with the sound of squeals as Letitia, from her seat on the sofa, bent to Grace's two-year-old daughter and tickled her. She also reached out to tickle Grace's four-year-old son until he collapsed to the floor in a fit of giggles.

'You're so good with them.' Grace leant forward to take another butterfly cake from the stand. 'Your cook's a real treasure, I hope you know how lucky you are.'

'Are you still having servant problems?' Letitia smiled at her. To the delight of both herself and Charlotte, Edward had not only been elected to Parliament, but had bought a house in Hampstead.

She nodded. 'Would you believe that I had to dismiss one of the parlourmaids only last week for inebriation?'

Letitia couldn't help laughing. 'It makes a change from the usual reason.'

Little Caroline was now looking at a picture book while her older brother played with the toy soldiers he'd brought. 'You're looking exceedingly well, Grace.' And she was, Letitia thought. Both marriage and motherhood suited her.

'So are you. Did you enjoy your stay in Ireland?'

'Yes, I always do.'

'I would so love to meet your friends after all these years. There is still no possibility of them coming to Eversleigh?'

Letitia shook her head. 'I'm afraid not. Katharine rarely travels, she dislikes it intensely.' It was strange, Letitia thought, how lies can develop a life of their own. It had been Mary who had come up with a solution as to how Letitia and Miles could continue to see each other without causing gossip about their previous relationship, or tarnishing Cedric Fairchild's reputation.

'If you were to spend a holiday in Ireland, and afterwards mention that you had made new friends, madam, nobody would think it amiss if you began to visit them.'

And so the subterfuge had begun, with not even Charlotte and Grace knowing the truth.

'Ella performed her duties well at dinner last week.' Grace began to laugh. 'Although I saw her eyes widen at the amount of food and wine that passed the lips of one particular guest.'

'He's an ass and I sometimes wonder how he retains his seat in Parliament.' Letitia's tone was dry. 'Although a title helps – Sir Charles Bentley does have a certain ring to it.'

Grace finished her cake. 'He's incandescent about Mr Lloyd George's so-called People's Budget. Edward, of course, is all in favour of it.'

Letitia smiled at her. 'Sitting on opposite sides of the House must lead to some heated debates.'

Grace laughed again. 'Yes.' She reached down and picked up Caroline, nursing her on her lap. 'As your oldest friend, may I say something?'

'Could I prevent you?'

'We both know that your single state is a conscious decision on your part because you've never really met the right man.' Grace hesitated. 'But don't you ever feel lonely?'

Letitia felt her composure slip, but managed a bright smile. 'I don't want to settle for second-best, Grace, merely to obtain the status of a married woman. And my hours don't hang at all heavy, not since I decided to support the WSPU. And don't look like that – I have no intention of becoming militant.'

Grace gazed at her. 'Edward's view is that such protests merely serve to engender resistance. But he does believe in women being given the vote.'

'Edward is a paragon,' Letitia said, 'I just wish he had a brother.'

Grace laughed. 'I've been thinking about Ella. Do you remember when we imagined there could be a reason you were brought into contact, to be part of each other's lives?'

'We used to talk a lot about fate, didn't we?' Letitia smiled at the little boy as she took one of Robert's toy soldiers from his outstretched hand. 'There has been nothing to enlighten me yet, but she has made a request to come and see me tomorrow morning. I wonder what that is all about?'

Chapter Twenty-Nine

As he walked along the broad treelined street in the southern end of Boston, Massachusetts, Rory couldn't help smiling as he heard the Irish lilt in the voices of two children playing hopscotch. They may have been born in America, but growing up in an Irish family meant they would never speak with a true American twang. He glanced up at the flickers of sunlight dancing among the leaves of the trees. Soon it would be the autumn – or fall, as they called it over here – bringing with it the most glorious foliage. He was looking forward to that, in fact he was feeling quite content with his life.

He turned into a new diner on East Berkeley Street where he had arranged to meet Sarah and saw that she was already waiting at a table in the corner. As he greeted her and slid in opposite, she frowned, unsmiling. 'You're late – you know how I dislike unpunctuality.'

'Sorry, something cropped up at the last minute.' Sarah's rebuke sat ill with him but as always, when he looked at her, Rory's burgeoning doubts dwindled.

'You look lovely.' Her fair hair was in an impeccable chignon, and blue always suited her. They had met six weeks ago in the grandeur of Boston's main Public Library, where she had been browsing among the history section. That was something else he liked about her: she knew she had a brain and was determined to use it. He found the attitudes of American women very different from those back home in England. Although still restricted to hearth and home, here the younger women were increasingly becoming free-spirited and keen to assert their independence. Although Sarah's parents, both academics, were unusual in allowing her to spend time alone with a young man they had never met.

'Thank you, but please can we order, I'm starving.'

He scanned the menu, trying to find a reasonably priced meal – having a girlfriend was playing havoc with his budget. Although he wasn't at all sure that Sarah thought of their friendship in that way, as the one time he had taken her hand as they walked, she'd removed it. But then they had been out in public.

'Have you chosen?'

'I thought I'd try the baked stuffed shrimp.'

He swallowed, noticing that her choice was the most expensive, then reminded himself that she had led a pampered existence and never felt the lack of money.

Rory chose the cheaper Maryland crab cake and, their order taken, Sarah put her elbows on the table and made a steeple of her fingers. 'How's the research going?'

'Well, I'm nearing the end. I'm into the eighteenth century now.'

'You *will* mention the Boston Tea Party and its significance?'

'Of course, it's such an iconic event in American history.'

She nodded. 'You mean in the American revolution.'

He stared at her, wishing she didn't always feel she had to correct him. 'Fully justified too – only the English could expect to levy taxation without representation!'

Her eyes narrowed. 'I agree, but we both know that any opinion of yours regarding the British Government will be coloured by resentment of their policies in Ireland.'

'And you don't think that relevant?'

'I think one should approach every aspect of history with a clear and unbiased mind.'

While Rory agreed with her in principle, he wondered whether she would be so impartial if her own government had allowed a million people to die of starvation. But he had no desire to spend their time together in political debate.

'As I said, you look especially lovely today.'

She gave a shrug. 'Looks are something one inherits and can take no credit for.'

When their food arrived, they began to eat in silence, broken only by Sarah's constant critical comments concerning her meal. But, when she proceeded to order an extravagant dessert and then complain about its quality, Rory was unable to control his irritation. 'Sarah, have you any idea how fortunate you are and always have been? I can't imagine that *you've* ever had to raid a dustbin for food.'

Her eyes registered her shock. 'Good heavens, no! And I can't believe that you have.' Her expression was one of horror, although her tone was still level as she protested, 'But you have a fine brain, a researcher, working for the most respected history professor in Boston.'

'One can have education and still be forced into poverty.' Rory hesitated. He had never revealed his full background to anyone other than Professor Dalton. But shouldn't it be different with Sarah, if he was hoping that they might have a closer relationship? In a few succinct words, he told her about the struggle it had been in London, his job as a pot boy, and his shame at being incarcerated in the workhouse. 'After my father died and I was released, what with my head almost shaved and shabby clothes, I found it impossible to find employment. I was both homeless and penniless, Sarah, and if I hadn't met Professor Dalton, I dread to think what path my life would have taken.' The incident concerning the wallet he had long decided was between himself and his Maker.

He watched the changing expressions on Sarah's face but if he had hoped for a sympathetic reaction, it wasn't forthcoming. Instead she was frowning. 'I was under the impression that, although Irish, you were from a similar background to me.'

There it was again, another subtle slight against his country. Even here, there was the same prejudice. 'I was,' he countered, 'until my father's downfall.'

She shook her head. 'Failure can never be countenanced, for whatever reason.'

Chilled, he stared at her and, with rising resentment, began to wonder whether Sarah had any understanding at all of human frailty. Their later conversation was desultory, her attitude cool, his own distant and, as they left the diner, Sarah said, 'Maybe I'll see you in the library some time? Thank you for the meal and I hope you enjoy the rest of the weekend.'

He watched her walk away from him, her steps small and restricted by her fashionable hobble skirt, undoubtedly elegant but having given him the proverbial brush-off. Boston was no different from any other city: it may not have the rigid class barriers of London, but it did have its own layer of snobbery. As he walked slowly along, Rory wondered whether he minded too much. After all, only his pride had suffered. He would have liked to have held her in his arms, if only to feel once more the softness of a young woman's body. His only chance so far had been at rare parties when he'd won forfeit and daring kisses.

But, overall, he was glad he had come to this city. Rory had been saddened when his initial year in New York with Professor Dalton came to an end. He felt so alive in this country, and knew that given the choice of returning to England or remaining on this side of the Atlantic, his preference would be for the latter. When the professor mentioned that a friend of his from Cambridge, now living in Boston, was in need of a research assistant, Rory had applied with alacrity, and, because of glowing references, had since never been unemployed.

There were so many aspects of the city he enjoyed and he was especially fond of hearing the mockingbird sing, the one that nested in the tree outside his room. Some complained, but he loved its repetitive song, enjoying the challenge of trying to guess which birds it imitated. Yes, he thought as he caught a tram, he had much to be thankful for, unlike the poor souls he'd left behind in the oakum room, most of whom would never again enjoy freedom.

It was the following week when Ella's latest letter arrived and he smiled; she'd written more often since the transatlantic penny post had been introduced. He took it out of his mailbox in the hall of the brownstone rooming house that he shared with two other young men, and slit it open.

Dear Rory,

Thank you for your last letter, I hope all is well with you. I am feeling rather excited. You probably don't realise, but I will be eighteen soon, the age when a young lady is considered to be 'grown-up'. This birthday is an important one because I have been very patient for a long time. Do you remember the hessian bag I clutched to me on the cart? I wrote and told you about the black silk purse inside containing my personal possessions. I'm still wearing the locket and try on the jewellery sometimes, and you know that I opened the long envelope a couple of years ago. But although I often browse through the journal, I've kept to my vow not to get it translated, not until I was old enough to understand it properly. But I'm ready now to show it to Miss Fairchild.

All is well here, except for stupid footmen who don't know how to behave themselves, but they don't get anywhere with me.

Your friend,

Ella x

PS: I have just begun reading Great Expectations *by* Charles Dickens.

Rory smiled, Ella always put a PS ever since the first time he'd sent her one. He scanned the writing again but couldn't find a single spelling mistake and her penmanship was now almost perfect. It had always intrigued him that the journal was written in a foreign language. And, as for the footmen, remembering that determined young figure marching up the drive to Eversleigh, Rory could well believe that she was capable of taking care of herself.

Chapter Thirty

It was only after Mr Forbes had spoken to the mistress, explaining that Ella found it difficult to read at bedtime without disturbing her companion, that she had been given a small attic room and, although the other maids scoffed that it was cramped and away from everyone, for Ella to have a room to herself was the ultimate luxury.

It had been then, knowing she would not be disturbed, that she had broken the seal on the long envelope, overjoyed to find her birth certificate and her parents' marriage certificate. And now, at last, she thought with growing excitement, she was going to show everything to Miss Fairchild, and hopefully discover what was written in the journal.

Letitia was idly awaiting her protégée, remembering that the last time Ella had asked to see her was about a year ago, to ask whether she would do her the favour of enquiring at the workhouse about an elderly inmate called Agnes.

'She was in the sewing room with me, madam,' Ella told her. 'I write to her sometimes, but it isn't easy in there to get paper and stamps. I'd just like to know how she is.'

Letitia had enquired of Mr Peaton and been faced with the task of conveying the sad news that Agnes had passed away six months previously. As the clock in the hall began to strike eleven o'clock, Letitia was hoping that if Ella needed her help again that there would be a better outcome.

The punctual knock on the door was firm and Ella came quietly into the room. 'Good morning, Miss Fairchild, thank you for seeing me.'

Never would Letitia have imagined that the half-starved child with the pinched face and stubby hair would develop into the lovely young woman coming towards her. She was, Letitia noticed, holding a black silk purse.

'It's just that I was wondering whether I could show you these.' Ella came forward. 'They're part of my personal possessions, which the Master gave me when I left the workhouse. There's some jewellery as well, but that's in my room.' She undid the drawstring of the purse, took out an already opened cream vellum envelope and held it out.

Letitia withdrew two official forms. 'Why, Ella, these are your parents' marriage lines and your birth certificate.'

'Yes, I wanted you to see them because they prove that I'm . . .'

'Not illegitimate?' Letitia's voice was gentle.

Ella nodded.

'I can understand how very important that is to you.' She glanced down at the date on the birth certificate. 'I see that you must now be eighteen. The years have passed so quickly, Ella. I hope you've been happy here.'

'Always, madam.' Ella hesitated, then said, 'It seems silly now, but the envelope looked so important that I felt scared to open it for ages.'

Letitia smiled. 'It was probably the red sealing wax.' She looked again at the birth certificate and saw that Ella's father was named as Justin Charles Hathaway and beneath the heading 'Rank or Profession' was the word 'Gentleman'. She frowned and read it again, feeling puzzled. After all, no respected family with means would allow one of their own to be incarcerated in a workhouse, especially a child. 'So you were born here in London?'

'Yes, madam – at least that's what it says.'

'And what a lovely name your mother had, Selina Maria.' Letitia frowned, surprised, and then glanced up and smiled. 'I see that your full name is Estella.'

'Yes, I like it.'

'But your parents were married in Cambridgeshire.'

'Yes. I went to the library and tried to find the actual place on a map, but couldn't.'

'It may have been a very small parish.'

Ella stood waiting as Letitia replaced the forms and returned the envelope. 'I would have shown them to you before, but I wanted to wait until I brought this.' Taking it out of the purse she said, 'It's my mother's journal.'

Letitia, even more intrigued as she saw the quality of its smooth tooled leather, opened the silver clasp and read the inscription at the beginning. When on turning to the first page to see that the writing was not only in an educated hand but, she exclaimed, 'It is written in French.'

'I thought it might be. I've seen French words on the wine bottles. I was wondering whether you can understand it, Miss Fairchild?'

'I would imagine I could, although I may be a little rusty. But a journal is a private thing, Ella. Are you sure you wish me to read it? Have you shown it to anyone else?'

'Only Mr Forbes, he thought it was in French too. I

wondered, unless it's too much of an imposition, whether you could translate it for me.'

Letitia gazed at her. 'And you have managed to wait all this time without knowing what it says?'

'I wanted to be old enough to understand my mother's thoughts.'

Letitia still felt a little uncertain. 'There may be some personal details, Ella.'

'I don't mind. I have seen the initial J in there, which I'm hoping refers to my father. I would just like to know more about both of them.'

Letitia's tone was gentle. 'Yes, of course, I can understand that. I never knew my own mother either.' She put the journal aside on the desk. 'I shall begin translating it this afternoon but, as I said before, it may take me some time, so please try to be patient.'

'Thank you, Miss Fairchild. Would you mind if I brought the jewellery to show you, on another day, I mean?'

Letitia was rapidly revising her suspicion that the jewellery would be paste. The names of her parents, the description of her father's occupation, even the quality of the journal and the fact it was written in French were in direct contrast to what she had imagined Ella's background to be. A memory stirred on the fringes of her mind, something that Ella had said a long time ago, that she believed that her mother had been killed deliberately.

'Yes, of course you may bring it,' Letitia said. 'I will let Forbes know when it is convenient.' She hesitated, then smiled. 'I would like to say, Ella, that I feel honoured by your trust in me.'

'When you gave me the chance to leave the workhouse, Miss Fairchild, I decided that I could once again believe in guardian angels.' Her smile lit up her face. 'And I may be an adult now, but I still think that.'

Startled, Letitia said, 'Why, thank you, Ella.' It was a lovely thing to say and, as she watched the slender figure of her parlourmaid leave the room, she wondered why she'd never before noticed that Ella bore all the signs of good breeding. One clue would have been her interest in literature, her ambition to become better educated. We see what we expect to see, Letitia thought, and, shamefully, that can easily blind us to the truth.

Chapter Thirty-One

That evening, even though her hour of solitude with a book was normally the highlight of her day, Ella's mind was racing far too much to concentrate. She was still mystified as to why the journal was written in French. If her mother *had* been French, surely she would have taught her daughter the language, and Ella would have repeated it in the workhouse? And wouldn't that have been scoffed at! Unless . . . Suppose there were secrets in there?

Becoming drowsy, she turned over on the narrow lumpy mattress, thinking that maybe she would sign herself as Estella when she next wrote to Rory.

'Sharpen yourself up, Ella, you're walking round like a wet weekend.' Cook's voice was shrill the following morning and Ella guessed that her varicose veins were playing up.

'Sorry, I couldn't get off to sleep.'

'Yes, well there's a new footman starting today, so it's just as well you're looking under the weather, we don't want to lose another one.'

Young Myrtle giggled, which brought her a scowl and a snapped order to wash the lettuce again. 'Two slugs I found, young lady. You'll have the next one on your plate.'

Ella made an effort to mollify her. 'Why don't I make you a nice cup of tea and you can put your feet up for a while.'

'What? With company tonight?'

'I could help. Harriet's such a quick worker that between us we've already set the table in the dining room.'

'That's true,' the butler said as he came into the kitchen. 'Well done, girls.'

Cook's mention of the new footman made Ella feel uneasy. She still hated to be the cause of two young men being dismissed without a reference, and kept reassuring herself about the poor dim Myrtle. Who knew what would have happened if either of them had been allowed to stay. Women should look out for each other, solidarity – wasn't that the word? The butler allowed her to have his previous day's newspaper, and Ella was following with interest the articles about Mrs Pankhurst and her brave ladies. The more she read the angrier she became about the injustices women had suffered for centuries. It was a man's world, that was for sure, and she hadn't forgotten the tales she had heard in the sewing room. By sitting quiet and keeping her eyes lowered, Ella had absorbed much that perhaps a girl of her age shouldn't have known. To learn that many husbands felt they had the right, not only to dominate their wives, but also to beat them and worse, had shocked her then, and it still did. 'It's no use calling the rozzers,' one weary woman had said. 'They can't interfere between man and wife, that's what they say. And there Alf was, knocking seven bells out of me.'

On her next half-day, Ella decided to go to Petticoat Lane. After all, hadn't she saved enough to buy a new hat? Not a straw one, because it was autumn now, and she had set her heart on velour with some nice feathers. Ella now possessed three outfits, as well as her uniform, and loved to change into something that made her feel a real person, rather than a servant. Not that she wasn't proud to work for Miss Fairchild and to live at Eversleigh, but she couldn't help but long for . . . She tried to think of a phrase she'd read recently. Feminine fripperies, that was it. Ella glanced down to admire her sage-green long jacket and skirt, made from a length of material – a Christmas present from the mistress. Whenever the seamstress visited Miss Fairchild and later took tea in the kitchen, Ella plied her with questions and, together with the basic knowledge she had learnt in the workhouse, she was now able to make her own clothes. However, she was still aware that nobody would take her for a lady. Not without an elaborate hat and kid gloves.

Later, after wandering around the market, Ella ventured into a Lyons Corner House, taking a seat at a corner table and ordering a cup of tea. 'Any cakes, miss? I can recommend the eclairs.'

The tea was enough of a treat for Ella, who wanted to save her money for a hat. She shook her head. 'Just the tea, please.' She watched the round-faced young waitress, smart in her black dress, white apron and cap, move around the room, knowing, with sympathy, that at the end of the day her feet would ache. Then, glancing around the room at the other customers, she began to try and guess what their lives were like, studying how fashionably they were dressed and wondering whether she was the only servant in there. When a tall dark-haired young man stood at the entrance before joining a young lady at a corner table, Ella thought of Rory, wondering how much he had changed. Maybe if she saved up to have her photograph taken and sent it, he might send her one of himself.

Enjoying the experience of being waited on, Ella tried to decide whether or not to buy a hat she had seen in the market. It had been the third one she'd tried on, in a lovely silver grey, with a wide brim and real osprey feathers, and it really suited her. It even had a ribbon around the crown, one that she could change to match what she wore. Second-hand it might be, but it was still too superior for a servant. It was that last thought that persuaded her. She didn't feel like a servant when she was away from Eversleigh, so why shouldn't she buy it?

Chapter Thirty-Two

On late Sunday afternoon, Letitia walked slowly around her garden, not to admire the autumn foliage, nor to choose yellow and bronze chrysanthemums for the house, but to mull over the astonishing discoveries revealed in Selina's journal. The written words of Ella's mother had drawn Letitia into another world. At first, the translation had seemed like a dutiful French exercise at school and she had found it necessary to search for a French/English dictionary in Eversleigh's library, finding one that had her own name on the flyleaf written in a round and childish hand. But, as time passed, she became so fascinated by this unknown woman's intimate thoughts that by the time she had completed her task, she was totally involved in the unfolding story. She had begun making a fair copy of the translation for Ella that morning after church and, thinking it unfair to keep her waiting, Letitia decided to send for her that very day.

It was at four o'clock that the bell in the corridor tinkled and minutes later the butler brought Ella's long-awaited summons.

'What? The mistress wants to see her again?' Cook looked surprised. 'She only saw her last week.'

'I think it might be about a book she wants me to read. She

couldn't find it before.' Ella, who over the years had tried to stop her habit of lying, was dismayed to find that this one came so easily.

'Is the mistress going to dismiss her?' Myrtle did manage her work as a scullery maid but, as Cook maintained, 'It was a waste of time to expect anything in the brain department.'

She now gave a heavy sigh. 'No, she isn't, and she won't be sending for you, either, so you needn't worry about that.'

'You mustn't keep Miss Fairchild waiting, Ella.'

'Sorry, Mr Forbes.' Swiftly, she went up to her room to retrieve the blue velvet box and pouch. Her heart was racing as she made her way down to the hall. Was she at last going to be able to read her mother's words? After a swift tap on the drawing room door, she went in to see her mistress seated on the sofa, and Ella could see that beside her lay the journal and a large brown envelope.

'Good afternoon, Ella.' Her greeting was warm. 'Good, you have brought your mother's jewellery, I was hoping you would remember.'

But Ella was unable to contain her eagerness. 'Did you manage to translate the journal, Miss Fairchild?'

She smiled, 'Yes, I did. But first, would you like to show me the jewellery?' Ella gave her the blue velvet box, then taking the tiny key out of its pouch, handed that over too.

The room fell silent with an apprehensive Ella watching as, once the box was unlocked, one at a time the two rings and the brooch were taken out, their stones sparkling in the reflected light from the long windows, their settings studied. Then it was the turn of the pearl necklace and earrings. Without comment, Miss Fairchild replaced everything in the box and, after turning the key, replaced it in the pouch.

'There was also a locket.' Ella undid the top buttons of her dress and, unfastening the chain, felt the warmth of the locket from where it had rested on her skin. She passed it over. Miss

Fairchild traced with a forefinger the delicate rosebud tracing.

'This is exquisite, Ella.'

Ella said quietly, 'There's a tiny curl of my baby hair inside.'

There was a rustle of silk as Miss Fairchild moved on the sofa, leaning forward. 'Oh, my dear, to find that must have meant the world to you.'

Ella found her throat closing with such emotion that she was able only to nod.

Miss Fairchild handed back the locket, then said, 'You don't need me to tell you how beautiful your mother's jewellery is. But you may not realise just what fine pieces they are, and I would imagine them to be extremely valuable. I'm intrigued to know where you have been keeping them safe from harm.'

Her heart racing at the news, Ella explained about the hessian bag and how she had hidden it at the back of her drawer.

Miss Fairchild frowned. 'Yet, like the rest of the staff you have no lock on your door. Perhaps, Ella, it might be advisable for me to keep them safe for you, at least until you have decided on their future.'

'I don't want to sell them, Miss Fairchild. They are all I have of my mother.'

'And your feelings are a credit to you. But it would be too risky for you to wear them until they are professionally valued and insured. You haven't mentioned them to anyone else?'

She shook her head, thinking that Rory didn't count.

'I do think it wise that I should put the box in my safe. But of course, it must be your decision.'

Ella was hesitating, reluctant to let it out of her possession. But then, it did seem the sensible thing to do.

'If you wish to have it back for any reason, please don't hesitate to ask. It is your property, after all.'

'Thank you, madam.' Ella couldn't help glancing at the large brown envelope.

Miss Fairchild smiled at her. 'You are naturally eager to know about the journal.' She paused. 'Your mother's proficiency in French was admirable and I have managed to translate it in full. In the journal she describes the last eight years of her life and I think, my dear, that when you have read what she's written, you will feel very proud to be her daughter.' She held out both items.

Ella found her hands unsteady as she took them. Would she at last discover why she had been sent to the workhouse, why there had been no relative willing to care for her? But, most of all, she longed to feel close to her mother, to understand her thoughts, her emotions. And since she hoped, after seeing her father's name on the birth certificate, that the initial 'J' stood for Justin, she was longing to find out about him. But she wanted to read the translation now, this minute, not to have to wait until she went to bed.

She glanced up to meet a sympathetic gaze. 'Ella, my dear, I think it would be unkind of me to expect you to wait until late this evening to read it. If you wish, you may go now to your room until six-thirty. I shall explain to Mr Forbes that you have my permission.'

Ella felt her eyes fill with tears at such understanding. 'That's really kind of you, madam, and thank you so much for all your help.'

'It has been a pleasure, Ella, and I would be interested in talking to you again, quite soon. Don't hesitate to ask Mr Forbes when you feel ready.'

Chapter Thirty-Three

Clutching the large envelope, Ella ran up the double flight of stairs to her room and closed the door behind her. Unlacing her boots, she removed them, took off her cap and put the pillow before the iron bedstead. Then, propped against it, she opened the unsealed envelope and withdrew several sheets of closely written paper.

Miss Fairchild's flowing handwriting took Ella into her mother's mind and heart from the very first entry, which began with the date 1890.

April 10th. My birthday present from my beloved J is this lovely leather journal. How I bless the serendipity that brought us together.

That meant 'J' did stand for her father! The words gave Ella a lovely warm feeling, although she would have to look up the meaning of 'serendipity'. But not now, she was too eager to continue.

May 21st. I have been unable to find the heart to write that my beloved mama and papa are no more. Papa suffered a seizure a month ago, and my poor mama was taken away by a bad bout of pneumonia. I am heartbroken. The Vicarage can no longer be my home and the new incumbent is due to arrive within days. With no other relatives, I am at a loss as to where to go.

Stunned, Ella could almost feel her mother's pain, her grief at losing both of her parents within such a short time. Grandparents she never knew and sadly never would. Poor Selina, having to leave her home and with no refuge. Ella closed her eyes against threatening tears, wanting to pause and think. If Selina had grown up in a vicarage, that could mean that her father had been a member of the clergy. Ella's only experience of ministers had been the one who came to the workhouse to thunder from the pulpit about the wickedness of the flesh, while the local vicar seemed only to be interested in those parishioners with wealth and position. She wasn't sure that she wanted to have religious blood in her veins.

She began to read again.

June 10th. I am afraid I do not write here as often as I should. But I am indeed fortunate. Due to the intervention of a kind parishioner, I am to be the governess of two dear children, aged six and eight. However, it is only for four months.

June 21st. J writes to me every day, but still his father refuses to meet me. We have become secretly engaged and I wear my beautiful ring on a chain beneath my dress. I despair of his father relenting as I have neither social position nor fortune.

July 30th. There is much friction between J and his father and I am full of guilt at being the cause. But how can I give him up when I love him so?

Ella became so absorbed, reading of the love between her parents and the obstacles in their way, that time ceased to have meaning. How, with her mother's position as governess coming to an end, the young couple decided to marry, Justin leasing a house in a small village many miles away, and Selina moving into lodgings for the necessary three weeks before the banns could be read.

December 30th. Our first Christmas together and while I originally decided to write in here in French because I knew that Mama would pry, now I bless the fact for I would not like others to read of my immodest thoughts. For I had never envisaged the marriage bed to be a place of such joy, such physical ecstasy. J and I are truly as one. I do love him so.

Weeks and months followed with entries describing their happiness, their pleasure in each other's company, shadowed only by Justin's sorrow that his father still would not recognise Selina. Then, on hearing that his father had been thrown from his horse and sustained a head injury, Justin went to see him.

October 12th. J is still at Riverside Hall, writing that he has succumbed to influenza. But it is two weeks now and I worry that I have heard nothing more, with my own letters unanswered. My anxiety is growing, yet I have such wonderful news to impart on his return.

October 30th. I can hardly bear to write these words. A letter came yesterday from J's father to say that my darling husband has died from pneumonia and is already buried. I was never given the chance to say goodbye, which breaks my heart. If it were not for our coming child I would pray to God to take me also.

Ella stared down in shock and disbelief that her father had died so young, so soon after their marriage, and had never even known of her existence. As for her grandfather's callousness, how could anyone be so cruel? Ella's anguished tears rained down her face – that her parents, so much in love, had been denied a future together. As had she, herself, because her childhood would have been so different if her father had recovered. There would have been no workhouse, no Miss Grint. Instead, she would have had a warm and loving home. If God was so all powerful, how could he let such a terrible thing happen, for her poor young mother to be left alone, grief-stricken and pregnant?

It was late that evening before Ella was able to continue reading, and was well past midnight before, emotionally drained, she came to the end of the translation. And by that time, her eyelids were so wet with tears and her mind in such a whirl that, despite her exhaustion, she found it impossible to sleep.

Chapter Thirty-Four

Rory, immersed in researching social changes in America in the eighteenth century for several hours, eventually leant back in his chair and flexed his shoulders. It wasn't the first time that his research had absorbed him so much that he'd allowed his muscles to become stiff. And Boston's Central Library was wonderfully conducive to study. He gazed up at its famous chandeliers, thinking again what a fine old building it was.

Rory began to gather his papers and, picking up the reference books, returned them to the shelves. What he needed was a brisk walk. He decided to make his way to the Public Gardens, there was something about being surrounded by trees. He smiled to himself, recalling those same thoughts all those years ago on Hampstead Heath. But, he thought as he strode along, the Heath had neither a lagoon nor Swan Boats. And to be on the water was just what he needed today. And later, as he took a seat with other passengers on one of the distinctive boats, he recalled that they had been inspired in the nineteenth century by the opera *Lohengrin*, in which the hero crosses a river in a boat drawn by a swan. It was exactly such small historical facts that he always found so fascinating.

It was later that evening, on his way home, that the accident occurred. A motor car had driven past him at an alarming speed and turned the corner ahead only for there to come screeching of brakes, a loud bang and shrill screams. Breaking into a run, Rory faced a harrowing scene. The car was halfway on the pavement, and partly beneath its wheels was the motionless figure of a man. Two ladies were clinging to each other in horror, continuing to scream. A male voice ordered, 'Be quiet, for heaven's sake,' and a tall thin gentleman bent to examine the victim. Rory hurried to peer into the vehicle and saw the driver collapsed over the steering wheel.

He turned to see other onlookers gathering and shouted, 'We need a police officer and an ambulance.' Relieved to see someone hurry away, he joined the other man. 'How badly hurt is he?'

'I am very much afraid that he is dead.' He rose, and it was only then that Rory saw the face of the deceased. God no, it couldn't be! His hand went to clutch his throat at his strangled cry and the other man said, 'You know him?'

Rory could only nod, his horrified gaze fixed on the familiar greying moustache and beard, the now vacant stare. His tongue clung to the roof of his mouth, and he could only manage a hoarse whisper. 'It's Professor Hamilton, I work for him!'

'I'm so very sorry, that must be an awful shock for you. How is the driver?'

Rory tried to clear his stunned brain, 'Unconscious, but breathing.'

'I'll go and have a look at him.'

To the accompanying gasps of shock and curious murmurings from the onlookers, Rory took out his handkerchief to lay it on his employer's face. A quiet man, who shunned society, he would have had no wish for his death to be a public spectacle.

A shout came from the small crowd, 'Did anyone see it happen?'

Rory shook his head. The other man called over his shoulder. 'I did. The driver lost control of his vehicle.'

196

'What a tragedy,' came another voice. 'The poor man didn't stand a chance.'

'If my friend hadn't stopped to tie his shoelace, it could have been him. It doesn't bear thinking about.' This was a woman and there was a sob in her voice.

'And a few seconds earlier, it could have been my wife.'

'All right everyone, stand back now.' The burly police officer and the ambulance arrived simultaneously, and Rory watched the sad proceedings until both the victim and the still unconscious driver were taken away. The officer was polite and efficient, writing in his notebook the statement of the witness and asking him to later visit the police station. Rory stood to one side, averting his eyes from the bloodstained pavement, still in shock, struggling to come to terms with the fact that a gentle man who lived only for his historical research had so cruelly lost his life.

The officer approached him. 'I believe you know the victim, sir. His address is in his wallet, but is there any way we can contact you, if necessary?'

'I didn't actually see the accident happen,' Rory told him but gave him his address. 'Professor Hamilton had no family, but there's a housekeeper, and if you could let them know at the university?'

'Procedures will be followed. And my condolences, sir.'

Rory made his way home profoundly shaken. Every instinct was in protest, in turmoil at the needless waste of an intelligent man's life, a man who had always treated him with the utmost consideration. And so it was, with a heavy step, that he opened the door to his shared brownstone building, fighting a terrible sense of loss and injustice.

Chapter Thirty-Five

Letitia was entering into her diary the date of the next WSPU meeting, feeling appalled by the images in the newspapers of the recent hunger strikes and incandescent at the flippant sarcasm with which they were reported. Surely, it was the perpetrators of the cruel degradation who demeaned themselves, not the brave women who had been forced to such lengths? But Parliament moved slowly, as well it might when one thought of some of the buffoons the public elected. The male public, she corrected herself. In the far, distant future, would women ever be allowed to become Members of Parliament? There would certainly never be any chance unless they were allowed to vote.

Letitia closed her diary and went to look out of the window. An image of Ella immersed in her mother's tragic story had been with her ever since the previous day and it was at that moment that Forbes came in. 'I'm sorry to disturb you, madam, but Ella is asking to see you again.' He frowned. 'I hope she isn't causing you inconvenience.'

She smiled at him. 'Not at all. Three o'clock this afternoon? If that fits in with her duties?'

He inclined his head. 'Of course.'

* * *

Ella had felt emotionally exhausted all morning, suffering from lack of sleep and unable to think of anything other than the journal. Her inattention had caused Cook to reprimand her twice, and so it was a relief that afternoon to follow the butler to the drawing room. Miss Fairchild was seated on the sofa, her expression one of concern and her voice was gentle. 'How are you, Ella? Have you read all of the journal?'

Ella nodded.

'I'm sorry, my dear, it must have been a very moving experience.'

Ella had felt her mother's presence and imagined her voice in every word and sentence, and was heartbroken when she reached the blank pages with all they implied. 'In places I was in tears. But I was angry as well. I hate unfairness.' Her eyes filled with tears and she blinked them away. 'She didn't deserve to be treated like that.'

'No, she didn't. She was a very courageous young woman.'

Ella gazed at her, hesitated and then said, 'Miss Fairchild, do you remember my once telling you that my mother had been killed deliberately, that the horses of a carriage had been driven right at her?'

'Yes, I do remember, Ella.'

'You probably thought it was childish imagination. But someone whispered that to me when I was taken away to the workhouse and I've never forgotten it.'

'What exactly did this person say?'

'It was a woman who was holding my hand as we watched from a window.' Ella even now could remember how she'd screamed at the sight of her mother's crumpled body lying beneath the hooves of the horses. 'She said, "*Dearie, promise me you will never forget what you saw. Your ma was killed deliberate, them horses were driven straight at her, and someone oughter pay for it.*"'

Miss Fairchild frowned. 'Do you recall anything about this

woman, her name, or what she looked like? Or know where you were living when this all happened?'

'I don't know exactly where we were living, but there were other people living there. And, although I've tried really hard, I can't remember anything about her, except that she had a sort of croaky voice.' Ella put her hand in her pocket and brought out the small note written in pencil. 'But as someone wrote this note – it was in the hessian bag – I wondered whether this could be the same person.'

Miss Fairchild read it aloud.

This bag was in a drawer in Mrs Hathaway's room. I put it in another to keep it safe. The rags and duster should keep it from nosy parkers. I sent it with the child. Violet Rutter.

She looked across at Ella. 'Violet Rutter is rather an uncommon name. You have no idea how old she would have been when she wrote this?'

Ella shook her head.

'It is possible she could still be alive.' There was a pause. 'Ella, why don't you give yourself a little time until you're feeling less emotional. And then, if you decide to look further into the circumstances of Selina's death, and wish me to help, I will.'

She felt a leap of gratitude. 'I'd appreciate that so much, Miss Fairchild.'

'I could, perhaps, begin by asking Mr Peaton details of how you came to be admitted to the workhouse. At least it would be a start.'

'Thank you, madam. It's really kind of you.'

'Then, shall we will leave it there for now? I promise to let you know if I have any news.'

Taking back the note, Ella left the room feeling lighter in heart than when she'd entered. She knew that she would read the journal again and again until she could remember it – she struggled to recall a word she had recently looked up in Rory's dictionary – verbatim, that was it. She wanted to keep her mother's words in her heart; after all, apart from her jewellery, they were her only inheritance.

Chapter Thirty-Six

Only a few days later, Letitia sat again in the Master's airless office. After their official business was finished, she said. 'Mr Peaton, I wish to raise another subject with you. A matter concerning Ella Hathaway, the girl I took into my household.'

'I always said she'd be trouble!' His wife had joined them for refreshment, and her reedy voice held a note of satisfaction.

'No, you are mistaken.' Letitia smiled at her. 'In fact, so far she has proved to be an excellent choice. But I would appreciate a little more information on her background. Could you acquaint me with the date when she was admitted to the workhouse and, if possible, also the circumstances?'

William Peaton frowned and turned to his wife. 'I don't suppose there's any harm in revealing such details.' Mrs Peaton rose. Dressed, as always, in unrelieved black, she selected a key from the bunch hanging from her waist, went to a side door, unlocked it and a few seconds later placed a large black ledger before her husband.

'She would be how old now?'

'Eighteen.'

The room fell silent as William Peaton turned the pages. 'Ah, here we are.' He ran his finger down a column of names, 'All in date order.'

'You are very methodical, Mr Peaton, I have always admired that quality in you.'

He nodded. 'A tidy mind, a tidy life. That's always been my motto. It says here that the girl was brought to the workhouse by a clergyman, the Reverend A Worsley.' His bushy eyebrows knit together. 'I quote, "orphaned by mother's accident". And the date of her admittance was the 13th February, 1897.'

'There is nothing else of note?'

He shook his head.

That evening, having found a copy of *Crockford's Clerical Directory* in Eversleigh's library, Letitia discovered that the Reverend A. Worsley's parish was situated only five miles away. And the following morning, taking great care with her wording, she wrote to him.

Two days later, resting on the salver that Forbes brought into the morning room, had been his reply.

Dear Miss Fairchild,
With reference to your letter of the 26th instant, I thank you for your kindness in praising the assistance I gave many years ago to a young member of your household. It is, indeed, most gratifying that you might wish to express your appreciation in a helpful way.

My church duties would allow me to be at your convenience on any Friday afternoon.

Again, my civilities to you,
I am your obedient servant in Christ,
Reverend A. Worsley

Letitia laid the letter down with a quiet smile. Her hint of a possible donation had brought the required result.

* * *

The following Friday, with a footman standing at the back of the carriage, Letitia was driven to an unprepossessing area and church. She frowned, and then, alighting from the coach, went to ring the bell of the adjoining and equally modest vicarage. A grey-haired woman, with a narrow face and body to match, opened the door, her expression curious as her gaze swept over her visitor. 'Yes, madam?'

'Good afternoon. Would you kindly let the Reverend Worsley know that Miss Fairchild would like to see him?'

The housekeeper – at least Letitia assumed that was her position – stood aside. 'Please, Miss Fairchild, come in. The Reverend is in his study, but I'm sure he'll receive you.'

I certainly hope so, Letitia thought as, when waiting in the narrow hall, she gazed at the framed prints of animals on the wall. Landseer's *Monarch of the Glen*, of course, it had been so favoured by Queen Victoria that Letitia doubted there was a gloomy room anywhere that didn't boast one. She liked the George Stubbs print of a prancing horse, but viewed with distaste one of a hunting scene entitled *The Kill*, and was relieved when the woman returned, accompanied by a tall cadaverous man with a long thin nose.

'My dear Miss Fairchild.' He rubbed his hands together. 'This is indeed a delight. Please, do come this way.'

Letitia followed him into a study dominated by an ill-carved mahogany fireplace and an overall impression of clutter, and not only of books and ancient tomes, as one might have expected, but a plethora of display cases containing pinned dead butterflies. She turned and smiled at him. 'I see you are a lepidopterist.'

He gave a thin smile. 'I think I can claim that distinction.'

She seated herself in the stuffed horsehair chair before the desk while he placed himself behind it. Making a steeple of his fingers, he said, 'May I ask, Miss Fairchild, exactly what made you contact me? Er, you mentioned something about a matter concerning a young member of your household. I will, of course be happy to help in any way I can.'

She inclined her head. 'Thank you, Mr Worsley, and you will find that I shall not be ungrateful. I am hoping that you possess a good memory. If I was to ask you to cast your mind back to February 1897, do you recall taking a child, a girl called Ella Hathaway, to the workhouse? She would have been about six years old at the time.'

'May I enquire your interest in this matter?'

She smiled. 'Let us say that she has become a protégée of mine.'

'I see. Yes, I do recall it, Miss Fairchild.' He shook his head. 'That was indeed a dreadful business.'

'Would you remember any details? Where the child had been living, or the circumstances from which you rescued her?'

He paused. 'She had been living in a small hotel owned by Mrs Frobisher, one of my parishioners. As to the circumstances, the child's mother, poor woman, was – please excuse the indelicacy – trampled to death by carriage horses.'

'You didn't see the incident yourself?'

He shook his head. 'I'm afraid not.' He sat back at a light tap on the door and the housekeeper brought in a tray, a china tea service resting on the starched and embroidered cloth. 'I thought, sir, that your visitor might appreciate some refreshment.'

From her proud expression, Letitia guessed that she had made a special effort and smiled. 'That is very kind of you.' She had to conceal her impatience as the tea ritual took place, waiting until the parson had finished the last of his three macaroons. 'You were saying, Mr Worsley, that you did not witness the incident yourself.'

He shook his head before dabbing his lips with a serviette. 'I informed the constable of that fact at the time.'

Letitia felt a leap of hope. 'So the constabulary were called?'

'Mrs Frobisher was most insistent. One of the servants had told her that the carriage was driven deliberately at the poor woman. It was all nonsense, of course.'

'I take it that was the conclusion of the constable on hearing her statement?'

'The witness was a menial, Miss Fairchild, and therefore not reliable. Unlike a most gracious gentleman who described the incident differently. He said that Mrs Hathaway stepped out into the road without looking. That the horses were reined in, but that it was too late.'

'Did anyone else confirm this gentleman's assertion?'

'Not that I recall.'

Letitia thought for a moment. 'You have been most helpful, Mr Worsley. I do have two more questions.' She smiled at him. 'I will then leave you to enjoy the rest of the afternoon. As you were the person sent for, do I take it that Mrs Hathaway and her daughter attended your services?'

He shook his head. 'I'm afraid not. The appeal for my help came from Mrs Frobisher. She wanted no scandal, you understand, and for the matter to be resolved as soon as possible.'

'And would you have the name and address of Mrs Frobisher's establishment?'

'I shall write it down for you.' He swiftly wrote down the details.

She picked up her gloves. 'I am grateful to you. Tell me, do you have any special fundraising project at the moment?'

He leant forward. 'Indeed we do. We sorely need repairs to our church hall, which is now so damp and chilly that it is quite unsuitable for parish gatherings.'

'A worthy cause, and one to which I shall be pleased to contribute.' She held out her hand. 'Good afternoon, Mr Worsley, you will be hearing from me.'

He ushered her out and Letitia went to her carriage and instructed Tom to drive home, thinking that if two people gave conflicting witness statements, surely their class should not be the criteria. Menial and unreliable, indeed – she wouldn't dream of describing servants in such a dismissive manner.

Chapter Thirty-Seven

In Boston, Professor Hamilton's death meant that for the first time since he came to America, Rory found himself in a quandary. There was no work available at the university, another research post was unlikely at such short notice, and, although he'd been prudent, his small savings would only support him for a short time. His fear was that to take a job as a clerk, shop assistant, or even waiter, would be a retrograde step with the danger of becoming permanent. But, knowing he had little choice, he scanned the Situations Vacant columns, circling any likely possibilities.

But his efforts resulted in dismay. Restaurants required experience, although kitchen work could be offered at a miserly wage. Shops were uninterested in his research references, needing retail experience. Clerical work, his highest hope, paid low wages on commencement, with the prospect of annual salary increments. Rory needed to earn enough now if he was to pay his present rent.

And so it was with despondency, after another rejection, that he began to walk home. Besides, he knew the closed world of academia. If he once moved out of its sphere, it would be difficult, perhaps even impossible, ever to enter it again. Going up the steps to his building, he inserted his key and, once inside, saw in his mailbox what he thought was a letter from Ella, but then saw the cramped handwriting of Professor Dalton. He gazed down at the envelope with some curiosity, then, taking it to his room, slit it open.

A few minutes later, he finished reading, feeling a sense of shock. Was there really such a thing as serendipity? He glanced down at the letter again.

Dear Rory,

I was saddened to read of the unfortunate death of Professor Hamilton, whose scholarship was respected worldwide. I am assuming that your own position is now untenable, and this has coincided with my decision to write a treatise on the Great Famine of Ireland and I recollect your interest in the subject.

I would consider it to be to our mutual advantage to work together again, if indeed you were willing to return to England. Your passage would, as a mark of my respect for your punctilious attention to detail, be at my expense. And your salary would of course be commensurate with your increased experience.

I would appreciate an early reply as I am now anxious to commence.

Rory drew a deep breath, his mind in turmoil, and minutes later he left the house to make his way to the Public Gardens, finding it easier to analyse a problem when walking in the fresh air and among leafy trees. And they were glorious at the moment, especially the maples with their rich red colour. As he strode along in the crisp, cool air, he thought of the coming London winter with its choking smog, casting his mind back to the staff at number 35. Would the butler, housekeeper and cook still be there? Charlie, the truculent footman he dismissed from his mind because, with a bit of luck, he would have moved on. Rory was torn. New England was a wonderful place to live, and he had come to feel content and settled in Boston. Was he willing to give all that up? But then he forced himself to be realistic; Professor Dalton had offered him a lifeline and to decline it could be a decision he would always regret.

Rory rose, aware that he was at a crossroads in his life, and began slowly to retrace his steps, pausing to watch some of the sailboats on the lagoon, and it was then, as he was leaving the gardens, that he saw Sarah walking towards him. Alone, as she so often was, and looking elegant in a rose-coloured coat and a cartwheel feathered hat in a deeper shade, she gave him a cool smile.

'How are you, Rory? I was sorry to hear of Professor Hamilton's misfortune.'

'It was rather more than that, but I'm well, thank you, Sarah.' He kept his tone casual.

'This will have affected you badly. I hope you won't find difficulty finding other employment.' Rory suppressed his anger at how the stigma of the word 'workhouse' had changed her attitude towards him. From being considered her equal, Sarah was now adopting a patronising manner equal to that of any English aristocrat.

His tone was cold. 'On the contrary, I have already been offered another research post.'

She looked surprised. 'Really? Anyone I know – in the academic world, I mean?'

'I have no idea, I doubt whether you are familiar with every member of the Royal Society.'

'In England, then?'

Rory nodded. 'With Professor Dalton again – if you recall, I told you about him. He's planning a book on the Irish Famine.'

'And shall you take it? I thought you Irish despised the English.'

'An intelligent person never generalises, Sarah.'

Colour rose in her cheeks, and she tightened her gloves. 'Whatever you decide, I wish you good fortune.'

Rory nodded, bade her farewell and felt not a jot of regret as he walked on. He'd had a lucky escape. Let someone else be duped by her cleverness and good looks. And it was then that an image of Ella came into his mind, sitting opposite him on the cart with shorn hair and drab ugly clothes; another time, raising her arms and running with joy on Hampstead Heath. He remembered their instant rapport, his instinctive desire to help her. He smiled. Bless her, she'd been a curious mixture of naivety and bravado, and her admiration had boosted his self-confidence at a sorely needed time. With the professor's offer making it a possibility, Rory found that he felt a growing urge to see this now eighteen-year-old Ella, and there was a spring in his step as he made his way home.

Chapter Thirty-Eight

Ella became obsessed with reading the journal every night. Her mother was now no longer a shadowy figure in the past, she was becoming almost a living, breathing person. And it was on realising how much she had been loved, what a happy child she had been, that slowly the pain of her harsh childhood began to heal.

Eventually the butler beckoned her to have a private word. 'You are not yourself lately.' He frowned. 'Ella, might I ask if there is something worrying you?'

She looked up at the face of the tall man who, in his black jacket and striped trousers, had so terrified her when she had first arrived. She still felt a wave of embarrassment at the memory of how she'd marched up to the front door of the house. She now had both liking and respect for him, but felt that she couldn't confide in him about the journal, not without Miss Fairchild's approval.

'There is something on my mind, Mr Forbes. But I am not yet at liberty to tell you, I'm afraid.'

He gazed down at her with wariness in his eyes. 'It isn't anything bad, is it, Ella?'

She shook her head. 'You don't need to worry, I promise.'

'Whatever it is, you shouldn't be allowing it to affect your work.'

'I'm sorry, I won't let it happen again.' She knew that she would feel more settled in her mind once Miss Fairchild told her what she had found out at the workhouse and on Saturday, when she heard the sound of the drawing room bell, she instinctively knew that it was for her.

'Please could you ask Ella to come and see me.' Letitia wasn't surprised to see swiftly concealed annoyance in her butler's eyes before he inclined his head and left. He would, of course, expect to be acquainted with any matter affecting a member of staff, and this wasn't the first time that Letitia had refrained from offering an explanation. Perhaps Ella would agree to include him in their confidence.

She turned at a tap at the door. 'Good afternoon, Ella. Please, as we will have much to discuss, do come and sit opposite me.'

Ella looked taken aback but walked across to the armchair and sitting, smoothed down her skirt. She looked discomforted, and Letitia remembered it being one of the butler's rules that no member of staff ever sat in the presence of their mistress.

'You have read the translation again?'

'Yes, Miss Fairchild, and you were right, I did need time to come to terms with it all.'

'Few girls in your position can be faced with such emotive revelations. I am so sorry, Ella, I confess that I found myself moved by your mother's tragic story, so your own feelings must have been overwhelming.'

She saw a suspicion of tears in Ella's eyes as she replied, 'Yes, Miss Fairchild, they were.' She hesitated. 'Did you find out anything from Mr Peaton?'

'Yes.' Letitia related the results of her visit to the Reverend Worsley. 'So you see, we do have information to help us.'

Ella's eyes lit up and she leant forward with eagerness. 'I could go to the hotel and talk to Mrs Frobisher.'

Letitia hesitated. 'Ella, I wondered how you would feel about our confiding in Mr Forbes. I feel he might be more flexible in terms of you having time off if he knew the circumstances. But of course, that decision can only be yours.'

Ella looked relieved. 'I'd like that, Miss Fairchild. He's been very good to me.'

Letitia rose and went over to her escritoire. 'Let me give you the address of the hotel.' Taking the small sheet of paper on which it was written she handed it over. 'Does the name seem familiar to you?'

Ella looked down with a puzzled frown. 'Balmoral? No, it doesn't seem to be.'

'You were very young at the time so perhaps that isn't so surprising.' Letitia paused. 'Ella, would you prefer to conduct your enquiries on your own? Only, if you would find it helpful, I would be happy to come with you.' She saw Ella hesitate and added swiftly, 'Whatever you decide, I would be most interested in learning the outcome.' She smiled. 'You may go now, Ella.'

'Thank you, Miss Fairchild.'

Letitia watched her leave the room, wondering how that slim figure would look in a couture gown, with her hair, most of which was concealed by her white frilled cap, properly dressed. And if she was to wear her mother's pearls around that slender neck . . . Letitia suddenly realised that her young parlourmaid had the potential to become an exceptionally beautiful woman.

Chapter Thirty-Nine

Rory received Ella's letter in the same mail that brought his anticipated steam ticket from Professor Dalton. He opened the one from the professor first and was relieved to see that the date of his departure was only ten days away. Although he had managed to find a few hours work in a bar, his savings were rapidly dwindling. Then, feeling surprised to hear again from Ella so soon, he went to sit by the window overlooking the maple tree outside and slit open the envelope. The letter wasn't copied in her 'best handwriting' this time, and she sounded rather excited.

Dear Rory,
I have such news for you. Miss Fairchild has translated the journal for me. It was written in French and it was so sad in places that it made me cry. But I'm even more sure now that someone killed my mother deliberately, and I'm going to find out who was responsible. I do wish you were here to help me.

Also, I took the jewellery to show her, you remember I told you about it and how I wear the locket beneath my uniform? Apparently, it is all valuable so she is keeping it safe for me.

At least I know now that I'm not quite the urchin who travelled with you on the cart that day. I hope all is well with you,

> *Best wishes*
> *Estella*

Rory smiled as he noticed the full signature, then frowned, trying in vain to remember Ella ever mentioning her mother's death. And she wished he could be there to help her!

It was the following day when Rory, letting himself out of the front door of the brownstone building, met the two other young men with whom he shared the rooming house. Joe, tall and gangly, who worked for a solicitor, and Pete, the freckle-faced teacher. They both grinned.

'I'm glad I've seen you,' Rory said, and, after telling them that he now had his sailing date and seeing the genuine regret in their eyes, felt a pang of his own to be leaving behind good friends. America had been kind to him; he liked its people, with their open-heartedness, even their often brash attitudes. Walking briskly to the nearest mailbox, he posted an acknowledgment to the professor that he'd received the ticket safely, wondering whether he would find London changed at all, although six years was, in reality, only a short period of time. And then his thoughts returned again to Ella as he paused at a news stand; he recalled her fierce expression when she'd vowed to 'pay back' an officer in the workhouse, someone called Miss Grint. The image made him smile. It would be so good to see her again.

As always, he enjoyed his walk to the Public Gardens and eventually reached a bench on which to sit and browse through his newspaper. But first Rory withdrew Ella's letter from his inside jacket pocket. Swiftly he scanned again the few lines, pausing at the sentence *it is all valuable so she is keeping it safe for me.*

If that was true, then the fact that it had not only accompanied Ella into the workhouse, but been given safely back to her when she left, was nothing short of a miracle. He frowned, wondering whether this Miss Fairchild was someone to be trusted. From all accounts, so far she had been good to Ella, but in his experience the moneyed classes were mainly snobs who guarded both their exclusivity and their wealth. Even if Ella did discover that she wasn't, as she had put it, an urchin, he couldn't imagine that a girl who had worked as a scullery maid would ever be accepted into their social circle. Rory replaced the letter and shook out his newspaper, feeling sure now that he had made the right decision to return to England. He was not only looking forward to surprising her, but Ella may need his protection, especially if she was going to search for someone who was capable of murder.

Chapter Forty

Ella, still unsure whether or not to go alone to the hotel, went outside to the old stables and, with a smile at the chauffeur, gazed at the gleaming motor car, wishing that Rusty was still there. She didn't know how long horses lived for, but was hoping he'd have ages yet to enjoy his life in Ireland. She looked again at the motor car, trying to imagine how it would feel to ride in it and in that instant made her decision. Mrs Frobisher would be far more inclined to help if confronted by someone of Miss Fairchild's status.

Shivering a little as she went back inside, Ella went to find the butler. 'Mr Forbes, please could I have a private word with you?'

He glanced up from a ledger. 'Certainly. Shall we say in half an hour?'

While she folded linen and tidied a dresser drawer, Ella kept glancing at the clock, hoping that Mr Forbes wouldn't take it amiss that she'd been so secretive all these years. And when she went into his room, it was with some hesitation that she told her story, explaining about the journal and how Miss Fairchild had been kind enough to translate it.

He stared at her in astonishment. 'In French, you say?'

She nodded. 'And the birth and marriage certificates proved that I'm . . .'

'Legitimate? You must be pleased to discover that.'

She nodded. 'I think I knew it deep inside, but that didn't stop the name-calling in the workhouse.' She told him of her concern about her mother's death. 'Miss Fairchild's already found out where it happened, and has offered to take me there to make enquiries.'

He looked taken aback and then gave an approving nod. 'I see. Is there anything I can do to help?'

'There is one thing, Mr Forbes. It's about my taking time off. For instance, my next half-day isn't for another fortnight.'

His tone was brisk. 'Don't worry about that. We are here to comply with our mistress's wishes.'

The following morning, it was with an apprehensive thrill that Ella climbed into the motor car, and when it began to move down the drive and, turning into the road, picked up speed, she hurriedly clutched at the door handle. But it wasn't long before she began to feel safer, although she still perched on the edge of the seat. She had expected to sit beside the chauffeur rather than beside Miss Fairchild, elegant in a petrol-blue coat trimmed with fur. Ella was conscious that, although she was wearing her Sunday best, a serviceable grey coat, both her gloves and boots instantly marked her as a servant. She'd made the right decision not to come alone. As Cook would say, 'money talks'.

'Do you feel nervous at all?' Miss Fairchild was smiling at her.

'More excited, really. I've waited a long time for this chance.' She hesitated, then added, 'Miss Fairchild?'

'Yes?'

'I wondered whether you would mind beginning, when we get

there, I mean. I think Mrs Frobisher might take more notice of you.'

'If you are sure? Then of course I will.'

Ella could sense a gradual change in Miss Fairchild's attitude towards her since translating the journal and seeing the jewellery. It was sad that people placed such importance on someone's background – after all, nobody could choose which class they were born into. Ella hadn't waited on a table at Eversleigh without having heard the phrase 'breeding always shows'. So what did that mean in her own case? That because her parents had been educated, then their daughter would also have the required social graces? Not, thought Ella with bitterness, when at the age of six she'd been sent to a workhouse.

The small private hotel was in a quiet street lined with poplar trees and looked respectable and prosperous, the servant in Ella appreciating the whiteness of the net curtains at the windows, the gleaming polish of the maroon front door. She stared up at the frontage but, to her disappointment, she felt no sense of familiarity. And then they were climbing the steps where Miss Fairchild, with Ella slightly behind her, pressed the bell. They were greeted by a harassed-looking maid in a black and white uniform who, on glancing down at the chauffeur and motor car outside, straightened her shoulders.

'Yes, madam?'

'Good morning, my name is Miss Fairchild, and I would very much like to see Mrs Frobisher.'

'If you would care to follow me, madam.'

Ella felt a tightening in her throat. She turned to look over her shoulder at the road. It must have been there, only yards from where she stood, that horses had trampled her young mother to death.

They were shown into a small parlour, comfortably furnished with a dark-blue velvet sofa and matching balloon-backed side chairs. Before the window, on a small table covered with a plush cloth, stood an aspidistra plant; there was a Queen Anne coffee table in the centre, with several copies of *Punch* and *Vogue* displayed. Miss Fairchild seated herself on one of the chairs, while Ella perched nervously on another, glad that she had someone with her. A carriage clock chimed the half-hour and Mrs Frobisher bustled in, a silver-haired woman with a kindly lined face, soberly dressed in pale grey, a cameo brooch at her throat.

'Good morning, Miss Fairchild.'

Letitia rose and Ella followed her example.

'Mrs Frobisher, it is kind of you to see me. This young lady is my maid.'

Mrs Frobisher gave a nod of acknowledgment to Ella. 'Please, do both sit down.' She herself took a seat on the sofa.

'Perhaps if I could explain that we have a mutual acquaintance. It was the Reverend Worsley who gave me your name.'

A pink flush rose in Mrs Frobisher's cheeks. 'Oh, I see.'

Miss Fairchild smiled. 'I am hoping that you will be able to shed light on a matter. About twelve years ago, there was a tragic accident outside your hotel involving a carriage and horses, and as a result a young woman lost her life.'

'I shall never forget it, a most distressing experience.'

'And she left behind a child, a little girl?'

Mrs Frobisher nodded, her expression now troubled. 'When nobody claimed her I am afraid she was taken to the workhouse. Something, I might add, that has lain on my conscience.'

'It seems odd that no one came forward,' Miss Fairchild said. 'Because would you consider the child's mother to have been a gentlewoman?'

'Oh yes, indeed. Mrs Hathaway was a most kind lady. But private, if you know what I mean.'

'So you knew little of her personal circumstances?'

Mrs Frobisher shook her head, and fingered her brooch. 'Not that I can recall. I do know that she was devoted to her little girl, I just can't remember her name.'

There was a pause, then Miss Fairchild said, 'Her name was Ella. This young lady is that child.'

'Well, bless the Lord, is she really?' Her eyes widening with astonishment, she stared at Ella. 'You've made a fine young woman, I must say.' Her gaze became one of anxiety. 'I hope they treated you well in that place, dear, and you don't think ill of me for letting them take you.'

'I wasn't your responsibility, Mrs Frobisher.'

'It was only because you were suffering with a cold that your mother left you behind, otherwise you might both have been . . .' Her voice trailed away.

Ella gazed at her in horror, realising how close she had been to being killed herself, because surely she would have been clutching her mother's hand as they crossed the street and the rearing horses would have . . .

Miss Fairchild said swiftly, 'Then we have much to be thankful for.'

'Mrs Frobisher, did you see the accident yourself?' Ella said.

'No dear, I was at the back of the hotel at the time. I have a small office there. But it was dreadful, what with the constable being sent for and . . .' She removed a lace handkerchief from her cuff and dabbed at her eyes. 'The sight of that poor woman lying out there. I was the one who had to identify her, you know.'

Ella's voice became almost a whisper. 'Do you know whether she suffered at all?'

She shook her head. 'It would have been instant, she didn't stand a chance. But I can tell you one thing, dear, her face hadn't a mark on it.' She dabbed at her eyes again.

Tears stung Ella's eyes, but at least that was a comfort to know.

'Beautiful, she was, even if there did seem something strange about her. I couldn't help wondering why she should stay here alone for all those months with never a visitor. Widowed so young, as well.'

There was a short silence and then Ella took a deep breath, mentally crossing her fingers. 'Mrs Frobisher, does someone called Violet Rutter still work here?'

'Indeed she does.'

Ella exchanged a sharp glance with Miss Fairchild. 'Would it be possible to . . .'

'Speak to her? Of course.' She rose. 'In the meantime, I shall arrange some refreshment for you.'

Ella felt stunned. Was she, at last, going to meet the woman whose hoarse voice had so haunted her? And then she reminded herself that this Violet Rutter, the woman who had written the note, might be someone entirely different.

Chapter Forty-One

Ella's every nerve was tense as she watched the door, and it seemed an age before a thin, wiry woman with wispy greying hair, scraped into a bun, came in. Dressed in a maid's uniform, she looked uncomfortable when her gaze rested on Miss Fairchild. 'You wanted ter see me, madam?'

Ella's spirits plummeted. It wasn't the voice she remembered. Nor did she look familiar.

Miss Fairchild said, 'Yes, and thank you for coming. But it is this young lady who has some questions for you.'

The maid turned and, despite her bitter disappointment, Ella gave her a warm smile. It was only due to Violet's honesty that Ella's precious personal possessions had survived.

She rose and held out her hand. 'Good morning, Violet.'

After a slight hesitation the maid shook it.

'Did Mrs Frobisher tell you why we have come?'

Violet shook her head. 'She had to hurry away to see to a guest.'

Ella smiled at her. 'You won't recognise me, and I didn't recognise you either. But then it was a long time ago. I'm Ella Hathaway. My mother and I used to live here, and then when I was six, she was knocked down and killed as she crossed the road. Do you remember?'

Violet gasped, her eyes wide with disbelief. 'Oh heavens, I can't believe it.' Miss Fairchild intervened. 'Violet, please do take a seat, this must be an emotional moment for both of you.'

'Thank you, madam.' She came to sit on a chair beside Ella, peering even closer at her. 'I can see a likeness now. I can't tell you how glad I am that things turned out well. Such a lost little 'un you looked when they took you away, it fair broke me heart at the time.'

'I believe I have you to thank for rescuing my mother's possessions. Do you remember that you found them in a drawer?'

She beamed. 'So the old duster worked, they didn't get pinched, then?' She glanced at Letitia. 'Begging your pardon, madam.'

Ella shook her head. 'No, they were kept safe.'

'And your little rag doll?'

'That was there too, on the top.'

'I knew kids weren't allowed to keep toys in the workhouse. And I hoped that anyone looking inside would think the rest was kids' stuff as well.'

'It was very clever, Violet. I'm really grateful to you.'

'It was real silk, that purse, I could tell as soon as I touched it, that's why I put it inside another one. I never looked inside neither.'

Miss Fairchild said, 'Violet, did Mrs Hathaway ever speak to you about her life before she came to the hotel?'

'No, she was real quiet, private like. Devoted to you, she was,' she said to Ella. 'She come in one day after going out to buy some new pencils, always drawin' she was, and seemed proper scared when she got back, clung to you so tight you were struggling to get free.'

'Do you remember when this was, exactly?'

'It was 9th February, I know cos that's my birthday and Mrs Hathaway give me some chocolates. That was the sort of lady she was, treated you proper.' They all turned to the door as it opened, and a plump smiling maid came in bearing a tray. 'Mrs

Frobisher says to tell you that she's been delayed, but will join you as soon as she can.'

Violet moved a few magazines aside so that the tray could be put on the coffee table. Ella watched as Violet poured two cups of tea, then sat back in her chair. 'Did you see anything that day that struck you as unusual about the accident?' She paused, unsure how to go on. 'All I can remember is holding someone's hand at the window.'

'That's right, mine. You buried your head against me, crying terrible you were.'

Distressed by the image, Ella fell silent.

Miss Fairchild said, 'Violet, would you be kind enough to think back and to tell us exactly what you did see? It really is rather important.'

'I've never forgotten it, madam. Gave me nightmares for weeks, it did.' She twisted her handkerchief in her lap. 'I did know that I'd seen the carriage before, drawn up along the street, and thought someone was visiting one of the houses. I only took notice of it because it was real nice, a sort of maroon colour with four black horses.'

'And it was there that morning?'

'It was the same one, all right. Little Ella was a bit tearful at being left behind so I took her to the window. Well, no sooner had Mrs Hathaway left and stepped off the pavement, the coachman whipped them horses and drove them straight at her. It were terrible.' Fishing inside the white cuff of her uniform for a small handkerchief, Violet was forced to wipe her eyes and her voice was trembling as she added, 'I swear it was deliberate. But this man come forward and said the carriage was already coming along the street and Mrs Hathaway never even looked. That was a downright lie.'

'Can you describe him?'

'He was definitely a toff, and a bit on the portly side, with a big sandy moustache.'

Ella, with desperation in her voice said, 'Violet, just before I was taken to the workhouse, someone said these words to me, "*Dearie, promise me you will never forget what you saw. Your ma was killed deliberate, them horses were driven straight at her, and someone oughter pay for it.*"'

Violet was staring at her. 'Well, fancy you remembering after all these years, word for word as well.'

'You mean it was you? But I remember a sort of hoarse, croaky voice.'

'I'd got a terrible sore throat at the time, there was that much flu about. But that's what I said, all right, and I stand by it. I told the constable the same thing but he took no notice. I heard him talking to the gentleman, who said that the word of a servant, a hysterical woman, couldn't be taken over his own. I was right mad about that, I've never bin hysterical in me life.'

It was then that Mrs Frobisher bustled in, and Violet immediately got up to pour her a cup of tea. 'Thank you, Violet. I expect you were surprised when you discovered who our visitor was.'

'I was that, and glad to see her again.'

'Violet has been most helpful,' Miss Fairchild said.

'Mrs Frobisher,' Ella said. 'I hope you don't think it an imposition, but I wondered whether it would be possible to see my mother's room?'

She frowned, 'Now let me see, it was . . .'

'Number twelve,' Violet said. 'I've just done it out.'

'Yes, of course, the guest left late last night. I'm sure Violet will show it to you. As for myself,' she replaced her cup and saucer, 'unless there is anything else I can help you with, I'm afraid you will have to excuse me.'

As Miss Fairchild thanked her for her courtesy, Violet whispered, 'Is she yer mistress, then?'

Ella nodded. 'She's been ever so good to me. If it wasn't for Miss Fairchild I might still be in the workhouse.'

'I can't think what your ma would 'ave said, you being a servant an' all.'

'You're one yourself, Violet. It's not so bad, really.'

'Me own ma was in service until she got married. But it don't seem right that you—' She broke off as Miss Fairchild joined them and with Violet leading the way, the three women went up a carpeted staircase to the first floor. Room twelve was at the rear of the hotel, comfortably furnished with a mahogany dressing table, wardrobe, chest of drawers and small armchair. Its window overlooked a narrow but long garden and Ella went to gaze out at the view that would have been her mother's. 'The furniture's the same, but the curtains and carpet were replaced only last year,' Violet told them. 'They were green and gold before. I liked them better than these brown ones'.

Ella was gazing at the bed. 'Did I sleep with my mother?' When Violet nodded, Ella tried to imagine herself as a child, lying beside Selina, their heads close on the white pillows. She turned. 'Which drawer did you find the purse in?'

'It was in the bottom one.'

Miss Fairchild said, 'You mentioned that Mrs Hathaway liked to draw. Do you know what became of her possessions – her sketchbook for instance?'

Violet looked uneasy. 'Mrs Frobisher sorted out her clothes. I think they mostly went to that church she goes to.'

'And the sketchbook?' Ella said.

'I was the only one who knew about that.' Ella saw a flush begin at Violet's thin neck before travelling to redden her cheeks.

Miss Fairchild's voice was soft. 'So you kept it as a keepsake?'

She nodded. 'I wasn't doing no wrong, it might have got thrown away.'

Ella was staring at her, hardly able to believe what she was hearing. Her mother's sketchbook was here in the hotel? Her pulse racing, she said, 'Violet, would you mind letting me have it? Please – I'd be so grateful.'

'Course yer can, it's only right and proper. I'll go and fetch it.' She hurried to the door, and after she'd left, Ella went to sit forlornly on the bed, touching with one hand the mahogany headboard, knowing that all those years ago her mother would have sat propped against it. 'If only it hadn't happened,' she said. 'It seems so unfair.'

Violet came back holding a sketchbook. 'I did use the pencils, but I never drew anything in this.' She gave it to Ella, then turned to Miss Fairchild. 'If there's nothing else, madam, I'd better be getting on with me work.'

'Of course, and thank you so much for all of your help.'

They returned to the front door, where Ella paused and drew Violet into a warm hug. 'Thank you,' she whispered, 'I'll never forget you.'

Miss Fairchild pressed something into Violet's hand, and as they went down the steps Ella glanced back to see the maid still standing in the doorway, a look of delight on her face as she gazed down at the value of the tip she'd been given.

Chapter Forty-Two

Rory enjoyed his return voyage across the Atlantic, especially as he had a small cabin to himself. Coming over, six years ago, he had shared a cabin with Professor Dalton's valet, whose sombre temperament had in no way lightened despite their close proximity. In fact, the man had rarely strayed on deck, even in his spare time, preferring to bury his head in a book.

But now, Rory soon struck up a friendship with a brother and sister who were travelling to England to attend a wedding. And he would have had to be blind not to notice the meaningful glances he received from the sister, whose wide smile and blonde curls attracted not a few admiring glances. But he was reluctant to embark on a shipboard romance and was thankful when her wiles were successful on someone else.

At last they reached England and, bidding farewell to shipboard acquaintances, Rory made his way to Hampstead. When he reached the familiar street and walked along to number 35, he couldn't help thinking of how hungry and scared he had been that first time, desperate to rid himself of his shame at finding and keeping Professor Dalton's wallet. Going down the basement steps, he stood back after ringing the bell, wondering whether a familiar face would greet him, only to grin on seeing Cook, herself, her broad face beaming. 'Well, talk about going out a boy and coming back a man. We've been expecting you, come on in.' As Rory leant forward and kissed her cheek, she flushed with pleasure. Leaving his trunk in the hall, Rory followed her into the kitchen where the staff were taking their afternoon break and sitting around the large table. The butler immediately rose and offered his hand. 'Welcome back.' His gaze swept over Rory's tall figure. 'America certainly agreed with you.'

'It did indeed, Mr Craven, and it is good to find you looking so well.'

The housekeeper was smiling at him and he smiled back, his glance sweeping the table until it reached the openly hostile glare of Charlie. He was still here, then. Rory gave a slight nod, which was ignored.

Mr Craven said, 'You know everybody, of course, with the exception of Arthur.'

Rory acknowledged the young man whose footman's livery hung loose on his thin body. Another of the professor's protégés, perhaps?

'I bet you're dying for a proper cup of tea,' Cook said. 'May, fetch Mr Adare another cup and saucer.'

Rory feigned astonishment. 'This young lady is never the May who used to be the scullery maid?' Her cheeks crimsoned as she poured him a drink and he took a spare seat at the table.

'Just listen to the charm on you.' Cook cut a slice of fruit cake and placed it on a plate for him. 'Is that what they're all like in America?'

'You would be in great demand over there,' Rory told the butler. 'They seem to think an English butler must have mixed with the aristocracy, if not the King.'

Everyone laughed, and Rory sat back and looked around him. Everywhere looked exactly the same, the only difference being that he was now referred to as Mr Adare, although he could sense Charlie's animosity, even from the other end of the table.

When she had travelled back with Miss Fairchild to Eversleigh, Ella had managed to resist the temptation to open the precious sketchbook in the car, instead holding it close against her, grateful that Miss Fairchild didn't question her or ask to look at the drawings. It wasn't until late that night when she was at last alone in her room, that Ella finally settled down to open it.

The fine sketches were pencil ones, the first page revealing a strong masculine face, the eyebrows well defined and beneath them deep-set eyes that seemed to gaze directly at her. Ella gazed down at the firm jaw, the way that his dark hair curled into the neck. He was the right age to be . . . Was she looking for the first time at an image of her father? There was almost a sense of recognition, of familiarity, and then she saw that his forehead was similar to her own, and his mouth – her fingers went to her own to trace the outline, only to find that her own was fuller, softer. On turning the following page, she saw another drawing of the same man, this time in profile. Surely this *must* be her father. She stared down at it for a moment and then slowly turned the page to see a manor house, one with mullioned windows and set amongst lawns edged with tall trees. It was without detail and Ella became thoughtful. Could this possibly be an image of Riverside Hall as described to Selina by Justin?

With mounting excitement, Ella turned to the next page to see the image of a baby, possibly twelve months old, lying asleep in a perambulator, its small head resting on a frilled pillow. Ella gazed down at the skilful shading, the peace of the child's expression and knew that it was an image of herself. She pored over the features, the long curved eyelashes, the small, perfectly formed nose, then, on turning the page, found an intricate sketch of a child of perhaps two years, her small mouth in a wide smile and Ella gazed down at her pretty smocked dress. She remembered the coarse material of the workhouse uniform, how it had often chafed her skin. The little girl was holding a small rag doll in her arms, the same one that had been at the top of the hessian bag. Ella stared down at the dangling legs of the doll and its pretty ringlets, wishing yet again that she could have had its comfort in the workhouse. Her fingers were poised to turn another page but her eyes were now blurring with tiredness. She closed the sketchbook and put it on her chest of drawers. There was always tomorrow.

Letitia, unsure of the situation downstairs, decided to discuss the matter with Forbes. 'I wouldn't want there to be any sense of unfairness among the staff, downstairs, because Ella is bound to need extra time off in the near future.'

'I don't think there will be any problem in that direction, madam. There is a certain sympathy for her, even a rather excited curiosity.'

'She has mentioned to you her suspicion about her mother's death?'

He nodded. 'But she hasn't disclosed that to the others.'

'Good, that was a wise decision. Thank you, Forbes. I would like to see Ella again today, shall we say at three o'clock this afternoon?'

'Of course, madam.'

When Ella came into the drawing room, Letitia was concerned to see dark circles beneath her eyes. 'You look tired, my dear.'

'I'm afraid I didn't sleep too well, madam.'

Letitia gazed at her. It was undoubtedly due to the sketchbook and she herself was curious to see Selina's drawings.

'The reason I sent for you, Ella, is to suggest that we include Mrs Featherstone and Mrs Melrose in your search.' She explained her reasons for doing so and was relieved to see Ella begin to nod her agreement. 'I thought that a few subtle enquiries about both the area where you were born and the name of Hathaway could be extremely useful.'

'And an MP would be able to do that?'

'I think it possible. For instance, someone in Parliament must represent that particular constituency.'

'Then I would be very grateful, thank you, Miss Fairchild.'

Letitia was thoughtful as she watched Ella leave the room. The difference might be subtle, but their relationship was undoubtedly changing.

Chapter Forty-Three

Rory, on being summoned to Professor Dalton's study, received a warm welcome.

'Delighted to see you again, young man.' The professor's smile lit up his face as he came forward to shake hands. The silver-haired man hardly seemed to have aged at all as he indicated the chair before his large mahogany desk. 'Please, do take a seat.' For Rory, that was the final confirmation of his increased status in the household, and a welcome recognition of his value and experience as a researcher. It was a good feeling.

The professor settled himself back into his leather chair. 'In a little while you must tell me all about Boston and your work there. But first, let us talk about my forthcoming book, as I am eager to begin writing. My motive for inviting you to return to England to help me wasn't merely a philanthropic one. Professor Hamilton's tragic death came, although it seems callous to say so, at a fortuitous time. I prefer to work with someone who has an enthusiasm or, shall we say, even a personal interest in the research involved.' He paused. 'My only hesitation was that you might find studying the Famine in such depth too painful an experience.'

'I don't deny that it will be an emotive subject,' Rory admitted, 'but my personal feelings are of no consequence, not if I can contribute to the truth being told.'

'Good, then we are of like mind. I believe you have been allocated a bedroom, which has an adjoining dressing room. And I instructed that it should be furnished with a desk and anything else you might need.'

'It is perfect, sir. And I'd like to say how good it is to be back and to see everyone again.'

'Indeed. And I have taken great pleasure in seeing how successfully you've managed your career in America. Boston is one city that, some time in the future, I fully intend to visit.'

Rory, knowing of his interests, told him about the city's universities, its wonderful old library, its broad treelined roads, and its vibrant culture, while the professor leant back in his chair and made a steeple of his hands as he listened and commented.

Then he leant forward and, opening a drawer, took out a sheet of paper. 'To come to matters of business, Rory, these are your new terms, salary, hours and so forth. I have based them on the normal rates paid at the universities.' He named a sum that compared well with the remuneration Rory had been receiving in Boston. 'That would, of course, include your living here.'

So much of Rory's previous salary had been depleted by rent and bills, not to mention food. Now, for the first time in his life he would be able to build substantial savings, to have some security. He swallowed. 'I don't know what to say, sir. That is indeed a generous gesture.'

The professor began to smile. 'I'll trust you will remember it when I ask you to work unsociable hours. I have a publisher's deadline to meet with this book, something I haven't experienced before.'

'You can rely on me, sir, I assure you.'

'I shall require you to begin first thing in the morning.' He pushed forward a Manila file on his desk. 'Find out all you can about exactly what was said and by whom in Parliament during the first six months of the period. That should include which political party the speaker belonged to. My intention is to present a balanced view, even if it portrays the English in a poor light.' He glanced over to Rory. 'I suppose you have no doubts about that?'

'No, sir.' Although, Rory was only too aware of how essential it was that he remained impartial in his research if he was to fulfil his duties without bias. But he also knew that it wouldn't be without difficulty, because hadn't he and his parents often discussed the very subject? And hadn't they all been filled with horror and anger at the cruel deaths suffered by two million of their fellow countrymen, including the elderly, women and children? No, it was not going to be easy.

Ella was wondering whether her last letter had reached Rory yet. She was never sure just how long the mail took. To remain in contact with him had become even more important to her as the years had passed. It had been Rory who showed her the way to improve herself, and reading was a way of escaping the humdrum existence of domestic duties. Her favourite literature not only included the classics, which she borrowed from Eversleigh's library, but she also browsed in the local bookshops for romantic historical fiction and would save up to buy the occasional novel. Besides, she thought, who else but Rory knew what life had been like in the workhouse.

However, now she was looking forward to settling into bed and looking at the sketchbook again. Moments later, she was turning the pages once more, pausing only briefly to look again at the beautifully drawn images of her father and herself, and then discovered that, interspersed with sketches of flowers, a small river and its wildlife, were further sketches of herself as she grew older, the last one being of Ella as a smiling little girl of perhaps six years, prettily dressed and with ribbons in her long hair. And then she turned to see a blank page facing her, then another and another, and tears stung her eyes as she realised that this must have been her mother's final drawing.

Chapter Forty-Four

Charlotte and Grace sat facing Letitia in the drawing room she had so often visited since a child, their expressions ones of surprise and then incredulity as she related the recent happenings.

Grace was the first to speak. 'I knew it. Didn't I say, all those years ago, that you could be meant to be in each other's lives? Where would the poor girl be now if she hadn't had the good fortune to attract your attention?'

Letitia smiled at her. 'You retain your belief in fate, then?'

'Absolutely. Otherwise I wouldn't have met and married Edward.'

Letitia looked at her friend who was now carrying her third child. Theirs was not only a successful match but a happy and fulfilling marriage, and Letitia glanced away before any suspicion of envy or self-pity could show in her eyes. She couldn't help wondering whether it really was too late for herself. And then she reminded herself that she was not yet thirty-four. A bachelor would look for a youthful bride, but might there not be some intelligent and caring widower with whom she could fall in love?

Charlotte interrupted her thoughts. 'Letitia, this is a far different matter than when you raised it several years ago. We must do all in our power to help the girl to find her right station in life.'

'I'm so glad that you're both sympathetic,' Letitia said with relief. She turned to Grace. 'I am hoping that perhaps Edward could make discreet enquiries for me.'

'An excellent idea,' Charlotte said. 'I am sure it won't be the first time that he's bought drinks for someone in the Members' Bar in the hope of extracting information.'

Letitia laughed. 'To the point, as always.'

'Why not? What other pleasure are we women allowed with all the restrictions placed upon us? Which brings me to the subject of the WSPU.'

'There are a lot of very brave women out there, inspired, of course, by Mrs Pankhurst,' Letitia said. 'I regret now that I didn't join the march on Women's Sunday, last June. Membership increased enormously after the publicity it brought.'

'That's how it may be,' Charlotte said. 'But don't forget that funding is crucial in the campaign and we both give generous support.'

'Yes,' Letitia said thoughtfully. 'But is it enough? You do have an excuse, Charlotte, in view of your health and age, but I am a relatively young woman.'

'All I will say is don't make any rash decisions.'

'How do you think I feel?' Grace said. 'I'm all for us having the vote, but I hesitate to become involved in the movement for fear of embarrassing Edward.'

'If he were other than a Member of Parliament, I would be distressed by that attitude,' Charlotte said, and gave a warm smile to her daughter.

'What you do have, Grace, is a daughter, and soon perhaps another,' Letitia said. 'I have a feeling that ours will be a long fight, and it may be that it will take the next generation to achieve equality for us.'

Charlotte laughed. 'I doubt whether being able to vote will mean that women will be considered equal to men, not in my lifetime, anyway, if ever.'

'Do you think we are?' Grace asked dubiously. 'I mean they are supposed to have finer brains.'

Letitia turned to her. 'Really, Grace. You can't honestly believe that.'

But Grace's voice was stubborn. 'I just know that Edward is much cleverer than I am.'

'Maybe, but you have an exceptional husband,' Letitia pointed out.

Charlotte was regarding them both with a quizzical look. 'I have no doubt whatsoever that if women received the same education as men, they would be equally capable in any field except that regarding physical strength.'

'But you don't think it will happen?' Letitia said.

'Not if our gentlemen friends can prevent it. They have far too much to lose. Power, for instance, control of their wives and households, domination of the world, need I go on?'

Now Letitia and Grace were laughing, although in Letitia's case the laughter was a little hollow. Because the words brought into her mind the memory of her father and how she had been subordinate to his every whim. And that, she thought, is surely not as a father–daughter relationship should be. And if she'd had a legitimate older brother, she would have had to obey his wishes too. Letitia bridled at the thought; achieving the right to vote wasn't enough. She wanted a democracy where the rights of women were recognised in their personal lives, rather than dismissed because – in the opinion of politicians – the poor creatures couldn't think for themselves.

* * *

Rory spent the first few days adjusting again to his surroundings and with Professor Dalton in his study, where the outline and aspirations for the new book were discussed in detail.

'I intend to write a full account of the Great Famine with unsparing detail, regardless of either the Government's lamentable part in the situation or that of a certain section of prominent Irishmen who used it to further their own interests. The truth needs to be told, Rory, and as I am English and you are Irish, I'm hoping that between us we will be able to present a balanced viewpoint. I endeavour not to let my personal opinion infiltrate my writing an academic treatise but, human nature being what it is, I don't always succeed. I shall rely upon you to remind me of that fact – don't be hesitant, you have my full permission.' He smiled across at him. 'And I will certainly point out any deficiency of your own in that direction.'

Once Rory had collated his notes, which would entail at least the first month's research, he began to think about contacting Ella. He had discarded the idea of surprising her on the Heath as impractical. After all, hadn't she said more than once how she missed going there? He decided to write.

Dear Ella,

Have you noticed the postmark? I had hoped to let you know that I was returning to England, but events overtook me. You'll be surprised, and I hope pleased to know that I am again researching for Professor Dalton. I'd thought of coming directly to Eversleigh to see you but considered that might cause you embarrassment.

I shall go to the Heath on Sunday at 2.30 p.m., but will understand if you're unable to meet me at such short notice. If not, perhaps you could write back and suggest a more convenient time. I'm looking forward to seeing you so much.

Your friend,

Rory

PS: I have brought you a present!

Ella's squeal as she opened the letter caused the rest of the staff to pause and wait with raised eyebrows.

'Heaven's above, whatever's happened?' Cook said, and lifted a floury hand to her perspiring forehead. 'Will somebody damp down that fire, it's autumn not flamin' winter. What does that letter say, Ella? Good news, from the way you've lit up like a Christmas tree.'

'It's from Rory! I can't believe it, he's back in England.'

'Glory be, how people do get about; America one day, here the next.'

'Hardly that, he's been gone six years.' Ella turned to the butler who had just come into the kitchen. 'I've a letter from Rory, Mr Forbes. He's come back and wants to meet me on the Heath on Sunday. Please,' she looked pleadingly at him. 'Is there any chance I can go? It's been such a long time since I've seen him.'

'Your next half-day isn't for two more weeks,' he protested.

'I don't mind a swap with mine,' Myrtle said, shyly.

Ella turned to her. 'You're an angel, Myrtle.' Her tone was gentle. 'But won't your mother be expecting you?'

She shook her head. 'She won't mind, last time she'd forgotten I was coming.'

Ella exchanged glances with Cook – they both had their reservations about Myrtle's mother. Then she waited with bated breath for the butler's answer to her plea as he seemed to be hesitating. 'All right, just this once, then.'

Brimming with excited anticipation at the prospect of seeing

Rory again, Ella wondered what had persuaded him to leave Boston. He had always said how happy he was there. And to return so suddenly, too. But she knew he would tell her. Hadn't they always found it easy to talk to each other? Although, later, a tiny doubt surfaced. What if that had changed and they were awkward together? After all, he would no longer be the lanky sixteen-year-old she remembered. She would be different too, very much so. Later, as Ella was polishing a gilt mirror, her mind ran ahead, planning what she should wear, then, seeing her reflection, paused. Would Rory think she was pretty?

Chapter Forty-Five

That same afternoon, Letitia, impatient to move on to the next stage of the investigation into Ella's background, stood at the long window in the morning room to gaze out at the garden. There were still autumnal shades to admire and she was remembering how as a child she loved to shuffle through the fallen leaves when the door opened and Forbes came in. Letitia turned.

'May I have a word, madam? It concerns Ella.'

Seeing his hesitation Letitia frowned. 'Surely there hasn't been some misdemeanour?'

He shook his head. 'Nothing like that. But she has received a letter from a young man named Rory Adare, with whom she has been corresponding since he left for America several years ago. Suddenly, and without warning, he has returned to England.'

Letitia gazed at him and said slowly, 'Are you implying, Forbes, that he may have returned due to learning of Ella's possible changed circumstances?'

He looked uncomfortable. 'I am afraid that thought had occurred to me, and Ella is meeting him on the Heath on Sunday afternoon.'

'Thank you, Forbes. You did right to inform me.'

After he'd left, she tried not to feel disturbed. After all, there could be some perfectly innocent reason Rory had returned to England and to Hampstead. But, although Ella's experience of life may have been harsh in her formative years, she had lived a sheltered life in Letitia's household for the past six. What did she know of the deviousness of people? She was almost as innocent of the male sex as Letitia had been herself, even though two young men had been dismissed because of inappropriate behaviour towards her, experiences that Letitia had never experienced and, fleetingly, could even regret. Some might regard her as a natural spinster, but there were occasions when, in the privacy of her bedroom, she would stand before her full-length mirror to gaze at her naked body. While her breasts would never have the full ripeness that Grace possessed, Letitia's own were high and firm and she was proud of her slender waist. And her curved hips seemed to invite childbearing. But then she would turn away and, with resignation, don her respectable nightgown. But Letitia had no regrets about her refusals. She was still determined not to settle for second-best, nor to fall for the wiles of a fortune-hunter.

She rose from the sofa, deciding to wrap up against the slight chill and to take a turn around the garden, hoping that the fresh air would clear her mind. And she would certainly send for Ella before Sunday arrived.

It was Saturday afternoon when the butler told Ella that Miss Fairchild wished to see her in the drawing room.

'You mean now?'

'Yes, now, Ella.'

'Perhaps she's got some news for you,' Lizzie said. 'Likely you'll be off to live in a castle or something, seein' as you think you're better than the rest of us.'

Ella swung round to her. 'That's rubbish. Were you born sour, or did you imbibe it with your mother's milk? If so, you must have been on a different breast than your twin, cos Harriet's got a much nicer nature.'

Cook intervened. 'Now then, you two, keep a civil tongue in your head, and Ella, shouldn't you be on your way rather than keeping the mistress waiting?'

Ella hurried into the corridor, checked she was neat and tidy and then went up the stairs to the main hall. After tapping on the door, she went in to see her mistress seated on the sofa, embroidery silks beside her.

'You sent for me, madam?'

She smiled. 'Yes, although I'm afraid there is no word yet from Mr Melrose.'

Ella watched as she threaded her fine needle through the linen she was working on and put it aside, then folded her hands on her lap. She was wearing a gown that Ella especially liked; one of shot silk, deep blue with a fine lace collar. 'I wanted to see you, Ella, because I understand that you have had a most welcome communication, a letter from a friend you've been writing to in America.'

'Yes, madam.' She guessed that the butler must have mentioned it.

'His return to England was unexpected, I believe?'

Ella smiled. 'He said he'd intended to write and tell me, but events overtook him.'

'Life can be like that. I suppose writing to him all this time, you have been able to confide in each other.'

Ella nodded. 'Yes, I tell Rory everything. I didn't think he counted, being so far away.'

'And he has come home to take up a position, I believe?'

'Yes, with Professor Dalton, as his research assistant.'

'He sounds a most enterprising young man.'

Ella felt a warm glow at the praise. 'His father was a journalist in Dublin, madam.'

'Indeed.' She smiled. 'Then I hope you both enjoy your reunion.'

'Thank you, Miss Fairchild.' Ella closed the door quietly behind her and, as she retraced her steps to the kitchen, thought how kind it was of the mistress to take such an interest. She heard the clock strike the hour and hoped that she would be able to retire to her room earlier than usual because she wanted to wash her hair and rinse it with diluted malt vinegar to make it shine. It would take ages to dry, but at least she could spend the time reading. She suspected that she would be too excited to sleep anyway.

Once the door closed, Letitia allowed her carefully schooled expression to relax. She rethreaded her needle and began to sew, with tiny delicate stitches, the outline of a flower. The finished antimacassar would be donated to the church bazaar, but her thoughts were far from Christian ones. Was she being suspicious, neurotic even, to think that the timing of Rory's return to Hampstead was too much of a coincidence? She had no doubt that he had genuine friendship for Ella; hadn't he been the one to sew the seed of her ambition to improve herself? And it had been a kindness to write to her all these years. But for him to learn of the mystery of Ella's background, coupled with her possession of valuable jewellery, wouldn't that be a temptation for an impecunious young man? Letitia pricked her finger and was annoyed with herself for being so distracted. She must remember that Ella was not a relative, and yet she had a growing desire to protect her. And once more Grace's belief came into her mind. That Letitia's life and that of Ella were fated to be intertwined. Fanciful though it was, could it be possible that there was some truth in it?

Chapter Forty-Six

On Sunday morning, Rory made his way to Mass, his temper still frayed by Charlie's barely disguised animosity. But the man was devious; so far his jibes had only been made when there were no witnesses present.

'Not coming with the rest of us like a decent Christian,' he'd just muttered, being the last to leave for church service with the rest of the staff. 'Popery used to be a crime in this country.'

'So did being a Protestant at one time. But I think we've moved on from that, at least intelligent people have.' Rory was rewarded by Charlie's freckled face reddening.

It wasn't the footman's sarcasm about religion that irritated him, or at least he didn't allow it to, but his constant derogatory remarks about the Irish. Rory found it difficult to understand why so many people held such prejudices. Even in America – although to a lesser degree – he had heard his countrymen referred to as the 'wild Irish, fresh from the bogs', and 'they breed like rabbits'. Weren't there large families here in England, ones with ten or more children? Or was it simply that mankind seemed to have a need to look down on others, finding some races an easy target.

On reaching the Roman Catholic church, Rory removed his

cap and, after crossing himself with holy water from the font, went into the familiar interior. After genuflecting, he took a seat in a back pew and, in the atmosphere of incense and candle wax, he looked around, admiring again the fine interior with its tile mosaics. He still had doubts about his faith and in Boston his attendance at Mass had not been as regular as the Church demanded, but this particular one held evocative memories and soon Rory rose and went to Our Lady's side altar to light two votive candles for the souls of his parents.

It was on returning up the aisle to his pew that he saw Mr Braithwaite. The abundant white hair might be far less, but the prominent nose, the bulbous wart couldn't be mistaken. If Rory hadn't gone to his assistance that day, hadn't escorted him to this church, then his life might have taken a different and ruinous path. However, as the old man's lips were moving and in his hands lay black rosary beads, Rory decided not to disturb him. There would be time later to renew their acquaintance.

Later, glad that the afternoon was bright with late autumn sunshine, and liking the feel of a slight breeze through his hair, Rory decided not to wear a hat, and he was smiling as, on his way to the Heath, he thought of Ella's hurried note in reply to his letter.

Dear Rory,
What a wonderful surprise. I've managed to get the time off to
meet you this Sunday, and can hardly wait.
Your friend,
Estella
PS: I hope we recognise each other!

His spirits were high as he waited in the same spot where they had previously met. The assistant in the exclusive shop where he'd chosen her present had gift-wrapped the box in silver and gold paper and tied around it a red silk ribbon. Ella would love it, he could recall, even now, the reverent way she had unwrapped the cheap crêpe paper around the dictionary he had given her. Of course, she could have changed, would have changed, but Rory was hoping she wouldn't have lost that capacity for delight. He gazed around the open spaces, his nostalgia shadowed by the memory of that first desperate night when he had sheltered beneath the large oak tree. How the following morning he had been trapped there by pouring rain and later raided a dustbin for food. Had he ever told Ella about that? Rory didn't think so, but of one thing he was sure – her reaction would have been far different from that of Sarah.

He began to scan the people wandering up to the Heath, his gaze passing over a fashionable young lady wearing a rather fetching hat. It shadowed her features – at least from a distance – but he admired the way she carried herself; straight-shouldered, with her head held high, displaying an eagerness for life. The silver-haired gentleman just behind must be her father. But then, as they drew nearer, the man's long stride overtook her and Rory realised that her lovely smile was actually for him. He stared at her in disbelief. 'Ella?'

She nodded, her gaze searching his face.

'But you're beautiful.'

She blushed. 'You look different too.' Rory was handsome in a way she had never expected, his dark hair lifting in the breeze, his grey eyes looking at her with admiration. All the way here, she had been nervous, her tummy full of butterflies, but she had known him immediately, standing there so tall and wearing well-cut clothes. She had dressed with care herself, proud of her outfit of a jacket and long skirt in petrol blue, with a white high-necked blouse. And this was the first time she had worn her new hat with the osprey feathers.

Rory held out both hands and she took them, joy rising within her. 'I can't believe you're actually here.'

He smiled down at her. 'Just look at you, all grown-up.'

'And so are you.'

He grinned, and released her. As they began to walk on, Rory said, 'We're lucky to have such fine weather at the beginning of October.'

'Mr Forbes calls it an Indian summer.' She gazed around at the expanses of grass, the trees and bushes, the people, children and dogs enjoying their Sunday afternoon outing. It had been such a long time since she'd been able to come here. But hopefully everything would change now that Rory was back. She turned to look up at him and when his gaze met her own Ella felt a little awkward, almost shy, and then they spoke simultaneously. 'Tell me . . .'

Rory laughed and said, 'You first.'

'Tell me what it's like to sail across the Atlantic. Were you scared?'

'Not scared, but, believe me, feeling seasick is not a pleasant experience.' He looked down at her. 'And when you get off the ship – disembark – you walk all funny, like this.' He demonstrated a rolling gait and she laughed.

'It must have been such an adventure.'

'It was, Ella. And you should see New York, I bet there's not a city like it in the world.' He grinned. 'And I'm sure most of the police come from Ireland, at least there's no lack of hearing the accent. I've got lots to tell you, but first of all have there been any further developments concerning your mother's journal?'

He listened intently as, haltingly, she told him of the visit to Violet Rutter, and that she now had Selina's sketchbook. 'There are drawings of me as a baby and little girl, and ones of my father. I'm convinced it is him, there's even a resemblance. Miss Fairchild says the next thing to do is to find out more about the Hathaway family.' Ella told him about Mr Melrose, who was an MP. 'We should hear something soon.'

He grinned at her. 'So, you have friends in high places!'

She laughed. 'Not me, Miss Fairchild.'

'She's been good to you, hasn't she?'

'She's my guardian angel.'

'Well, we all need one of those.' He was glancing over to the right-hand side. 'Can you remember the tree we sat under last time, just before I left?'

She nodded. 'I showed it to Jack the last time we came up here.'

Rory was startled. 'So, you have a young man. You kept that secret, not that I'm surprised, Ella,' he glanced down and met her gaze. 'My little urchin has grown into a very attractive young lady.'

She smiled up at him. 'No, Rory, I haven't got a "young man", as you call it. Jack used to be one of the footmen and he was a good friend, that's all. But he left to marry the daughter of a publican. I think he felt all of his Christmases had come at once!'

He laughed. 'I can imagine. But public houses and inns are hard work, I know that from experience.'

She looked around. 'That's the tree over there, and the ground is dry, although . . .' She hesitated, glancing down at her best clothes.

'Estella Hathaway, what do you take me for?' Rory removed his jacket and, when they reached the tree, he placed it on the ground. 'Sir Walter Raleigh and I have much in common.' Seeing her look of enquiry he said, 'He was supposed to have laid down his cloak so that Queen Elizabeth wouldn't have to walk through a puddle.'

'You seem to know everything.'

'I wish that was true.'

Ella, guessing that her present must be inside the briefcase he'd been carrying, couldn't help darting a glance at it and he smiled at her, waiting until they were settled with their backs against the tree, before saying, 'No, it isn't a picnic in there, which is what you thought it might be last time.'

She turned to smile at him. 'Yes, I remember.'

Rory opened the briefcase and took out a shiny box. 'There you are, all the way from Boston. Apparently, these are what all the young ladies in high society use, so naturally I thought of you!'

Ella, taking the present from him, gazed with delight at the pretty ribbon and wrapping paper. 'It's too nice to undo, I want to keep it just like this.'

'No, you don't! You're dying to see what's inside.'

'Of course I am.' She turned to him with shining eyes. 'But can't I wait a little while? I'm enjoying just holding it.'

'You can do whatever you like.'

'Then I will.'

The rapt expression on her face was one he remembered, and suddenly the years fell away and he was sitting beside that twelve-year-old girl, thinking how much shorter her legs were than his own. Now, Rory looked down to see that, below Ella's long skirt, her polished black boots still didn't reach the full length of his legs. It was the hat, he thought, with its feathered plume that had made her seem taller. And almost as if she had read his thoughts Ella, whose gloves now lay in her lap, reached up and removed it, lifting a hand to gently fluff her hair, now glossy brown, the colour of ripe chestnuts. 'I still love to feel the breeze in my hair, let the fresh air and sunshine bathe my face.'

And she always will, Rory thought, after spending her childhood incarcerated in a workhouse.

Ella, acutely conscious of his gaze, remained still, the silver and gold box resting on her lap. Her fingers smoothed out the ribbon, and then she turned to him. 'Have you noticed that I'm wearing the locket? I usually keep it hidden beneath my clothes, but I wanted you to see it. I had to wait until I was away from the house, though.'

'Why?' Rory leant closer.

'Because Miss Fairchild wants me to keep the jewellery a secret. It's still locked in her safe.' She held the heart-shaped locket up for him to see. 'Look at the tiny rosebuds around the edge,' and then she pressed the small catch and it sprang open to reveal a tiny lock of baby hair. 'I can hardly believe this is mine. When I first saw it, Rory, I was in tears.' She turned to him. 'It made me feel that I was someone who had been loved.'

Impulsively, he reached out to take her hand. 'Ella, you are one of the bravest people I have ever met. You deserve to be loved.' And when her shining eyes met his own, and he felt the coolness of her skin, Rory felt such a rush of feelings that he felt bewildered. Even though they had corresponded all these years, in his mind had always been the image of a young girl with a thin pale face and ugly cropped hair. And now, to feel like this. His mouth was dry as he released her hand and watched her click shut the exquisite locket. If the rest of her mother's jewellery was as fine as this, his Ella should hopefully never be destitute again. And then he thought of her comment that Miss Fairchild was keeping it all in her safe. A place that Ella wouldn't have access to. He felt a flicker of unease. Life had taught Rory that many people weren't to be trusted, and it did seem unusual for Ella's mistress to be taking so much interest in the affairs of one of her servants. Was she indeed, as Ella thought, truly her guardian angel?

Chapter Forty-Seven

For Ella, to be sitting beside Rory on the Heath on this lovely autumn Sunday afternoon was as near to heaven as she could imagine. Every nerve in her body was alive with awareness of his body almost touching her own, of his long legs and broad shoulders. And the sensation she had felt when Rory reached out and held her hand had left every sense tingling. She may have daydreamed, sometimes, of a romance between herself and Rory when he was thousands of miles away in America – what young girl wouldn't when receiving letters from a young man? But it had always been a fantasy and she'd laughed at herself, thinking that even if by some miracle she did see him again, it was unlikely that she'd be attracted to him in that way. They were good friends, that was all.

But Ella had known as soon as she'd seen Rory scanning the approaching visitors to the Heath. Hadn't her heart leapt into her mouth, and not just with joy at seeing him again? And now, as she tried to hide her confusion, she glanced up at him from beneath her lashes, her gaze tracing his profile. He was so handsome, she couldn't believe what a difference six years had made to them both.

'Are you ready to open your present yet?'

She looked down at it, knowing that he wanted to see her pleasure. Part of Ella wanted to show off the beautiful way it was wrapped to the other servants. But then she lifted her head and seeing the amusement in his eyes mixed with a plea, she was lost. She didn't think she could refuse Rory anything. She began to undo the ribbon, removing it with care, before unfolding the silver and gold paper to reveal a square box, which, when opened, released a delicate aroma. Nestling inside were four small pretty soaps, individually wrapped in their different colours; white, pink, cream and pale blue, with tiny gold labels. One at a time, she lifted them out and held them briefly to her nose. 'Rose,' she murmured with pleasure. 'The others are lavender, vanilla and geranium. Rory, they're lovely, the nicest present I've ever had.'

'I remembered that harsh carbolic in the workhouse, so I knew you'd like it. And I don't suppose you're supplied with toilet soap, even now.'

She shook her head. 'Thank you!' A little shyly, she leant towards him, intending to kiss him on the cheek, but just then Rory turned so that instead her mouth touched his. Hot with embarrassment she drew back.

'No, don't,' he murmured, and, slowly drawing her towards him, his mouth met hers in a gentle kiss and when they drew apart he said, 'That's to say hello. After all, we didn't even shake hands.'

Feeling shaken, Ella smiled up at him. 'And it's a "thank you" kiss from me. I love my present.'

Rory said, 'If that's my reward I must buy you more. If I'd known that you had grown into such a beauty I would have come back to London ages ago.'

'Really?'

He laughed. 'Perhaps I was meant to wait until you were eighteen.'

* * *

At Eversleigh, Letitia found herself listening for the hall clock to chime as the afternoon lengthened, wondering whether Ella would bring Rory to the house, perhaps to introduce him to the rest of the staff. That would certainly be allowed as long as his stay was brief, and she decided to take a stroll around the garden in the hope of seeing Ella return. The path the servants used, leading to the kitchen door, was adjacent to the old stables, and if Letitia remained within sight of it, this would afford her a glimpse of the young Irishman. But until what she judged to be the appropriate time, she would continue with her embroidery. It wasn't an activity she especially enjoyed, but at least it was creating something, because, apart from providing employment, she often felt that she was achieving little in her life. I mean, she thought, as she snipped a thread with small sharp scissors, what was I put on this earth for? At the moment it was neither to give nor receive love, or to raise a family. Social niceties, expensive clothes and jewellery were all very pleasant, but a spinster's life was not only lonely, but one that could easily become shallow. She sighed as she sewed, knowing that she should push such negative thoughts to one side. Didn't she visit the workhouse and continue her father's donations? Wasn't she supporting women's suffrage in her own way?

It was soon after she went to take the air in the garden that she saw Ella, looking extremely fashionable, walking towards the kitchen door. She was alone. Ella drew nearer, carrying an expensively wrapped gift. Her face was glowing with happiness. The reunion had obviously been a success, as well it might with this young Irishman returning to find the pinched-faced girl he'd left behind transformed. He already knew about Ella's valuable jewellery and her hope of discovering more about her background. Would he now set out to charm her? Letitia couldn't bear to think of Ella becoming hurt; she'd had so much misfortune in her life.

Later that evening, Letitia went to her escritoire. Time was of the essence, as she knew only too well how young love could swiftly blossom. And if Rory's father really had been a Dublin journalist, then she knew exactly who would be able to check his background and that of his family. She would write to Miles.

After completing her letter, Letitia then mused on the name of Professor Dalton. She wondered whether Charlotte or Grace knew of him, even whether they had any slight acquaintance. Could that be another avenue to explore in order to discover more about Rory?

Chapter Forty-Eight

Ella decided to show Rory's present to Mary Blane first, reasoning that, as a lady's maid, she would have seen such fragrant soaps before.

'My, these are very fine indeed,' she said. 'That young man of yours has excellent taste.'

'He's just a friend, Miss Blane.'

'Aye, and best it should stay that way.'

Ella was startled. It was a remark she hadn't expected and wasn't sure whether to ask for the reason, but already Cook and the two parlourmaids were crowding round them.

'Far too good for the likes of you,' Lizzie said, taking one of the soaps and sniffing at it.

Ella snatched it back. 'And why is that, then?'

'Because you might fancy yourself as better than the rest of us, but once a servant, always a servant.'

'You do talk claptrap,' Cook snapped, and Ella handed her one of the soaps and saw the dumpy woman's eyes widen with pleasure at the flowery aroma. 'Lovely, that's what they are. I hope you thanked him properly, Ella.'

She lowered her eyes, hoping her blush wasn't too obvious. 'Yes, of course I did.'

Myrtle, after wiping her hands on a rough towel, gently touched the silver and gold wrapping paper. 'Isn't it pretty? I've never seen anything like it.'

Ella looked at her wistful expression and felt a pang of sympathy for the girl. With a bully for a father and a feckless mother, a child with limited intelligence wouldn't have had an easy life. But at least nobody here taunted her, at least not when Ella was in hearing distance.

But she was now rewrapping the box and moving away. It was still her half-day and she couldn't wait to be alone. Her steps were light as she ran up the backstairs and up a further flight to her room. And, after taking off her hat and boots, changing out of her good jacket and skirt and hanging them up, Ella slipped on a plain but serviceable dress and propped up the pillow before the iron bedstead. Then, closing her eyes, she settled down to relive every moment, every word spoken during that exciting afternoon. She still couldn't believe that Rory had kissed her, even now she could feel the touch of his lips on hers, and that had been the most wonderful moment of all.

On the following Wednesday, Letitia was shown into the Featherstones' drawing room to the sound of laughter.

'You sound in good spirits,' Letitia said, as she went to kiss Charlotte and Grace each on the cheek before taking a seat in an armchair.

'Mama was relating to me an anecdote about her childhood – I had no idea she could be so naughty. Apparently, when she was ten years old, she took a strong dislike to one of the maids who had a habit of pinching her when nobody was looking.'

'And it hurt. I think she hated not only me but anyone she regarded as privileged,' Charlotte said. 'Of course, I didn't tell anyone. In fact,' she said drily, 'I rarely saw my parents.'

Grace looked across at Letitia, her eyes brimming with

merriment. 'So Mama got her own back. She used to evade her lazy governess and creep up to the servants' quarters with a couple of earwigs in a matchbox and tip them into her bed.'

'Wasn't I a horror?' Charlotte said. 'I hate creepy-crawlies now. I do remember that I always kept it to one species, otherwise she would have suspected.'

Letitia too was now laughing. 'So what happened?'

'She became too scared to sleep in case more earwigs appeared during the night and, after a week, she gave notice. I feel guilty now, but felt very clever at the time.'

'It served her right for being cruel to you,' Grace said. 'I hope my children will tell me if such a thing ever happened.'

'Grace, my love, you are a far better mother than mine ever was to me.'

Charlotte's voice was wistful.

Grace smiled at her. 'I'm merely following your example, Mama.' She turned to Letitia. 'And what news do you bring, my friend?'

She told them about Rory's return from Boston, and her fears that he would turn Ella's head. Then, with apologies, she revealed that in her personal safe lay items of valuable jewellery that were rightfully Ella's.

'On first seeing them, I was too mystified and shocked to say anything. Then, thinking it wise, I extracted a promise from her that the matter would remain between us. But Ella decided this didn't apply to Rory, because he lived in America.'

'And you think that's what prompted his swift return to England?' Charlotte frowned.

'It does seem rather a coincidence.' Grace was glancing at the plate of scones, butter and pots of strawberry jam on the tray that a maid had just brought in, and Letitia decided to wait until after their refreshment before broaching the subject of Professor Dalton.

But, when she did, Charlotte disappointed her. 'I'm awfully sorry, but I cannot claim even the slightest acquaintance with him. The name is completely new to me.'

Grace was licking jam off one of her fingers, and Letitia and Charlotte exchanged indulgent glances. 'If this professor writes historical tomes,' she said, wiping her fingers with a serviette and replacing it, 'then it's almost certain that Edward will have a copy. I think that if he has read one of Professor Dalton's books, and as broadly speaking we live in the same area, that could be considered a valid reason to ask him to dinner.'

'Excellent,' Letitia said. 'And, Grace, I hesitate to remind you, but has Edward any news for me yet?'

'He mentioned it last evening, Letitia, and intends to write to you.'

'What a blessing that man is,' she said, with satisfaction, and then as her gaze rested on Grace's rounded stomach, added, 'In more ways than one.'

'Letitia!' The other two women spoke simultaneously, which caused even more laughter.

And as she was driven home after such an enjoyable afternoon, Letitia felt in good spirits. As soon as Edward's letter arrived, which could even be the following morning, she would let Ella know. She would also try to find out whether Rory had given any reason for his sudden decision to leave Boston. After all, Letitia thought, as, after the short distance, the chauffeur alighted to open the gates to Eversleigh, it might even be because of some scandal. But would that reason be any less worrying than her suspicion that he may have returned with the deliberate intention of taking advantage of a vulnerable girl?

Chapter Forty-Nine

For Rory, the day began with another clash with Charlie, whose increasing animosity was now making him careless.

'Off to sit on your arse again all day,' he muttered after breakfast.

Rory glanced away. 'If you mean that I'll be doing research in the British Library, then my answer is yes.'

'Yer think you've got the professor wrapped round yer little finger, but you'll get yer comeuppance one day, I promise.'

'Charlie!' The butler's not inconsiderable voice came from behind them. 'I'll have a word, if you please!'

Startled, Charlie left the kitchen and turning, Rory saw that Cook had also heard the exchange. 'Don't you take any notice of 'im, he's a nasty piece of work that one.'

'I don't know why he hates me so much,' Rory said, frowning as he picked up his gloves and briefcase. 'He did, right from the very first day.'

'Then he was just showing off, he thinks it clever to put people down.' She paused from peeling Bramley apples. 'Since you've come back, though, it's the green-eyed monster cos you've made something of yerself. You're better-looking too.'

'Why, Mrs Marriott, I didn't think you cared!' He grinned at her. 'I ain't so old as I can't look, you know.'

He laughed and then looked with something approaching fondness at the woman who had made him welcome on that never-to-be-forgotten first day. Although, it was unlike her to be so critical about another member of staff; she had endless patience, even with the butcher's boy's stutter. 'Don't worry about Charlie, I've suffered worse slights.'

'Aye, I'll bet you have.' She looked sharply at him. 'Mind you, there's bin something different about you these past few days.'

Rory just smiled. Did it show on his face? The happiness he felt every time he thought of Ella and their reunion on the Heath? Being with her had felt the most natural thing in the world. The only cloud in his mind after walking Ella home to Eversleigh's gates had been the knowledge that it might be weeks before he could see her again.

An hour later, he was immersed in reading about the Irish Famine and, as he turned page after page detailing the cruelty, starvation and ruthlessness that had taken place, he became profoundly moved. Men, women, children and animals had died from extreme starvation, many at the roadside or in cold dark ditches. Yet, over the water, here in England, so much could have been done to prevent such suffering. Rory's anger would rise so much that, at times, it threatened to choke him and he would have to bend his head to hide his tears. Men didn't cry, and certainly not in the British Library.

When the post arrived that morning, Letitia recognised immediately Edward's unmistakeable handwriting.

My dear Letitia,
I hope that you are well, and I look forward to seeing you again

shortly. As you are aware, I have been making enquiries in
the House on your behalf and believe that I have discovered
information that will be helpful to you.

Riverside Hall is apparently a small seventeenth-century
manor house near Canterbury, long in the Hathaway family.
Grace feels intrigued by the mystery, which has led me to look
favourably on an invitation to a social event being planned
by the MP in whose constituency it is situated. I believe that
Sir Justin Hathaway is expected to attend, and I wondered
whether it would appeal to you to accompany us?

With affection,
Edward Melrose

Letitia raised her head. A title? Surely this couldn't be the same man? Then she read again Edward's suggestion that she should accompany them. She had never visited Canterbury. Of course, Hathaway could merely be a common name in that area, and the name Justin coincidental, but if there was even the slightest chance that Sir Justin could be the girl's grandfather, then the matter concerned Ella rather than herself.

'I do feel that,' Letitia confided, as that evening she sat at her dressing-table while her maid dressed her hair. 'But I can hardly ask Mr Melrose to include her in the invitation as well.'

Mary, who was taking a keen interest in Ella's search, paused, one hairpin in hand. 'Och, that's no problem. I take it that I would be accompanying you?'

'Of course. We both know I would be considered either eccentric or facing poverty to go without my personal maid. Neither would it reflect well on Mr Melrose.'

'But it doesn't have to be me, does it, madam?' Mary inserted the hairpin and stood back to survey her handiwork.

Letitia twisted round and gazed up at her. 'What do you mean?'

Mary nodded. 'Nae doubt there will be two or three weeks beforehand, enough time for me to give some instruction to Ella on the duties of a lady's maid.'

'You mean for her to go in your place?' Letitia was taken aback, unsure how she would feel about Ella performing such intimate tasks. And that, she realised, was in itself a tacit admission that their relationship was developing into far more than employer and servant.

Mary said, 'She's a fine, intelligent girl and I'm sure you could trust her.'

'And you wouldn't mind?'

'If I'm honest, madam, I've been wanting to be away to visit my aunt in Edinburgh, she's not been too well.'

'Mary, you are a fount of inspiration. I shall talk to Ella tomorrow.'

'Ella, the mistress wants to see you in the morning room.' The butler beckoned her as she paused in her task of holding a skein of wool for Miss Blane. 'Lizzie can take over.'

Ella turned to the other maid and held out her arms to transfer the wool.

'I hate doing that, it makes my arms ache.' Lizzie got up with reluctance from the long kitchen table. 'Besides, I was late coming down for my morning break.' She gave Ella an envious glance. 'I suppose it's about your posh background again.'

'What the mistress wants to see her about is none of your business.' The butler's voice was sharp.

'Sorry, Mr Forbes.' With a sullen expression, Lizzie took the chair that Ella had vacated, while Ella hurried out to run up the backstairs and along the black and white tiled hall to tap on the door of the morning room before entering.

'Good morning, Ella.' Miss Fairchild was holding a letter in her hand. 'I thought you would like to know that I've heard from Mr Melrose.'

Taking it from her, Ella read the contents, swiftly at first, then went back and read more slowly. 'I'm not sure that I understand. This Sir Justin Hathaway has the same name as my father.'

'Hathaway is probably a local name; it could be that your grandfather was a distant relative and had some position at the Hall.'

That made sense, Ella thought. 'Shall you go, Miss Fairchild?'

'I think it is an opportunity not to be missed. But, as you know, I never travel unless accompanied by a maid.' She paused. 'And as this directly concerns you, Ella, Miss Blane has suggested that in this particular instance you should take her place.'

Ella stared at her. 'You mean to come with you as your personal maid?' She was flabbergasted at the thought. She might be able to look after clothes, even pack them, but she didn't know anything about dressing hair.

'Yes, I do. There should be enough time for Miss Blane to give you some training, at least enough for us to manage together. And it would only be for a limited time.'

Ella felt breathless. Wasn't she a quick learner? 'I'd do my best, madam.'

'I know that, Ella. Miss Blane will tell the rest of the staff that she needs to visit relatives in Scotland, which is true as her aunt is unwell. Although this must remain between ourselves for the moment.' She smiled. 'After all, we don't even know the date yet, except that it will be soon.'

Ella was trying to keep calm. She had never been anywhere other than Hampstead, and to travel all the way to Canterbury was going to be a real adventure. But then she realised it might mean that she would miss seeing Rory.

'You look troubled, Ella.'

Ella hesitated, unsure whether it would be proper of her to mention her time off. Such things were always arranged through Mr Forbes. 'I want to come, madam, of course I do, and I'm grateful for the chance. Only I was remembering that I've arranged to meet Rory again on my next half-day.'

Miss Fairchild looked thoughtful. 'If the dates clash, then perhaps you could take your half-day when we return. Shall we wait until we have more details?'

Relieved, Ella nodded.

'I'm not sure whether it would be a good thing, though, for you to mention to anyone yet about Sir Justin Hathaway. The fewer people who know of the real reason we are going on the visit, the better. Don't you agree?'

Ella nodded to show she understood, but when, minutes later, she made her way back to the kitchen, she decided that of course she would tell Rory.

Chapter Fifty

With the date for the trip to Canterbury being confirmed within days, Ella hurried to write:

Dear Rory,
I'm sorry, but I won't be able to meet you on the Heath like we arranged. I am going with Miss Fairchild to Canterbury that weekend, acting as her personal maid. It is all to do with my background and the name Hathaway, but I'll tell you more when I see you.

I shall wait for you this coming Sunday afternoon instead, and hope you can meet me then. I'm glad it's sooner, because I've really missed you.

She hesitated. Should she sign it, love Ella, or best wishes Estella? Deciding on the latter, she added, *PS: I have already used the rose-scented soap.*

And, though puzzled when he didn't reply, and wearing her new hat again despite an overcast sky, on Sunday afternoon she waited at the same spot where they'd met previously. When time began to pass with no sign of Rory, after an hour she had to face the fact that he wasn't coming. Ella wasn't sure what to do – she could hardly go to Professor Dalton's house, even though she now had the address. She would hate to cause Rory embarrassment. After waiting a while longer, she was forced to give up when darkening clouds threatened rain and, with bitter disappointment and hunched shoulders beneath her umbrella, made her way back home.

The following Friday, Letitia leant back against the leather upholstery of Edward's Daimler, having chosen to travel with her friends, while her own vehicle travelling behind held Ella, Grace's maid, Alice, and Edward's valet. When, after the first few miles, Edward began to study some papers and beside him Grace seemed thoughtful, Letitia relapsed into silence with only the occasional comment. Instead, she gazed out of the window enjoying the journey and reflecting on the coming weekend. Eventually, although the drive was a comfortable one, and undertaken at a civilised hour, Letitia guessed that Grace, as she did herself, was feeling relieved when they stopped for refreshment before at last reaching their destination.

Ella found every minute of the journey fascinating, thankful that Alice, a pale-faced woman of about forty, remained quiet most of the time. She seemed to be religious, holding a black Bible which she read slowly to herself, her lips moving with each word. The valet sat in the front beside the chauffeur. But although Ella loved seeing the changing scenery and was delighted that in the fields there were actual sheep and cattle, her thoughts kept returning to Rory. She had never received a reply to her letter and had dithered about writing again. But there had been so much to do, learning about her duties as a lady's maid, and her final fitting for a black dress with a detachable white lace collar and cuffs took place only the day before they were supposed to leave. She could only hope that he wasn't ill, and consoled herself that at least he knew not to wait for her on the Heath this coming Sunday.

The home of Harold Pincham MP was, as Letitia and Grace agreed, a most charming manor house with its mellow stone and ivy-covered walls. Their host made little effort to control the two lurchers who raced to greet the new arrivals and, against their noisy welcome, Edward introduced Grace and Letitia, while Ella and Alice went to supervise the unloading of their mistresses' luggage, and the valet, that of his master.

It wasn't until later that small and vivacious Mrs Pincham made an appearance, apologising for her tardiness when she came into the drawing room to join them. 'Merely a slight indisposition, which, I'm delighted to say, has passed.' Once the introductions were complete, she commented that they were the first of their expected guests to arrive. 'I'm pleased to say that we have a delightful gathering this weekend, and dinner tonight will be a slightly informal affair. Unlike tomorrow evening, when we hope to be honoured by the presence of Sir Justin Hathaway.'

So it still wasn't certain that he would join them, Letitia thought with dismay. She had decided, and also reminded Ella, who was using the surname Brown, that it would be unwise to reveal their interest in him beforehand.

That first evening, Ella felt terribly nervous about actually attending Miss Fairchild. At Eversleigh, Miss Blane had provided a wig for her to practise on, but touching Miss Fairchild's actual hair and seeing her in a state of undress was going to seem so personal and even impertinent. But her mistress made light of Ella's occasional clumsiness.

'That necklace has always been a little tricky to fasten. I rather think I would prefer the pearls, anyway,' she said, and when Ella had put out the wrong silk chemise, merely smiled and asked her to change it.

'We shall do very well, my dear,' she said when at last Ella had completed her task. Ella breathed a sigh of relief, even though she still felt nervous about the following evening when a more elaborate hairstyle would be required.

Later, down in the kitchen, when Alice had already gone up to bed, Ella sat chatting to one of the parlourmaids, who told her what good people Mr and Mrs Pincham were to work for. The wrinkled and bent butler, who looked as if he should have retired years ago, had been allowed to stay on. 'Got nowhere to go, had he?' she confided. 'That wouldn't have happened at my last place. We was under constant threat of dismissal. One girl was given the boot just because she dropped a glass. But the worst thing was' – even though they were sitting in a corner distant from the others, she dropped her voice – 'avoiding the master, if you know what I mean. Randy old devil. He'd come at you wherever you were, you know – 'aving a feel.'

Ella stared at her. 'Don't tell me he—'

'Not with me, he didn't. But there were others younger.' She touched the side of her nose. 'Let's say that more than one of his bastards ended up in the workhouse. Some of these toffs have got morals like polecats. What's your mistress like to work for?'

'She's very fair,' Ella said.

'Worth a lot, that is.' She yawned. 'Well, I can't sit here all night, I'm off to me bed.'

They both rose together and went their separate ways, Ella finding Alice kneeling by the side of the double bed they were to share. She moved around the room silently, performed her ablutions and slid beneath the laundered sheets. It seemed ages before Alice ended her whispered conversation with God, and Ella felt the mattress dip as she climbed into bed. With her mind still racing at the thought of the following evening, it was a long time before she managed to drift off to sleep, her last thought being that even if there was no possibility of her actually meeting this Sir Justin, she was determined to find some way of seeing him.

Chapter Fifty-One

One of the aspects Rory enjoyed about his work was that, when immersed in the written word, especially when he needed to take notes, hours could pass without him even being aware of them. At least he never had to suffer the tedium of boredom. The professor had warned Rory that he would find the content of this new book an emotive one, but he was now delving into the testimony of witnesses and discovering corruption on a scale he'd never imagined. He found himself reading tales of human degradation so appalling that his heart filled at first with shock, then with fury. That anyone could inflict or even accept such hardship being suffered by one of their own kind was a sacrilege in itself. He had known the subject he would be researching, hadn't fooled himself that he would be immune to its horrors, but constantly reading of what his countrymen had been forced to endure was beginning to affect his every mood.

And so the prospect of seeing Ella on Sunday was like a balm to his troubled thoughts. Even an image of her made his heart beat faster, and his desire to see her again grew with every passing day.

When the time came, he took especial care with his appearance, even gazing into the mirror to wonder whether he should begin to grow a moustache. Rory decided that he would sound out Ella's views. If she preferred him to remain clean-shaven, then so be it. With care, he brushed his jacket, polished his shoes, wore a clean stiff collar and, picking up the small box of chocolates he'd bought, set out for the Heath. It was a fine day with only a few clouds in the sky and, confident that it wouldn't rain, he left his umbrella in his room. Wouldn't he need one hand free to take Ella's hand? Rory didn't think he was being foolish to be so optimistic. There had been a definite rapport between them last time, and one not merely of friendship. If, as he hoped, Ella was longing to see him as much he was to see her, then the afternoon held a wealth of promise.

He arrived early at the meeting place and, feeling relaxed and happy, waited with keen anticipation. It seemed impossible now that on the previous occasion he hadn't recognised her, had even thought the silver-haired man behind to be her father, because every detail of her lovely face, her smile, was etched in his mind and heart. He had been meant to return to England, he was sure of it. Rory had no doubts that he and Ella had been fated to meet, because the strength of emotion she aroused in him was unlike anything he had ever experienced. The thought that at any moment she would walk up towards him, her eyes alight in her own special way, was such a tantalising one that it wasn't until he took out his fob watch that he realised just how late she was. Rory frowned to see the time had already overrun by fifteen minutes. And then, as the time ticked by without any sign of her, he shuffled his feet a little and flexed his shoulders. It was true autumn weather, with a bright sky and deceptive sunshine – certainly not warm enough to stand for so long. Rory turned and walked briskly for several yards and then turned to walk back again. When the overdue time reached forty-five minutes, his growing concern turned into anxiety. Could it be that she was ill? Rory waited until the full hour had passed, and then decided to go to Eversleigh.

As he walked along the treelined road that led to the tall black wrought-iron gates and then opened them, he could only imagine how nervous Ella must have felt that first time on seeing the substantial house. Rory swung left along the broad path, which, as he'd expected, brought him to the rear of the house and, glancing at a large well-kept garden, approached a green-painted door and tugged on the bell pull. Within a couple of minutes he was facing a pretty young maid in a green uniform with a heart-shaped face, fair hair beneath her cap, and blue eyes that widened on seeing him.

'Good afternoon. I've come to enquire about the well-being of Miss Ella Hathaway.'

Her mouth gaped, and he realised that the poor girl didn't have all her wits.

'What's your name?' he said gently.

'I'm Myrtle.'

'And do you know Ella?'

Her expression lit up. 'Oh yes, Ella's nice.'

There came a strident voice behind her. 'Myrtle, haven't I told you not to answer the door.'

'There was nobody else, Cook.'

A plump woman in a white apron appeared, a white cap almost covering her greying hair. She gazed at him with suspicion, 'Yes?'

'I'm sorry to disturb you,' Rory said. 'My name is Rory Adare and I was wondering whether Miss Ella Hathaway is quite well. We had arranged to meet earlier this afternoon.'

Her expression changed. 'I'm sorry, she isn't here.'

Rory frowned. 'I'm not sure I understand.'

'The mistress has gone to Canterbury for a few days, and Ella with her to act as lady's maid. Right thrilled, she was.' She looked puzzled. 'I'm sure she wrote and told you.'

Myrtle, behind her, was nodding. 'I saw the envelope. It had a stamp on it.'

Rory stared at them both and slowly shook his head. 'I haven't received it.'

'They're coming back tomorrow, all being well.'

Rory saw Cook's gaze sweep over him, her eyes alight with curiosity. 'Shall I tell her you called?'

'That would be most kind. And please will you give her my regards.'

'Of course, Mr Adare.'

'Thank you.' Deep in thought, Rory turned and walked back down the drive to open and close the gates. Still disappointed not to have seen her, he wondered why he hadn't received her letter. He had heard they could sometimes go astray, but it seemed odd for it to happen within such a short distance. At least he knew that Ella wasn't ill, and he smiled to himself as he imagined how much she would enjoy both travelling and acting as lady's maid to Miss Fairchild. It would be good for her to see more of England, that was something he hoped to do himself. London might be its capital, but he knew that many counties had their own distinctive character. Perhaps one day he and Ella could explore different locations together.

The house was quiet as Rory let himself into the wide black and maroon tiled hall with the stained glass of the fanlight over the front door allowing the sun's rays to stream in. He went straight to the mahogany settle by the wall on which mail would rest in readiness for the butler to sort. Rory first bent to look, in vain, down the back, before kneeling to peer underneath, then to slide his hand to its rear. There was no envelope nor any sign of one.

Getting up and straightening his clothes, he made his way down to the kitchen.

Cook glanced up from her Sunday newspaper from which she delighted in relating any juicy scandals. 'You're back early.'

Rory gave her an absent smile, and going to the dresser began to search its shelf. There was nothing. He turned to the few members of staff there.

'I don't suppose any of you have seen a letter lying about, addressed to me?'

There was only shaking of heads.

'When would it have come?' Cook said.

'I'm not sure, probably a few days ago. Only I'd arranged to meet someone on the Heath, and apparently she'd written to cancel it.'

'Go on, she's probably just stood you up! Can't say I blame her.'

Rory turned on Charlie. 'For heaven's sake give it a rest. I wouldn't put it past you to have hidden it just to spite me.'

'Hidden what?' The butler paused in the kitchen doorway.

Rory explained. 'Mr Craven, I don't suppose you can recall whether there was a letter delivered for me during this past week?'

He didn't hesitate. 'Yes, there was. You had already left for the British Library, so I followed my normal routine and left it here on the dresser.'

'I'm afraid it wasn't there when I returned. And it was important.'

The butler came further into the kitchen. 'Do you have any basis to accuse Charlie of such a crime? Because interfering with His Majesty's mail is a serious offence.' He swung round to glare at the young footman. 'There is not much I miss in this house, and I haven't been unaware of your hostility to Mr Adare since he returned. In fact, I remember you had the same unfortunate attitude towards him all those years ago.'

There was a heavy silence in the kitchen as everyone turned to look at Charlie. Cook's face was red with indignation, while the housekeeper compressed her lips.

'Speak up, I shall discover the truth one way or another. Did you, or did you not, take a letter addressed to Mr Adare?' Charlie's face was now crimson, his forehead beaded with perspiration. 'It was a joke,' he muttered.

This, on top of all of Charlie's insults and nasty innuendos, made bile rise in Rory's throat. He was furious. 'Fetch it!'

'I ain't got it no more.'

The butler's expression was one of fury. 'So you won't mind your room being searched.'

Charlie sprang up in indignation. 'I didn't mean no harm by it.'

'But it did do harm, didn't it? I'll ask you again, have you still got the letter?'

Charlie hung his head and mumbled, 'Yes.'

'Then you will bring it down here, hand it over to Mr Adare, and apologise.' He raised his voice. 'Do you hear me?' He glanced at the younger footman who was staring after Charlie, his mouth agape. 'Close your mouth, Arthur. What have I told you, dignity at all times.'

'Well, I never heard the like,' Cook said, so furious that she had to fan her hot face with her apron. 'I've always said he was trouble, that one. Shall you tell the professor, Mr Craven?'

The housekeeper was tutting and nodding her head, the two parlourmaids exchanging delighted glances. Rory discovered later that they'd found it best to keep out of Charlie's way. 'Wandering hands,' one of them confided.

'I have yet to decide what action to take.' He turned to Rory. 'I only hope this won't cause you any lasting embarrassment.'

'Certainly misunderstanding, I'm afraid.' Rory was finding it difficult to contain his anger. Even more so because once he had read Ella's letter, he realised that she too would have stood and waited in vain on the Heath. And with her stunning good looks, she would surely have attracted attention, even been approached by someone with ill intent. He dismissed a sudden fear that she may have thought that he hadn't bothered to come, there was too much trust between them for that. He was now even more desperate to see her again.

As for now, Charlie had better keep out of his way, because Rory's every instinct was to give the lousy rotter the pasting he deserved.

Chapter Fifty-Two

That first night in Canterbury, Letitia had found it a pleasant enough gathering at dinner, although having now made their acquaintance she found the three other couples rather earnest, with a penchant for discussing the moral decline of the country since Edward VII had acceded the throne. Mrs Pincham, though, had a delightful sense of humour, which had been a saving grace when the ladies had withdrawn.

She was also disappointed when the subject of Sir Justin wasn't introduced; instead the conversation was about the differences in fashions worn by ladies in the home counties and provinces to those worn in London.

The languid, pale-faced wife of another MP stated, 'I do believe that we, in the capital, provide the example for the rest of the country to follow.'

'How very true.' This time it was a woman so stout that Letitia expected her ample breasts to split her silk bodice. 'But then the news from Paris reaches us so much sooner.'

Mrs Pincham was looking a little defensive, and Letitia went to her aid.

'I think most of our sex wish to dress well, after all doesn't our toilette take up a large part of our day? Deciding what to wear for different occasions, dressing for dinner?' She stifled a smile, noticing that her use of the word 'sex' had caused eyebrows to raise. Undeterred, she continued, 'Personally, I am hoping that women will in the future have more weighty matters to consider.'

There was a hushed silence, then, 'Am I to take it that you are one of these . . .'

'Suffragettes? In my own way, I suppose I am.'

'Unfeminine, my husband calls it!' This came from the third of the guests, a woman called Clarissa Horton who Letitia had instinctively disliked. Cold and haughty, her voice haranguing her maid had earlier drifted along the corridor between their rooms.

Grace remained silent, as always the perfect political wife.

Mrs Pincham, conscious of her role as hostess, intervened. 'Well, ladies, it is a free country and we are all entitled to our opinions.'

Letitia smiled at her. 'But of course. And may I say, Mrs Pincham, what an excellent meal you gave us.'

She beamed. 'And tomorrow, I have planned an excursion to Canterbury. I thought the cathedral, followed by a little shopping, before returning for a late luncheon. This will allow plenty of time for a rest before dinner when, as you know, I am hoping that Sir Justin Hathaway will join us.'

When Saturday morning dawned, Letitia went down to breakfast to be met by Edward with the news that Grace was feeling rather tired and had decided to remain in her room and rest.

Reassured that he wasn't unduly concerned, Letitia greeted the other weekend guests, resigning herself to a morning in Canterbury with the other women without the company of her friend. Upon discussion of travel arrangements, Edward offered his own car, and

Harold Pincham his, but Letitia swiftly asked whether she could travel in her own vehicle. 'I would like to give my maid a chance to see Canterbury,' she said.

'I'm assuming that you don't anticipate her joining our party?' It was the haughty woman speaking, her thin nostrils pinched at the thought of such indignity.

'Of course not. It's simply that she's an intelligent girl who wishes to learn as much as she can.'

There came a sniff from the same woman. 'I'm not sure I agree with the working classes being educated.'

Letitia, about to retort, reminded herself that this weekend, although ostensibly social, also had its political side and that she was Edward's guest. Instead, she went to the sideboard and gazed down at the silver tureens. The bacon looked crispy, the scrambled eggs creamy, but it was the kedgeree with its spicy aroma that tempted. She took a liberal helping and returned to the breakfast table.

'It will be quite an expedition,' beamed their host, but while Letitia was keen to see Canterbury Cathedral, with its famous history, she did not feel so enamoured of the planned shopping trip.

Later, when they all filed out of the cathedral, it was in silence. Letitia realised that the others too had found it a sobering experience to stand before the exact place where Thomas Becket had been so unjustly murdered, and also to see his marble effigy. She loved the tranquillity of old churches, both grand and small. It was almost as if the prayers said down the ages had seeped into their stone walls. She didn't regard herself as a religious woman, but was realistic enough to know that her attendance at services was a necessary social obligation. However, there were times when she could be moved almost to tears by a certain something in the atmosphere in these holy places, and this morning had been one of those times.

And so it was with a twinge of guilt that, as they left the cathedral, she invented a headache as an excuse for needing some quiet time alone. 'No, truly, please do go on without me. I'm sure that a little exercise in the fresh air will be more beneficial than to join you in shopping.'

While expressing concern, the others left her to her own devices. 'You'll never go to heaven,' Letitia chided herself as, despite the chill in the air, she began to stroll by the river. 'But I couldn't have stood that ghastly woman a moment longer.'

The same evening, Letitia sat before the mahogany dressing table in the room allocated to her, watching Ella's intense concentration with a certain amount of sympathy. The hairstyle she was attempting sometimes taxed even Mary's skill. Letitia's anxiety changed to relief and pleasure as she gazed at the reflected elaborate arrangement when Ella held up a hand mirror.

'Ella, that is a credit to you. I've always liked wearing my hair this way.'

'That's what Miss Blane said, so I've been practising.'

'And an apt pupil, if I may say so.' She twisted round to gaze up at her. 'You didn't seem inclined to talk earlier. Did you explore the cathedral?'

'I thought it was wonderful, Miss Fairchild. But that poor man, Thomas Becket. Do you think the King really did intend him to die?'

'That, my dear, is a question that has occupied historians through the centuries. And there's no denying that he said, "Will no one rid me of this troublesome priest?"'

'And the four knights interpreted it to mean his death.' Ella's voice was thoughtful.

'I'm afraid so.' Letitia looked at the rose silk gown hanging outside the wardrobe. 'I do hope we have chosen well, I have a feeling that I shall need all of my confidence tonight. You are sure that the dining-room table has been set for twelve?'

'I had a peek in.'

'So Sir Justin must be joining us. You have gleaned little about him from the other servants?'

'I haven't asked any questions yet, Miss Fairchild, as we agreed, but I did hear someone say that he was a bit of a recluse.'

'Then we must feel honoured that he has bothered to put in an appearance. And I promise to find out as much about him as I can. You're sure you'll be able to see him for yourself?'

Ella nodded. 'Yes, Miss Fairchild, I know exactly where I'm going to stand.'

The position Ella had chosen was at one end of the gallery, which overlooked the broad, stone-flagged hall. Shadowed, it would give her some seclusion while her view of anyone arriving would be a clear one. She reminded herself of the letter her mother had copied into her journal, sent by Justin's father shortly after the one informing her of his son's death.

As he married you against my wishes, you will never be welcome at Riverside Hall. But I acknowledge on his behalf a responsibility and will therefore instruct this firm of solicitors to administer to you a modest allowance. Here is their address. Please do not contact this house in future.

It had been so cold, so cruel. And the letter that Selina had sent, informing him that she was expecting his grandchild had been returned unopened, with the solicitors mentioned informing her

286

that they had been instructed not to forward any communication. And if the man who would shortly come through the door below, was the same one responsible for such callousness . . .

She was beginning to feel anxious that another member of staff would see her loitering when at last she heard the doorbell jangle and saw the butler move towards the front door. 'Good evening, Sir Justin.'

'Good evening.' His voice was a pleasant baritone. There was a pause, with Ella able to see little except the butler receiving a hat, gloves and cape.

'Please come this way, sir.'

And it was then, as the lights from the chandelier shone on his face, that Ella saw the man she had come to find out about.

Chapter Fifty-Three

In the drawing room, the buzz of conversation momentarily ceased. 'Sir Justin, how good of you to join us.' The voice was the calm one of Harold Pincham and, with a swish of silk, his wife bustled forward to greet their guest of honour.

Stunned, Letitia tried not to stare. This tall clean-shaven man was only in his early forties! She shot a wild glance across the room to meet the perplexed gaze of Edward and Grace, then tried to remain calm as the small group came towards her.

'May I present Miss Letitia Fairchild, who has accompanied Mr Edward Melrose and his wife?' Harold Pincham's voice was quiet, while his wife's face was pink with pride.

'Miss Fairchild.' His gaze was inscrutable.

She smiled and inclined her head. 'Sir Justin.'

'We shall leave you two dear people to converse,' trilled Mrs Pincham.

Letitia gave an inward sigh. People were always so obvious when there were two unattached people.

'Shall we? Converse?' He was smiling, and she decided that he'd had exactly the same thought, then glanced with annoyance at the portly man who insinuated himself between them. With a thin reedy voice, and married to that atrocious woman Clarissa Horton, he had scarcely spoken to Letitia the whole weekend. Now he ignored her, introduced himself and proceeded to dominate the conversation. Sir Justin's dark moustache – he was otherwise clean-shaven – gave a slight twitch.

'And you, Miss Fairchild?' Sir Justin seized a pause to interject. 'This is a political gathering, do I take it that you too take an interest?'

Before she could answer, their companion said with contempt, 'My wife informs me that Miss Fairchild supports votes for women.'

'Indeed, I do,' Letitia said sweetly. 'Does that make me a social pariah?'

Sir Justin turned to her and smiled. 'Not in my eyes.'

It was then that Clarissa Horton came to join them and to be introduced. 'And what delicious gossip have I missed?'

Her husband, whose face was now crimson with affront, said, 'Sir Justin seems to have sympathy with the absurd suggestion that women should have the vote.'

'Surely not, you must be mistaken,' she snapped. 'Although I confess to be intrigued, Sir Justin, to know why you have remained distant from London society.'

'Indeed?'

'Having now met you, may I say that our capital is the poorer for it.'

'You are free to say what you like madam, just as I am free not to answer.'

Her thin face paled and, taking her husband's arm, she hurried him across the room to begin, with sidelong glances, to whisper to another couple.

Letitia said quietly, 'I see you speak your mind, Sir Justin.'

'It is the one entertainment I have.' She couldn't help laughing and it was then that someone else joined them and, seeing Mrs Pincham trying to attract her attention, Letitia excused herself and went over to her.

'I have placed you beside Sir Justin at table,' she whispered. If there was one thing that incensed Letitia it was to be the subject of matchmaking and normally she would have been furious, but now her reaction was one of exhilaration. This would give her the perfect chance to question Sir Justin, to discover more about his family. She felt a quickening pulse at the prospect and it was not just because of finding the answers she sought.

'That is indeed kind of you.' With a grateful smile Letitia turned to join Edward and Grace, whose expressions mirrored her own bewilderment. 'I was expecting white hair,' Grace whispered, while Edward frowned, obviously thoughtful.

When dinner was announced, they all went into the dining room where the table displayed arrangements of hothouse flowers whose scent wafted pleasantly in the air. And once seated Letitia was immediately conscious of the physical presence of the man beside her. Their chairs were close, his thigh in perfectly tailored trousers near her own and he was the most attractive man she had met in years. In fact, she thought, glancing across the table to Grace, since the first time she had met her friend's beloved husband. But then Letitia reminded herself of the reason she was there. She owed it to Ella not to let personal feelings distract her.

'Do you have a family, Sir Justin?'

He turned from his consommé, and she could see a knowing amusement in his eyes. 'I do not even have a wife. And yourself, Miss Fairchild?'

She laughed. 'I think I would have noticed.'

They conversed easily together, interspersed, as convention

demanded, with politeness to other guests, and then she said, 'Hathaway is an unusual surname. Is it one often found in this area?'

'Not as far as I know.'

'And your Christian name, is that a family one as so often happens? Do you have relatives bearing the same first name?' She laughed, trying to make it into an amusing remark. 'I have a friend whose father and brother are called Robert, and so are two of her cousins. It tends to cause much confusion.'

'I can imagine.' He paused as the butler served the fish course of salmon garnished with cucumber. Then said, 'I'm not aware that it's a family name. I'm afraid any relatives I have, cousins you understand, were burdened with Arthur and Ernest. My mother had a little more imagination.'

As each course followed another, Letitia came to realise that she had never been in a man's company with whom – apart from Miles – she had felt so attuned. But even when she had thought herself in love with Miles, she had never experienced this strange sensation when her gaze met his, a sort of sweet stirring within her. And, at times, his own gaze seemed intense. Did he, too, feel the attraction between them or was that her own wishful thinking and vanity? A man of such substance would have had the pick of the county, the cream of the feminine population. Why would he look twice at a thirty-four-year-old spinster?

And why had he never married?

It was late when Letitia eventually came up to her bedroom to find Ella, her face pale, her eyes dark with anxious enquiry, waiting to attend her. With a qualm, Letitia realised that the girl's own shock must have been even greater than her own. 'I know, my dear. I was taken aback to see him as you must have been.' She turned so that Ella could unhook her dress and put it on its padded hanger, then

Letitia slipped into a blue satin peignoir. 'Also, Ella, I'm afraid I discovered nothing that will help us. There are no other relatives in the family called Justin, and apparently Hathaway isn't a common surname in this area.'

Ella didn't reply, and Letitia glanced to see that she seemed agitated. 'What's wrong? Are you feeling unwell?' Letitia had never seen her in such a nervous state.

'Once I have completed my duties, Miss Fairchild, then please – I need to show you something.'

Chapter Fifty-Four

With a rapidly beating heart, Ella hurried along the carpeted corridor outside Miss Fairchild's room and then up the brown varnished stairs to the servants' quarters, where, on entering her room, she saw Alice rising from her knees, her interminable evening prayers obviously over. She glanced over at Ella and yawned. 'Finished your duties?'

'Not quite, I need to go back.'

Alice slid beneath the bedclothes and turning over so that she wouldn't face Ella, drew the burgundy eiderdown over her shoulders. 'Well, try not to wake me when you come in, I'm done for.'

Feeling sick with nerves, Ella bent to her carpet bag and took out Selina's sketchbook to hold it for a brief moment against her, trying to calm her emotional turmoil. She saw no one else on her way back and, after a light tap, went into the room to see Miss Fairchild seated on a velvet chair near the glowing embers of the fireplace. She looked at the sketchbook clutched in Ella's arms and said, 'Please do bring that other chair and come and sit beside me.'

Ella obeyed while trying to stop her hands from trembling. With a throat that was dry with tension, she began, 'I haven't shown you any of these drawings before, although I was intending to. I brought Selina's sketchbook with me because I wanted my grandfather to see what a talented daughter-in-law he'd spurned, but now . . .' her voice broke. 'Please, look at the first page.' She handed over the sketchbook.

Ella saw her gaze down, heard her intake of breath, her eyes widen with shock. 'But this is . . .'

'And the following one with the sketch of the same man,' Ella whispered. The sound of the page being turned echoed in the silence.

'This means . . .' there was a catch in her voice. 'I can't believe that I didn't see the resemblance earlier. Those hazel eyes, a certain turn of the head, even the same brown hair. But your father died before you were born, didn't Selena write an account of it? How can this be possible?'

Ella's eyes were bright with tears. During the long hours of the evening, she had tried to imagine the scene when, in the early stages of her pregnancy, Selina had received that terrible letter informing her of her husband's death. Her grief would have been so overwhelming, despairing, it would never have occurred to her that the tragic words were lies. In misery she burst out, 'You don't think that he could have known what my grandfather did? That he didn't love my mother, after all? That he regretted his marriage?'

'Ella, we can't assume that. Don't you think it more likely that writing to tell Selina that her husband had died – from pneumonia, if I recall – was his father's way of excluding her from the family, rescuing his son from what he saw as a disastrous marriage?'

'But that wouldn't explain why Justin abandoned my mother, never tried to find her. He *must* have known and agreed to it all, perhaps even her death.' She was now on the verge of sobs. 'How could he?'

Miss Fairchild took both her hands. 'My dear, we have no reason for thinking such a terrible thing. Of course he loved her, why else would he defy his father to marry her? Besides, how do we know what sort of lies Justin was told? We mustn't jump to conclusions, Ella.'

Ella was facing the realisation that gone was the chance to challenge her grandfather, to let words of hatred and contempt pour forth. She had hoped to shock him into facing the truth about himself, make him ashamed of his despicable actions. But such a harsh and cruel man probably wouldn't have had a conscience anyway.

Her mind kept evading the knowledge that, unbelievably, her father was alive. The joy she should have felt at the discovery was tainted by her suspicious dread that he, too, had been involved in Selina's tragic betrayal. And if that was true, then in her veins would run the blood of not only one evil man but two.

Chapter Fifty-Five

For once, Ella blessed the fact that Alice preferred to read her Bible rather than to chat during the long journey home. And, as the car continued on its steady journey, Ella found herself wrestling yet again with the knowledge that her father hadn't, as she had believed for so many years, died before she was born. At times, she had to blink tears away as she stared blindly out of the window, wishing with all her heart that she could feel joy and excitement. Miss Fairchild might speak well of Sir Justin, saying that she found it difficult to believe that he could be guilty of such a heinous crime, but Ella's thoughts were dark. She did try to take as much interest in the passing scenery as on the outward journey, but somehow she felt withdrawn from reality, lapsing into long silences and staring into space.

And then, at last, the car was driving up to Eversleigh with footmen emerging to remove Miss Fairchild's luggage. Feeling tired, Ella said goodbye to Alice, collected her own carpet bag and made her way to the kitchen to be greeted with a shy smile by Myrtle. 'I've missed you.'

Ella gave her a hug. 'I've missed you too.'

Her face red with importance, Myrtle said, 'Somebody came to see you yesterday.'

'Glory, let the girl get in!' Cook turned to Ella. 'It was that Mr Adare, the one you call Rory.'

Ella felt a leap of excitement.

'Of course, madam here answered the door, even though she's not supposed to. He said he'd waited for you on the Heath yesterday afternoon and wondered if you were all right.'

'But I wrote to him and explained I'd be away.'

Cook shrugged. 'Obviously he didn't get it.'

'Did he leave a message?'

'Just sent his regards, that's all.'

'Is he your sweetheart?' Myrtle was carrying, with care, a cup and saucer, and Ella sat at the long table gratefully to sip the hot sweet tea.

'You shouldn't ask such personal questions,' Cook chided.

'If he is, I feel sorry for him,' Lizzie muttered, who was darning a ladder in her stocking.

'And you, my girl, need to mend your manners.' Unseen, the butler had come into the kitchen. 'And you should be doing that darning in your own time. Off you go about your duties.' He turned to Ella. 'Welcome back, I trust all went well?'

'I managed well with attending to the mistress, Mr Forbes.' Ella slightly raised her eyebrows and gave a slight shake of the head to show that she hadn't found her grandfather. Later, she would tell him everything.

Sleep came slowly that night as Ella lay restless, unable to put out of her mind all that had happened. And she was heavy-eyed the following day when, because Miss Blane hadn't yet returned from Scotland, Ella had to attend to Miss Fairchild in addition to some of her parlourmaid duties. She wondered whether she should write to Rory again, but then the next morning, when she made her way down to the kitchen for elevenses, it was to be greeted by an excited Myrtle. She pointed to the dresser. 'You've got a letter.'

Ella hurried over, her heart dancing when she saw Rory's familiar handwriting, and put the envelope in her pocket. But within minutes, she went out to the downstairs lavatory to read the single page in growing fury, before hurrying back to the kitchen.

'Oh yes,' Lizzie sneered. 'Sneaked off to read your love letter, then.'

'The sooner you find a young man of your own the better,' Ella snapped. 'It might stop you being such a jealous cow.'

'If it was from Mr Adare, does he know why he didn't get your letter?' Cook said.

'He most certainly does!' Ella told her what had happened.

'Now, why should anyone do such a thing? Interfering in other people's business.' Cook was bristling.

'Apparently he's been sacked.' Ella swung round to the butler. 'Mr Forbes, please can I have Sunday afternoon off? Rory has written to ask if I can meet him.'

He nodded. 'You deserve it after Canterbury.'

Hugging to herself the prospect of seeing Rory so soon, Ella's mind was already darting to what clothes to wear.

Having given Grace a chance to recover from the previous weekend's visit, Letitia telephoned her on Wednesday and arranged for them to meet with Charlotte that afternoon. She was pleased to see her friend looking relaxed as she sat in the drawing room opposite her mother.

'I didn't bring the children,' Grace explained. 'We need to think clearly, which is impossible when you're constantly interrupted.'

'Quite so,' Charlotte said. 'But I'm hoping that doesn't mean that I won't see them very soon.'

'Of course not, Mama. You know how they love to come here.'

Charlotte's health had improved during the past few years, partly Letitia suspected, because of the joy she found in her grandchildren.

'I do feel for Ella,' Charlotte said. 'It must have been a terrible shock to realise that Sir Justin was actually her father. You are sure of that, Letitia?'

She nodded. 'There is no doubt. One has only to see Selina's sketches of her husband.'

'What sort of man is he, Letitia? Grace tells me that you and he were often in conversation.'

'Mama, they had eyes only for each other.'

Letitia held up a hand. 'I protest, Grace, that wasn't true at all.' But, to her embarrassment, she felt colour rise in her cheeks.

She saw Charlotte give her an appraising look and was forced to smile.

'I do admit that I found him charming and intelligent.'

'He's also extremely handsome,' Grace teased.

Charlotte's voice was quiet. 'You were attracted to him, Letitia?'

She hesitated, but who else could she confide in. 'Yes, I was. But, as he has remained single all these years, I would doubt that he is looking for a wife.'

'My dear, I cannot remember the last time you were attracted to anyone at all. I shall look forward to meeting this paragon.'

Letitia's voice was tight as she said, 'He's hardly that, not if he was compliant with his father's appalling treatment of Selina.'

'We need to find a way of bringing him to London.' Charlotte's voice was decisive. 'And Grace tells me that Edward has already come up with a plan. He intends to invite Sir Justin to a dinner party at the end of the month.'

Letitia felt doubtful. 'What makes you think he will accept?'

'Because,' Grace told her, 'Edward intends to add on his invitation an offer of a personal tour of the Houses of Parliament, and also a visit to the theatre.'

'But even so.'

Charlotte leant forward. 'Don't you see, my dear, we are hoping that there is a mutual attraction between you and Sir Justin. And if so, that will be another incentive for him to come.'

'And if he declines?' Letitia saw the answer in their eyes, one she didn't want to contemplate. Although wasn't she used to disappointment?

Charlotte broke into her thoughts. 'Of course, assuming that he does accept, there will still be problems to overcome. Ella certainly has the right to meet her father. I'm afraid you will have to arrange that.'

'Thinking of Ella reminds me of another part of Edward's plan.' Grace paused to pop a crystallised fruit in her mouth. 'He had thought to include Professor Dalton. Do you remember we spoke of it?'

'I do, and it's an excellent idea,' Letitia exclaimed. She hadn't, as yet, received a reply to her letter to Miles concerning Ella's young man. Tracing Rory's father was obviously proving to be a more difficult task than she'd supposed. Could it be that he had been lying about his background?

Chapter Fifty-Six

Sunday morning arrived and, although there was a chill in the air, to Ella's relief there was no forecast of rain. Even though she had so much to tell Rory, overshadowing that was an ache within her to simply be with him again. She had decided to wear the same petrol-blue skirt and jacket she had worn that first time, knowing that it flattered her figure. The service in the well-attended church seemed to last forever and it was with relief that she saw the vicar, and not his stammering curate, climb up to the pulpit to deliver the sermon. Even then, she hardly listened; all her thoughts were of the coming afternoon.

At two o'clock she walked down Eversleigh's long drive, carrying the hessian bag, the translation and the sketchbook. Due to a sudden breeze, she was forced to put a hand to her best hat and make the hatpin more secure but, as she made her way to the Heath, nothing could dim her spirits, not with the prospect of meeting Rory, and she felt a surge of joy as she saw that he was already waiting for her, his face lighting up as he saw her come up the slight incline.

'You're even more beautiful than I remembered.'

'And you're even taller!' She felt an unsteady catch in her

throat. He was so wonderful, she could hardly believe how happy and confident even the sight of him made her feel. He made a slight movement towards her, and caring not a jot that they were in public, Ella lifted her face and felt his cool lips press her own in a swift but welcoming kiss.

Rory held out one hand to take what she was carrying, the other to take her own, and holding hands they began to walk on. 'Tell me how you liked being a lady's maid. That's a huge jump from a scruffy little scullery one.' He laughed down at her.

'Gosh, I must have looked a real fright then. It was all Miss Grint's fault.'

'But did you like it, dressing hair and so on?'

She nodded. 'I was grateful for the training, but it was only temporary, for that particular weekend. I'm angry, though, with that flaming footman of yours.'

Rory grimaced. 'Charlie his name was. I just think he was eaten up with jealousy. We're all thankful he's gone.' He indicated the bag. 'You said in your letter that you were dying for me to look at your personal possessions. Shall we go straight to our tree and settle down to it? That's if you won't be too cold.'

She shook her head and with daring said, 'I can always snuggle up to you.'

'Why, Estella Hathaway,' he released her hand and put an arm round her waist. 'What an excellent idea!'

Ella was beginning to feel almost lightheaded with the easy aura of affection between them. And yet it was all happening so quickly. Maybe it was because they had written to each other so many times while Rory was in America that she felt so at ease with him. Once they were settled on the thankfully dry grass beneath the spreading branches and their fast diminishing autumn leaves, Ella removed her gloves and relieved Rory of the translation and the sketchbook. She was longing to tell him her news about her father, but forced herself to wait as she watched him begin to undo the hessian bag.

'That was how Violet disguised the black purse and there was a rag doll and dusters on the top.'

He raised an eyebrow when he saw the softness of the silk and, on removing the journal, she watched him finger the quality of its leather and silver clasp, then open it to read the name on the flyleaf. His voice was quiet. 'You must have been astounded when you first found this.'

'I was.' She passed over the brown envelope containing the translation. 'But, thank heaven, I knew Miss Fairchild.'

Removing the neatly written transcript, he began to study it while Ella moved closer to him. Sometimes she would look up at him, thinking that his intent expression must be his usual one when doing research, and her gaze would drift to his hands, which she could remember being calloused when she'd first seen him on the cart. Now they were the smooth hands of a gentleman and Rory would not be out of place at any of the dinner parties held at Eversleigh. It was secluded where they were sitting with their backs against the gnarled trunk of the old tree and Ella closed her eyes, savouring being so close to him, feeling the brown tweed of his coat against her cheek. Her own clothes were a fine wool so she didn't feel too chilled, although she knew it had been vanity not to have also worn her coat. And that was because, although it might be warm and suitable for someone in service, its subdued grey did nothing for her complexion.

When at last Rory lowered the pages of translation, she moved so that she could turn and face him. 'You've read it all?'

He nodded, his face grave.

'It broke my heart. I couldn't stop crying for ages.' Ella paused at the remembrance of herself alone and tired, late at night in her narrow room. 'I still believe my mother was murdered.' She told him about Violet Rutter, of her whispered words, how she had seen the carriage driven directly at Selina. 'The police dismissed her evidence because she was only a servant, instead taking the word of a gentleman who suddenly appeared on the scene, although Violet swears she'd never seen him at the time.'

Rory's forehead was furrowed in a deep frown. 'You know, coupled with the fact that your mother was afraid someone was watching her . . .' He leafed through the pages and read aloud, "*I feel so vulnerable, so alone. I have this feeling that someone is spying on me. 'Tis foolish, maybe, but I cannot shake it. I must protect my child, and, although I hate the thought, perhaps it is time to move away from here, to find other lodgings.*" This was written before Selina came to live in Hampstead. And we know she had earlier moved twice. It sounds as if she was always trying to find anonymity and failing.' He closed the journal and said, 'One can't help wondering about the lawyer. She would have had no choice but to notify him of any new address.'

'Otherwise she would risk losing the allowance.' Ella's eyes widened. 'But surely a lawyer wouldn't . . .'

Rory shrugged. 'Let's not forget that it was your grandfather who was his client. And there's an old saying, "He who pays the piper calls the tune".'

Ella's tone was one of fury. 'I can't believe that I carry that hateful man's blood in my veins.'

'Are you absolutely sure of that?'

She nodded, and began with increasing vehemence to tell him all that had happened the previous weekend.

Rory was staring at her, his eyes wide with shock. 'Are you saying that . . . ?'

She nodded. 'Yes, it seems that my father is alive, after all. I knew as soon as I saw him. But first let me show you the marriage and birth certificates.' She took the envelope out of the one that had contained the translation.

He studied them for a few moments, then said, 'May I see the sketchbook?'

Ella bent and removed it from the bag. 'It's the first page and the second one.'

She waited, watching the changing expressions on his face as he looked down at the sketches. 'You're right, Ella, about this being your father, there's a definite resemblance. To think that for all these years you've thought him dead.' As he leafed slowly through the rest of the drawings, he shared smiles with her, murmuring what a beautiful baby she'd been, his expression becoming sad when he reached the final page. She saw his lips tighten. 'Well, my love, you're not alone in this any more. I know Miss Fairchild has done a lot to help, but you're not as precious to her as you are to me and I'll help in any way I can.'

Then he put everything down on the grass beside him and said, 'Sweetheart, can we just for now put all this aside? Because having met you again has meant the world to me, and I don't think I can wait another minute before I kiss you properly.'

Ella willingly went into his outstretched arms and raised her lips for a kiss that left her breathless with its intensity. She lifted a hand to stroke his dear face, and then her mouth sought his again, and again. The sweetness of their kisses made her breathless, heat rising in her body only for them to be forced to break apart as the rustle of grass announced that they were no longer alone. A middle-aged man, his bristly moustache quivering with indignation, glared with disapproval as he strode by.

'Has he never been in love?' Rory murmured.

'Is that what we are?' She ran her finger along his jawline and then up to his mouth, tracing its firm outline. 'It's all so soon.'

'I don't care. I am, sweetheart, and unless you are too, then you're a shameless hussy.'

She laughed, and he kissed her again, and this time his hand came down to cup her breast. She could feel his warmth through the thin wool material, a longing for him to undo the tiny buttons, to feel his skin against her own. How she loved being touched by him. 'I wish we weren't in public,' she whispered.

He lifted his head for a swift look around. 'There's nobody around.' But he drew back. 'We'd better behave before I lose control. You're a temptress, young woman.'

'This has all happened so quickly,' she murmured. 'I never expected it, did you? I mean when I first knew you were coming back.'

'I didn't know what to expect.' Rory smiled down at her. 'For all I knew you might not have changed a bit.' He gently lifted a soft tress of her hair, which was now uncovered, with her hat lying on the ground. 'I did guess, though, that your hair would be longer, although I never imagined it would be this rich chestnut brown.'

Ella felt a flush of pride. 'I do brush it 100 times every night.'

'Well, I think it's lovely. You know, I think you and I were meant to be released from the workhouse on the same day.'

'Suppose I'd come out a week later. We might never have met.' She was horrified, and then began to dust a few fallen leaves off the front of her skirt.

'You'll be getting chilled,' Rory said. 'Let's walk on for a while and get some exercise.'

'I hope that doesn't mean you won't kiss me again.' She stood and, swinging round, realised that she needed to dust off even more leaves from the back of her skirt. Rory did the same with his coat.

He smiled down at her. 'I'd never stop if I had my way.'

Dusk was falling when they eventually parted, Rory having insisted on accompanying her back to Eversleigh. Outside the gates he kissed her on the cheek. 'I can't bear to let you go.'

She drew his hand up to her lips. 'I know.'

'I'll see what I can find out for you, Ella. I'll write to you, anyway.'

She watched his tall figure stride back along the road and walked up the drive with sunshine in her heart. Rory was in love with her and that would sustain her whatever the future held.

Chapter Fifty-Seven

Rory spent the following evening in deep thought. The afternoon had been wonderful in so many ways and an involuntary smile played around his lips as he remembered how often they had claimed Ella's soft ones when they were up on the Heath. It was hard to believe that they had only met twice since he returned. But the earlier part of the afternoon was also much on his mind. He wasn't sure that Ella fully realised the implications of what she had discovered about this Sir Justin Hathaway. If he was indeed her biological father, Ella being in possession of both the marriage and birth certificates, then legally her position as his daughter was irrefutable. And unless Sir Justin's estate was entailed, and of course he was still young enough to father a son, then Ella's position in society would dramatically change. It was with desperation and panic that he tried to distract himself from the unpalatable fact that an impecunious young Irishman would hardly be considered a good match for an heiress.

Instead, Rory's thoughts turned to the malevolent streak shown by her grandfather in his letters to his daughter-in-law, and a shudder ran through him. Someone who could be so callous, so harsh would, in Rory's opinion, easily be capable of planning the ultimate crime of murder.

Letitia was writing letters when, a few days later, a telephone call came from Grace. 'Professor Dalton has written an acceptance. I'm sure you'll be able to find a private moment to mention Rory to him. But there has been nothing yet from Sir Justin. Although it's early days and no news is good news.'

'Let's hope so.' Letitia turned to gaze out at the rain lashing against the windows.

'You really like him, don't you?' Grace's tone was soft.

'I remember asking you the same question just after you'd met Edward. And my answer is the same as yours, yes I do.'

'Then I hope it all works out as well for you as it did for me.'

'There is a mountain to climb first, Grace. Even if he reciprocates my feelings, there is much to worry about concerning his character.'

'I know, my dear. I'll be in touch.'

Letitia replaced the receiver and tried to calm her mind.

And then, the following morning, the awaited letter from Ireland arrived. There was an account of Miles suffering a cold, of little Letty also succumbing, and then an answer to Letitia's question.

There was certainly a Seamus Adare living in Dublin, who wrote regular political columns for the national newspapers. You ask about the young man Rory. I can only tell you that there was a son of the same name, known as something of a scholar. However, soon after his wife died, Seamus became ill, it is believed with cancer, which led to him falling on hard times. He and his son left Dublin for London and little has been heard of them since.

Letitia put down the letter and mused that Seamus Adare had breathed his last in a workhouse. She could imagine that his pride would prevent any reports of it in the press. So at least Rory hadn't lied about his background.

She was so deep in thought that the shrill sound of the telephone startled her.

'Letitia?' Grace's voice sounded excited. 'I have such good news. We have received an acceptance from Sir Justin.'

'You have?' Her feeling of relief was so strong that her legs felt weak.

'Don't you see what this means? I doubt he would be coming except for a desire to see you again.'

'We can't be sure of that, Grace.' Letitia tried to steady her voice.

'The date is only a fortnight away, so we shall soon find out. I think this calls for a new dress, don't you? Perhaps one with a lowish neckline?'

Maybe Grace has a point, Letitia thought as she replaced the receiver. Always conscious that her own small breasts, even if firm and well-shaped, compared unfavourably with others more generously endowed, Letitia rarely revealed her small cleavage. She'd been toying with the idea of arranging an appointment at one of the new London fashion houses as an alternative to using her regular dressmaker. This would seem to be the perfect opportunity. Then, going over to the fireplace, Letitia placed her hand on the silken bell pull, thought for a moment, then gave it a slight pull.

Within seconds, the door opened and Forbes came in. 'Yes, madam.'

'I would very much like to speak to Ella when her duties permit.'

'I shall send her along directly.'

'Thank you, Forbes.' She smiled at him. 'I have good news for her.'

He gave a slight bow of his head before he left, but not before she had seen an answering smile. Her butler took his responsibility for discipline downstairs very seriously, proud of his fairness and lack of favourites. But she suspected that he had a soft spot for Ella. And Letitia was becoming increasingly conscious that same sentiment applied to herself. She was also finding it difficult to continue treating her as a servant.

It was another half-hour before Ella tapped at the door and came in. 'You wanted to see me, Miss Fairchild?'

Letitia nodded and explained about Edward Melrose's invitation. 'I have just heard that Sir Justin has written to accept.'

She saw Ella's eyes widen with shock. 'You mean that he will actually be here, in Hampstead?'

'Indeed he will, and very soon. At least then we should be able to ascertain the truth.'

'That's what I'm afraid of,' Ella whispered. Letitia was now so involved in the situation that she could feel the girl's pain. She seemed to be hesitating before saying, 'Rory has read your translation of the journal and seen the sketchbook, and he has some suspicion about the lawyer's part in it all.'

Letitia felt troubled. 'I hope he realises that this must all be kept confidential, it wouldn't do at all for it to become public knowledge.'

'You don't need to worry about that, madam. He does a lot of research for Professor Dalton, he knows how to be discreet.'

Letitia smiled at her. 'I'll keep you informed of any further developments, I promise.'

Ella straightened her shoulders. 'Is there any way that I'll be able to meet Sir Justin? As you can imagine, I need to ask him some questions.'

'I think you both have the right to meet each other. Don't worry, I'll find some way of arranging it.'

'Thank you, Miss Fairchild.'

Letitia watched Ella leave the room and, with sympathy, could only guess how she must be feeling. She, herself, could sense a knot of apprehension building about the coming dinner party. To sit beside Sir Justin yet again was going to be an exquisite torture. Because, despite longing to see him again, in one way she was dreading it. What if she discovered that the man she was in danger of falling in love with had feet of clay?

Chapter Fifty-Eight

When she left the morning room, Ella's mind was in such an upheaval that she had to seek sanctuary in her attic bedroom. She could hardly believe that within a fortnight she would be able not only to meet, but actually talk to this unknown man who was her father. The man who could have been responsible for her mother's tragic life, whose neglect could have caused her own unhappy and harsh childhood. If it hadn't been for the intervention of Miss Fairchild, Ella might still be in that hell of a workhouse now. Even the thought of the coming confrontation made her feel sick with nerves, and it was some time before she felt calm enough to go downstairs and try to behave as if nothing had happened.

It was not until the end of that afternoon, after studying in the British Library, Rory was able to turn to a clean page of his notepad and write at the top the name 'Sir Justin Hathaway, Riverside Hall near Canterbury'. Blessed with a retentive memory, Rory tried to remember Selina's actual words concerning her husband's death. In the normal way of things, a high-born family would announce such a sad occasion in *The Times*. But he decided it would be futile to go to the newspaper's archive, because how could Ella's grandfather have inserted such a lie, when his son was still alive? No, the place to begin was to investigate the firm of lawyers who had acted for the Hathaway family at that time, and he thought it a pity that Selena had never mentioned their name. Fleetingly, he wondered about the original letters, but it was more than likely that they'd been destroyed on Selena's death. A guest in a hotel who never had visitors? Letters and bills would most likely have been burnt. His hope was that changes or alterations had been needed to Riverside Hall and its estate, which would be recorded at the Land Registry in Lincoln's Inn Fields. Ancient families rarely changed their solicitors.

The following morning, when he received Ella's letter saying that her father was coming to London and she was to meet him, Rory knew how tense and worried she must be feeling. He tried to think how he could help and it was then that the idea came to him of taking her to a music hall to take her mind off things. After all, he had never taken her out, at least not properly, because walking on the Heath would hardly fit the description. And wouldn't she just love it?

Ella sat in the stalls of the Hippodrome enthralled. They left the theatre arm in arm, Ella laughing up at Rory with delight. 'I've never seen anything so wonderful.'

'Which act did you like best?'

'All of them,' she said promptly, and felt more light-hearted than she'd managed to be ever since Canterbury. The convivial atmosphere in the theatre, the music, the bawdy performances had been the perfect distraction from the constant shadow in her mind concerning her father. And now she pushed even the memory of that away, unwilling to allow anything to come between herself and Rory; their times together were far too rare and precious.

Rory bent and lightly kissed her. 'Where would you like to go now? Or are you like Cinderella, you have to be home by midnight?'

'Midnight?' She was horrified. 'I can't stay out that late, Mr Forbes would have a fit.'

'I'm only joking. I just don't want to let you go.'

She leant her head against his shoulder. 'I know. I want to be with you all the time.'

'More than anything, I want us to find a place where we can be together, just the two of us.'

'But can I trust you, Mr Adare?' She gave him an arch glance.

He whispered into her ear, 'Only if you don't lead me astray.'

She laughed. 'Oh, I do love you.'

'And I love you.'

'For ever and ever?'

He smiled down at her. 'For ever and ever.'

They parted at the gates of Eversleigh with Rory saying, 'I don't know what the outcome will be when you meet Sir Justin, but try not to worry, I'll always be there for you.'

And so it was with a lighter heart that, later, Ella quietly opened the back door to the kitchen at Eversleigh. One of the songs that Vesta Tilley had sung on the stage, was running through her head and she sang softly, *'I'm Burlington Bertie, I rise at ten-thirty . . .'*

'No need to ask if you've had a good time.' The butler was alone, seated in his shirtsleeves and reading. 'I was about to turn in, so I'm glad you're safely home.'

'Oh, it was wonderful, Mr Forbes.'

He smiled. 'Yes, I enjoy a good music hall myself. But there are other forms of theatre, Ella. Opera, ballet and a good play. I used to be a bit of a thespian myself, in my younger days.'

She stared at him. 'You were on the stage?'

'I've not always been a butler, you know.'

'I can't think of you any other way.'

He smiled. 'And that's how it should be. Off you go now, and sleep well.'

'Thank you, Mr Forbes, you too.'

People were full of surprises, Ella thought as she climbed the first, second and then third flight of stairs to her room; she sometimes had to restrain herself from kissing the butler on the cheek she'd become so fond of him.

The word 'kiss' made her think wistfully of the brief and circumspect ones she and Rory had shared on the way back. Were they always to be only together in public? And later, as she undressed for bed and hung up her clothes, Ella bent to remove her black woollen stockings and gazed down at her white, silky smooth legs. She'd seen dark hairs on Rory's wrists, would his legs also be hairy, his chest? She tried to imagine their bodies naked against each other, beginning to understand how Rosie had fallen pregnant. Because if she'd felt about the baby's father the way that Ella did about Rory . . .

Chapter Fifty-Nine

On the evening of the dinner party, Letitia, seeing Mary Blane's rather startled expression, felt a stab of anxiety. 'You think it is too revealing?' Her gown, which had cost an inordinate amount of money, moulded to her figure in a way she wouldn't have thought possible.

'Not at all, madam. It's just that you look braw bonnie! The colour of that material is as vibrant as any jewel.'

Letitia felt her spirits soar. This new Couture House, affiliated to one in Paris, had created a dress surpassing, in style and fit, anything Letitia had ever worn.

'That is quite poetic, Mary.' Letitia had chosen a ruby silk embellished with tiny cream rosebuds and the décolletage was cut and boned cleverly to hint at enticing breasts. The front skirt might be narrow, but an elegant flounce outlined her hips before trailing down the back. And, as always, Mary had created the perfect upswept hairstyle.

'I thought, perhaps, the pearl necklace?'

Letitia nodded and clipped on the matching drop earrings.

Once Mary had left, Letitia rose and went to her full-length mirror seeking more reassurance. She couldn't remember ever feeling so nervous and it was a heady thought to know that only one person was responsible. No matter how she tried to warn herself that on this second occasion she might not find Sir Justin so attractive, her heart was telling her otherwise. This was going to be a momentous evening in many ways. She was only too aware that it could be the forerunner to disillusionment for not only herself but also for Ella. Letitia could only imagine how the poor girl must be feeling tonight, knowing of the plan for tomorrow morning. Would she be able to sleep at all?

Lights were streaming from the tall windows as Letitia's car was driven up the Melrose's drive to their Georgian house. Her throat was tight with nerves as she greeted the familiar butler, and accompanied him along the spacious hall to the murmur of voices from the open door of the drawing room. Grace saw her immediately and came forward, kissing her cheek. 'Letitia, you look marvellous, I've never seen you look better.' She lowered her voice. 'He isn't down yet. I'm afraid there was a problem with the hot water. I feel so embarrassed.'

Letitia laughed. 'Isn't that just typical?'

'Edward is not at all pleased.'

'Grace, it can happen in the best of households.'

'But why did it happen tonight!' She took Letitia's arm. 'Never mind, it will give you a chance to talk to Professor Dalton.'

Slim, and dignified, with a neat silver moustache and goatee, he turned to her with a warm smile and she discovered within minutes how perceptive he was. Determined not to let the chance slip, after a few pleasantries, she said in what she hoped was a casual way, 'I believe that our households are acquainted, Professor. I have a parlourmaid, a protégée of mine, who is friendly with your research assistant, Mr Rory Adare.'

His pale-blue eyes studied her own. 'Ah, I see. And you would probably find it reassuring to know something of his character.'

Relieved to be able to speak plainly, Letitia nodded. 'I admit to having become rather fond of her.'

'A sentiment which does you justice. I will certainly enlighten you. Rory came to me as a youth of sixteen who, through no fault of his own, had fallen on hard times. But you probably know that.'

'I know that he spent some time in the workhouse.'

The professor inclined his head. 'He was from a good family and had the makings of a scholar, all he needed was the start I gave him, and I've never had cause to regret it. I hold him in high esteem, Miss Fairchild, and can only say that the young lady in question is very fortunate.'

Letitia smiled at him instinctively knowing that this man was not one who would be easily fooled. 'Thank you, I appreciate your candour.'

Letitia's attention wavered, drawn to the tall figure of Sir Justin arriving on the threshold. Her breathing quickened, he was even more handsome than she remembered.

She turned her gaze back to Professor Dalton, whose slight smile revealed again his perception and she said, 'I'm sorry, it's just that . . .'

'I quite understand, my dear.'

For Letitia, the atmosphere in the room was now heightened by Sir Justin's presence, and her heart beat faster when she saw Edward bringing him over.

'You remember Miss Fairchild?'

His gaze met and held her own. 'Of course, it is a pleasure to see you again.'

She felt her colour rise. 'And mine to see you, Sir Justin.'

Then Professor Dalton was introduced and pleasantries exchanged before Edward excused himself, and then, within seconds, Grace came to say, 'Professor Dalton, might I steal you away? I'd rather like you to meet my mother.'

For a moment there was a silence, then Sir Justin gave her a quizzical smile. 'So, Miss Fairchild, we are left alone, which means I can compliment you on that becoming gown. And if we are not seated together at the table, I shall take considerable offence.'

She laughed, already feeling at ease with him, just as she had in Canterbury. 'I have no patience with pretence. Considering that Grace is my closest friend, I doubt you have cause to worry.'

'Then I look forward to a most delightful evening.'

The booming voice of Charles Bentley made her turn and she felt a stab of dismay as, glass in hand, he came to join them. 'Letitia, you can't keep the guest of honour all to yourself. Besides, my wife wishes to know the name of your dressmaker.'

She forced a smile. 'Sir Justin, may I introduce Edward's uncle, Sir Charles Bentley, MP.' The two men shook hands. Charles immediately began to pontificate about one of his favourite topics, his political achievements, and Letitia cast an apologetic glance at Sir Justin and excused herself.

A few minutes later she managed to get Charlotte alone to relate the professor's opinion of Rory.

'That is one worry less, then.'

Letitia nodded. 'Especially as my friends in Ireland confirmed his background.'

Keeping her voice low, Charlotte said, 'As for Sir Justin, he is devastatingly attractive. I shall be sitting opposite him at the table and I believe one can learn much of a person's character by observing their facial expressions.'

'So you've given yourself the task of vetting him.'

'Let's just say that my heart won't be ruling my head, which from the glow in your eyes leads me to suspect that yours might. We mustn't forget the shadow hanging over him, Letitia, I'm anxious that you might get hurt.'

'I am willing to take the risk.'

Charlotte smiled. 'And so would I be if I were twenty years younger.'

Later, on going into dinner, Letitia was relieved to see that Charles Bentley was seated at the far end of the table, and it was with a pleasurable flutter that she took her own place beside Sir Justin.

'You do realise that it was in order to see you again that I accepted my host's generous invitation.' Sir Justin's words were low, meant for her alone.

'I rather thought it might be the lure of visiting Parliament.'

'That, too, I confess. But would I have travelled up to London if you hadn't been here? I doubt it.'

Letitia's own voice was low. 'Then I can only say, Sir Justin, that I am very pleased you made the effort.'

'Our acquaintance may only be brief, but do you think we could dispense with the formality. I'd like to call you Letitia, if I may.'

She smiled into his eyes. 'Of course, and I shall call you Justin.' Her pulse was racing at the speed at which the situation seemed to be developing. But then the moment was broken as a bespectacled elderly gentleman on her other side spoke to her, and it wasn't until the first course was served that she was able to return to Justin.

'Welcome back,' he murmured.

'And you.'

'I've been hearing of your not inconsiderable virtues.'

Letitia laughed. 'Grace and I have been friends for years.'

'So I gather. I must say that she and her husband make a fine couple.' She saw his eyes cloud over. 'Letitia, I am not a sentimental man, but I do believe that some people are fortunate enough to find their soulmate.'

'But can that happen only once?' Despite herself, her tone was wistful.

'Damn fine soup this, Grace.' The loud voice resounded around the table.

'Edward's uncle appears to be a man who enjoys his food,' Justin commented, not answering her question.

Angry at the interruption of what could have been a crucial moment, she retorted, 'That is the understatement of the year!'

Justin had to put his napkin to his lips to stifle his laughter.

'You are priceless! But tell me, Letitia, is your home fairly near?'

'Yes indeed, only a short drive away in Hampstead.'

'Is it one where you spent your childhood?'

She nodded. 'If you can call it that. My mother died when I was born, and my father was a disciplinarian. I had every material advantage, but I'm afraid there was little affection.' She turned to look at him. 'I don't know why I'm confiding this to you, it is most unlike me to reveal personal matters.'

His gaze met hers and she could see in his eyes not only sympathy but also a deep concern. 'It distresses me to think of you being unhappy.'

She gave a slight shrug of her shoulders. 'I don't suppose my upbringing was different from many children of my generation. Parents tended to remain distant to their offspring, relying instead on nannies.' She smiled. 'Fortunately, Edward and Grace don't subscribe to that ethic.'

'Then they are rare.'

'And what of your own childhood?' Letitia's voice was quiet.

'Not dissimilar to your own. I, too, grew up without a mother. My father did remarry but his new wife died within twelve months.'

She caught her breath. 'That seems so unfair.'

'That was how he viewed it, or so I imagine. Perhaps that's what made him so bitter, I only know that he was not an easy man to live with.'

She shot a glance at him. Was he about to elaborate? But they were interrupted by the butler hovering to pour wine, and as the evening went on, conversation became more general around the table. Dinner was never uneventful with Charles Bentley present, who was fond of holding forth on any topic that arose. That was, Letitia thought, when he could tear himself away from the plate before him.

'I see what you mean,' Justin muttered.

'He's always the same. I wonder why Grace doesn't have his food served in a trough!'

He began to laugh. 'You are delicious, do you know that?'

Yet again their gaze met and held, and a thrill ran through her at the undisguised warmth in his eyes. She hadn't been mistaken in Canterbury, he too felt the connection between them. He leant back as the butler refilled his glass and she glanced down at his wrist resting on the table, his hand was so close to her own that she felt tempted to inch it closer, to feel the touch of his skin. Letitia could fool herself no longer. Despite their short acquaintance she was falling in love with this man, there was no question of a fleeting infatuation, not at her age and sensibility. I have waited so long for him to come into my life, she thought, I cannot bear to think of outside influences robbing me of my last chance of happiness. And yet there were such high stakes here and it was time the mystery was solved.

'Justin?' He was smiling across at Charlotte and turned to her.

'Letitia?'

'May I ask if you are a churchgoer?'

Startled he said, 'Only when duty demands it, I'm afraid.'

'Then could you possibly come to Eversleigh tomorrow morning? Shall we say eleven o'clock? There is something I would like to discuss with you in private.'

He looked surprised, and then gave an amused smile. 'I know you sympathise with the suffragette movement. Tell me, am I to expect a proposal?'

Her riposte came swift and light. 'It is only the vote we seek, not to emasculate our men.'

He laughed and then his expression became serious. 'You have intrigued me. In fact, wild horses wouldn't keep me away. I feel so mystified that I feel I shall scarcely sleep tonight.'

'Oh, I think if you, later, take more than your usual amount of brandy that should provide the solution.'

He roared with laughter, and across the table Letitia saw Charlotte glance across, raise her eyebrows and smile.

As Justin turned to speak to Grace, Letitia's emotions were in chaos. How could she reconcile the man beside her with the monster that Ella suspected he might be? Edward had earlier murmured to her that he also found it difficult to believe, while Grace said that he'd been delightful with the children. And then, because of the nature of the evening, her musing thoughts were interrupted not only by another course to be served, enjoyed and commented upon, but the necessity of contributing to the general conversation. With every nerve in her body aware of Justin's proximity, Letitia tried not to imagine the dramatic scenes that would be taking place the following morning. And now, to her dismay she was beginning to feel a sense of unease. With the growing rapport and affection between them, was she being disloyal not to warn Justin, to prepare him? But Ella wouldn't wish that and it was not Letitia's decision to make.

Chapter Sixty

Ella was called to the morning room immediately after breakfast and the request made her heart race so much that she could hardly breathe. Most of the night she had been tossing and turning, thinking of the previous evening's dinner party and wondering whether Sir Justin had accepted the invitation to visit Eversleigh. She knew the answer as soon as she entered the room and saw Miss Fairchild's expression.

'He's coming?'

'At eleven o'clock.'

Ella caught her breath. No matter how many times she'd agonised over this moment, she still felt unprepared.

Miss Fairchild too seemed nervous. 'You won't change your mind as to what to wear?'

'Why should I pretend to be something I'm not? I am a servant, due to his neglect.' Her tone was bitter. 'I shall wear my uniform.'

'Ella, please try not to prejudge him. You are sure you want to talk to him alone?'

She nodded. 'Positive. If you could just tell him that there is someone who wants to meet him.'

'I shall do exactly as you wish. And if you need me at any

time, just ring for Mr Forbes. He knows the situation.'

'Are you quite well, Miss Fairchild?' Ella thought that she'd never seen her mistress look so pale.

'I'm afraid I didn't sleep well. And the morning will undoubtedly bring its problems. And how about you, my dear, how are you feeling?'

'Terrified.'

They both laughed, which helped to ease the growing tension.

Then Miss Fairchild frowned. 'Tell me, did Rory have any success in discovering the name of your grandfather's lawyer?'

Ella shook her head. 'I had a letter from him this morning. Although he still thinks they were involved in some way.'

'Why aren't you coming to church, Ella?'

'It wouldn't be wise.'

'How do yer mean, it wouldn't be wise?' Cook was frowning as she bustled to the mirror to adjust her Sunday hat.

Ella whispered, 'I've got the runs.' She returned Cook's searching look with wide-eyed honesty, because that might even happen the way her stomach was churning.

'That's two down then, what with Mr Forbes having a sore throat. Glory, I hope it ain't anything catching.'

Eventually the door closed behind the churchgoers and, as soon as they were alone, Ella glanced at the new footman who was left on duty. 'Harry, I can keep an eye on things, there's nobody expected. Why don't you take the chance to slope off to your room and read that book you've just started?'

His thin face reddened as it always did when she spoke to him. 'Are you sure?'

'Yes, you can owe me a favour some time. Just make sure you're back in the kitchen when they come back.'

'Thanks, Ella.' Within seconds he was gone.

Glancing at the clock, she saw that it was ten minutes to eleven. Sir Justin could be here at any time, and she hurried to the mirror to check on her appearance. When the butler came in she whirled round. 'Mr Forbes, you startled me.'

He glanced around the kitchen. 'The footman?'

'Upstairs, reading his book.'

He gazed at her, his forehead creasing with concern. 'This is a momentous occasion for you Ella. Are you sure you'll be all right?'

She nodded. 'Yes, I think so.'

'I am going up to the hall now and shall remain there.'

'I'll go and fetch everything I need, then come up once he's safely in with Miss Fairchild.'

And it was on the second landing, as she returned from her room carrying the journal, its translation, the long envelope and the sketchbook, that Ella heard the peal of the doorbell.

In the morning room Letitia, who had been tense for most of the morning, rose from the sofa on hearing footsteps cross the hall, and gathered as much dignity as she could muster. Her fingers went up to touch the lace collar on her blouse, the pearl necklace at her throat, and then the door was opened for Sir Justin Hathaway to be announced.

Hardly conscious of Forbes closing the door behind him, her gaze met his own, and he came swiftly forward. 'You look lovelier than ever in daylight.'

'Thank you, and good morning, Justin.' To see him in her home was a heady experience. 'Welcome to Eversleigh'.

He gave a warm smile. 'It is a privilege.'

'Can I offer you some refreshment?'

'Coffee would be pleasant, and if it comes with biscuits, even better.'

She laughed, delighted with his informality, and went to the bell pull. For the next few moments they talked of his impending visit to the House, and of a play they were to see in the company of Edward and Grace. When the butler brought in the refreshments and impassively withdrew, Letitia saw surprise in Justin's eyes. 'My staff always attend morning service,' she said. 'Normally I do too, I feel it is expected of me.'

He reached out to take a biscuit. 'But you made this morning an exception.'

She poured their coffee. 'Yes.'

Taking his cup and saucer from her, Justin said, 'I would like to think that was because of your delight in my company, but last night you mentioned that there was something you wished to discuss in private? I confess that I am still mystified.' His tone was light, but his gaze met and held hers, and she could see in his eyes a wariness.

Letitia was hesitating. 'First of all, Justin, I want you to know that despite what may follow, I would have invited you here anyway.'

His gaze held hers. 'Because?'

'I think you know the answer to that question.' Her voice wasn't quite steady.

He smiled. 'Is this to be a confession of past misdeeds?'

She shook her head. 'There are no skeletons in my cupboard, at least not really.' Knowing that she could delay no longer, Letitia took a deep and unsteady breath. 'Justin, I shall now send for Forbes to remove the tray and afterwards it is my intention to leave the room. Because there is someone waiting to see you and she is insistent that you should be alone. I can't stress how important this is, Justin. I can only tell you that it was not by accident that we met in Canterbury.'

He looked startled and then his eyes narrowed.

Despite herself, her voice began to tremble. 'I don't think you will ever know how hard this is for me, Justin.'

She saw his jaw harden.

'Then for heaven's sake delay no longer and ring for the man.'

Chapter Sixty-One

Waiting in the hall, Ella's tension was becoming unbearable, and then, at last, she saw the butler bring out the tray. As planned, within minutes, Miss Fairchild followed him, closing the door behind her.

Ella exchanged glances with them both, then after taking a deep breath she gave a light tap on the door and entered the morning room.

The wintry sunlight was pouring through the windows as the man seated on the sofa rose to face her. Her gaze fixed on the features she had so often studied in sadness, seeing again the curve of the fine eyebrows, the eyes so similar to her own. She was, without any doubt, standing before her father.

'I'm sorry,' Sir Justin looked puzzled. 'Miss Fairchild said there was someone who wished to meet me, if you have come in to . . .'

She shook her head. 'I am not here as a parlourmaid.'

He frowned. 'I don't understand.'

Ella's throat closed in panic, despite having so often rehearsed what she would say when this moment arrived. She could only stare at him and then somehow the words came out clear and strong.

'My name is Estella Maria Hathaway. I am the daughter of Selina Maria Hathaway, and I believe you, Sir Justin, to be my father.'

The silence that hung heavy in the room was punctuated only by his sharp intake of breath and she saw his eyes widen first with shock and then anger.

'Is this some form of joke?'

Her voice was now tight with the bitterness she had suppressed for years. 'No, it is not a joke.' Ella moved nearer to him so that the light from the window shone full on her face. 'Perhaps you would care to look at me more closely.' She lifted her hands and unpinned her cap so that her hair cascaded to her shoulders. 'I have never seen an image of my mother, but perhaps I resemble her.'

He was now staring at her in growing bewilderment. 'Are you insane?'

Relentless, Ella said, 'And my eyes, are they not like your own?'

He took a step backwards, shaking his head in disbelief. 'You are claiming to be my daughter?'

'I know that I'm your daughter.' Her voice shook. 'I have my mother's journal, plus her marriage lines and my birth certificate to prove it.'

He was now staring at her, his gaze roaming over her features with speculation. Then his glance fell to the envelopes and the sketchbook she was holding. With a peremptory gesture he held out his hand. 'May I?'

Ella passed to him the long envelope and taking out the certificates he began to study them. It was when he read the birth certificate that she saw his expression of disdain deepen. He shook his head, and his tone was one of impatience. 'My wife Selina died at least six months before the date this says you were born. I'm sorry, I have no idea how you came upon the marriage certificate, but the birth certificate has to be a forgery. Whoever has put you up to this has been misinformed.' His gaze travelled over her features again. 'Yes, I admit that in appearance

331

you could be mine and Selina's child, but it is just not possible.'

With an unsteady hand, Ella undid the top buttons of her uniform and unfastening the gold locket, held its chain and passed it over to him. 'Maybe you might recognise this.'

He took the fragile jewellery in his hand and traced the rosebuds around the edge before pressing the tiny catch to look down at the curl of baby hair.

'Where did you get this?' His voice was quiet.

'It was in my personal belongings when Miss Fairchild rescued me from the workhouse. There was also other jewellery, which she is keeping in her safe.'

He looked sharply up. 'Workhouse?'

There was a silence.

'What did you say?' His voice was harsh.

Ella was relentless. 'When I was taken to the workhouse, a servant whispered these words to me. "*Dearie, promise me you will never forget what you saw. Your ma was killed deliberate, them horses were driven straight at her, and someone oughter pay for it.*"'

'You have certainly learnt that off pat. However, I have to inform you that my wife drowned in a storm.'

'I don't know who told you that, Sir Justin, but it was a lie.'

He stiffened, then demanded, 'You mentioned a sketchbook.'

She handed it to him. 'If you would look at pages one and two?'

The look on her father's face as he gazed down at the undoubted sketch of himself caused a rush of emotion in Ella. She had never seen anyone look so stricken. 'I remember . . .' Slowly he turned to the following page.

'Is that of Riverside Hall?'

He nodded, and in a low voice said, 'Selina must have copied it from a rough sketch of mine. She only saw the house once and that was from a distance.'

He said sharply, 'Who gave you this?'

'The same maid who safeguarded my personal possessions.' Ella said quietly, 'Please look at the next page.'

It was on seeing the sketch of the baby that he was visibly shaken, and Ella had to force herself to remember that this anguished man could have been responsible for her mother's heartbreak and eventual death.

She put both the journal and the translation on a small table. Her voice taut she said, 'These are my mother's own words written in French. Miss Fairchild kindly translated for me. I think, Sir Justin, that you will need to be alone when you read them.'

Still turning the pages of the sketchbook, at first he didn't reply. Then he glanced at the table and on seeing the leather journal with its silver clasp, his hand stilled. Ella gazed at him for one long moment before leaving in silence.

In the drawing room, after Ella had told her what had transpired, Letitia forced herself to wait at least forty-five minutes before she went into the hall to take a glass of brandy from the tray Forbes offered.

She opened the door to see that Justin was standing before the tall window, one hand holding the translation of the journal. Slowly, Letitia walked over to him and gently touched his arm. He turned, and seeing the brandy, silently took it.

She said quietly, 'I'm so very sorry, Justin.'

'So am I.' His voice was harsh.

Was he feeling betrayed that she had tricked him into coming to Eversleigh?

He drained the brandy and at last looked at her, his eyes so despairing that it took all of her control not to fold him in her arms. 'I didn't know. Believe me, I didn't know. Thank God that

Selina fled to her father's friend in London, and he and his wife cared for her when she had the baby. I still can't believe that Ella is actually mine.'

'I think the evidence is indisputable.'

'Letitia, I can't thank you enough. She would never have found me without your help.'

'And you forgive me for enticing you here to Eversleigh?' Her voice was soft.

'Of course I do. She's beautiful, I still can't believe she's mine.'

'She thought you were dead until that evening in Canterbury. When you came into the hall, she was waiting on the landing above expecting to see her grandfather.'

His expression hardened. 'I wish to God he was still alive. He and I have an account to settle.'

'Justin, I think Ella has more questions, ones that you will find painful.'

'Then, my love, I shall need another brandy. Because what I have to tell her will not, I fear, reflect well on me.' He buried his head in his hands, his voice strangled. 'I shall never forgive myself! How could I have been such a trusting fool?'

Chapter Sixty-Two

Rory was finding it impossible to concentrate on anything, even during the eleven o'clock Mass. He felt restless, anxious for fresh air, which always enabled him to think clearly. And as he emerged from the church doors and began to walk briskly away, it didn't take long for him to come to a decision. Ella was not only the most precious person in his life, he was the only one who truly loved her. How could he let her face such a difficult and momentous happening in her life without offering his support?

It was as he strode along the pavement towards Eversleigh's gates that he saw a group of people ahead, walking slowly in twos and threes. Rory raised his hat as he passed by them, recognising the angelic face of the scullery maid. And then a plump woman in a plain brown hat called out, 'Good morning, Mr Adare.'

'Good morning.'

'If you're hoping to see Ella, I'm afraid she isn't well.'

He paused, then guessed it would have been a ruse to remain behind alone. 'It's Cook, isn't it?' She nodded. 'I'm sorry to hear that.'

He continued to walk, passing the gates as if his destination was different, only to double back after a few moments. As he had thought, there was now no sign of the staff, and he hesitated only for a second before going up the drive directly to the front door. He was neither a servant here nor a tradesman. His ring was answered instantly, and the tall balding man who stood there was undoubtedly the butler.

'Good morning, you must be Mr Forbes.'

He inclined his head.

'My name is Rory Adare, I'm a close friend of Miss Ella Hathaway. I'm sorry to call uninvited, but I know you are in her confidence and I wondered whether it would be possible for me to remain quietly in the background. Just in case she has need of me.'

After a searching glance, the butler's expression relaxed. 'Yes, of course.' He stepped aside for Rory to enter and took his hat. 'Perhaps if you would wait in the study?' He led the way along the hall and ushered him inside. 'I shall let Miss Fairchild know of your presence.'

'Thank you.' Rory couldn't help admiring the book-lined room with its comfortable leather armchairs, but he was still restless, his nerves on edge. Suppose Ella's father could not explain his actions, suppose he really had been involved in her mother's death. How on earth would she cope with such terrible knowledge?

It was when Letitia returned from the morning room that the butler said, 'Mr Adare is here and I have put him in the study, madam. He thought Ella might be in need of him.'

'I see. Thank you, Forbes.' Letitia stood for a moment in uncertainty, then made her way to the drawing room where Ella sprang from the sofa as she came in.

'Has he read it?'

Letitia nodded. 'He has, and, Ella, he's devastated. I truly don't believe he had any idea you existed.'

'He accused me of lying.' Her eyes were wet with tears.

'Selina's journal has changed everything.'

'I hate to say it, but I liked him.' Ella's eyes were despairing. 'How can I, when I suspect him of being guilty of such evil things?'

Letitia spoke slowly. 'I set much store by instinct, and I cannot believe that he is. However, Sir Justin is now prepared to answer all your questions.'

'Then shall we get it over with, Miss Fairchild?'

'I must first tell you that Rory is here. He thought you might have need of him.'

Ella's face lit up. 'Could he be present?'

'You mean when we return to the morning room?'

Ella nodded. 'He gives me confidence.' She added in a quiet voice, 'I feel scared. I mean, what will I do if my father can't explain? I shall owe it to my mother to go to the police.'

Letitia looked at the anxious, vulnerable girl before her and knew that she had no right to deny her request. She nodded. 'He's in the study. If you would bring him in to meet me first?'

Ella went to the door as if she had wings on her feet, and she brought in a tall, dark-haired young man with a serious expression on his face. Letitia remembered that he, too, had been in the workhouse, although his manner towards her was by no means subservient.

'I'm delighted to meet you at last, Miss Fairchild.' He held out his hand.

Letitia took it, noting the firm handshake, and smiled warmly at him. 'Ella has spoken much of you.'

'So is it all right for Rory to join us?' Ella's voice was tense.

'If you feel it will help.' Letitia was hoping with desperation that Justin wouldn't object. After all, the subject under discussion was intensely personal.

337

But in the morning room, Justin was immersed yet again in the translation of the journal and looked up with a face etched with sadness. His gaze went first to Ella, only to frown when he saw Rory. He rose. 'I don't believe . . .'

Rory stepped forward. 'I apologise for the intrusion, Sir Justin. My name is Rory Adare and I am here at Ella's invitation.'

Letitia said swiftly, 'Shall we all take a seat?' She left the sofa vacant for the young couple and went to sit opposite Justin. For a moment nobody spoke, and then Justin looked across at Ella. 'I'm sorry for the way I behaved earlier.' His smile was strained. 'I can only say that I wish I'd known of your existence years ago.'

Ella looked at him with sadness. 'I wish I had known of yours, maybe then I wouldn't have ended up in a workhouse.'

'My dear, I cannot bear to think of it.'

She hardened her heart. She owed it to her mother to find out the absolute truth. 'Then, Sir Justin, perhaps you could bear to give me an explanation?' Ella's gaze searched her father's eyes, which were so much like her own, and could see a man whose soul was in torment.

He said, 'Ella, I can only tell you that your mother and I were the happiest couple alive. No man loved a woman more. But as you know from Selina's journal, my father could never reconcile the fact that I chose, as my wife, the daughter of a clergyman. He even refused to meet her. When he told me that she'd drowned, weakened as I was after pneumonia and pleurisy, at times I even wished to follow her to the grave. I was very ill for several weeks and afterwards my father sent me to Madeira for six months to convalesce.' His lips twisted. 'I can see now that his motive wasn't entirely altruistic.'

There was silence in the room, and Ella's gaze never left him as he tried to compose himself. 'I'm sorry, it is a bitter blow to discover my father could be so cruel. He was always manipulative, but after that fall from his horse when he received a severe blow to his head, he developed dark and unpredictable moods. There was no reasoning with him at times. But never could I have imagined him capable of deceiving his own son, of writing those terrible letters to Selina.' His face was pale and drawn.

'But he was capable of far more, Sir Justin. I believe him to be behind my mother's murder.'

Sir Justin's lips tightened. 'Could you elaborate on exactly how my poor Selina did die.'

He listened as Ella related all she knew, his gaze never wavering from hers, and she saw both shock and despair in his eyes.

'The coachman couldn't have been Burton, he was a gentle soul, a family man too. He only retired a couple of years ago. My father must have hired someone, and also a carriage, because the Hathaway carriage was black and always drawn by matching greys.' He looked angrily bewildered. 'I'm finding it difficult to believe such monstrous evil. The description of the man with the sandy moustache resembles a man called Norman Morrison. A friend of my father's who I always disliked, he was often a guest at Riverside Hall and I do know that he had considerable gambling debts.' His voice was full of contempt. 'I would imagine he could well put personal gain before honour.'

'Is he still alive?'

He shook his head. 'Unfortunately not, otherwise I would have ensured that he was brought to justice for his perjury.'

There was a silence. Ella almost hated the way she was interrogating the man before her, who was looking unutterably weary. If he really was as innocent as he claimed, this must be one of the worst days of his life. But there were still questions she needed to ask.

'Did you never go back to the home you shared with my mother, to find out exactly where she died?'

'Yes, I did, but it was only after I returned to England. By which time other tenants were in the house.'

'But her clothes, your possessions?'

'All given to the poor, according to my father, to protect me from painful memories as he'd been concerned as to my state of mind. Lies!' He smote one hand against the other. 'Nothing but a parcel of lies.'

'Wasn't there a housekeeper or servant who would have known the truth, seen my mother pack and leave?'

He looked at Ella. 'It was not a large house and we had no live-in servants, wanting privacy and a simpler life. Two sisters came in to clean and cook, but I was told they'd left some time ago for America.'

'Your father probably paid their passage.' Ella said in a tight voice.

'I'm beginning to think he was capable of anything. In the village, people said they had heard about the accident, and I had no reason to doubt them. But as we all know, it is easy to start a rumour. The house was situated by a river and Selina loved to walk along its banks, sketching the wildlife. At the time I rode to Riverside Hall there were widespread heavy storms, which was when I got soaked through and, afterwards, ill. I was told that the little bridge she used to walk over had been swept away in the floods. That part, at least, was true, because I saw its replacement. I was also told that her body was never found.' His lips twisted with pain. 'All I could do was to place a memorial stone in the churchyard where her parents are buried.'

The room fell silent.

It was Letitia who spoke first. 'Justin, is Grace expecting you back for luncheon?'

He shook his head. 'Not necessarily.'

She smiled at him. 'Excellent, because Forbes is arranging an early one. I thought that might be welcome. If there are further questions, perhaps they could wait until later. He will serve us himself, and I will ask him to set an extra place for Rory.' She turned to Ella. 'Perhaps, my dear, you would care to change from your uniform.'

'I would like to think that she will never wear it again, nor work as a servant!'

Sir Justin's voice was harsh.

For the first time, Rory joined the conversation. 'While I agree with your sentiment, Sir Justin, I think Ella will make up her own mind about that, at least in the short term.' Ella flashed him a grateful glance. She hadn't battled through life on her own for all these years, only at the age of eighteen to give up her independence.

Upstairs in the attic, even as she removed her uniform and slipped on a burgundy skirt and white high-necked blouse, Ella's mind was feverish, going over and over Sir Justin's explanations. To realise that he was not the evil person she had imagined, to know that she felt drawn to him, was a dream come true. Because his horror on discovering that his father had lied about Selina's death couldn't have been faked. Hadn't she seen for herself the despair and sorrow in his eyes?

And, now he had acknowledged her as his daughter, nobody could ever again accuse her of being a bastard.

And then, she began to hurry, to tidy her hair and to lift the gold locket and chain to hang outside her blouse, wondering what they were thinking downstairs about only Mr Forbes serving in the dining room. When they discovered she wasn't in her room, they'd assume she'd gone for a walk in the fresh air. Never would they dream that in the room where she waited on the gentry, their parlourmaid would be seated as a guest.

Rory, having accepted a glass of sherry from the butler, was beginning to feel ashamed of his previous suspicions now that he'd had the chance to meet Miss Fairchild. As for Sir Justin, normally Rory had little time for the aristocracy, but he found himself instinctively liking him. And there was no doubt that he was overwhelmed to find he had a daughter, which meant that Ella would no longer feel an isolated orphan. It also seemed certain that her father was innocent concerning Selina's death. However, her grandfather was a different matter. That man had no scruples; not even a blow on his head could excuse his dreadful actions. Rory intended to discuss his theory regarding the lawyer with Sir Justin, as he still believed that he had been involved in the conspiracy. Hopefully, he, at least, would still be alive. As he sipped his drink, Rory thought what a handsome couple Sir Justin and Miss Fairchild made, he in a silver grey jacket with velvet lapels, Miss Fairchild wearing an ivory blouse with leg-of-mutton sleeves and an elegant green skirt. At that moment, she looked up at the tall man beside her and there was no mistaking the way their gazes lingered on each other. Rory could only once more wonder at the power of fate, but then he had seen its impact on historical events too often not to recognise its existence.

Chapter Sixty-Three

Luncheon was not a comfortable affair. Despite making an effort, Justin was understandably rather withdrawn, and it was left to Letitia to keep the flow of conversation, conversing mainly with Ella and Rory. She found herself drawn to the young Irishman, and when she saw Justin's gaze often rest on Ella, thought how sad it was that father and daughter had been unaware of each other's existence for so many years.

Letitia was beginning to feel uncertain, even anxious, knowing that Justin's mind must be full of memories of his beloved Selina, but towards the end of the meal he seemed to come out of his reverie, and her heart sang when he looked across at her with a warm smile.

It was not until later, when Ella and Rory left to go for a walk on the Heath, that Letitia and Justin at last had the chance to spend some time alone. And once in the drawing room and seated beside each other on the sofa before the cosy crackle from the log fire, he said, 'Is Forbes likely to come in?'

She shook her head. 'Not now. He would have no reason to.'

'In that case,' he turned and they gazed at each other for a long moment, and then slowly he leant towards her and Letitia raised her lips to meet his firm warm ones. Their kiss was tentative, gentle and when they drew apart Justin said, 'Am I rushing things, Letitia? It's just that I've waited so long to meet you.'

'I know exactly what you mean.' Her voice was soft and he kissed her again, this time more searching, intimate and she felt as if she wanted to melt into his very bones. He lifted his head and tenderly touched her mouth.

'What can I say? I'd thought that we would spend more time discussing Ella, but I think you have bewitched me.'

Letitia was smiling at him in a way she had never smiled at anyone. Couldn't he see how happy she was, how much in love?

He turned to her, his gaze keen. 'Letitia, we have reached this stage almost too swiftly, are you sure of your feelings?'

Her voice was soft. 'Are you sure of yours for me? This has been an emotional day, after all.'

'I am absolutely sure. Since I lost Selina I had given up hope of anyone touching my heart in the way that you have. You're so lovely, so intelligent, Letitia, I can't understand how you've remained single for so long.'

She fell silent, knowing that she should tell him about Miles. What if it changed his feelings towards her? But, if they were to have a future together, then there had to be honesty between them.

'Letitia?'

Her gaze met and held his. 'Naturally, I had suitors, Justin. But there was only one I thought I loved.' Haltingly she related the sorry tale. 'I was heartbroken,' she said. He listened in silence as she told him how two years after her father's death, Miles had returned and come to see her. 'That last night when he came to Eversleigh, my father told him that no court in the land would ever marry us.'

Justin frowned. 'I don't understand.'

Letitia was finding the words difficult to say. 'I was not my father's only child, Justin. Miles discovered that he was his illegitimate son, which made us half-brother and sister.' She saw his shock and swallowed hard. 'There was nothing physical between us other than a few kisses. But, when I found out, the shame of it nearly destroyed me.'

'But it wasn't your fault.' He drew her against him again and resting her head on his shoulder, she whispered, 'No, but I did have feelings for him which were terribly wrong.'

'Where is Miles now?'

Letitia told him about Katharine and her little namesake. 'I have these "imaginary" friends in Ireland, and visit at least twice a year. Not even Grace and Charlotte know the truth.'

Justin lifted her chin and kissed her gently. 'You are a good person, Letitia. Never doubt that. You were young, probably more in love with the idea of being in love than anything else.'

'And it doesn't make any difference? To us, I mean?'

He shook his head. 'Of course not. Ever since I first saw and talked to you in Canterbury, I've been unable to get you out of my mind. Why else do you think that I came to London, if not to see you again?'

She smiled up at him. 'I was hoping that was the reason, because Canterbury was the same for me.'

'That makes me feel more happy than you can imagine.'

They were then quiet, each with their own thoughts, until Justin said, 'I have to confess, Letitia, that I've sought little company these past years, although one has occasionally to accept social engagements. But that didn't mean that I wasn't at times lonely, missing having someone to share my life with. Once you've known true love, you don't want to accept second-best, which it would always have been, until now.' He turned and smiled into her eyes. 'It's early days, I know, but I do feel that we are meant to spend the rest of our lives together.'

Her gaze met his and she could see in his eyes both determination and a question. Her heart gave a leap and then Letitia tried to be sensible. 'I think we would cause a scandal if we made such a decision so soon. Besides,' she began to tease him, 'how do you know that I don't have all sorts of awful habits you couldn't live with?'

He laughed and drew her into his arms again, whispering, 'I was told by my nanny that I was a very obstinate little boy.'

'Hopefully, you will have grown out of it,' Letitia murmured, and then Justin was claiming her lips again in a delicious interlude.

'Do you really care what people think?' She was still within his arms, and seeing the plea in his eyes, Letitia relented, and shook her head.

'Neither do I.' Withdrawing from her, and rising from the sofa Justin knelt on one knee before her. His expression solemn he said, 'Miss Fairchild, I fear I cannot live without you, please would you do me the honour of becoming my wife?'

'Then, in order to save your life, Sir Justin, I would be delighted to marry you.'

He rejoined her again on the sofa and taking her left hand looked down at her third finger. 'I must buy you a ring. Shall we go together so you can help to choose?'

She smiled at him. 'Yes, please. But Justin . . .'

'Yes, my darling?' He was stroking her hair, and she cared not a jot that he was disturbing its arrangement.

'Can we not announce our engagement until the end of the week? It would seem sort of . . .'

'A little less mad?'

She laughed. 'Something like that.'

'And can I make a request of you?'

'Anything.' She leant forward to kiss him.

'Please say we don't need to wait a long time before the wedding.'

'If we did, I think you would need to make a respectable woman of me.'

He threw back his head and laughed. 'Do you know how you delight me with your honesty?'

Afterwards they talked of his discovering Ella, or as Justin said, his daughter discovering him, and then, as lovers do, of their lives before they met. When the grandfather clock in the hall struck four, Letitia said, 'It will be growing dark on the Heath, so they should be back soon.'

'It's really rough out there, do you think she'll be all right?'

She smiled at him. 'Justin, she's managed for eighteen years without harm coming to her, and she isn't alone.'

He frowned. 'This Rory, what do you know about him?'

Letitia related what Professor Dalton had said. 'You've met him, Justin, so you'll understand why I respect his opinion.'

'But shouldn't she be given the chance to meet other more eligible young men?'

'Justin,' she said softly. 'Ella will never be able to ignore her past, or the fact that she spent six hard years in a workhouse. Rory understands all that, has suffered too, in his own way. Don't you think that augurs well for their future? Ella could marry someone wealthier, yes, but what if one day her past came between them? People can be such terrible snobs.'

His expression became one of sadness. 'And I, more than most, should understand that. I have to admit that I like the young man and that was a very good point he raised during luncheon, about the lawyer. I intend to follow it up.' His jaw tightened. 'I can promise you one thing, if there is anyone left alive who was involved in Selina's death they will be tracked down and dealt with. And I also intend to discover where she was buried. However, as regards the situation between these two young people, I shall have to give it some thought.'

Chapter Sixty-Four

Up on the Heath, Ella and Rory were battling against an oncoming wind. His shoulders hunched, one hand tightly holding Ella's, Rory shouted. 'Are you sure you still want to be up here?'

'It's so wild and free, can't you feel it?' She glanced at him, her eyes full of mischief. 'Rory Adare, if you don't kiss me again and soon, I shall die of neglect.'

His answer was to twist round and, holding her tightly against the wind, kissed her so hard that she gasped. 'I'll die if I can't breathe too.'

'Don't you dare! You and I, Ella Hathaway, are going to have a long and blissful life together.' He took her hand and, bent against the increasing wind, they began to hurry back. As they went through the gates to Eversleigh, Ella thought back to that first time when, as an ignorant child, she had approached the front door. She was tempted to do so now, but conscious that she was still the parlourmaid, pulled on Rory's hand to guide him to the back of the house.

He resisted. 'Hey, we came out through the front door!'

'Maybe, but I'm still a servant here, remember.' In truth, Ella wanted Rory beside her when she braved the kitchen staff. She could well imagine the gossiping that would have taken place because, although only Mr Forbes had served in the dining room, it would have been the other parlourmaids and a footman who cleared away. And the fact that there were four places set, with no advance information of guests, would have caused a lot of speculation. They'll never have guessed, she thought with some hilarity, not only that a titled gentleman was one who happened to be my father, but that Rory and I were the other guests. Ella opened the green back door with Rory following.

'Well, and where have you been young lady?' was Cook's greeting as they entered the kitchen. 'I thought you were ill.' She glanced at Rory. 'Oh, you met up with her, then?'

'I did indeed, Mrs Perkins.' He gave her his warmest smile.

'Well, there's been all sorts of goings-on upstairs. Mystery guests, that's what, and Mr Forbes not saying a word.'

Ella didn't reply, instead she took off her coat and, taking Rory's, hung them on a peg in the corridor before coming back in and saying, 'We're dying for a cup of tea.' She lifted the heavy kettle, filled it and was putting it on the hob when, on seeing Lizzie sidle up to smile at Rory, she snapped, 'You can stick your tongue back in, madam, he's spoken for!'

Lizzie flounced away. 'As soon as you open your gob people will know you're a workhouse brat. No matter what happens, you'll never be any different.'

Ella was furious with herself. It was ages since she'd reverted to such expressions, but Lizzie had always got under her skin.

But Rory didn't let it go. 'Lizzie, is it? As I'm also a workhouse brat, do you consider my future is ruined too?'

The girl's face flooded red. She turned her head away just as the butler came into the kitchen.

'Here she is, after all, Mr Forbes,' Cook said. 'Gone out to meet her young man. Look at her, all dressed up.'

He didn't comment, instead, looking at Ella, he said, 'The mistress would like to see you both in the drawing room.'

Ella switched off the gas beneath the kettle.

'Sounds like you're in trouble, young lady,' Cook said with triumph.

'Serves her right!' Lizzie muttered, causing her sister Harriet to glare at her. Ignoring her, after tidying her hair, Ella went with Rory up the backstairs to the black and white tiled hall. 'Go on,' she whispered, turning to Rory. 'Kiss me up here, I dare you!'

'You're brazen,' he whispered back. She'd only meant a brief peck, but somehow it developed into something else entirely, and it was only on hearing a cough that they drew apart.

Ella muttered, 'Sorry, Mr Forbes.' With a disapproving expression he opened the door to the drawing room.

Miss Fairchild and Sir Justin were standing before the long window and turned towards them when they came in.

'Did you enjoy your walk?' Sir Justin said.

Ella's gaze had gone immediately to her new-found father. He was, she suddenly realised, a very handsome man, it was no wonder that Selina had fallen in love with him. And then an astonishing thought swept over her as she noticed how closely he and Miss Fairchild were standing together and she almost stammered, 'Thank you, we did, although it was blowing a bit of a gale.'

'Come and sit down, both of you,' Miss Fairchild said. 'I'll ring for some tea, you must be chilled.' She rose and went to the bell pull, but must have seen Ella's alarm because she added, 'Don't worry, Forbes will look after us himself. But after today, my dear, Sir Justin and I really do think we'll need to discuss your changed circumstances.'

* * *

It was two days later that Miss Fairchild sent for Ella, who had spent the last few minutes yet again fending off questions about the frequent visits of Sir Justin.

'Come in, my dear, do take a seat.'

Ella went to sit opposite her and waited.

Miss Fairchild smiled. 'I wanted to talk to you about the dinner party on Friday. Sir Justin will be a guest and he has specifically requested that you and Rory are invited.'

Ella was startled. She may have joined the mistress for luncheon that day, but a formal dinner party was a far different proposition.

'I know you normally wait on us, but Forbes tells me that he can make alternative arrangements. I have already sent a written invitation to Rory. And I've been most careful in my choice of guests, Ella, so you have no need to worry.'

Ella, her mind in a whirl about all the implications, could only say, 'Thank you, Miss Fairchild.'

'I understand that you haven't yet revealed your relationship with Sir Justin to the other staff.'

'I wasn't sure what to do, I knew how awkward it would make things.' And she still felt troubled about it, unsure what was going to happen in the future. Her mind was forever going over possibilities, and the last thing she wanted at the moment was to lose her sense of security downstairs.

Miss Fairchild was smiling at her. 'Would you be happy to carry on as normal until Friday morning, when perhaps you could announce your news? Then your presence at dinner that evening won't seem at all strange.'

Ella nodded. 'Yes, I can see that.'

'Afterwards, I shall tell Forbes that I wish you to accompany me to London, as you will obviously need something new to wear.' She must have seen Ella's worried expression. 'Don't worry, Sir Justin has opened an account in your name at one of the top stores.'

Ella stared at her. 'You mean . . .'

'That if you find something you like, then, my dear, you will merely need to charge it.'

Shopping for clothes at a top store in London? To Ella it felt like she was entering a fairy tale, and it was almost in a daze that, a few minutes later, she left the drawing room to return to her own world downstairs.

On Friday morning, Cook was the first to speak. 'Well, I'll go to the foot of our stairs! Was this Sir Justin that mysterious guest last Sunday?'

'I'm afraid so.'

Lizzie was cutting. 'You'll have a more swelled head than ever.'

'Does that mean you're a princess?' Myrtle's voice was shy.

One of the footmen nudged the other and said, 'Cor, to think we've been working with a toff's daughter.'

'I'm still the same Ella.' Her cheeks were hot with embarrassment.

'Well, I'm glad for you.' Harriet came forward and gave her a hug. 'A proper Cinderella story, that's what it is.'

'Yes.' Cook's voice was emphatic. 'I'm pleased for you an' all. When I remember the scrawny kid who came from the workhouse, against my better judgement I might add, I'm glad you've had some good luck. You were always a good worker, Ella, I shall be sorry to see you go.'

'Is Ella leaving?' Myrtle's eyes filled with tears.

Ella went to hug her. 'I don't know what will happen yet. Let's wait and see.'

One of the two young footmen demanded, 'How come you grew up in a workhouse, then?'

Ella hesitated. 'It's complicated, but I would never have been sent there when my mother died if Sir Justin had known about me.'

'Why didn't he?' This time it was Cook asking the question and the butler intervened. 'There will be plenty of time for explanations another time. You need to get ready to accompany the mistress, Ella.'

'Yes, Mr Forbes, I'll go and change.' As, with some relief, she left the kitchen she heard him saying, 'I need to talk to you all about this evening's arrangements.'

Chapter Sixty-Five

On Friday evening, Rory, wearing evening clothes he had bought in Boston, was shown by the butler to the drawing room to be greeted by Miss Fairchild and Sir Justin.

'Ella will be joining us any time now.' Miss Fairchild smiled at him. 'She and I have had a most successful visit to London as her father wished me to help her choose a new gown. Ah, here she is.'

Ella came hesitantly into the room, and Rory caught his breath. Her slender neck was revealed by an upswept hairstyle, while the pale-green silk dress outlined her figure and its embellished lace revealed her shapely shoulders. Was this vision his urchin who ran like the wind on the Heath?

'Ella, you look absolutely beautiful.'

She smiled at him. 'I'm wearing my mother's pearls and earrings.'

'I remember so well buying them for Selina, as I do the other items of jewellery,' Sir Justin said. 'She would be proud that you are wearing them, Ella.'

Her voice was quiet. 'They mean a lot to me.'

Miss Fairchild said, 'More guests will shortly be arriving, but we wished to have a little time alone with you both.'

She turned to Sir Justin, her smile radiant, and he said, 'We have some news and we wanted Ella to be the first to know.' He paused. 'Miss Fairchild and I are engaged to be married.'

There was an astonished silence and then Rory went to shake Sir Justin's hand. 'Sir, may I offer you my sincere congratulations, and also to you, Miss Fairchild.' He turned to Ella who seemed stunned. 'Ella?'

'My congratulations too, I think it's wonderful news.' She made a hesitant move towards her father and, with some shyness, kissed him on the cheek.

Miss Fairchild said, 'I shall be so happy to have you as a stepdaughter, Ella.'

Startled, Ella realised that would be true and on impulse went to hug her. 'I'm so thrilled,' she whispered.

'We know it seems rushed,' Sir Justin said. 'But we have both waited a long time for happiness. And we are very certain of our feelings.'

'And before we announce it to anyone else, I must inform Forbes.' Miss Fairchild went over to the silken bell pull, and when he came in, the engaged couple went over to talk to him.

'It's all happened so quickly,' Ella whispered. 'It almost seems as if it was meant to be. My coming here, I mean. Otherwise they would never have met.'

Rory said in a low voice, 'I'm hoping they have a son.'

'Why?'

'Because then you won't be an heiress, and I won't be thought a fortune-hunter. Of course, the estate could be entailed anyway.'

'What does that mean?'

He smiled at her. 'Look it up in your dictionary.'

She smiled up at him. 'You look so handsome dressed like that.'

Miss Fairchild came back to them. 'I've told Forbes to make the announcement downstairs and to later serve the staff a glass of champagne.' Ella could just imagine their surprise and shock. She was almost dizzy herself at the news, still hardly able to believe that one day soon the mistress would be her stepmother. And it was only then that she realised that she could never be part of the 'downstairs' world again. That part of her life was now in the past, and she felt only a fleeting regret to be replaced by a flutter of excitement. She glanced at Sir Justin, wondering whether he would like her to call him Papa. And then a thought struck her and her gaze drifted to Miss Fairchild. Whatever would she call her after the wedding?

It was after the last guest had left that Rory went over to Sir Justin and, in a low voice, said, 'Might I have a private word, sir?'

'But of course.' He turned to Letitia and Ella. 'Please excuse us, perhaps we could take advantage of the study?'

The two men each chose one of the leather armchairs so that they faced each other. Sir Justin waited.

Rory tried to conquer his feeling of nerves, but knew that it was a question he needed to ask. 'Sir Justin, in these new circumstances, when you and Ella have found each other, I can't help wondering . . .'

'What my feelings are regarding Ella and yourself?'

Relieved at his perception, Rory nodded.

Sir Justin leant forward. 'I can see that you and Ella are extremely close, Rory, and believe me I am grateful for all the encouragement you've given her. She has even shown me the dictionary you bought her at a time when you were financially insecure.' He hesitated before adding, 'And I do like you.'

There was a short silence and Rory felt a cold knot of apprehension.

'However,' Sir Justin's gaze was steady. 'I am very conscious of her youth. Ella has little experience of the world, and I am sure you will understand when I say that I have both the means and every intention of showing it to her. Also, I wonder whether you have fully realised that as my daughter, she will need to take her rightful place in a cultured society.'

'Sir Justin, I can assure you that Ella's happiness means everything to me.'

'And I believe you. But as I have said, I feel strongly that, as befits her birthright, Ella should be given the chance to travel, to mix with her own class.'

'And you think that I would hold her back?' Rory was struggling to remain calm while fighting rising panic, knowing that as Ella was under age, her father had the authority to forbid their relationship. Was this what he was leading up to? 'We love each other, surely you aren't suggesting that we should part?'

'It would take a cruel father to insist on that. And, after my own experience, you can imagine that is the last thing I would do. But might I ask, Rory, that you consider exercising patience? To consider a total separation? I'm not suggesting forever. Perhaps a year? Just so that you give her the chance to spread her wings. She has, after all, so far led a very sheltered life.'

Rory was appalled. A whole year without his lovely girl? Not to be able to see her, to hold her in his arms, or even to write to her? 'Have you mentioned this to Ella?'

He shook his head. 'I would ask you to discuss it with her. And I'm sure that, at first, she will oppose it. Ella is a strong-minded young lady, her character forged, I'm afraid, by my culpable neglect. I shall never forgive myself for the hardship she's suffered. However, I am afraid that entering society will not be easy for her, and I hardly think that you would want her to be at a disadvantage.' He smiled and rose as there came the sound of the clock striking the hour. 'I can see that this has come as a shock to you, Rory, but do remember that it is her entire future that is at stake.' He held out his hand, and took Rory's in a firm clasp. 'I am confident that you will do the right thing.'

Afterwards, Rory was never sure how he managed to remain in control of his feelings when they both returned to the drawing room. He did remember that, soon afterwards, Letitia pulled the bell cord to summon Forbes, which enabled him to leave swiftly, to ignore Ella's bewildered gaze. And, declining the use of the carriage, Rory walked back to number 35, hardly noticing the icy wind that had arisen. Never had he imagined that the evening would end this way; his hope had been that Ella's father, knowing that his daughter was so much in love, would have given them both his blessing. But then, he thought with bitterness, nothing actually changes. He recalled his perceptive and intelligent father, his gentle mother, and knew that even with their considerable attributes, the English aristocracy would have looked down on them. And, despite their good manners and friendliness, it would seem that Sir Justin and Miss Fairchild were no different in their outlook. Rory wasn't considered good enough and, proud of what he had achieved, he felt totally humiliated.

But by the time morning arrived, after a restless night tossing and turning, with reluctance Rory had to accept that in one respect, Sir Justin was right. Unless Ella learnt about art, sculpture, theatre and music, how would she be able to converse with people to whom such things were part of their lives. No, he was perfectly happy, eager even, for Ella to travel and experience these things. It was the prospect of being parted from her that lay like a black cloud over him.

Ella was impatient to see Rory again. It had been obvious when he'd returned to the drawing room with her father, that something had happened between them. So, when a couple of days later they met on the Heath, after a warm hug, she was swift to confront him. 'What was it you wanted to talk to Sir Justin about the other night? You looked so serious when you came back.'

Rory hesitated. 'I needed to know how he felt about me, with regard to you, I mean.'

She linked her arm in his as they began to walk along. 'He likes you and so does Miss Fairchild.'

'Liking isn't enough, though, is it? I have nothing to offer you, Ella, you must realise that.'

She gazed up at him. 'You have good references and will soon get another position after you leave Professor Dalton.'

'Ella, you have got to think of the different life you'll be living from now on. You would like to visit other countries, to see famous art galleries and cultural sites, wouldn't you?'

She nodded, enthralled at the prospect. 'Is that what he's suggesting?'

'He's insisting upon it.'

But Ella's excitement was tempered by a sudden thought. 'How long would I be away for?'

'I suppose the time would vary.'

'That would mean being away from you.'

Rory didn't answer, and she glanced sharply at him. 'There's something else, isn't there?'

She listened in growing disbelief and fury as Rory told her of his conversation with Sir Justin. 'How dare he try to separate us?' she burst out. 'He has no right to suddenly come into my life and tell me what to do!'

'The problem is, sweetheart, that, as your father, he has. Until you come of age, anyway.'

'You didn't agree?' Ella felt horrified.

'I was too stunned to say much at all.' She saw his jaw tighten. 'And so angry I hardly slept.' Rory paused. 'But I've thought long and deep about this, Ella. There's another aspect to it. Have you never thought that you've had little chance to meet any other young men?'

'Why would I want to?' She was devastated he could even think such a thing. 'Well, I'm going to refuse. I'm not being parted from you for a whole year and that's final.'

'I know exactly how you feel, but once you've had time to think about it, you'll realise that we don't have any alternative. It would be selfish of me to try and persuade you otherwise.'

She gazed up at him in anguish. 'Surely you can't think we should do it?' Her eyes were brimming with tears. 'Won't you mind being parted from me?'

He drew her to him. 'I hate even the thought of it.' His mouth claimed hers as if he would never let her go. 'Don't you know how much I love you?'

'And I love you. Haven't you said that we're soulmates? And we couldn't even write to each other?'

'A complete separation, your father said.'

Ella's tears spilt down her cheeks. 'But I need you, I can't not see you for a whole year.'

Rory held her close. 'Haven't you proved how strong you can be? Ella from the workhouse can do it, even if you doubt Miss Estella Hathaway.'

Chapter Sixty-Six

Letitia was finding herself in somewhat of a quandary. And, as she had so often in the past, she turned for advice to Mary Blane, who had both met and approved of Sir Justin. 'I simply don't know what to do for the best.'

'About Ella?' Mary's voice was calm as she brushed out Letitia's hair.

'I'd love her to be a bridesmaid, but can you imagine the shocked whispering in the congregation? Even as a guest she will be the subject of gossip.'

'You mean because people know that she was a servant here?'

Letitia nodded.

'Then, if I might, I suggest a break with tradition, madam. Is there any reason that you and Sir Justin might not marry in Canterbury? Ella will receive stares, yes, as his newly discovered daughter, but you could have a small, private wedding.'

'With only true friends invited who would be discreet.' Letitia turned to gaze at her. 'It would be more difficult to organise, though.'

'You'll manage, and Ella can help. Anyway, spending more time at Riverside Hall before the wedding will make her feel more confident.'

'And then she *could* be a bridesmaid. Her father will like that.'

'And you could still have Mrs Melrose's little girl as another, and the boy as a pageboy?'

Letitia nodded. She would have loved to invite Letty over from Ireland, but she and Miles had decided it would be safer to uphold the fabrication that Katharine found travelling difficult and, as for himself, he obviously couldn't attend. But Letitia planned for them to meet her new husband very soon, at least in the spring. 'And you are sure, Mary, that you're happy at coming to live at Riverside Hall?'

'Where you go, madam, I go. Besides, I told you, I get on well with the staff.'

'I just wish I could take Forbes with me, but perhaps it's for the best that I leave him in charge of Eversleigh. Sir Justin has promised that we will often come and stay, so I won't lose touch with my friends.'

'Mrs Melrose will miss you.'

Letitia laughed. 'I think she has her hands full with this new baby. Apparently, she's far more trouble than the first two.'

The wedding took place in the charming village church where the Hathaway family had worshipped for over two hundred years. Orchids, carnations and delicately scented freesias stood in magnificent displays, while crimson silk garlanded the end of every pew. On the altar were vases of deep crimson roses. With the organ playing softly, it was an intimate yet exciting scene to greet late-arriving guests entering to be ushered to their seats.

Ella, as chief bridesmaid, was waiting in the porch, within her charge little Caroline and Robert, both wearing pale-blue satin. The children were wide-eyed and overcome by the solemnity of the occasion, whilst she was trying to quell her own increasing nerves. She loved her dress of crimson velvet and the band of fresh flowers in her hair, but that didn't mean that she wasn't aware that her presence would attract many wondering glances. And she was struggling not to be anxious because she knew that this day was one she would remember all her life.

And then the gleaming limousine with its white ribbons was drawing up outside the beribboned lychgate, and Ella drew the children aside as the bride, on the arm of Edward Melrose, began to approach the entrance. Breathtakingly radiant, Letitia had chosen the elegance of a white satin sheath with a cascade of lace trailing behind. The softness of white fur was around her shoulders, and her dark hair shone beneath her mother's wedding veil, on top of which was a sparkling tiara. She gave a warm smile to Ella and then, as the inner doors were being opened, came the strains of the opening bars of Handel's *Arrival of the Queen of Sheba*. The congregation slowly rose, some heads already turning to see the bridal procession and, as she walked sedately behind the children, Ella caught a glimpse of Mr Forbes and Miss Blane, but her gaze was searching for Rory and her heart lifted when she saw him near the front.

At the head of the aisle stood her tall father, his expression one of pride and happiness as his bride approached. Ella took from Letitia her bouquet of exquisite red roses and guided the little ones into their place on the front pew.

And it was then that, for the first time, she listened to the age-old words, *'We are gathered here today in the sight of God . . .'*

It was three weeks after the wedding when, late one evening, Letitia stood on the balcony of their penthouse apartment in Madeira. She gazed at the scene before her with a full moon shining down on the glistening sea, and realised that in another week they would be going back to England. Enjoying the sensation of a slight breeze wafting through the diaphanous fabric of her white nightdress and lace peignoir, she was about to turn when she sensed his cologne then felt his arms around her waist. Justin said softly, 'Hello, my wife.'

'Hello, my husband.' She nestled back against him. How she loved this man.

He lifted her hair and bent to nuzzle the nape of her neck, and, knowing what was to come, she twisted in his arms, her mouth eagerly seeking his. Taking her hand, Justin led her back to the bedroom with its huge double bed, the sheets turned back over the blue satin coverlet, an ice bucket and champagne by its side. Small lamps sent a soft glow over the room, and Letitia stood while Justin removed her peignoir and slowly slipping down first one strap of her nightdress then the other, let it fall to reveal her breasts. She heard his intake of breath and then he was removing his black silk pyjama jacket and holding her against him whispering, 'I want to feel your skin against mine, every minute of every day.'

Pressed against him, she could feel the hairs on his chest against her nipples, and, moving towards the bed, they lay on the crisp linen sheets, his mouth coming down on hers, his hands moving and caressing. Afterwards, relaxed and sated, their limbs entwined, she lay against her beloved husband, smiling as she remembered wondering whether she would ever know the secrets of the marriage bed.

Chapter Sixty-Seven

Grace had been the one to solve the problem of where Ella should live for the month following the wedding.

'That's really kind of you,' Ella said, although the fact that Mr Melrose was an MP still made her feel shy in his presence. 'Perhaps I could help with the children.'

'That, my dear, would be a godsend.' Grace smiled with genuine friendliness.

And so it was settled. Ella enjoying playing games with the little boy and girl, and listening to them read. But it was their baby sister who was her real joy. She had never even held a baby before and cuddling the warmth of her tiny body became precious moments. But although Nanny made Ella feel welcome in the nursery, she knew better than to take advantage. She was also treated as a guest, taking her meals in the dining room with her hosts but, by mutual consent, she had a tray in her room if they gave a dinner party.

'To protect you, really,' Grace said. 'Several of our friends will have dined at Eversleigh and we wouldn't like you to feel uncomfortable. Give it time, Ella, and all this will pass.'

And Ella could see the sense in it. And also why Charlotte Featherstone came to offer her advice. 'You will find yourself in unfamiliar situations, my dear,' she said. 'In society circles, I am afraid that what most sensible people would consider trivialities assume far too much importance.'

Full of admiration for Charlotte's elegance, Ella found herself straightening her back, and being conscious of the position of her feet. 'I'm very grateful.'

But she was unused to being idle, and although she loved having the chance to read more, that didn't prevent her from becoming restless at times, even bored. It was after reading yet another report in the daily paper denigrating the efforts of the women fighting for the vote, that Ella decided to offer her support to the WSPU. She wasn't sure yet about being militant, but she wrote to ask if the movement needed a willing helper, delighted to receive confirmation that her assistance would be appreciated in an office involved with pamphlets and publicity. She knew that Letitia supported suffrage, so surely her father couldn't disapprove?

But Ella's overwhelming delight was that until the honeymooners returned she was able to meet Rory up on the Heath. And so each Sunday afternoon, just as before, they would meet, walk and talk for ages, despite any inclement weather, and sometimes went again to the music hall. But now there was no warm study for them to be together, even if, for the sake of convention, it was only for a limited time, and they could only seek 'their' oak tree to shelter beneath the branches.

With her chin tucked against the rough wool of his coat, her head resting on his shoulder, they would sometimes stand against the rough bark of the trunk content to be in each other's arms. But that never lasted long, because soon Rory's lips would find hers, his demanding mouth filling Ella with a longing she knew no respectable young lady should feel. He would slip his hand beneath her coat, his hand searching for her breast beneath her blouse. Despite the cold, her body was hot for him and she could sense his frustration as with a groan he would fasten her coat and hold her close as if he would never let her go.

But the final time, the one she had been dreading, arrived only too soon and, knowing that she had to say goodbye, Ella clung to Rory in tears. He took out his handkerchief and gently wiped them away. 'Aren't I the gentleman,' he teased, although his voice was husky. 'Don't I have at least three of them?'

She managed a weak smile. 'I bet you've used your sleeve before now.'

'I've had no choice, same as you.'

But Ella's tears continued to rain down her cheeks, and her breath caught in a sob. 'I don't want to leave you.'

'And I shall feel as if I've lost my right arm when you go.' He held her close against him, and she wanted to remain there forever, safe and loved. It wasn't that she didn't feel excited at what lay before her, what girl wouldn't, but to Ella a year seemed like an eternity.

'Promise me one thing, sweetheart. When we do see each other again, you'll tell me the truth. I shall understand if you've met someone else.'

'But I won't . . .'

He placed a finger against her lips. 'Life can be full of surprises.'

'Then you must promise the same.'

'Oh, I shall be Jack the Lad while you're away.'

She knew him better than that, but he was going to miss her, and loneliness could easily lead to temptation. Ella couldn't bear the thought of him with someone else.

Then Rory said, 'These past months, since I came back to London, have been the happiest of my life, sweetheart. Whatever happens, I want you to remember that.'

Ella reached up to kiss him, and placed her hand lovingly

against his cheek. 'Exactly one year from now, on the Sunday nearest today's date?'

He nodded. 'I shall be counting the days.'

Seeing the pain in his eyes, with tearstained cheeks, she turned and walked away. When she looked over her shoulder, it was to see Rory still standing to watch her and it took all of Ella's resolve not to run back to him. Feeling as if her heart was breaking, she lifted her hand in one last farewell wave.

When Rory saw Ella enter the house and the door close behind her, he felt as if a light had gone out of his life. And in the following weeks, his devastation at knowing he was losing her for a whole year affected him so badly that it took a reprimand from Professor Dalton to puncture his self-absorption. Appalled that he had made errors in his research, Rory realised that he was foolish to allow his emotions to affect his work. Wasn't he totally dependent upon the reputation he'd worked so hard to build? He would have even less to offer Ella if he couldn't find another research post when this current book was finished. And so, although he found it almost impossible, he managed to consign their separation to a separate compartment in his mind, instead pursuing further knowledge and, at weekends, taking exercise by exploring London's historic sights and walking in its beautiful parks. Hampstead Heath, he tended to avoid. And, although Rory had advised Ella to regard herself as free, he saw no need to apply that concept to himself. He had already found the love of his life.

Chapter Sixty-Eight

1911

Ella, leaning against the rail of the ship, looking at the vast expanse of water before her, was trying to decide which had been her favourite city. Was it Rome with its culture and history, or Paris where she and Letitia had chosen an evening gown each in one of its famous fashion houses? Ella would never forget the delectable pastries in the coffee shops of Vienna, nor the wonderful paintings she'd seen in Madrid's art galleries. Her father and Letitia were presently in their stateroom and, as always, she was being careful not to intrude on their privacy. But she did not remain alone for long and, even before he joined her, she could sense him approaching. He didn't touch her, just stood by her side and murmured, 'Not long now.'

She nodded. 'Yes, we'll soon be back in England.'

'Do you go straight to Canterbury?'

'No, to London, to Lady Hathaway's home in Hampstead.'

His hand came to cover hers. 'Ella, you know how I feel about you.'

She turned and looked up at the face that had now become so familiar. They had met in an art gallery in Rome, and James, in his mid twenties, was the heir to a large estate in Wiltshire. Somehow, their paths had often crossed in Europe, whilst their friendship was in no way discouraged by her parents. And she had liked him right from the beginning; the way his fair hair curled at his neck, his straightforward manner and his dry sense of humour.

At his words she hesitated, then her voice was quiet. 'I did tell you about Rory.'

'Yes, you did. And you've never given me false hopes.'

'I do like you, James, very much indeed.'

His smile was rueful. 'But I'm not him.'

She shook her head. 'I'm sorry.'

'Then I hope he realises how lucky he is.'

But behind Ella's gentle smile was a dread that was increasing with every passing day. A year was a long time. There had been no contact between them, not even a letter. Whatever would she do if Rory had met someone else?

Later that evening, in their stateroom, Letitia and Justin were discussing exactly the same subject.

Letitia was shaking her head. 'I don't know if she would be able to bear it if Rory has met someone else.'

'That, my darling, is out of our hands. Just as it is if it does prove that she has formed an attachment to the eligible James. You must admit that she can now hold her own in any society situation. I'm so proud of her, Letitia. I know you won't mind my saying that she has inherited much of Selina's natural grace.'

'Justin, I know how important Selina was to you, I never mind our talking about her.' Letitia smiled at him. 'I'm perfectly secure in your love for me, especially now that we are to have a child.' She glanced down at her still flat stomach. 'Ella is going to be thrilled.'

'Are you going to tell her before we land?'

Her smile was one of utter contentment. 'I'm longing to, but not yet.'

Justin became thoughtful. 'Let us just imagine that Rory's feelings haven't changed. He gave me the impression of being a young man who was rightly proud of his achievements. But he only had live-in accommodation and we don't even know whether he is still with Professor Dalton – after all, the book might be finished. How will he provide a home for Ella?'

She looked at him with growing anxiety. 'Suppose Rory decided to take up a university post in America again?'

'I would do all in my power to prevent it.' His jaw tightened. 'I missed the first eighteen years of her life, I'm not prepared to lose her again.'

Letitia said quietly, 'Then, if needs be, we must be prepared to come up with some sort of solution.'

In her cabin, Ella was turning the pages of a journal, but this time it was not one belonging to her mother, but her own. It had been Rory's gift to her that last time up on the Heath, and he had written on the flyleaf, *For my darling Ella, so that you can keep memories of your first travels. Always yours, Rory xxx*

She glanced down at one entry. It was a fleeting note, of a wedding she had seen in Turin. There had been such an aura of romance, of magic, around the young couple, but Ella had laughed aloud to see the bride's Borzoi dog wearing a collar of flowers. Rory would so enjoy reading about that. Ella had absorbed European culture as if born to it, loving every minute of the time spent with her father and Letitia, but that didn't mean that she hadn't missed Rory terribly. Would she soon be showing him the records she'd kept of all the wonderful galleries, museums, churches and scenery she'd seen? She looked again at the flyleaf. Was he, she wondered, still 'always hers'?

Or would he meet her on the Heath only to say that she had been away too long? He could even be married. Ella's logic kept warning her, yet in her heart she clung to the intensity of their kisses, the passion they'd shared. And now every day was seeming an eternity.

Chapter Sixty-Nine

The long-awaited Sunday morning found Rory with a dread in the pit of his stomach. And even at the breakfast table his gloomy distraction was noticeable.

'What's the matter with you then, Mr Adare?' He'd hardly touched the plate of bacon and eggs that Cook had put before him. 'You did say you weren't fasting for Communion this morning.'

'I'm sorry, I was miles away.' Hoping that it would calm his nerves, he made more of an effort. But although later, during Mass, he knelt and stood at the appropriate times, all his thoughts, his emotions were centred on the coming meeting on the Heath. Never for a moment did he doubt that Ella would be there. She would never break a promise.

But with their reunion now imminent, he couldn't rid himself of the rising fear that Ella's feelings for him would have changed. I am wrong for her on so many levels, he told himself. Only he knew that he had once descended to theft, but there, for all to see, were his lower social status, his lack of a university education and the fact that he didn't even own his own house. What titled father would welcome such a suitor? Sir Justin might have seemed kind but there was steel in his character, and Rory had no desire for

Ella to marry without her father's approval and thus cause a rift between them.

And so he went to their rendezvous early, uncaring of curious glances as he stood alone. He wanted to watch her coming towards him. Rory didn't need to hear the words, he would know by the way she walked and the moment he looked into her eyes.

Ella took great care in choosing what to wear. While part of her longed to flaunt her new and fashionable clothes bought in Paris, she didn't want to dress so expensively that, to Rory, she seemed like a stranger. And so, although the forest-green skirt had its own matching coat, her hat was simplicity itself, trimmed only with tiny feathers.

The butler was in the hall as she came down the staircase and he moved to open the front door.

'Thank you, Mr Forbes.'

'It's Forbes now, Miss Ella.'

Her gaze met his and she smiled. 'Please would you let Lady Hathaway know that I've gone up to the Heath?'

He inclined his head. 'Of course.'

And then she was walking down the long drive and making her way to the rendezvous. Her stomach was churning with nerves, but she was also full of excitement at the thought of seeing Rory again, at last. Too impatient to wait, she had set off early and knew that Letitia and her father would be watching from the window. They had been wonderful, not once had they tried to influence her. I shall know, she told herself, in an instant. He won't even have to tell me, I shall see it in his eyes. Her mind pushed away the thought of heartbreak. She would try to be brave, unselfish, wanting only his happiness.

As she neared the Heath, Ella slowed her step, hardly able to believe that the moment had at last arrived. And then she could see his tall figure outlined at the top of the slight incline, the breeze ruffling his dark hair, a so familiar image. With her throat full of apprehension, Ella began to walk towards him and, as she drew nearer, could see mirrored in his face her own longing and uncertainty. For one intense moment their gaze met, anxious, searching, and then the smiles came and she was going into his outstretched arms. His hug was fierce and, as she clung, he murmured against her hair, 'I've so missed you, my beautiful girl.'

'And I've missed you. I love you so much.' Ella's words were muffled by joyful tears.

'I could never love anyone else.' He released her and, glancing at people passing, said, 'Sweetheart, remember a certain tree?'

Minutes later she was leaning against the familiar gnarled trunk and at last feeling the pressure of Rory's lips against her own. In his impassioned kisses she could sense his past loneliness, even while she gloried in the sensations his warm mouth aroused. 'Rory,' she whispered. 'At Eversleigh, there's an empty study with a warm fire. And, hopefully, no one will disturb us.'

'You mean so that you can tell me all about your travels?' His lips twitched.

It was, she thought, as if they had never been apart.

'Maybe that could come later?' Ella smiled up at him, feeling exultant. She knew that her father would now wish to talk to him, but not today. Today he was going to be all hers.

It was several days later when Rory received a letter from Sir Justin, or rather it was more of a note, albeit written on his own headed writing paper.

Rory, I wonder whether you would be able to dine with us on Friday evening at 8 o'clock? I would appreciate the chance to talk to you privately beforehand in the study.

So, it had come. The summons he had both expected and dreaded. Professor Dalton's manuscript on the Irish Famine had been returned by his publisher for final corrections and, once Rory had completed them, his services would no longer be required. Already, the professor had gently probed as to what Rory's future plans were, but everything had rested on Ella's return.

Arriving at what he judged to be the appropriate time, Rory and Forbes greeted each other in their usual friendly yet formal manner and being shown into the study, Rory looked around the now familiar room with appreciation. The book-lined walls and comfortable leather chairs were his ideal environment, and a smile curved his lips as he remembered the previous Sunday when he and Ella had settled themselves in there. Ella had helped him to undo her blouse, laughing at his frustration at the tiny buttons. Their passionate kisses had been full of relief and longing, her need for fulfilment seeming to match his own. It had been Rory who managed to calm things down and not only because of the risk of someone coming in. He needed to love and protect his lovely girl, not to take advantage of her outside marriage.

But now he turned as Sir Justin came in to join him. 'Good evening, Rory.' He went to a decanter. 'May I offer you whisky?'

'Thank you, sir.'

Taking the chair indicated, Rory accepted the glass and waited.

Sir Justin settled himself in the chair opposite. 'I think you probably have an inkling of why I need to talk to you alone. I'm sure you know that Ella's happiness is of paramount importance to me.'

'As it is to me.' Rory gazed steadily at him.

'I am inordinately proud of the way she has adapted to her new background. Tell me, do you see a change, a difference in her?'

'An amazing difference, she is much more confident and poised. And obviously had a wonderful time. It has been fascinating to read her journal.'

'I think she was writing it especially for you.' He frowned, his keen gaze searching Rory's. 'I trust that you didn't find any other distraction while she was away?'

Rory shook his head. 'You can rest assured on that count, sir.' He took a sip of his whisky, feeling its warmth flow through him, and tried to feel more relaxed.

'I'm relieved to hear it. However, my daughter's future remains unsettled and I find that troubling.'

'The problem is, sir, that my own is presently unclear, which is why I haven't yet ventured to formally request her hand in marriage.'

'And she has left me in no doubt as to what her answer would be.' He smiled. 'A very determined young woman is my daughter.' He paused. 'Am I correct in thinking that your present position will shortly come to an end?'

Rory nodded. 'Yes, Professor Dalton's book is completed.'

'And you haven't made any definite plans?'

'I was unable to, not until Ella returned.' There was a silence, then Rory said slowly, 'I confess to finding myself at an impasse. I foresee no difficulty in obtaining another research post, but although I have managed to save a decent sum from my salary, it would not be enough to give Ella the home she deserves, especially here in London.'

Sir Justin drank some of his whisky and leant forward. 'You are not considering returning to America?'

'Certainly Ella would love Boston, and in some ways it might be easier for us there.' Then Rory shook his head. 'But to ask her to leave you and her stepmother would be too selfish of me.' He looked at the impeccably dressed man opposite and gave a wry smile. 'Besides, I imagine that you and she wouldn't wish it.'

Sir Justin's nod was a firm one. 'Tell me, Rory, do you have ambitions other than being involved in research?'

Unsure of where the conversation was leading, Rory thought for a moment. 'I've often thought that I'd like to enter journalism, like my father. But experience has taught me that credentials are not always enough, one needs influential contacts. At least to be given a first chance.'

'And if that chance was given?'

'It would depend entirely on the quality of one's articles.'

'And this writing could be done in addition to undertaking a research post?'

Rory frowned. 'I'm not sure . . .'

'Where this is leading?'

He nodded.

'Rory, we have to be realistic. While you and Ella are in love and naturally wish to marry, there is this barrier of practicality. And yet, knowing of your earlier difficulties, Letitia and I respect what you have achieved and are conscious that you value your independence. But we do have a suggestion that might prove to be the answer.' He paused while Rory, feeling wary, gazed intently at him. 'To put it simply, Letitia would be delighted if, once married, you and Ella could take care of Eversleigh. She doesn't wish to sell her childhood home, preferring to use it as a base when in London. But she's not keen on it being occupied only by servants.'

Rory stared at him, his mind in a whirl. To be able to marry

Ella and for them to live in this fine house? To work here in this comfortable study?

'This is in no way a charitable gesture, even though there would be no household expenses involved,' Sir Justin said. 'But my daughter would have her true status, you would be able to continue your research, and eventually it could be a way to achieve your journalistic ambitions.'

Still stunned at the vista opening before him, Rory managed to say, 'It is a most kind and generous offer, sir.' He took a deep breath. 'Have you discussed it with Ella?'

Sir Justin shook his head. 'I thought it only right to approach you first.'

Rory had no doubts of Ella's delighted reaction, nor of his own. 'I think I can accept on behalf of both of us, sir, and can only express my heartfelt gratitude.'

'Then shall we join the others?'

Rory drained his glass and rising held out his hand. 'Thank you again, Sir Justin, I shall be everlastingly in your debt.'

As they walked across the hall, Rory was euphoric.

'I'm so pleased that Riverside Hall is a manor house instead of a huge stately home,' Letitia was saying as they went into the drawing room. 'You liked it too, didn't you?'

Ella nodded. 'It was lovely walking in the fields and along by the river.' She turned and smiled at Rory, then felt puzzled as she sensed his excitement.

Sir Justin went to join Letitia on the sofa who looked questioningly at him and smiled when he nodded.

'Ella, my dear,' she said. 'We didn't want to raise your hopes about this until after your father had spoken to Rory.'

Rory, who was now seated opposite, smiled as Ella shot him a swift curious glance. Then, as she listened to the plan, her excitement began to build. 'Isn't it wonderful, Rory? I'm so thrilled I don't know what to say.'

'A kiss would be good,' her father said smiling, and she rose and when she went to kiss him on the cheek, he whispered, 'It was Letitia's idea.'

Ella turned to look at the woman who had done so much to change her life, her eyes brimming with tears. 'I'll never be able to thank you enough for all you've done for me. I always said you were my guardian angel.' She impulsively went into Letitia's welcoming hug.

Rory's voice was husky. 'My gratitude is overwhelming.'

Letitia smilingly turned to Justin. 'Is this a good time to tell them?'

'I can't think of a better.'

Letitia said, 'We have further news for you. I visited my doctor yesterday afternoon and he confirmed what I suspected.' Her face was radiant. 'I am expecting a baby.'

Ella's intake of breath was so audible that her father laughed, even as Rory shook his hand.

'It's the most wonderful news! That means I shall have a half-brother or sister!' She kissed her stepmother and again her eyes filled with tears. 'I'm sorry, I just feel so emotional.'

'An occasion for champagne, I think,' Justin said, and went over to the bell pull.

'I have everything I've always longed for,' Ella said, going to take Rory's hand. 'To marry Rory and to be part of a family. Although I never imagined that I'd be able to live at Eversleigh as—' She stopped.

'Its mistress?' Letitia began to laugh. 'At least when I'm at Riverside Hall. Do you not have any ambition unfulfilled?'

There was a short silence.

'Miss Grint!' Ella said, her expression hardening.

Letitia stared at her. 'Do you mean that officer at the workhouse, the one I saw striking you?'

'She hated me,' Ella said. 'And I've always vowed that one day I'd get my own back.'

'Oh, my dear, soon after you came here, I took it upon myself to insist on her dismissal.' Letitia turned to Justin. 'If you could have seen the ugly clothes she made Ella wear when she was released. I saw her from the window as she came up the drive.'

Astonished, Ella said, 'I didn't know! And you mean that all these years . . .'

'She wasn't able to be cruel in that workhouse again and, with no reference, one would hope not in any other.'

It was then that Ella felt the last vestige of resentment about her childhood drain away. Agnes had told her that life wasn't always fair, and it certainly hadn't been for Selina. But as for herself? Ella looked around at the people she held close in her heart. Wasn't she now the most loved and fortunate young woman in the world?

Acknowledgements

My appreciation to the wonderful writing group JustWrite
in Leicester. I still miss my friends there.
And my gratitude to Biddy Nelson for her perceptive advice.
My thanks also to my lovely agent Ros Edwards and to Julia Forrest
for her professional editing skills.
And to Allison & Busby for their warm welcome and my
fabulous book cover.

Born and educated in the Potteries in Staffordshire, MARGARET KAINE now lives in Eastbourne. She began writing with short stories and her debut novel *Ring of Clay* won the RNA New Writer's Award and the Society of Authors' Sagittarius Prize.

margaretkaine.com
@MargaretKaine